SERAPH

John Graham

KDP

Published by KDP

ISBN 978-1-70312-384-5

Typesetting services by BOOKOW.COM

Contents

THE JUNGLE

D EEP space took days or weeks to traverse, even at faster-than-
light speeds. The nondescript freighter that arrived on the
edge of the star system had been in Q-space for almost a month.
Travelling on conventional engines, it took another six hours to
reach its destination.

The planet's surface was a patchwork of green and blue with
streaks of sandy brown in the subtropical latitudes, and solid
clumps of white at the poles. Deep oceans covered one half and
tropical vegetation covered the other half. Its atmosphere was
a tolerable oxygen-nitrogen mixture and its surface teemed with
life.

The freighter lumbered into geosynchronous orbit above the
equatorial continent. Once in position, a slit opened in its flank
and a transport shuttle was propelled into space.

As the shuttle cruised down towards the planet, its underside
began to glow from the friction of atmospheric entry. The heat
intensified, engulfing the shuttle's hull in a cushion of fire that
burnt bright in the alien sky. Once the shuttle had reached the
upper troposphere, it ignited its engines and began a more steady
descent.

The surface was obscured by ashen clouds, pulses of lightning
flashing intermittently within. As the shuttle plunged through
the storm cell, the passengers could actually hear the rain drumming against the hull. The impact of millions of droplets melded

with the droning bass note of the engines to produce a rumbling roar.

"Do you prefer Dr Shelton or Mortimer?" one passenger asked another.

The man known to the other passengers as Dr Mortimer Shelton had a head of grey hair, steel grey eyes, and a small silver moustache. He was much older than the other two men, judging by the faint wrinkles on his face, and far less comfortable with flying.

"Dr Shelton is more dignified," Mortimer replied, "but either one is fine."

The occasional peal of thunder could be heard outside, making Mortimer worry whether the shuttle's hull could withstand a lightning strike.

"Do you want to see something cool?" the man asked Mortimer.

Mortimer nodded and his fellow passenger activated a viewing screen, angling it so they could both see. They were looking at a live camera feed showing the jungle stretching for hundreds of kilometres across the landscape.

"All I see is rainforest," Mortimer said, confused.

"Wait for it," the man responded.

Sure enough, something appeared in the corner of the screen. It was a sprawling network of structures made of white stone and arranged in concentric, geometric shapes leading up to a central complex at the top of a low-lying peak: a city.

"This planet is the homeworld of an intelligent alien species," the man explained, "and this city is one of dozens of settlements all over the jungle."

"How advanced are they?" Mortimer asked.

"Advanced enough to use fire and build giant stone cities," the man replied, "they have writing, mathematics, and metalworking skills too!"

It was a fascinating view. The alien city was a glorified hillfort compared to Asgard City, but it was still impressive in its own right.

"Why do you have a base on a planet which already has alien life?" Mortimer asked.

"Why wouldn't we?" his companion countered rhetorically.

"Don't you remember the 2nd Prime Law?" Mortimer reminded him, "'No unauthorised contact with alien species.'"

"It's not as if we go down and talk to them!" his companion laughed, "and we're not planning to, either. Besides, it's a bit late to start worrying about breaking the law."

Mortimer fell silent. His companion was right: he had abandoned his life on Asgard and allowed these people to smuggle him to this forsaken corner of the galaxy. By this point, he was either presumed dead or a fugitive from justice. Why worry about the law when you're already on the run from it?

"Are you studying them?" he asked.

"You could say that," the man answered, "but not for xenoanthropology's sake."

"Why build a base so close to where they live?" Mortimer asked, "There have to be some uninhabited areas on this planet far enough away."

"Maybe," his companion responded, "but none of us were part of the Network when the facility was built, so we have no idea."

"*We're beginning the final descent!*" the pilot announced over the intercom.

Mortimer checked his safety harness whilst his companion folded the display away and double-checked his own restraints. The turbulence outside flared up, shaking the shuttle as it braved the storm winds.

"Couldn't we have waited for clearer weather?" Mortimer asked nervously.

"We're not totally careless with the natives," his fellow passenger explained, "It's a lot harder to notice an unknown flying object in the middle of a thunderstorm."

The shuttle dropped and Mortimer's stomach dropped with it, making him glad he hadn't eaten beforehand. The passenger compartment wasn't much bigger than a storage closet, and the sounds of the raging storm did nothing to reassure him.

"Has anything ever happened to a shuttle during a storm?" Mortimer asked, afraid to be more specific with his question.

"Don't jinx it!" another passenger sitting opposite yelled at him.

"Spacer," the first passenger said with a roll of his eyes, "superstitious bunch the lot of them. But the short answer is no."

As he spoke those words, there was a deafening bang followed by a blaring klaxon as emergency lights illuminated the passenger compartment with a crimson glow. The shuttle lurched violently to one side then the other, causing the passengers to cry out in panic.

"*Lightning strike!*" the pilot shouted, "*Port engine's gone! Brace for a hard landing!*"

"I told you not to freaking jinx it!" the spacer shouted at Mortimer.

"Like that makes a fucking difference!" the first passenger shouted back.

The shuttle dropped suddenly and swerved like a roller-coaster, causing another round of panicked yelling as the pilot struggled to keep the beleaguered craft airborne.

"*Homebase! Homebase! This is Sparrow One!*" the pilot yelled, his words audible over the intercom, "*We've been struck by lightning! The port engine is gone! We're gonna crash!*"

"*Roger, Sparrow One,*" a calm voice answered, "*A retrieval team is being mobilised, keep the VIP safe at all costs. Good luck.*"

Mortimer guessed that he was the 'VIP', but was too frightened to think much of it.

Was this how it was all going to end? Had he seriously come all the way out here just to die in a shuttle crash on some back-of-beyond planet?

And what if they survived the crash? No doubt the jungle was filled with monsters that could kill them before they were rescued. There was also a primitive alien civilisation living in the jungle. How would they react to visitors from beyond the stars? How violent were they? Did they practice cannibalism? Did it count as cannibalism if they were a different species?

That last thought was a strangely superfluous concern given the circumstances, but it was all Mortimer could do to distract himself from impending death.

The shuttle did a barrel roll, and the passengers screamed again as they were thrown upside down before the shuttle righted itself. The shuttle then swerved sharply again and tilted to the other side as its descent accelerated.

Mortimer could only guess the shuttle's movements from the way his innards were thrown back and forth by inertia. Once again, he was glad that he hadn't eaten before the ill-fated flight. Dying on an empty stomach was better than being sick in his final moments.

"*The ground is coming up fast!*" the pilot shouted, "*Brace yourselves!*"

* * *

Mortimer's vision returned as his blackout cleared only to discover that gravity was pulling him towards the ceiling. The shuttle had survived the crash intact but had landed upside down. His companions were also groaning and stirring as they recovered.

"Is everyone ok?" the man sitting next to him asked.

"I'm fine," Mortimer replied groggily, "more or less."

"You freaking jinxed the craft in mid-flight, you freaking idiot!" Spacer cursed at him furiously, apparently unhurt by the crash.

"Enough!" barked the other passenger, "let's get out of here!"

Everyone struggled with their restraints before managing to get free. Mortimer fell out of his seat and landed on the ceiling while his two companions dropped down and started retrieving emergency equipment. Getting back on his feet, Mortimer stumbled towards the cockpit door and tried to open it, but the handle was stiff and wouldn't budge.

"It's gonna need more than a strong tug," his fellow passenger explained.

Mortimer stepped aside as the man raised a two-handed axe with a hammerhead on the reverse of the blade. He brought the hammerhead down on the cockpit door's handle, smashing it clean off and breaking the lock with it.

Entering the cockpit, Mortimer saw the pilot strapped into his seat upside-down, immobilised but alive. He tried to undo the safety harness, but the buckle wouldn't open. Axeman pulled out a survival knife and cut through the restraints.

"Tools always trump bare hands," he remarked.

The pilot groaned as Mortimer caught him and hauled him out of the cockpit. Axeman leant a hand, and together they moved the semi-conscious pilot into the passenger compartment, laying him down on the floor – or the ceiling, rather.

"Now, we just wait for the retrieval team to follow our beacon," said Axeman.

"Did the tracking beacon survive the crash?" Spacer worried aloud.

"…Check…the panel…" the pilot murmured, pointing weakly towards the cockpit.

Mortimer clambered back into the cockpit. The display was covered in warning lights, but thankfully the emergency beacon was still working. He put on a spare headset and pulled the speakerphone down to his mouth.

"Um…hello," Mortimer said hesitantly, "this is…Sparrow One, can anyone hear me?"

"*Sparrow One, this is Homebase!*" a voice responded, "*Is everyone alright?*"

"The pilot is injured," Mortimer replied, "but otherwise, we're all alive."

"*Good to know*," the operator sighed with relief, "*the boss is already furious.*"

"We're still inside the shuttle," Mortimer continued, "but the storm outside is still pretty strong, we're not sure if it's safe to go outside."

"*It's not,*" the operator replied, "*if the storm doesn't get you, the predatory fauna will. Stay exactly where you are until the retrieval team arrives.*"

"Understood, Homebase," Mortimer acknowledged, "We'll stay put."

"*Keep in radio contact,*" the Homebase operator instructed, "*The natives in the jungle aren't a friendly bunch. If they venture out to investigate, we'll let you know.*"

"Roger that," Mortimer replied nervously.

The comm. line went dormant and Mortimer removed the headset.

"Seems like we're stuck here till morning," Axeman stated the obvious.

* * *

The storm began to dissipate an hour after the crash. Once the clouds cleared, dawn truly broke as a brilliant white star became visible in the morning sky. Axeman opened the hatch and poked his head out. Mortimer tried to follow suit.

"Get back in the shuttle!" Axeman snapped, pushing Mortimer back inside, "you're the VIP, so if your head gets bitten off by some jungle monster, we'll pay the price."

Mortimer caught a brief glimpse of a verdant canopy of trees – or things that looked like trees – stretching out in all directions. The shuttle had crashed near the edge of a small clearing halfway up a mountain covered in rainforest.

"It's a beautiful view outside," Axeman reported back, shutting the hatch again, "but the retrieval team isn't here yet."

"Of course not," replied Spacer, "they haven't hailed us yet."

The communications array squawked suddenly. Mortimer scrambled back into the cockpit and hooked the headset back over his ears.

"*Sparrow One! This is Homebase, come in!*" the operator hailed them frantically.

"This is Sparrow One," Mortimer replied, "We're still here, what's the problem?"

"*A hunting party of natives is approaching!*" the Homebase operator explained, "*100 metres distant, and they're moving fast – in YOUR direction!*"

"Frick!" Mortimer cursed, "how far away is the retrieval team?"

"*One kilometre distant and closing,*" the Homebase operator replied, "*but the natives will get to you first, just a heads-up.*"

"Uh…what should we do?" Mortimer asked.

"*Hold tight and pray for luck,*" the Homebase operator answered.

The line went dormant again.

"Did you hear all that?" Mortimer asked.

The looks on his fellow travellers' faces made it clear that they had. Spacer made sure that the hatch was locked while Axeman checked on the pilot.

"What kind of weapons do the natives have?" Mortimer asked.

"They've made it to the Iron Age," Axeman responded, "but most of their weapons are made of stone or wood – or the local equivalents."

"Could we get a look at them with that camera?" Mortimer suggested.

"Assuming it survived the impact," Axeman replied, pulling the viewing screen down.

The camera module was underneath the shuttle's nose, and having landed upside-down it was the right way up to view the outside world. Axeman tapped the screen experimentally and sure enough, it reactivated.

The view wasn't quite as spectacular as the glimpse through the hatch, but Mortimer was still impressed by the endless sea of vegetation. Panning the camera around, the group saw a crude path leading from the clearing down into the rainforest.

As they watched, the native hunting party arrived. A dozen figures emerged from the undergrowth riding snarling war-mounts resembling terrestrial lizards with strong hind legs and grasping forearms. The creatures sniffed the air, baring saw-like teeth while chomping impatiently at the bit.

The riders were green and lithe with wiry limbs, sinewy bodies, tapered snouts, and bony ridges on their heads. They wore padded armour and wielded stone-tipped lances. Some had bows slung over their shoulders and quivers full of arrows attached to their saddles. The crashed shuttle was hard to miss, and they surrounded it with lances poised.

One of the hunters brought its war-mount to a halt just short of the shuttle and poked it experimentally with its lance. The passengers huddling inside heard the stone tip clang against the metallic hull, trying not to utter a peep.

On the screen, the passengers saw the alien warrior raise its lance and plant it in the dirt with the tip facing upwards before dismounting. Whilst its comrades stayed mounted, the alien warrior approached the crashed shuttle, reaching down to its belt and drawing a heavy club with a smooth stone head.

The alien warrior walked with a precise and graceful strut. Its skin was as green as the surrounding vegetation. As it approached, the camera was able to pick out the flaming orange colour of its eyes and the way its lips peeled back to reveal a row of carnivorous teeth. Then it swung its club down and up again in a sweeping arc, striking the side of the shuttle.

The blow was jarring – to the hull and the passengers' nerves. Mortimer bit his hand to stop himself yelping. Axeman gripped his axe while Spacer squeezed a safety handle. They watched on the screen as the alien warrior raised its club for a second swing.

A brilliant blue lance of energy cut through the humid morning air and struck the alien warrior with perfect accuracy. The target died instantly, exploding in a spectacular shower of evaporated blood and flash-boiled gore. The scouting party's warmounts yowled in fright, thrashing about as their riders struggled to pacify them.

Soaring on wings of fire, a menacing figure descended from the morning sky and made a dramatic landing in the middle of the scouting party. It released a localised shockwave as it landed, sending up a cloud of dirt and knocking the mounts off their clawed feet.

The anthropomorphic figure had mechanical limbs and stood three times the height of a Human. Its hull was matte black with crimson trim and its 'head' was a kickball-sized sensor pod housed inside an armoured cradle. Mounted on its shoulder, and extending from a module on its back, was the barrel of a cannon still giving off wisps of smoke.

The figure stood there in a semi-crouched stance, poised like a wrestler as it waited for the alien scouting party to recover their wits.

The mounts righted themselves, snarling and snapping at the strange metal warrior as their riders readied their lances. The mount whose rider had been killed had nothing to restrain it, and it released a shrill squeal before charging forward.

The metal warrior seized the creature by its open jaws and forced it to the ground, bringing one foot up and stomping down hard on the animal's throat. The fearsome mount's squealing jumped by an octave as the metal warrior crushed its voice box, and it began to choke spasmodically as it struggled to breathe.

The other alien warriors drove their mounts forward, charging at the metal demon with lances aimed at what they assumed was its heart. The stone-tipped lances skidded off its armoured skin without leaving a scratch, but the mounts barrelled into the metal warrior.

As the metal warrior was knocked over, the mounts moved in for the kill, trampling on its torso as they clamped their jaws around its limbs. But the metal warrior's armoured skin was impervious to enamel and stone alike, and the mounts reeled back in pain as they spat out bits of broken teeth.

The metal warrior climbed back to its feet as the alien riders dropped their lances and drew their stone-headed clubs, swinging with all their strength. Their blows rebounded from their opponent's skin with audible clangs of metal stopping stone.

The metal warrior fired its shoulder-mounted cannon again, this time at point-blank range. The cannon spat out a beam of blue light accompanied by a zap and a hiss as the ultra-hot beam instantly vaporised the moisture in the air.

The beam hit one of the mounted alien warriors directly in the face, causing its head to explode in a sizzling shower of vaporised gore, and causing the mounts to rear up and squeal in alarm. The rider's headless body tumbled from its frightened mount, the stone-headed club slipping from its clawed grasp.

The metal warrior fired a second time, this time taking aim at one of the war-mounts. The deadly beam of energy struck its target in the flank, cooking its innards to a crisp in a fraction of a second.

The mount exploded from the inside out, its skeleton bursting open and showering crimson viscera all over the clearing. The rider was launched into the air, flailing like a ragdoll all the way up and all the way down, emitting a warbling scream that echoed out across the landscape before it hit the ground with a hard crunch.

The remaining riders realised the futility of battling this enemy and fled, their mounts galloping back into the jungle as fast as their clawed feet could carry them.

The metal warrior fired one last parting shot, hitting one of the riders in the back. The rider's torso exploded from within, launching its limbs and head into the air. Its already terrified mount stumbled over its own feet and rolled into the undergrowth, shrieking and yowling long after it was out of sight.

The passengers watched the whole thing play out on the tiny screen. There was no doubt that the combat platform was part of the retrieval team, but the gruesome, one-sided fight was unnerving to watch all the same.

As the combat platform surveyed the aftermath, the barrel of its primary weapon reoriented until it was vertical before retracting into the module on its back. It turned sideways and fixed its sensor pod on the crashed shuttle, regarding the wreck with a cyclopean optical sensor that glowed electric blue.

Something approached from the opposite path. It was a skimmer vehicle, its humming antigravity engine keeping it suspended just above the ground. The chassis resembled a trilobite with a flat body and a cockpit sticking up from the front like a bulbous head.

The combat platform raised a hand, acknowledging the skimmer's arrival, then pointed at the shuttlecraft. Following the instruction, the skimmer turned in a slow arc until it was parked alongside the crashed shuttle. A small ladder extended down from the flank and a hatch opened on the side.

Mortimer opened the shuttle hatch so that Axeman and Spacer could haul the wounded pilot out first, then he climbed out after them. The heat and humidity slapped him in the face as soon as he emerged. It was stiflingly hot and the moisture in the air clogged his throat.

The scenery was beautiful, but the abattoir-like aftermath of the fight was a literal stain on the landscape. Mortimer felt his empty stomach roil as he saw the explosive patterns of alien blood and viscera spattered across the ground.

Next to his feet, he noticed the head of the alien warrior who had taken a swing at the shuttle. Its lips were peeled back in a razor-toothed snarl and it glared up at him with ferocity frozen into its fiery eyes. It was definitely dead, but the look on its face at the moment of death was well-preserved and he was mortified by it.

Once the injured pilot was safely aboard the skimmer, Spacer and Axeman grabbed the stupefied Mortimer and pulled him inside. The oppressive humidity and heat vanished as he entered the air-conditioned interior.

Spacer and Axeman strapped the pilot into a medical bed before strapping themselves into their seats. Mortimer sealed the hatch and did the same.

"Seraph, this is Rhino One," said the skimmer pilot, "all survivors are aboard, including the VIP. We're heading back to Homebase."

"*Good*," replied a gravelly voice, "*I'm staying here for a while.*"

"Acknowledged," the skimmer pilot replied, "do you need additional support, sir?"

"*Did I need support against those primitives earlier?*" came the gruff response.

"Uh…no, sir," the skimmer pilot replied nervously.

"*Then get out of here and don't let anything happen to the passengers*," Seraph ordered, "*especially Mortimer Shelton.*"

"Understood, sir," the skimmer pilot answered, "We're moving."

The pilot hit the accelerator and the skimmer powered away, cruising back up the way it had come. Spacer and Axeman relaxed in their seats, relieved to be on their way to safety.

Mortimer had frozen up.

He had recognised the voice of 'Seraph' instantly, even though it had been 45 years since he had last heard it. The grammatically flawless Standard Human Speech with textbook-standard pronunciation was unmistakable. So was the precise cadence and blunt tone. That was how Directorate operatives spoke, and only those from certain branches.

The person who had spoken was supposed to be dead.

* * *

Seraph watched the skimmer craft disappear up the mountain path, the cockpit's HUD providing him with an array of telemetry on the craft. The scene of the massacre he had just committed was filtered through the sterile and digitised view in front of him. Not the biggest or the longest skirmish he'd ever fought, but stimulating nonetheless.

One of the war-mounts was lying dead on its flank, its throat crushed by his mechanical foot. There was hardly anything left of the other one he'd killed; what remained of its ribcage resembled a blooming skeletal flower dripping with blood.

Seraph turned back to the crashed shuttle, the combat platform's mechanical feet creating little tremors as he stomped forward. Lying on the ground was a stone-headed club with a slender clawed hand wrapped around the long wooden handle. Next to the club was the severed head of the wielder, a ferocious snarl fixed permanently on its ugly alien face.

Seraph reached down, the articulated joints of his combat platform allowing him to bend over and extend a mechanical hand to the ground. He picked up the severed head and turned it around, locking eyes with the alien's own.

The alien's eyes were as fiery as the look on its face in death. Its thin lips were peeled back to show its mouthful of razor-like teeth. Apparently, they had evolved from the same genetic stock as their mounts, and the family resemblance was clear. This one had been a warrior of some note, judging by the sigils ritually burned into the bony ridge on its head.

Seraph looked out at the verdant landscape. The endless sea of greenery was all that the naked eye could see, but his eyes weren't naked. Through his HUD, he could see the alien capital in the distance, particularly the grand palace and the temple complex poking above the treeline and the rest of the city.

For such a primitive species that still used stone clubs and loincloths, it was hard to believe they could construct anything as sophisticated as a city. Even so, that was all the more reason not to underestimate them.

Seraph looked up at the sky. The storm clouds had cleared away, leaving only thin wisps of cirrus and the glare of the morning sun.

His HUD singled out the aerial surveillance drone and zoomed in, highlighting its bulbous body and the four turbine engines that held it aloft. It soared high above the jungle, beyond the sight of the tree-dwelling primitives below. Its hull was also outfitted with a visual distortion field generator, and Seraph could only detect it thanks to his HUD.

Still holding the dead warrior's head, Seraph stomped back over to the centre of the clearing. The lance was still stuck in the ground with the spearhead facing skyward, and he reached up and planted the neck stump on top of the spearhead, ensuring that the head was facing back towards the jungle path.

* * *

After the skimmer had brought them to the 'Homebase', the four rescued passengers were sent to the medical wing for a checkup. The pilot went into surgery while Mortimer was given a quick injection and then led away by a guide.

He was brought to a viewing room with a giant monitoring screen on the wall. There were several technicians present, including one operating a set of pilot's controls. The screen featured another live camera feed displaying the stone city he had seen earlier.

The operator zoomed in on the crowded central concourse. The resolution was so clear they could see the outfits and headdresses worn by the aliens as they rippled back and forth. A smaller group was walking down the middle of the concourse. Mortimer counted nine figures moving in single file near the front as several dozen attendants accompanied them.

"Those are the surviving riders that attacked you earlier," Mortimer's guide told him.

"Quite a welcome they're receiving," Mortimer remarked.

His guide smirked wryly and gestured to the drone operator, who adjusted the camera controls again, zooming in as far as possible.

Mortimer could now see that each rider was tied to the next by a long piece of rope around their waists. The attendants were wearing scaled headdresses and embroidered cloaks, and wielded two-handed staves as they escorted the riders down the concourse.

"They're prisoners?" Mortimer asked, sounding horrified.

"Worse than that," his guide explained, "the aliens are incredibly superstitious, and the lesson the boss taught them seems to have come across as a bad omen."

"So they're gonna sacrifice the surviving riders in a ceremony to appease the 'gods'," the drone operator explained, "although, they were probably going to do that anyway given how terrified they are of storms."

The camera zoomed out again and panned upwards. The concourse ended at the foot of a set of stone steps leading up to an open-air shrine. At the back of the shrine complex was a stone ramp, overlooking an enormous black pit.

"That's a naturally occurring sinkhole," the guide explained, "but the natives think it's a gateway to the underworld."

"It actually leads into a cave network deep inside the bedrock," the operator added, "the network extends all the way through the—"

"That information is 'need-to-know'," a familiar voice interjected, "and right now, our guest doesn't need to know it."

Everyone snapped to attention and saluted as 'Seraph' entered the room. Mortimer simply froze up rather than stand to attention.

"At ease," Seraph ordered.

As everyone else returned to their duties, Mortimer remained fixed to the spot as a man he hadn't seen for almost half a century approached him.

He was tall and well-built with muscles sculpted by intense physical training. He had a chiselled jaw with light skin and a head of short dark hair trimmed to a military buzz cut. He also had a grizzled and veteran look, as if the weight of experience were weighing him down. In fact, he resembled his son aged by half a century.

His most eye-catching feature was his eyes – they were an iridescent green.

"It's…been a while," Mortimer ventured hesitantly.

"About 45 years," Seraph replied, smiling with his mouth and glaring with his eyes, "so I hope you haven't forgotten my name."

"Of course, not," Mortimer answered.

"Then say it," Seraph ordered, injecting steel into his voice.

Mortimer gulped as he looked up at Seraph and obeyed.

"Alexander Thorn."

* * *

Mortimer was led out of the viewing room through a maze of corridors by his host and new boss. It was like a military base with plain surfaces and pipes running everywhere. It all looked the same to Mortimer, but Alexander seemed to know his way around by heart.

The facility had to be decades old. Most of the machinery was ageing but functional, but in a few areas, the equipment looked brand-new. Mortimer couldn't guess how much it must have cost to build a facility this large, but it did make him wonder who had funded it, not to mention how it had been built right under the noses of the natives.

And what was it all for? Mortimer still knew virtually nothing about the 'Network', let alone its agenda. Hopefully, Alexander would enlighten him – particularly regarding what had happened to him during the past 45 years.

After a long trek through the facility, Alexander brought Mortimer to a meeting room, much smaller than the viewing room they had been in. Mortimer sat down in one of the chairs and waited for his host to start speaking.

"How was the trip?" Alexander asked, pouring himself a drink from a glass flask.

"Apart from the crash, it was fine," Mortimer remarked jokingly, "thanks for swooping in to rescue us, by the way."

"The idiot who authorised an atmospheric flight during a lightning storm has already been punished," Alexander said matter-of-factly.

Mortimer gulped.

"Why do you look so shocked?" Alexander asked, "The whole point of the extraction mission was to get *you* off of Asgard and over here. If you'd been killed in that crash or been torn apart by the natives, it would have all been for nought."

"I see…" Mortimer replied hesitantly.

"Do you want a drink?" Alexander asked, raising the glass he was holding.

"No thanks," Mortimer answered politely.

"Good," Alexander replied, "this stuff was synthesised from the venom of various local fauna. All paralytic neurotoxins. It would kill you in minutes."

He downed the whole glass in one go.

Mortimer didn't react. He knew for a fact that Alexander's metabolism would clean out the neurotoxins. He had personally designed the original enhancements.

"That brings me to your purpose here," Alexander continued.

"You want my expertise?" Mortimer guessed.

"Yes," Alexander responded seriously, "for something very specific."

He put the empty glass down and stared hard at Mortimer, his glowing green eyes revealing rage simmering just beneath the veneer of calm.

"Do you remember what happened to me?" he asked.

"…All too well…" Mortimer replied, his pulse quickening.

The look on Alexander's face turned into a grimace and then to absolute stone.

Mortimer felt immobilised by that gaze. He remembered very clearly what Alexander was talking about and it made him very afraid. Had he been brought halfway across the spiral arm just so his former friend could personally exact revenge?

"Every 24 hours I get at least one episode," Alexander explained with a layer of fury in his voice, "this wave of pure rage that I can't control, and it's all thanks to you, on the orders of the DNI and the bionic-eyed bitch who runs it."

"And you want me to find a permanent solution?" Mortimer asked.

Alexander pulled an inhaler out of his pocket and stared at it as though he hated it.

"Whenever I have an episode, this counteracts it," he growled, "the effect is strong enough to last me as long as an episode would."

"It might be difficult to design a permanent—" Mortimer began to explain.

Alexander dropped the inhaler and launched himself at his guest faster than he could blink. Mortimer felt a hand close around his throat and squeeze his windpipe. Then he felt himself being lifted bodily out of the chair and into the air.

He wriggled and flopped about like a fish yanked out of the water, his eyes bulging as he struggled to breathe. Alexander held him at arm's length and stared into his eyes with a murderous look, giving him just enough air to stop him from passing out, never moving his arm and not blinking once.

After a while, Alexander relaxed his grip on Mortimer's throat and let him go. Mortimer dropped from mid-air and slumped back into the chair, clasping his throat and hyperventilating. Alexander loomed over him, the murderous look in his eyes barely softened.

"Why do you think I brought you here in the first place?" Alexander snarled, his voice brimming with rage, "why do you think I had you synthesise that mind-altering gas in case the first plan failed? Why do you think I went to all the trouble required to get you off of Asgard and all the way out here undetected?"

Mortimer was completely taken aback, and he didn't dare utter another word.

"I arranged all of that," Alexander said dangerously, "because I want to put an end to these episodes. *You* designed whatever botched enhancement causes these episodes, and as a result, I almost murdered my own wife and son!"

Mortimer kept his mouth shut as Alexander pulled off his shirt and tossed it to one side. His torso was made of chiselled muscle but marred by seven scars across his chest. Seven non-lethal bullet wounds permanently etched into his flesh.

"Fortunately, Jez was a good shot," Alexander continued, "and you were a good enough scientist to ensure that my regenerative abilities saved me, none of which absolves you of responsibility for all this. So if even *you* cannot find a permanent solution to the problem that *you* created, I may as well kill you right now."

Mortimer was acutely aware that choosing his words poorly would make them his last.

"I...said it would be difficult..." he ventured bravely, "...but not impossible."

"For your sake, that's very good to hear," Alexander replied, picking the inhaler off the ground and putting it back in his pocket, "the only other thing I want to hear from you is a list of things that you need to get it done."

"Well," said Mortimer, rubbing his neck, "the first thing I'll need is a lab."

* * *

Mortimer did his best to keep his distance from Alexander without losing sight of him. He knew, of course, about the rage episodes. It had been the biggest crisis in the Voidstalker Programme's history; and, given that he had been the head of research at the time, Alexander was right that the fault lay with him.

Alexander didn't say a word. However severe his loss of control, he was clearly still rational enough to know that he needed Mortimer alive. It remained to be seen how long Mortimer could count on that.

"Your biometrics have already been added to the security system," Alexander explained as they approached a reinforced door, "you can access any part of the facility that I permit, including this area of the research wing."

The sensor flash-scanned Alexander's eyes and the door opened.

"This is will be your new lab," he said, showing Mortimer inside.

"What kind of computing resources do you have?" Mortimer asked.

"Nothing compared to the Directorate, I'm afraid," Alexander replied, "but we do have a top-of-the-line quantum server which should be adequate."

"There may be other things I'll need," Mortimer added.

"Give me a list by the next solar day and I'll have the Network acquire it," Alexander answered, "I have plenty of connections."

It was a far cry from the facilities Mortimer had used at the DNI, but it was impressive nonetheless; and judging by the brands, the equipment was indeed top-of-the-line.

"I'll have two androids sent to serve as your lab assistants," Alexander continued, "but you will not be working with any of the rest of the staff. Understood?"

That last part was an instruction and a threat, and Mortimer nodded.

"I've also given you access to my medical records," Alexander added.

"What are the rest of the labs for?" Mortimer asked.

"Other research," Alexander answered, "the nature of which is 'need-to-know'."

"Do they have anything to do with the natives?" Mortimer pressed.

Alexander walked up to Mortimer, cornering him against a worktop.

"Which part of the phrase 'need-to-know' do you not understand?" Alexander growled.

Mortimer refrained from answering.

"The short answer is 'yes'," Alexander added, turning to leave, "that's all you need to know until you produce results...which reminds me."

Without warning, he grabbed Mortimer and threw him to the ground. Mortimer barely had time to break his fall as Alexander pinned him to the floor. He then pulled Mortimer's head back and pressed something against the back of his neck. The collar closed and locked itself around Mortimer's neck, a little green light winking into existence.

"What the frick are you doing?!" Mortimer demanded, struggling ineffectually under Alexander's weight, "what is this thing?"

"Something to ensure your cooperation and obedience," Alexander responded, getting off of Mortimer and letting him stand up again.

The collar fit snugly around Mortimer's neck without causing him any discomfort, but whenever he tried to tug on it, it constricted sharply.

"If the collar's countdown reaches zero, it will inject a toxin into your bloodstream," Alexander explained, "unless I enter a code on the back of the collar."

"...How much...time is in the countdown?" Mortimer asked falteringly.

"45 hours," Alexander replied, "one for each of the intervening years."

Mortimer wanted to faint with fear, but his limbs were frozen so he couldn't do even that. This was more than just a means to keep him in line, Alexander evidently hated him and wanted revenge almost as much as he wanted a cure.

"Take as long as you need to find a cure and get it right," Alexander ordered, "but in the meantime, you're not going anywhere."

He departed the room and locked the door behind him, leaving Mortimer standing there wondering exactly what he had gotten himself into.

* * *

The underground tram came to halt. The engine fell silent and the headlamps died, leaving the glow-strips on the walls as the only source of light. A dozen people disembarked and began to unload caskets and other equipment. Once they were ready, the team continued down the tunnel on foot, lugging their equipment with them.

The mountain was an extinct volcano, and the magma produced aeons ago had excavated this network of caves, permeating the mountain like a web of igneous capillaries. The cave walls were covered with millions of micro-crystals that refracted the light from the glow-strips, creating hypnotic subterranean rainbows.

There were no navigational markers, so they relied on their wrist-top computers to guide them to what looked like a dead-end. The path widened out into a bowl shape with walls that narrowed into a vertical shaft stretching all the way up to the surface. It was a sinkhole half a kilometre deep, and at the very bottom was this dead-end cavern.

The team began setting up, laying the caskets to one side and assembling the machinery. Above their heads, a ring of devices bolted into the chamber's ceiling glowed, their light refracting through the micro-crystals and scattering across the cavern. The glittering cascade of light gave the cave a heavenly aura – ironic, considering its real purpose.

"Get ready!" the team leader shouted.

Everyone rushed to make sure the equipment was ready before racing to the edge of the cavern. Sitting in a monitoring booth, one of the men brought up a live video feed showing a bird's eye view of the sinkhole and the surrounding area.

From above, the sinkhole looked like an opaque abyss – an optical illusion created by the holographic projectors around the cavern roof. The mouth of the sinkhole was surrounded on all sides by the alien temple complex. Nine figures were standing near the edge as the priests and guards prepared to throw them in.

The alien priests were dressed in garish outfits, adorned with multi-coloured feathers and bones bleached white by the sun. The temple guards wore ceremonial armour and wielded two-handed staves while the prisoners awaited their deaths with stoic patience.

Once the sun's rays were aligned with the sinkhole, two priests seized the first prisoner, ran him along an ornate stone ramp, and tossed him in. As the crowds behind them cheered and chanted, the priests repeated the action with the rest of the sacrificial prisoners one by one until they had all been thrown to their supposed deaths.

The artificial gravity projectors were activated as a tiny speck appeared far above, its silhouette barely visible until it fell through the holographic distortion field. Warbling as it fell, the first prisoner was caught by the gravity projector, slowing its fall dramatically as a pair of technicians ran over with an open casket.

The prisoner fell straight in, and a set of restraints wrapped themselves around the writhing alien, tightening in response to its struggles. The casket sealed itself automatically and the two technicians dragged it away as fast as they could.

This procedure was repeated with practised speed until all nine 'sacrifices' had been captured and locked inside the waiting caskets.

With all nine alien prisoners seized, the team prepared to leave. Once the equipment had been shut down and packed away, the caskets were carried back to the waiting tram to be transported back to the facility. The caskets were stood upright along the wall of the carriage with the rest of the equipment stacked in a corner.

The alien prisoners were still conscious, and they squirmed and thrashed inside their atmospherically controlled caskets. Their struggles were futile and their warbling shrieks were inaudible to the Human technicians.

As the tram began to move, one of the technicians stood up and walked over to one of the caskets, peering in through the glass observation window. The alien inside was still raging and thrashing, its blazing orange eyes bulging and its leafy green lips peeled back to reveal its razor-sharp teeth.

When the prisoner saw the technician, its rage faded. It had never seen a Human before and as the technician stared it down, the alien stared back.

"Welcome to hell," the technician said with a cold sneer.

THE INVESTIGATION

Everything around him was pitch black. It was so dark the gloom was almost like a physical substance. He still felt the manacles securing his limbs and gravity pulling on his body, reminding him that this wasn't a dream. He didn't know how he'd ended up here; all he remembered was a shock-dart piercing his skin and excruciating pain.

A helmet of some kind had been secured around his head, presumably to monitor his neural activity, but it was unusually bulky for a neural monitoring device. It wasn't causing hallucinations or disorientation, so it wasn't a torture device either.

"*Why did you meet with Mortimer Shelton prior to the attacks?*" asked a disembodied voice through an electronic filter.

"He's a friend of mine, so I paid him a social visit," he repeated for the twentieth time, "and I still have no idea what attacks you're talking about."

"*Don't lie, Gabriel,*" the voice commanded.

"You know perfectly well that I'm not lying," Gabriel replied patiently.

The voice would speak to him periodically, informing him of events that had occurred whilst he was away and demanding to know his role in them.

"*The sooner you confess, the sooner you will be free, Gabriel,*" said the voice.

"I told you, I have nothing to confess," Gabriel answered.

"*If you don't tell us the truth–*" the voice began to speak.

"I *am* telling you the truth!" Gabriel interrupted sharply, his patience wearing out, "and by now, you should already know that!"

There was a long and ominous pause as Gabriel wondered if there was any point in answering back to the darkness.

Then the darkness evaporated, revealing a bare holding cell with a door at the far end. As Gabriel's eyes adjusted to the light, the door opened and a figure entered.

She wore a midnight black uniform with an admiral's insignia. Her jet black hair was tied back in a bun, and her slightly pale face conveyed no emotion whatsoever. Her organic left eye was hazel-coloured, but her right eye was a bionic implant with a laser-red iris. Her official title was the Director-General of Naval Intelligence, but the obvious nickname had stuck.

"This is not the welcome I would like to give you," Red-eye said as she approached, "but unfortunately, a lot has happened in your absence."

"Enough to snatch and question one of your own operatives?" Gabriel asked wryly.

"I'm afraid so," Red-eye replied, "Although the neural imaging scanners have shown you to be innocent…or an insidiously good liar."

"So why am I here?" Gabriel demanded impertinently.

"Do you remember being exposed to that hallucinogenic chemical in Dr Shelton's lab?" Red-eye asked, "And the box with the injector that was sent to you?"

Gabriel's anger cooled as he remembered both.

"That same chemical was used in the terror attacks which killed 60 people and poisoned thousands of others," Red-eye continued, "and before that, it was used to poison a team of our operatives who proceeded to gun down a dozen innocent people due to its influence."

What remained of Gabriel's anger evaporated as the words sank in.

"Furthermore," Red-eye added, "you were named during the investigation."

"Into the attack?" Gabriel asked, straining to believe a word of this.

"No," Red-eye replied, "the investigation launched by the Internal Security Department to root out and capture the mole who facilitated Dr Shelton's escape from the planet."

For a moment, Gabriel found himself unable to speak.

"A…a what?" he stammered.

"A mole," Red-eye replied calmly, "he was a data analyst who, when asked who had directed him to sabotage the Directorate's surveillance network, named you."

The mere fact that there *was* a mole was shocking enough. A deluge of questions came to the tip of Gabriel's tongue, but he simply stared in disbelief.

"You did well to eliminate the hive-ship," Red-eye continued, "but we have a new crisis, and whether or not it implicates you, it certainly involves you."

Gabriel remained dumbstruck.

"In any case," Red-eye summarised, "you are clearly not the one behind these attacks, let alone the wider conspiracy, so you are free to go."

"Is that what the headgear was for?" Gabriel asked.

"Yes and no," Red-eye responded, "a farfetched theory occurred to me that you might have been enthralled during the Loki mission last year."

Gabriel didn't know whether to be shocked or outraged or just burst out laughing.

"Thanks to the device, that theory was disproven," Red-eye added, "this latest incident has nothing to do with the Swarm as far as we can tell."

"Your vote of confidence in my loyalty is appreciated," Gabriel replied sarcastically.

* * *

As a courtesy to a senior operative – or as an apology for kidnapping and interrogating him – the DNI arranged a private sky-car to take Gabriel home. Before he left, Red-eye handed him a debrief summarising the events that had transpired in his absence. The details were so bizarre that Gabriel was scarcely able to believe them.

When the sky-car arrived at the apartment tower, Gabriel left the report in the vehicle and disembarked, making his way to his front door. The biometric sensor flash-scanned his eyes and he stepped inside.

He was home, and it certainly felt good to be home.

Aster was still at work and the children were still in their learning pods. Gabriel was exhausted; nonetheless, he decided to check on his children first.

He went to their bedroom and stood in the doorway. The holographic displays were dimly visible through the translucent canopies of the four pods; he could even see their fingers poking and swiping at the images in front of them. He opted not to disturb them.

Returning to the master bedroom, he saw one of the household androids standing watch over the crib where baby Emerald was sleeping. Gabriel let her sleep and went to the bathroom, the lighting strip above the mirror illuminating automatically.

He had a head of short black hair, light skin with a clean-shaven face, and a perpetually grim look on his face. Then there were his eyes with irises that shone a luminescent green. It was a genetic marker engineered into his genome by the DNI, marking him as a voidstalker.

"*Would you like a drink, sir?*" the household android asked, its voice electronically distorted and stripped of Human inflexions.

"Nutrient juice," Gabriel replied gruffly, waving the machine away.

"*Yes, sir,*" the android nodded politely before turning away.

Gabriel returned to the bedroom, still thinking about the debrief report. The mole naming him as his handler was obviously a lie, but it was a lie intended to sow doubt about the extent of the infiltration. Even so, why name him?

Then there were the two packages Mortimer had sent to his home. The antidote was one thing, but the second package, intended for his family, was more disturbing.

The android returned with a glass bubbling with fizzy nutrient juice. Gabriel took the glass, draining it dry before handing it back to the android. It tasted like fizzy water, but it was the nutritional equivalent of a full meal.

The sound of the front door opening and shutting reached Gabriel's ears and he marched to the hallway. His sense of urgency faded when he saw who it was.

"...Welcome home," Aster said awkwardly.

She approached Gabriel and walked into his waiting arms. He stroked her shoulder-length brunette curls and teased out the blonde highlights. They stood like that for a moment, savouring each other's presence before Gabriel finally broached the subject.

"The Directorate told me about the package," he said gravely, "the one Mortimer Shelton sent to you while I was gone."

Aster looked up at him with light brown eyes, then nodded slowly.

"Then we have a lot to talk about," she said, extricating herself from the embrace.

Aster went to the master bedroom and Gabriel followed her. She checked on baby Emerald first before turning to face him with pursed lips and a hard stare that he had never seen her give him before.

"What is the Voidstalker Programme for?" she demanded.

Gabriel flinched.

"Why would you want to know that?" he asked.

Aster unloaded with her version of events, including Mortimer Shelton's message sent through the tablet drone – something the debrief report hadn't included. By the time she had finished speaking, Gabriel was left speechless.

"Do you seriously have nothing to say?" she demanded.

"What exactly do you expect me to say?" Gabriel demanded in response.

"Something!" Aster snapped, "Something that fucking tells me you didn't know that your bosses were raising your own children to be lab rats!"

"What the fleek are you talking about?!" Gabriel snapped back at her.

"Weren't you listening to a word I just said?!" she exclaimed, "you're a puppet in a giant experiment being run by the DNI, and my children were born into that experiment!"

"You mean *our* children," Gabriel corrected her through teeth gritted in anger.

"Yes," Aster said coldly, taking a brave step towards Gabriel and glaring up at him, "that's precisely how they got entangled in this mess in the first place."

There was an angry standoff with Aster barely able to keep from quivering as Gabriel glared back at her. He could tell that she was angry, but so was he.

Baby Emerald began to cry, and Aster broke off the staring match to tend to the baby. She lifted the wailing infant out of her crib and rocked her gently. She kept a wary eye on the father as she sat down on the bed and cradled her daughter protectively.

Gabriel stormed out of the room.

* * *

The Spire was the most secretive building on Asgard as well as the most conspicuous. The structure itself jutted out from the ground like an iron spike, its jet black surface absorbing everything along the electromagnetic spectrum. It stood as a dark and humourless rebuke to the surrounding civilian opulence.

The Spire never slept. All Directorate operations in the sector were coordinated from this building, and legions of analysts worked in shifts at all hours. Crises of one kind or another were constantly flaring up, but the past few weeks had been particularly hectic.

The Spire had dozens of operations centres, one of which had been requisitioned to hunt for the perpetrators of the gas attacks. Having run out of leads, it was now tasked with rooting out any other moles that might have infiltrated the Directorate.

"We've finished running through every social connection the mole had," the analyst informed Red-eye, "there's absolutely nothing to indicate that he knew Colonel Thorn."

Red-eye nodded.

"Keep up the search," she ordered, handing the analyst a flexi-tablet, "in the meantime, there's another lead I want you to investigate."

The analyst looked at the flexi-tablet and furrowed his brow.

"I don't understand," he said quizzically, "this happened almost half a century ago."

"This is a separate lead that I want re-examined," Red-eye explained, "It has nothing to do with the mole, but it could shed light on the identity of his handlers."

"Understood, but…what could have been overlooked?" the analyst asked.

"The fate of the cargo that the ship was carrying," Red-eye replied.

"Understood," the analyst said before leaving.

Red-eye turned back to her wrist-top. It was a custom model made especially for her with a screen whose contents were only visible through the filters in her bionic eye.

She was looking at two incident reports, each of which had happened 45 years ago. One was stamped with a tier 2 classification and the other with a tier 4 classification. The analyst had been sent away to investigate the tier 4 incident.

The two incidents were more than merely connected; one had led directly to the other. The mystery was what had transpired afterwards. She doubted that the analysts would discover anything new, but it was still worth an attempt.

* * *

The passenger compartment was unusually cushy for a transport shuttle, complete with padded leather seats and deceptively comfortable safety harnesses. There was even a decent-sized viewing screen installed inside the armrest for inflight entertainment. Even so, Jezebel felt no less a prisoner now than she had in prison.

The trip in the cargo ship had been boring but bearable, despite the revoltingly grimy interior. Her mysterious rescuers had given her a private cabin for the journey, but despite the apparent hospitality, she knew better than to believe that she was truly free.

The viewing screen was a touch-sensitive panel made from a single pane of glass. The light from the cabin made her reflection visible, and even though it wasn't a proper mirror, seeing her own face again gave her pause.

Her lips were blood red, and her hair was jet black with blonde highlights and styled into a corn-braid. She regarded her reflection through hazel eyes with a look of aristocratic superiority on her face crinkled with disdain for the hideous spacer uniform she was wearing. Even so, there were no other clothes available, and it was a relief to be out of a prison jumpsuit.

She activated the viewing screen, beholding a vast expanse of verdant vegetation on the video feed. The topography was also highlighted, showing an enormous mountain looming over the landscape, a mass of greenery covering its slopes all the way up to the summit.

Having spent her whole life on the hyper-urbanised planet Asgard, Jezebel found the natural beauty of this alien world dazzling. Even when viewed on a screen from high above, the endless verdure looked luscious and unspoilt.

Near the foot of the mountain, a whole area of the rainforest had been cleared away and in its place was a geometric arrangement of structures. It was a city, a vast alien city made out of white stone, with some buildings standing several storeys tall.

What kind of world was this and why had her rescuers – or kidnappers – decided to bring her here? They were well beyond the frontiers of Human space, of that she was certain. That made perfect sense if the point was to evade the long reach of the law, but why choose a world that was already inhabited, even by primitives?

The journey timer flashed in the corner of the screen, alerting her that the shuttle was five minutes away from its destination.

Jezebel switched off the screen and folded it away. The inertial dampeners prevented her from feeling the turbulence outside, but they couldn't prevent her stomach from physically moving as the shuttle dropped dramatically. Feeling the altitude change in her gut made her double-check her safety harness.

Just a few more minutes and she would get to find out why she had been brought to this backwater planet…just a few more minutes.

* * *

The hangar entrance was built into the side of the mountain, and the shuttle swooped straight in through the open blast doors, unseen by the natives. Once the shuttle was inside, the blast doors sealed up again, concealing the entrance with a facade of foliage.

Inside the hangar, a robotic arm plucked the shuttle from the air and pulled it into a docking cradle. Then the hatch opened and Jezebel exited the shuttle.

As soon as she stepped out, her ears were assailed by a cacophony of industrial noise. The mechanical whining of robotic arms and the humming of automated loader trucks was distractingly loud. Jezebel covered her ears in discomfort until one of her escorts handed her a pair of earmuffs, which she gladly accepted.

Jezebel's escort guided her down the length of the hangar deeper into the mountain. As they walked, she saw dozens of other shuttlecraft held inside docking cradles along the walls. It wasn't just shuttlecraft; there were all manner of ground vehicles and atmospheric craft as well, many of them sporting hardpoints on their hulls.

Jezebel's legs were exhausted by the time they reached a reinforced door near the far end. Her escort activated the intercom and spoke into it.

"She's arrived," he said.

The heavy door unlocked from the inside and swung open. The escort allowed Jezebel in first before following her inside, leading her down a corridor and up a flight of steps.

It wasn't long before they arrived in what looked like the living room of an apartment. It was fully furnished, complete with couches, an elegant carpet, and a high-backed chair in front of a replica fireplace. This was evidently someone's private quarters, and the decor stood in bewildering contrast to the rest of the facility.

"Leave us," a male voice commanded from behind the chair.

The escort saluted and departed, leaving Jezebel frozen to the spot.

"Do you still remember me?" the voice's owner asked as he stood up.

Jezebel didn't answer. She remained motionless with shock as the figure approached, looking at her with emerald eyes that shimmered under the light.

"I...killed you..." Jezebel stammered in disbelief, "...didn't I?"

"That's the least of the catching up we have to do," Alexander replied.

* * *

Alexander and Jezebel sat down opposite one another, the host waiting patiently for his guest to come to terms with the fact that her 'late' husband was still alive.

"How was prison?" he asked after a pause.

"Awful," she replied, her cool tone sharpened by her flute-like upper-class accent, "I thought I would lose my mind in that tiny box."

"I hear you have only yourself to blame for ending up there," Alexander remarked.

Jezebel's eye twitched, but she opted not to respond.

"I'm assuming that you've got plenty of questions of your own," Alexander said, "so what would you like to ask me?"

"How are you still alive?" Jezebel demanded.

"The DNI's medics saved me," Alexander explained, "then they transported me off the planet, and 45 years later I had you broken out of prison and brought here."

"You're skipping a big chunk of time," Jezebel pointed out.

"It's not relevant at the moment," Alexander replied.

Jezebel strongly disagreed.

"What is this place?" she asked.

"It took a long time to build," Alexander answered round-aboutly, "especially given that we had to hide the project from the attention of the locals. But this complex now serves as the nerve centre for the Network's operations both on this planet and elsewhere."

"Would it be too nosy to ask who your bankrollers are?" Jezebel asked suspiciously.

"Not at all," Alexander replied with a cunning smile, "given that they don't exist."

"You expect me to believe that *you* funded all of this?" Jezebel demanded.

"Whether or not you believe it," Alexander answered, "that's what happened."

Jezebel glared at him.

"I'm afraid I can't tell you the purpose at this point," he added.

"If there's no one above you, that makes you the one in charge," Jezebel pointed out, "so why can't you tell me the purpose?"

"It's complicated," Alexander responded.

"It always was with you," Jezebel said sharply.

Alexander said nothing.

"Why did you break me out of prison?" Jezebel demanded.

"I need your connections," was the reply, "specifically your connections to the political and business circles on Asgard."

Of course there was an ulterior motive.

"My sources tell me you've built quite a business empire," Alexander remarked.

"Did they also tell you that I murdered my husband and used the life insurance payout as the seed money?" Jezebel asked acidly.

"As you can see, those rumours are false," Alexander laughed.

Jezebel replied with a stony stare and cold silence. It wasn't funny in the slightest.

"However, you are correct that I didn't have you broken out of prison due to altruism," Alexander continued, suddenly businesslike, "the Network is still growing and will receive an enormous boost from your connections."

"So you want me here as a business partner?" Jezebel asked.

"That's one way to think of it," Alexander replied.

They both knew that she was in no position to refuse. Even if she could leave, she was a fugitive within Human space and couldn't start over in the alien-infested frontiers beyond. Her only leverage was her usefulness to his plans – whatever they might be.

"I presume this facility has a communications array?" Jezebel asked.

"Of sorts, yes," Alexander answered, "but since we don't want to expose our location to the rest of the galaxy, the setup is a bit more elaborate than usual."

"Well, if you're going to use my connections," Jezebel continued, "you'll have to be more specific about what you want."

* * *

Gabriel lay on the couch in the living room. Aster's words had left a sore wound and red-hot rancour smouldering in his mind. First the Directorate had suspected him of betrayal, and now his own wife – even referring to the children as 'hers' as if they needed protection from their own father.

He clenched his fist and glared at the ceiling like he wanted to punch it. The wall was closer, and he wondered how much force it would take to make a hole. It was a dangerous feeling to have, and as long as he felt this way, it was best to keep his distance from his family, or at least until his head was clearer. Besides, he needed to think.

The Directorate probably still suspected that there was a connection between himself and this obscure network of infiltrators. Now that his innocence had been established, however, there was no way Red-eye would allow him anywhere near the investigation. He was simply too close to the whole thing.

Maybe that was for the best. Once again, he had made it home alive and reasonably unharmed. Once again, his children would get to see his face in the flesh and not in a memorial photograph at his funeral. It wouldn't be long before he got bored again and wanted to take on another mission, but for now he should enjoy being home.

The pitter-patter of small feet reached his ears. Eight-year-old Orion, six-year-old Rose, four-year-old Violet, and two-year-old Leonidas snuck into the living room, peering over the couch's armrest with shimmering green eyes.

"I'm home, sweethearts," Gabriel said to them with a welcoming smile.

They didn't reply. Normally they would pounce on him with joy, happy to see their father again. Instead, they filed around to the front, approaching with sombre looks on their faces. Gabriel sat up on the couch to face them.

"What's wrong?" he asked, worry creeping across his mind.

The children looked at each other, wondering who should speak first.

"Are your bosses going to take us away?" Rose asked mutedly.

The question made Gabriel's chest tighten.

"Of course not," he answered emphatically, "why would you think that?"

"Because they heard and saw the message from your old friend Mortimer Shelton," Aster explained, appearing in the doorway cradling Emerald in her arms, "including the part about you and the other voidstalkers being the Directorate's 'greatest creations'."

Gabriel felt floored. Throughout all their arguments about the secrecy of his work, his frequent absences from home, and the directives of his mercurial superiors in the Directorate, the children had always remained blissfully ignorant.

Not anymore.

"They have a lot of questions for you," Aster added sternly, "and as their father, you owe them the truth – certainly more of it than you've ever given me."

With that gratuitous parting barb, Aster departed the room, leaving Gabriel to face his children's interrogation alone.

No one said anything initially. There was silence as the children exchanged awkward looks with one another, wondering what they should ask first.

"Why do our injuries heal so quickly?" Orion spoke up.

Gabriel dreaded to think what could have prompted that question, but he noticed Violet wince and clutch her arm defensively.

"Violet got hurt while you were away," Orion added.

"Let me see," Gabriel said to Violet.

Violet pursed her lips but approached, reluctantly extending her arm. Gabriel took his daughter's arm in his hands and examined the skin, looking for the wound.

"The scar went away," Rose blurted out, "but there was lots of blood–"

"No! No! No!" Violet squealed in distress, covering her ears and shutting her eyes.

Gabriel wasn't surprised that his children had inherited his enhancements, but Mortimer had assured him that all of the military-grade enhancements had been left recessive.

Evidently not.

"Well, you take after me," said Gabriel, pulling up his trouser leg, "I got hit in the leg on my last mission and had a scar here."

"What scar?" Leonidas asked, looking for the wound.

"It happened a week ago," Gabriel explained, "so it's all healed up."

They stared at his unharmed leg in fascination.

"You're all doing extremely well in the learning pods," Gabriel continued, "in fact, you're learning the material exponentially faster than other children your age."

"What's 'exponentially'," Violet asked.

"When a value grows proportionally to its derivative," Orion answered immediately.

"What's 'drib-a-tiff'?" Leonidas asked.

"'Deh-rih-vah-tive'," Orion corrected his brother, "speaking properly, you dummy."

He gave Leonidas a playful thump on the arm.

"Don't hit your brother!" Gabriel snapped, his temper flaring suddenly.

The children flinched and took a collective step backwards.

"Apologise to your brother," Gabriel ordered Orion.

"But Leo pronounced it—" Orion tried to say.

"Now," Gabriel ordered, baring his teeth like a wolf.

Orion gulped.

"I'm sorry, Leo," he mumbled sheepishly, "for hitting you."

"Don't ever hit each other," Gabriel admonished them.

The children nodded slowly.

"Back to the question," Gabriel continued, "you're learning faster than other children your age, and that's something you got from me as well."

"Will we get other powers from you?" Violet asked.

"Maybe," Gabriel answered uncertainly.

"Are you…sure they won't take us away?" Rose asked fearfully.

"They won't," Gabriel replied bluntly, "I'll kill them if they try."

The children nodded, only partially convinced. Gabriel knelt down on the carpet and pulled them all into a group hug, squeezing them against his chest. They reciprocated, hugging their father and each other close.

* * *

SC-0611 had been a shadow courier: a stealth ship built to transport sensitive cargo between Directorate facilities. The vessel had departed Asgard 45 years ago bound for a facility in another star system and had never arrived.

"What exactly does the director-general think was overlooked the first time?" one of the analysts asked in exasperation.

"If I knew that, we would be finished by now," the lead analyst replied, resetting the simulation, "now let's try this again."

The simulation displayed the gravitational fields of the stars and planets, shading them according to their strength at a given point in space. The shadow courier was depicted as a blue dot navigating a path of least gravitational resistance through Q-space.

"From the beginning," said the lead analyst.

"The SC-0611 departs the Helheim facility and sets course for the edge of the system," one of the analysts repeated wearily, "approximately five hours after departure, it reaches the edge of the system and initiates the jump to Q-space. All of that is based on telemetry picked up by the in-system sensor network and is therefore verifiable."

The blue dot duly set off from the shaded bubble representing the Asgard star system, snaking between the animated bubbles representing neighbouring star systems.

"Now we get to the puzzling part," the lead analyst recounted, "almost exactly halfway through the journey, the shadow courier's Q-space transponder sent an automated message registering a shipboard anomaly."

The blue dot stopped dead in the middle of the star map and the simulation paused.

"Q-space isn't known to exhibit 'anomalous behaviour'," said one the analysts.

"System failure during Q-space then?" another analyst suggested.

"A technical failure would have been logged and transmitted automatically by the Q-space transponder," the lead analyst pointed out, "Also, if the ship's Q-engine failed in transit, the ship would have been forced out of Q-space entirely."

"What about sabotage?" someone else suggested.

"Every crewmember was subject to background checks," the lead analyst reminded everyone, "we would know by now if this was deliberate."

He didn't sound convinced by his own words, and neither was anyone else. Recent events had made the possibility of sabotage uncomfortably strong.

"What kind of cargo was it carrying?" another analyst asked.

The lead analyst brought up the cargo manifest on the main screen. Besides the usual supplies, there was only one item on the manifest: a stasis pod, but the identity of the occupant was blacked out by a tier 2 classification.

"So everyone on board except for the cargo passed background checks," one of the analysts pointed out, "and we know the 'cargo' was dangerous because that's why the ship was carrying him or her – or it – away from Asgard in the first place."

"And no one thought to flag this up at the time?" someone else asked in disbelief.

"Of course not," another person snorted, "can't you see the classification?"

"Enough," the lead analyst ordered, "The point is, we've found our saboteur."

* * *

Rather than start his assigned project, Mortimer spent an hour examining his new collar and bitterly regretting the choices that had led to him wearing it.

The collar was made of an elastic composite material whose colour blended in with his skin. Whenever he touched it, the collar would turn black and a countdown indicator would appear on the front showing him how much time was left. The actual interface was on the back, however, preventing him from entering the reset code himself.

There was no safe way to remove the collar, and no doubt the material was impervious to being cut or burnt. Apparently, Alexander had put it around his neck instead of his wrist to make it even harder to remove. If that was true, his former friend-turned-captor had given him too much credit: Mortimer wasn't sure he could stomach chopping off his own hand.

In all honesty, the device itself was ingenious. What kind of sociopathic hatred would motivate someone to design something like this?

Stupid question. He knew exactly what kind of hatred was at work here, he had already been given an earful about the 'incident'. That meant his best chance of getting rid of the collar was to fix the consequences.

His personal laboratory was a far cry from the DNI's facilities, but it was still better than the tiny medical clinic he used to work in. Nonetheless, it needed some upgrades. Stepping out of the lab, Mortimer wandered around with a data slate looking for signs of life.

The corridors were sterile and unadorned, and every door was sealed with a biometric lock. There was a map on the wall, but when Mortimer tapped it he realised it was a printed diagram, an oddly low-tech feature for a facility like this to have.

There was a pounding noise.

He raced towards the source of the noise and came to a lab with a wall-sized observation window. Inside, he saw several people dressed in hazmat suits trying to wrestle a green-skinned alien onto a medical bed while the alien thrashed about as it fought to be free.

Finally, they managed to clamp a manacle around each of the creature's wrists, and then both its ankles. Once its limbs were secure, one more binding was extended to cover the creature's torso, tightening hard enough to pin it down.

Mortimer watched as the alien's struggles weakened until the restraints finally did their work. Having subdued their test subject, the lab attendants went to their work stations and began preparing whatever experiment they were about to perform.

"Do you need something?" a voice behind him asked sharply.

The person challenging him was a woman dressed in medical overalls. Her skin looked pallid as if she hadn't been exposed to natural sunlight for years, and she glared expectantly at Mortimer with a pair of mud-brown eyes as she waited for an answer.

"I've...got a requisition order," he replied nervously, handing over the data slate.

The woman took the data slate and glared at the screen as she read it.

"Quite a wish list," she remarked.

"One which the boss himself wants fulfilled as a matter of priority," Mortimer added.

"Yes, he did say something about that," the woman replied, slipping the data slate into her coat pocket, "I'll get it to the procurement team once I'm done. In the meantime, feel free to watch if you're still curious."

"What are you going to do?" Mortimer asked.

"We're about to conduct a toxicological resistance analysis," the woman answered.

"You're going to poison it?" Mortimer asked with horrified incredulity.

"Yes," came the detached reply, "and then monitor its bio-chemistry in real-time to see how its immune system reacts."

"But that's…" Mortimer tried to protest but the words failed to come.

"Crude? Cruel?" the woman said, unconcerned by his misgivings, "There's a multitude of reasons why we do it this way but suffice it to say that this way is simpler."

After shooting down his objections, she entered the lab and shut the door behind her.

Not once in his decades-long career had Mortimer used, or been asked to use, live test subjects, not even alien test subjects. Everything had been done with quantum computers that could simulate the biochemistry of an organism down to the minutest detail.

So why were they experimenting on these aliens?

* * *

Alexander found the natives fascinating. To the authorities that governed Humanity, the only alien species worth worrying about were spacefaring races and pathogens. Alien flora and fauna, and any other species too primitive to pose a threat were ignored.

He reclined on the couch in front of a wall-sized screen, watching the live video feed. The lights had been dimmed to create a cinema-like atmosphere, making the viewing screen the only source of light. There were thousands of films and serial shows he could watch, but the reality outside was far more interesting than fiction.

The stealth drone was equipped with a camera powerful enough to be mounted on a spy satellite. It soared far beyond the gaze of the clueless natives, enabling Alexander to watch as the assembled armies of two rival city-states clashed in the jungle.

The readout on the screen counted approximately ten thousand infantry on each side along with several thousand predatory mounts being used as cavalry. The camera also had a sophisticated thermal filter, allowing it to see through the tree canopy and pick out the shapes of the individual alien warriors as they battled and brawled.

The door opened and someone walked in. Since no one else had access to this wing of the facility, it had to be Jezebel.

"How are you settling in?" Alexander asked without turning around.

"Well enough," Jezebel replied as she approached.

"There's plenty of space on the couch," Alexander said, beckoning to her.

Jezebel sat down at the far end of the couch, keeping her distance. She had changed out of her dirty spacer overalls and was wearing her trademark business suit instead.

"This probably isn't to your taste," Alexander said, "but I find it strangely entertaining."

"What are they doing?" Jezebel asked, squinting at the countless dancing shapes.

"The city-state at the foot of this mountain had its territory invaded by another city-state to the north," Alexander explained, "so the two armies are fighting it out."

"Is this why you've set up shop on this planet?" Jezebel asked, subtly shifting the topic, "so you can watch primitives killing each other?"

"It's an entertaining distraction," Alexander replied, "but no, it's not the main purpose. This planet is outside settled space, Human or alien, which makes it a convenient hiding spot for a dead man like me or a fugitive like you."

"There are plenty of uninhabited planets," Jezebel pointed out, "why this one?"

Alexander didn't answer.

"I told you I need to know more about what you're up to here if I'm going to leverage my 'connections' for you," Jezebel pressed him.

"Yes, you did," Alexander responded, pursing his lips, "well, this facility also includes a sizeable R&D wing, and much of the research is not strictly legal."

Jezebel shifted uncomfortably on the couch, wanting to get up and leave.

"It's got nothing to do with xenotechnology, in case that's what you're worried about," Alexander clarified, "although, I'm surprised that you would be uncomfortable with illegality given the nature of your former business empire."

"I didn't touch anything xenotech-related," Jezebel replied, then conceded, "although I have backed some legally questionable ventures."

"Bad girl," Alexander smirked.

"Don't call me that," Jezebel said sharply.

"Will you shoot me again if I do?" Alexander laughed.

"What the fleek is wrong with you?" Jezebel demanded angrily, "How can you joke about something like that?"

"It takes the edge off of things," Alexander responded.

"I'd prefer you just tell me what happened to you in the intervening decades," Jezebel said bitterly, "because so far, your story is that the DNI locked you up and took you away, and somewhere along the line you got free."

Alexander remained silent.

On the screen, the massed alien armies clashed in the undergrowth. Whatever strategy the opposing commanders might have devised fell apart as the two sides engaged in a vicious free-for-all. They rarely took prisoners, and then only as sacrificial offerings.

More test subjects for the R&D team.

"Aren't you curious about your son?" Jezebel asked.

"Very," Alexander answered, "I hear he's joined the Voidstalker Programme."

"The what?" Jezebel asked, mystified.

"Oh, of course, the DNI didn't bother to tell you about that," Alexander said, "or that I was part of the programme myself, hence the 'incident' that parted us."

"Did you know he married a colonial girl?" Jezebel asked, her lip curling in disdain.

"Yes, and raised quite a brood," Alexander replied.

"I should have guessed you would be well informed," Jezebel remarked, sliding a little closer, "which makes me wonder why you need my connections at all."

Alexander picked up on the unstated question and turned to her.

"I need customers," he answered.

"What are you selling?" Jezebel asked.

"Do you really want to talk business now?" Alexander asked back.

"Since 'business' is why you broke me out of prison in the first place," Jezebel pointed out, "we'll have to talk about it at some point."

"Very true," he conceded, "this planet is a proverbial goldmine, but its isolation makes it difficult to cash in on its riches."

"What kind of riches?" Jezebel asked.

Alexander pointed to the screen.

The aliens were still hurling spears, swinging clubs, and clawing each other to death. The carnivorous mounts were lashing out at anything that moved, including their own side, trampling on them or tearing them to shreds.

"This planet is overflowing with biomedical research potential," Alexander explained, "The dominant species alone has a fascinating biochemistry."

Jezebel understood what he meant, and she didn't look comfortable with it.

"That's a pretty sordid business plan you have," she remarked with a grimace.

"There's no xenotechnology involved," Alexander reiterated, "so there's no reason for the authorities to take an undue interest."

"That doesn't convince me," Jezebel said sceptically.

"It's not quite illegal," he replied, "just like being a vulture capitalist isn't quite illegal."

Jezebel's eye twitched.

"Yes, I know you moved away from that industry," Alexander continued, "but the point is you're already in too deep to start worrying about morality or legality."

"I want to hit you," Jezebel hissed.

"That would be an improvement over shooting me," Alexander quipped.

"Are you too much of a coward to just ask about how your family has been for the past half-century?" Jezebel exclaimed.

There was no reply.

"Or have you turned from a demon to a sociopath?"

Alexander snapped and lunged at Jezebel, grabbing her wrist and pulling her towards him. His face was twisted with rage and his iridescent emerald eyes were ablaze.

"I have done my level best not to think about you or Gabriel for 45 years!" Alexander snarled, "I almost killed my own family because of what the DNI did to me! So excuse me for preferring not to relive that!"

Jezebel was frozen as Alexander visibly seethed with fury as if the effort of containing his anger was almost unbearable.

Suddenly, he pushed her back onto the couch and pulled something out of his pocket, turning his back to her as he pressed it against his face and inhaled deeply. He stood there hyperventilating as his breathing slowed. When he turned around, his rage had evaporated.

"Every 24 hours I have an episode," Alexander explained in a quiet voice, "and it was during one of those episodes that I attacked you and Gabriel."

Jezebel didn't move or speak.

"The DNI locked me in a stasis container and shipped me off to Terra knows where," Alexander continued, looking greatly subdued, "the ship never reached its destination because I broke out. After that, I made myself as hard to find as possible."

There was a solemn pause.

"Speaking of this biomedical research you're conducting," Jezebel ventured cautiously, "does it have anything to do with your condition?"

"I've talked enough about me," Alexander answered, sitting down again at a distance, "the battle's nearly finished."

The counter on the screen had dropped considerably, and it looked like the defending army had won. The invaders were breaking and scattering, and the defending army was busy hunting down stragglers.

"What will they do to them?" Jezebel asked out of morbid curiosity.

"They'll be paraded through the streets of the capital," Alexander replied, "after which they'll be ritually tortured and executed or thrown into the sinkhole in the heart of the temple complex which they think is a gateway to the underworld."

"And then you catch them and experiment on them," Jezebel concluded in distaste.

Alexander shrugged.

"It's no worse than what they do to each other."

THE PRISON

EVERYONE was up early in the Thorn household, but the atmosphere was less than happy. Gabriel had answered as many of his children's questions as he could if only to reassure them that they wouldn't be snatched away in the night. Whether they believed him or not was another matter.

The family was seated around the table quietly eating breakfast. Aster was in the master bedroom looking after baby Emerald – partly to avoid having to talk to Gabriel.

"Daddy, are we better than everyone else?" Orion asked.

"What do you mean?" Gabriel asked.

"Your bosses did things to you to make you better than other people," Orion reasoned, "and you said yesterday that we got those things from you. So that should make us better than other people, shouldn't it?"

He should have seen that sort of question coming.

"We all have certain traits that make us *physically* superior," Gabriel clarified, "but that doesn't mean that we're morally superior."

"Woss 'morary'?" Leonidas asked through a mouthful of food.

"Good and bad," said Rose.

"If we're morally the same but physically superior," Orion continued, "That still means we're superior on average, doesn't it?"

Aster entered the room with Emerald in her arms.

"We have a budding philosopher in the family," Gabriel noted with amusement.

"If daddy is better than other people," Orion explained, "and we all inherited what makes daddy better, that should make us better as well."

Aster smiled a bit.

"But mommy doesn't have daddy's genes," Rose pointed out.

"So that makes us better than mommy," Orion concluded cheekily.

"No it does not," Gabriel said sharply.

The children flinched at their father's tone.

"Thanks for your vote of confidence," Aster said to Gabriel disapprovingly, "but you don't have to be so mean in saying it."

Gabriel didn't scowl, but he gave Aster a hard stare, and she returned the stare, holding Emerald close to her chest. The children looked on in awkward silence, unaccustomed to seeing this sort of tension between their parents.

"I don't want to be better," Violet mumbled.

She had stayed silent this whole time, staring sheepishly at her empty plate as the rest of the family's eyes turned in her direction.

"Why not?" Orion asked, bewildered by his sister's statement.

"It's creepy," she replied.

Gabriel got up and approached his daughter, squatting down to eye level with her.

"Is it because of your arm?" he asked.

"Yes," Violet mumbled.

"But you're ok," Gabriel pointed out, "and it's because of your genes that you're ok."

"I don't want to think about it," Violet said, squirming at the memory.

"You don't have to," Gabriel reassured her with a smile.

"You hardly ever smile, daddy," Rose said with a smile of her own.

Gabriel's smartphone started buzzing.

"Since everyone's finished eating," he announced, pulling his phone out, "I think it's time to get into your learning pods."

Gabriel stepped out to take the call while the children left the table and the household android cleared the plates away. Aster watched him go with a worried look on her face as Gabriel glared at his phone before accepting the call.

"Hello," he said.

"*Colonel Gabriel Thorn*," said the person on the end, his voice electronically distorted, "*Victory Sovereign One Seven Zero Seven. This is the Directorate.*"

"Confirmed," Gabriel replied.

"*Colonel Thorn*," said the voice, "*this call is to confirm that you have been placed on leave until your next assignment.*"

"You could have simply texted me that," Gabriel remarked.

"*You were cleared of any wrongdoing during questioning*," the voice continued, "*but because of the evident interest that this Network has in you, the director-general doesn't want you involved in the investigation.*"

Gabriel suspected as much.

"You think I'll get in the way?" he asked.

"*Your involvement would complicate the investigation*," the voice replied, "*especially given your personal ties to the suspects.*"

"What 'suspects' would I have personal ties to?" Gabriel asked suspiciously.

"*Irrelevant*," the voice rebuffed him, unfazed by the slip, "*you are expressly forbidden from involving yourself in this matter. The director-general herself ordered it.*"

"Understood," Gabriel answered.

"*Have a good weekend*," the voice concluded before hanging up.

'Suspects'. The speaker had inadvertently used the plural. His connection to Mortimer was undeniable, but what other suspects could there be with whom he had personal ties?

"I've been placed on leave again," Gabriel informed Aster.

"And they had to phone you up to tell you that?" she asked sceptically.

"Evidently," said Gabriel, "have you spoken to anyone else about this?"

"No," Aster replied.

"Are you sure?"

"Yes, I'm sure," Aster shot back defensively, "the only other person I spoke to was your mother, and that was *before* this all started."

"You spoke to my mother?" he asked incredulously.

"After I came home to find Violet miraculously healed from her injury, I decided to call her to ask about Mortimer Shelton and your father," Aster explained.

Gabriel looked at her.

"She always gets angry whenever someone mentions him, so I asked her," Aster added even more nervously, "why does it matter?"

"It doesn't," Gabriel lied, "never mind."

* * *

With access to Alexander's medical records, Mortimer was able to get a basic idea of how to treat his condition. He wanted to explore the rest of the facility, but given how his 'host' had almost choked him to death, it probably wasn't a good idea.

Meanwhile, the elastic collar was deceptively comfortable. The fact that it would kill him without Alexander's periodic intervention was a morbid distraction, and he couldn't help tapping it to check the timer.

39:28:17
39:28:16
39:28:15

The door to the lab opened and Alexander walked in without announcing himself. Mortimer looked uneasily at him but kept working.

"It will take some time before my operatives can acquire everything on your shopping list," Alexander informed Mortimer.

"Well, I've already made a start," Mortimer replied.

"Don't you already know how to fix it?" Alexander asked, "I know for a fact that you fixed this problem with the next generation of voidstalkers."

"I fixed the underlying cause and prevented it from occurring in other operatives," Mortimer explained warily, "but I didn't actually cure the condition itself."

Alexander gave a burning glare.

"I'll also need to observe an actual episode in real-time," Mortimer added.

"Didn't you get a good 'observation' earlier?" Alexander asked sardonically.

"You said you experience at least one rage episode per day," Mortimer tried to explain, "but simply losing your temper isn't strictly speaking an episode. I need to monitor one of these episodes from start to finish without your usual treatment."

Alexander appeared to consider it.

"I suppose it could help," he said in agreement, "I'll contact you with a suitable time."

He kept watching Mortimer from the corner of the lab with an iron gaze.

"Does Gabriel have the same enhancements as me?" he asked.

"Uh…yes," Mortimer answered hesitantly, "but the first generation voidstalkers were also given many other enhancements on top of the initial batch."

"If Gabriel and his fellow voidstalkers are the first generation," Alexander wondered, "what does that make me?"

"Zero generation," Mortimer replied, "Gabriel's generation of voidstalkers were the first to be incorporated as a distinct black ops programme, so your generation was retroactively named the 'zero generation' to avoid confusion."

"And what happened to the other zero generation lab rats?" Alexander asked sharply.

"As far as I know, the rest continued serving in the military and intelligence services or retired," Mortimer answered, avoiding the obvious barb.

Alexander didn't respond, he just continued to glare.

"What kind of experiments are you doing on the natives?" Mortimer asked bravely.

"Biomedical experiments," Alexander replied, "though not the kind you were tasked with performing on me or my son."

"But why are you experimenting on them?" Mortimer pressed.

He was wary of angering Alexander. Then again, Alexander needed him to fix his rage episodes, so he did have some wiggle room.

"I've been searching for a cure ever since the incident," Alexander explained, "but I never held out hope of getting help from the very people who were responsible, so I began pulling together individuals from various quarters and finally set up shop here."

"So you found the biochemistry of the natives to be useful?"

"Very," Alexander replied, "extracting you from Asgard took planning and skill, but locating you in the first place was pure luck. So until my agents found you in the Undercity, I'd been using research on the aliens as a reference point."

"So why continue to experiment on them?"

"And why would that matter to you?" Alexander asked through gritted teeth.

"I mean…" Mortimer said haltingly, "I should be able to create a proper cure without having to use them…the natives, I mean."

"That's good to know," Alexander replied, "seeing as the continued experiments on the natives have nothing to do with my medical concerns, and therefore do not concern you."

"The quantum computers you have here are decent," Mortimer added apprehensively, "they should be enough to create an accurate simulation of your biochemistry and the effect that the cure will have on it."

"Your point being that you can iron out any kinks beforehand?" Alexander asked.

"The mistake my team made," Mortimer answered carefully, "the mistake that I made was not being totally thorough in that regard."

There was another awkward pause as Mortimer continued to work on the machines under Alexander's dark gaze.

"Was there...something else?" he asked nervously.

"Now that you ask, yes," Alexander replied, approaching him from behind.

Mortimer held still as Alexander held him by the shoulder with one hand and entered a key code combination into the back of his collar with the other. The collar chimed and the timer re-illuminated as it was reset.

45:00:00

44:59:59

44:59:58

"That was all," Alexander said simply, "I just wanted to check on your progress and make sure there was plenty of time left on your clock."

"Understood," Mortimer replied as his guest departed.

* * *

Alexander kept walking until he reached the next wing, the incipient fury in his head simmering below the surface. Of course, it was always there, drumming at the inside of his skull, clamouring to be free. The inhaler medication kept it subdued, but every small setback and every minor inconvenience reminded him of its presence.

The biometric reader flash-scanned his eyes and the doors opened into a research wing organised in a doughnut shape with the outer walls lined with work stations.

As he entered the chamber, one of the researchers approached.

"Sir," she reported, "we're still having trouble with the neural-control devices."

"Still can't flip the switch properly?" Alexander remarked.

"We can now reliably trigger the berserk response at will," the researcher explained, "but we can't reliably shut it down."

"What specifically is the problem?" Alexander asked.

"The natives' overdeveloped sympathetic nervous system amplifies the fight-or-flight response by an order of magnitude," the researcher explained, "one gentle jolt from the neural-control device sets off a positive feedback loop in the limbic system, but it takes sustained lack of stimulation before the positive feedback loop dissipates."

"And if we interfere with the positive feedback loop it would undermine the very reason why they're such valuable test subjects in the first place," Alexander concluded.

"Indeed," the researcher confirmed, "we can keep tinkering at the edges until we find a workable solution, but if you want to accelerate the programme…"

"Fast-tracking the development of subpar specimens? Absolutely not," Alexander said firmly, "keep working at the problem until you find a solution, but no shortcuts."

"Yes, sir," the researcher said before returning to work.

Using the controls on the railing, Alexander summoned one of the stasis pods. A robotic arm planted its gripping claws on one of the pods, plucking it out of its alcove and carrying it across the chamber to his position.

The specimen inside was a young, healthy adult. Its skin was a leafy green hue and the bony ridge on its forehead was fully developed. Its eyes and mouth were closed, concealing its fiery orange gaze and carnivorous teeth as it rested in artificially-induced sleep.

They truly were remarkable: omnivorous, warm-blooded amphibians descended from tree-dwelling jungle critters. They had clawed their way up the evolutionary ladder through an environment filled with vicious predators, debilitating diseases, horrific parasites, violent weather, and even some carnivorous flora to reach the late Iron Age.

Of course, their hair-trigger propensity for violence was difficult to tame, but it couldn't be watered down without watering down their very essence as a species. Their violence made it hard to believe that they had already mastered writing and urban planning.

Alexander stared at the specimen as if he could read its sleeping thoughts. He knew better than anyone else ever could what it was like to have such rage smouldering in his core, barely contained by his higher brain functions. The difference was that these aliens had evolved this way, whereas his own condition was the result of incompetent tinkering.

The reminder was like a splash of fuel on burning coals and he squeezed the handrails, his composure holding through sheer force of will.

* * *

A century of terraforming had given Asgard a breathable atmosphere and an Earth-like climate, but outside Asgard City and the sprawling web of satellite settlements, much of the planet was semi-arid plains. Fields of hardy desert grass covered vast tracts of the planet, giving way only grudgingly to barren rock.

The local star was high in the sky, a bright white disk illuminating the deep blue clouds of the gas giant Odin around which Asgard orbited. Thanks to the light from the star, Odin was illuminated by a partial corona even in the middle of the day, casting a cerulean glow across the landscape.

Flying high over the plains, the transport craft's path dipped low as it approached its destination. The transport had a bulbous hull with four atmospheric engines sticking out of its flanks like the stubby legs of a bumblebee. It cruised through the air with a grace that belied its plump body, a ring of blue fire crowning the exhaust port of each engine.

Just over the horizon, its destination came into view: a gigantic structure resembling a stack of building blocks in the wilderness.

It was made of innumerable cubic modules, moving and shifting like a 3D puzzle constantly rearranging itself.

The bulbous transport cruised towards the top of the facility where a communications pylon jutted up from the centre. The transport slowed to a halt above a landing platform beside the pylon, extending a set of landing legs and descending to the ground. Once the transport had landed, its engines powered down and a hatch opened in its flank.

A group of men and women in official suits disembarked, gathering on the terrace and squinting under the sun. Asgard City was visible in the distance as a forest of towers stretching across the horizon, the reflected sunlight rendering it visible through the haze.

At the base of the command tower, a door opened and a man came out to greet them. He was tall and lanky, dressed in a grey warden's uniform with the collar open. The left arm of his uniform had a wrist-top computer woven into the fabric and he checked it repeatedly as he approached the delegation.

"Ladies and gentlemen," the warden said, his mildly fluty accent giving him away as a native of the Clouds, "my name is Daniel Lawless, Chief Warden of the Bentham Penitentiary Facility. It's an honour to welcome you."

No one remarked on the irony of Warden Lawless's name as they shook his hand one by one, certainly not the last person in the delegation. He was a tall and well-built man with light skin, and looked more like a military man than a government inspector, even with a thin pair of dark eyeshades.

"Pleased to meet you, sir," said Warden Lawless with a pleasant smile.

"Likewise," said Gabriel, returning the smile.

* * *

Voidstalkers were lone-wolf operatives trained in deep-space black operations, so they were well-versed in infiltration, just not this kind of infiltration.

Gabriel may have been barred from the DNI's mole hunt, but his security credentials still counted for something. As luck would have it, there was an official delegation from off-world today, and he was able to tag along. He would get in trouble for this, but the Directorate had been keeping plenty of secrets from him, so he didn't feel all that guilty.

Aster was a different matter. He had told her that the DNI had called him in for another debriefing and she had taken him at his word. That gave him an excuse to be gone from the house, but he didn't feel totally comfortable lying to her. Then again, she had set him on this line of inquiry by talking to his mother whilst she was in prison.

This prison.

The warden led the delegation inside the command tower. Once they were out of the sun, the delegates put their eyeshades away, all except Gabriel who kept his on.

"So this is the famous Bentham Prison," remarked one of the delegates.

"The facility is named after a jurist and philosopher who lived almost a thousand years ago," Warden Lawless explained as they filed into the elevator.

Once everyone was aboard the elevator pod and the door was shut, Warden Lawless selected a destination on his wrist-top and the elevator began to move.

"This facility's namesake once conceived of a prison called a panopticon," the warden explained as they descended, "a prison in which all the cells would be arranged around a central guard tower, rendering the inmates entirely visible to the prison guards whilst keeping the prison guards invisible to the inmates."

"Modern security cameras render that idea obsolete," someone pointed out.

"On the contrary," the warden replied, "technological limitations were the reason the panopticon was never built, but later inventions made the original idea feasible again."

"And what is that idea?"

"That you can control an enormous incarcerated population with minimal monitoring," the warden answered, "if the inmates can never be sure when they're being watched, good behaviour is incentivised without the need for full-time monitoring."

Through the wall-sized window, they could see that the facility was arranged like a hollow cylinder around the command tower. The cells themselves were mobile pods just like the elevator pod, moving along electromagnetic rails or housed in docking alcoves.

"This is the panopticon concept brought to life," the warden declared, "but with a twist: we don't just watch the inmates, we also control their sense of location through a modular architecture which allows us to rearrange the layout of each cell block at will."

"And what would be the point of that?" Gabriel asked sceptically.

"The more the inmates cooperate, the greater the consistency in their surroundings," the warden explained, "insubordination is punished by changing their surroundings. Even the simulated day-night cycle can be altered in order to confound their perception of time."

The delegates gawped and chattered, visibly and audibly impressed so far.

"What's the recidivism rate?" Gabriel asked, dampening the excitement.

"For violent offences, it's the same as the average for other prisons on Asgard," the warden replied, "for all other crimes, it's about 10% below the average."

The delegates nodded approvingly. Gabriel didn't.

"You don't seem convinced," the warden noted.

"A prison is supposed to confine criminals and rehabilitate them so they can rejoin society," Gabriel elaborated, "I fail to see how this facility's unique design accomplishes either goal or anything else besides playing mind games with the prisoners."

"I respectfully beg to differ," the warden answered, "as I said, the recidivism rates for most categories of crime are below the average for Asgard, and the unique means of control that this prison affords is certainly a factor. As for security, it's astronomically difficult to break out of prison when the prisoner doesn't know where they are."

"So you've never had a breakout attempt since the facility opened?" Gabriel asked.

"No," the warden replied, "never."

* * *

The elevator pod came to a halt halfway down the command tower and opened its doors. The delegation disembarked into a communal area lined with access gates for other pods.

"Depending on their behaviour, and the nature of their crimes, prisoners are allowed a certain amount of socialisation time in spaces like this," the warden explained as he continued the tour, "this decreases aggression and aids rehabilitation."

"What do you do with the most dangerous prisoners?" someone asked, "it must be risky allowing them out of the super-max wing."

"There is no super-max wing," the warden replied, "The ability to control the prisoners' surroundings obviates the need for distinct layers of security. We simply keep the most dangerous prisoners separate from the rest of the prison population."

That would make it harder for Gabriel to locate his mother.

"Next, we'll head to the sub-levels to see the central server," said the warden, "to head to this area you'll all need to be biometrically scanned. Just an extra precaution."

Everyone re-entered the elevator pod and duly lined up to have their eyes flash-scanned. Gabriel's DNI credentials would grant him access, but he didn't know if his true affiliation would be visible to the warden. If it was, there would be trouble.

He removed his eyeshades and allowed the reader to flash-scan his eyes.

The light flashed green and the elevator pod began to move. Gabriel put his eyeshades back on and said nothing. His eyes made this sort of infiltration mission difficult, and since the scanner had let him pass, it was impossible to claim that they were implants.

The elevator pod shifted on its tracks, catching everyone by surprise. Warden Lawless furrowed his brow and jabbed at his wrist-top.

"I thought we were going to the server room?" someone asked.

"We are, but…apologies, it seems the system is redirecting us."

"Where?!"

"Uh…it's not clear," the warden answered, trying to sound calm.

"If this is some kind of joke or stunt–" one of the delegates spoke up.

"It's not!" the warden snapped, "Just let me reset the controls."

The pod looped around and away from the command tower before cruising towards the upper level of the prison's inner ring and docking with one of the alcoves.

The pod doors opened, revealing a barren hallway devoid of furnishings and lined with security doors. The delegation ventured cautiously out of the pod while the warden continued to struggle with the controls.

Once they had all exited, the elevator pod doors sealed behind them, trapping them in the hall. The delegation descended into fearful murmuring as some people opened their own wrist-tops and smartphones.

"There's no signal in here!" someone said in a panic.

"Electronic communication is blocked for unauthorised devices," the warden explained.

"What about *your* device?!" someone shouted.

"It's short-range only!" the warden snapped back, "I can't get a message out!"

The fearful murmuring died down into fearful silence. They were trapped with no way to signal the outside world, and the warden had lost control of his own prison.

"*Gabriel Thorn,*" said a computerised voice, "*please step forward.*"

Everyone exchanged confused looks, everyone except for the man just named.

"*Gabriel Thorn,*" the computer repeated, "*please step forward.*"

It was obvious they weren't going anywhere until he complied, so Gabriel took off his eyeshades and stepped forward.

"*Please surrender your firearm,*" the facility's computer instructed him.

"Why would I do that?" Gabriel demanded.

"*Failure to comply will result in the activation of appropriate countermeasures to ensure your compliance,*" the computer warned.

The delegation began edging away from him, and out of the corner of his eye, Gabriel saw the warden look him up on the wrist-top. A profile from the prison's database appeared, showing Gabriel's mugshot with a list of offences allegedly committed.

The warden looked up with terror in his eyes and the delegation huddled behind him in fear when they saw what was on the screen.

"It says here that you're guilty of corporate espionage, blackmail, and murder," said the warden, "and that you're meant to be serving a life sentence."

"But if he's an inmate," one of the more level-headed delegates pointed out, "how did he come with us on the visit to the prison?"

"*Please surrender your firearm,*" the computer repeated, "*failure to comply will result in the activation of appropriate countermeasures to ensure your compliance. You have 10 seconds to comply…9 seconds …8 seconds…*"

Gabriel whipped out his gun and pointed it straight at the warden's head. The warden froze with terror as the delegation scrambled away from the line of fire.

"*Threat to innocents detected,*" the computer announced, "*countermeasures activated.*"

Gabriel grabbed the warden and swung him around as an automated turret protruded from the ceiling and opened fire. The shock-dart hit the warden in the back, puncturing his clothing before zapping him and paralysing his muscles.

The delegates screamed and scattered, only to discover that the doors were locked. The security turret fired at them as well as its real target held up the warden as a Human shield.

Gabriel realised what a reckless and idiotic plan this was. His plan had been to locate his mother's cell and use his clearance to get a face-to-face meeting with her. That way he could interrogate her about his father and his connection to the DNI's mole investigation.

It had all worked out fantastically well.

Keeping the warden's body between himself and the turret, Gabriel looked into the biometric scanner, causing the light to flash green and the door to open. He then dragged his hostage inside and sealed the door before keying in the landing platform as the destination.

Why the prison had identified him as a dangerous inmate and yet still allowed him to override the system with his biometric credentials was a paradox he didn't have time for right now. He just had to get out of this facility.

* * *

Mortimer still had fond memories of the Rand Block and its state-of-the-art equipment. His new lab, by comparison, was rather underwhelming. Granted it was still well-furnished, but the calculations he needed to perform would take hours or days instead of minutes.

Alexander had yet to confirm a time or place to observe one of his rage episodes, and until he did, the simulations were the only available substitute. In the meantime, he decided it couldn't do any harm if he explored a bit, and a short elevator ride brought him down to the hangar where he had first arrived.

The ceiling and walls of the hangar were polished rock whereas the floor was made of composite panelling. Airborne service drones flitted through the air like plump insects while wheeled maintenance drones raced across the floor. Sticking to the walls, Mortimer walked down the length of the hangar, gazing up in awe.

There were rows of vehicles and shuttlecraft housed in the docking cradles all along the walls. The ground vehicles were an impressive array of wheeled, tracked, and antigravity craft. There were also combat drones and piloted gunships with hardpoints on their hulls. Judging by the size of the engines, these craft were also capable of exoatmospheric flight.

Mortimer came to the end of the hangar and looked right, realising that it was just one section of the subterranean armoury. Built at a ninety-degree angle from the docking hangar, the main cavern around the corner stretched on as far as the eye could squint. Instead of vehicles, the walls were lined with stacks upon stacks of heavy weaponry.

Chain guns, plasma cannons, missile pods, flamethrowers, high-powered lasers, and sundry other weapons of war were locked away in these racks. Thousands upon thousands of power packs and ammo modules were visible as well. The amount of firepower on display was enough to lay siege to half the planet.

Hugging the side of the cavern, Mortimer moved down the length of the armoury, awestruck and more than a little horrified by what he was seeing. As he progressed towards the end, he came to a much larger cage containing a hulking humanoid contraption with hardpoints on its shoulders, standing more than three times a Human's height.

It was a piloted combat platform looming over the armoury, its metallic hands curled into fists, and its dormant optical socket glaring down at him. The retracted barrel of its primary weapon was sticking up from behind its shoulder, and a pair of Human engineers were tweaking the power module that fed it.

Mortimer recognised the black colour scheme with crimson trim and gulped: It was the combat platform that Alexander used.

* * *

Mortimer made it to the end of the armoury without incident and disappeared through a side door, his head swirling with more questions than before. Never mind how Alexander and his Network had acquired so much military gear, what did they need it for?

He entered a new room and saw two people look up in surprise.

"Uh, can we help you with something?" one of them asked.

The room was part-lounge, part-monitoring room with a video feed being projected onto the opposite wall. The room's two occupants were sitting on the couch with refreshments arrayed on the table in front of them.

They were still waiting for his answer.

"I was just...walking around," Mortimer explained lamely.

"How'd you get through the door?" the second person asked.

"The biometric scanner let me through," Mortimer pointed out.

The two men looked at each other, then shrugged their shoulders.

"We almost never see you scientists around here," the first person replied, "but if the system doesn't have a problem with you, neither do we. Care to join the viewing party?"

"Sure," Mortimer said hesitantly, taking a seat.

The screen was showing an aerial view of the polished stone buildings and concentric geometric districts of the alien capital. There was some kind of festival taking place, judging by the throngs of aliens dancing in the streets. The stealth drone's camera was even able to pick out the feathered and scaled headdresses and outfits of the priests and celebrants.

"Quite a party they're having," Mortimer remarked.

"They had this huge battle this morning against an invading army," the second person explained, "they crushed the invaders and now they're giving thanks to the gods."

The first person adjusted a control.

"The natives are a sadistic bunch," he added, "as you can see."

The camera panned sideways and zoomed in on a raised, square platform surrounded by a colourful panoply of banners. One by one a bound alien prisoner was taken up onto the platform by a group of temple guards and killed.

"They skin some of their captured enemies, dry their hides out, then stitch them together into big long scrolls," the first person explained.

"What the frick for?" Mortimer exclaimed in horror.

"Writing," the second person answered, "once the scrolls are ready, they record their history, like the history of this battle they just had."

"Of course, they do have peacetime writing materials," the first person clarified, "but recording your victories on the remains of your defeated enemies is gruesomely poetic."

"They also toss a portion of their prisoners into the sinkhole, alive and unharmed, so the underworld gets its fill," the second person added, "which means more test subjects for you guys in the research wing."

Mortimer saw a chance to pry further into the Network's agenda.

"How did you guys get recruited?" he asked.

"We come from all sorts of backgrounds," the first person replied, "mostly disreputable if I'm being totally honest. I was discharged from the Navy."

"Dishonourably," the second person added.

"If you want to get specific," the first person said, rolling his eyes, "I got in a fight with an officer and shot him by mistake. He survived, but the court-martial didn't care."

"I was a security officer in an interstellar shipping firm," the second person said, "When the Network offered me money and adventure, I took them up on it."

"I, on the other hand, was recruited after being discharged," the first person continued, "There aren't many employers who hire ex-cons unless those employers are already on the darker side of the law. So I signed up as well."

Mortimer was confused. Besides extensive resources, the Network clearly had tendrils all over the place, including agents on Asgard itself, and yet these two men seemed more like mercenaries than highly motivated operatives.

"How much is in it for you guys?" Mortimer asked.

"They didn't explain this to you?" the first person asked in surprise, "we're basically all equity partners in the Network. Which means that all the money the Network makes is divided by the total number of operatives and that portion is given to each operative. You can also make a little on the side, as long as it's in the service of the Network."

"Of course, not everybody's in it for the credits," the second person added, "I know a few people who are ex-DNI or anti-government zealots. They're insane if you ask me, but you can't fault their commitment."

"Enough about us," the first person said, "How did you get recruited?"

Mortimer hesitated. He wasn't sure if Alexander would want him talking about this.

"Don't be all mysterious with us," the second person said jokingly, "even if we wanted to spill your secrets we've got no one to spill them to."

"Well..." Mortimer began, "I used to work at a medical facility in Asgard City. I got in trouble with the authorities and Network operatives whisked me off the planet."

"You must be pretty valuable to the boss," the first person remarked.

"How did he get so many people to follow him?" Mortimer asked, shifting the topic.

The two men fell silent and the mood chilled somewhat.

"We're not totally sure," the second person answered, "no one really knows where he came from, but he can be nearly all things to nearly everyone, and even though we're all entitled to an equal share, no one questions his leadership. We certainly don't."

"And like I said," the first person continued, "we were each recruited from all sorts of backgrounds, but there is a cadre of people who aren't just mercenaries, they're zealously loyal to him. Don't ask us why."

Silence fell over the room again. The two men looked very reserved all of a sudden, it was obvious they didn't like this topic.

* * *

The decor in the living quarters was decent, if not totally to Jezebel's tastes. The carpeting was plain, the furniture was comfortable, and the simulated fireplace was a nice touch. It wasn't as well-furnished as her penthouse in Asgard City, but it was better than sleeping in a bunk bed aboard a cargo ship.

The door to the living room opened and Alexander walked in. Jezebel felt apprehensive as he approached but kept her composure nonetheless.

"I have some names for you," she said, offering him a flexi-tablet.

Alexander accepted the tablet and began to read.

"They were always reliable contacts," said Jezebel.

"Interesting list of names," Alexander noted as he read.

"The names I give you will depend on what you intend to ship, and to whom."

"True..." Alexander replied, keeping his peace.

"It had better not be xenotech–" Jezebel began harshly.

"It's not," Alexander cut her off, "for one thing, I don't have any xenotech to sell. For another, trafficking in xenotech would attract attention from the wrong people."

"Narcotics?" Jezebel ventured.

"No," Alexander replied, "possibly pharmaceuticals, but not narcotics."

"Some of the people on that list dabbled in both," Jezebel noted.

"Any non-entity with a chemistry degree can make and sell their own custom pills," Alexander responded, "but most of them aren't smart enough to evade the authorities."

"And you know this how?" Jezebel asked suspiciously.

"Because I did a stint as the enforcer for one such venture," Alexander replied without remorse, "I worked my way up under a false identity, expanded the business, then cashed out and vanished before the authorities swooped in."

"And then used the money to fund the construction of this place," Jezebel concluded.

"Well, there were some intermediate steps along the way," Alexander added, "but the gist of my rogue-to-rich story is exactly that: I'm self-funded and have no bankrollers, which therefore makes me beholden to no one."

"So how did get you so many people to work for you?" Jezebel asked.

"Don't you know the expression about cats and curiosity?" Alexander rebuffed her.

"Is that a threat?" Jezebel asked with a scowl.

"Not at all," Alexander replied, "you're just getting ahead of yourself."

"If I'm going to help you with this business venture of yours," Jezebel continued, "I'd like to know what's in it for me."

"Besides not being returned to the tender care of the law to serve out the rest of your sentence for corporate espionage, blackmail, and murder?" Alexander said coolly.

"I may still legally be your wife, I can even be your business partner," Jezebel said before jabbing her finger into his chest and hissing defiantly, "but I will not be your lackey."

Alexander looked at her, then leaned forward and kissed her. She pulled back in surprise, pushing him away as she did so.

"What the fleek was that for?" she demanded.

"Old time's sake," Alexander said with a smile.

Jezebel harrumphed in response.

"So, how about a deal then?" Alexander continued, "You bring me these contacts and I'll give you a cut of the proceeds equal to my own."

"Very generous of you," Jezebel remarked, still sounding sceptical, "but my assets and accounts have been frozen by the authorities."

"That will certainly complicate things," Alexander conceded, "but in the meantime, you can still be useful. As a business partner, not a lackey."

"That's good to know," Jezebel replied, "no man gets to command me."

"What about women?" Alexander asked with a smirk.

"Definitely not other women," Jezebel countered sharply, "I spent years building up my businesses, becoming rich enough to buy the best life possible on Asgard, and I didn't do that by subordinating myself to the bigger fish in the pond."

"I'm glad Gabriel had such a strong mother growing up," Alexander remarked.

"That's more gratitude than he's ever shown me," Jezebel said, turning bitter, "he ran off to join the military and came back with some upstart hussy from the colonies."

"Yes, Aster," Alexander said, "she sounds quite plucky, actually."

"You're entitled to your admiration," Jezebel replied, wrinkling her nose with contempt, "but I can't stand her. Maybe Gabriel married her to spite me."

"I bet the feeling is mutual," Alexander pointed out, "given that you made a fortune fleecing colonies like the one where she grew up."

"Probably," Jezebel admitted, "but I don't really care how she feels about me. I just have no idea why Gabriel married that woman."

"Well," Alexander looked Jezebel in the eye, "why did you marry me?"

* * *

The warden's wrist-top was a detachable sleeve wrapped around his forearm, so Gabriel ripped it off and wrapped it around his own forearm. The warden was still lying paralysed on the floor, his eyes bulging and his limbs contorted into a comic pose.

Gabriel searched for his name in the database, and sure enough the name, photograph, and alleged crimes of prisoner no. 11631 were displayed on the screen. Just as the warden had said, his alleged convictions were for corporate espionage, blackmail, and murder, the very things for which his mother was serving time.

He typed in the name 'Jezebel Thorn'.

His mother's name, mugshot, and list of convictions came up on the screen, listed accurately as corporate espionage, blackmail, and murder. Her prisoner number was listed as '11631', identical to the one Gabriel supposedly had. How was that possible?

The pod switched direction without warning. On the wrist-top, he saw that the prison computer was rerouting him to another part of the facility.

That made it pointless to use the pod to get back to the command tower. If the computer could just override him, he would be stuck in an endless loop of commands and counter-commands. To escape, he would have to do something drastic.

Gabriel accessed the master controls on the wrist-top. The prison was almost entirely automated, with the central computer rearranging whole sections at random. The only person with more authority than the computer was the warden who, via his wrist-top, could shut down the entire facility and the central computer along with it.

The wrist-top's master control menu presented Gabriel with two options: a lockdown and a shutdown. Locking down the facility would trap him in the prison for good, so Gabriel selected the shutdown option.

'*Warning: initiating a facility-wide shutdown will disable power to all systems.*'

Gabriel couldn't fathom why the designers of the prison would install such an option. Then again, he couldn't fathom why they would put total control of the prison in one device worn by a lone warden. Whatever their reasons, it was a stroke of luck for him, so he pressed the confirmation button.

'*Confirmed*,' the wrist-top noted, '*facility-wide shutdown initiated.*'

The power died in the blink of an eye and the pod lurched violently on its rails, causing Gabriel to lose his balance. Through the pod window, Gabriel saw the lights die all across the facility as incarceration pods and facility sections froze in their tracks.

Then the magnetic rails failed and the pod dropped like a stone.

THE MESSAGE

Prisoner or guest? That was what Jezebel had really wanted to ask her back-from-the-dead husband. Either way, it beggared belief that Alexander simply wanted her corporate contacts. He had broken her out of prison and smuggled her out of Human space to be brought here. If his contacts were that good, he didn't need her help.

There were many other questions circling in her mind, not least of which was the nature of his organisation. Was it a spy ring? A corporation? A private militia? A combination of those? The questions wouldn't let Jezebel sleep, so she climbed out of bed.

Stepping out of her bedroom, she saw another room at the end of the corridor with the door ajar. She crept towards the door and peered inside, glimpsing a circular room with a holographic projector in the centre, simulating a blazing orange sun.

Someone was in the room gazing at the simulated sun. Every minute or so he would turn his back to the hologram and adjust something before turning around again. Apart from the hologram, it was too dark to see anything else in the room.

Jezebel watched for a while before turning away. If Alexander caught her standing outside the door he might get suspicious. Besides, there was a far better chance of learning more through their 'business' discussions than by sneaking around. She crept back towards her bedroom, making it all the way to the door.

"Can't sleep?" a male voice asked.

Jezebel flinched in surprise. She hadn't even heard him approach.

"What the fleek are you doing?" she demanded.

"I was going to ask you that," Alexander replied.

Jezebel kept her mouth shut.

"If I thought you were a security threat I wouldn't have given you a room in my own private section," Alexander reassured her with a smile.

Jezebel nodded appreciatively but didn't believe a word of it. Alexander was being his polite and pleasant self, with no hint of his temper.

"So, are you still not tired?" he asked.

"Not really," Jezebel replied, "did you want to talk about something?"

"Sure, if you're not doing anything else."

Cautiously, Jezebel opened the door and invited Alexander inside. He entered the room and flopped himself down on the bed as Jezebel shut the door and joined him.

"How has Gabriel been doing since you last saw him?" Alexander asked.

"I haven't seen him for a whole year," Jezebel replied.

"Well, that makes you a lot more up-to-date on him than me," said Alexander.

"He seemed well enough last time we spoke," Jezebel remarked, "he talks exactly like you. Perfectly standard pronunciation, no accent, and no inflexions."

"So he doesn't talk like a Human flute?" Alexander asked jokingly.

"He used to when he was growing up," Jezebel continued, "but he's completely shed the accent, although I'm sure he could still speak that way if he wanted to."

"Does our daughter-in-law talk like a colonial?"

"She curses like one," Jezebel remarked with a disdainful sneer, "but no, she's lived on Asgard long enough to shed whatever dialect she used to speak."

"And the grandchildren?"

"They speak normally," Jezebel replied, then added with a grimace, "Although I hear hints of an accent when they're excited. Gabriel's not around enough for his military-speak to have an effect on how they talk."

Jezebel's grimace turned into a scowl.

"And their mother does all she can to keep them away from me," she added bitterly.

"Given how much you hate her, I'm not surprised," Alexander noted.

"Whose fleeking side are you on here?" Jezebel hissed at him.

Alexander held his peace on that question.

"She called me to ask about you," said Jezebel.

"In prison?" Alexander asked.

"Yes," Jezebel confirmed, "first she asked about someone called Mortimer Shelton, then about you, and I gave her your name. I couldn't stand to hear your name or even a reminder of you for so long, especially with all the whispers about how I killed you."

Alexander reclined on the bed and stared up at the darkened ceiling.

"Was there ever anyone else?" he asked.

"Are you jealous?" Jezebel asked, reclining next to him.

"Half a century is a long time to wait," Alexander pointed out.

"I did a perfectly good job of raising Gabriel on my own, so I never felt the need to start over," Jezebel said, then turned to Alexander, "but then you probably already knew that."

"Why do you say that?" Alexander asked.

"You clearly have an extensive information network," Jezebel argued, "and you already knew that Gabriel has a family. So you must have been monitoring me as well."

"Well, I wouldn't have known which prison you were sent to without contacts to tell me," Alexander partially admitted.

"So why did you break me out?" Jezebel interrogated him.

"I need your network to expand my own," Alexander replied simply.

"Nonsense," Jezebel countered, "I was in prison for a year and still had another three decades to serve. I no longer have any influence that you would need. So why did you really break me out and bring me here?"

Alexander didn't respond, but Jezebel sensed that her assertions were correct.

"Are you monitoring Gabriel's movements as well?" she asked.

"Enough," Alexander replied gruffly, "we both need to sleep."

He lay down like a log and closed his eyes. Jezebel didn't remember inviting him to sleep over, and she looked at him as he dozed off. At least he wasn't hogging the bed, and she lay down beside him. Slowly, she extended a hand and rested it on his shoulder.

It was still hard to believe that he had been alive all this time. Only touching his skin and feeling the warmth of his body under her hand made the fact real to her.

* * *

Gabriel found himself on the floor of the elevator pod. The power was down and the lights were out, apart from a set of emergency lighting strips. Picking himself off the floor, He drew his gun and activated the under-barrel light. The door of the pod had opened and beyond was a morass of darkness, barely illuminated by the emergency lighting.

He had done it: he had successfully shut down power to the entire prison. Now what? This was supposed to be a simple information-gathering mission. Finding his mother in this vast prison – if she was even in the prison at all – was now the least of his concerns.

Gabriel stepped out of the pod, moving forward into the darkness with his weapon ready. He panned his gun from side to side and the under-barrel light cut swaths through the darkness, illuminating banks of dormant computer servers. He had ended up in the prison's server room after all, exactly where the warden had planned to take the delegation.

He could restart the facility's systems from here. Then again, what good would that do as long as the computer thought he was a convict on the loose? He would have to remove his name from the database before reversing the shutdown. But before he could access the database, he would have to power up the computer again by reversing the shutdown.

Most of the wrist-top's functions were unavailable due to the shutdown, but there was still a map of the prison. Given that one of the selling points of the prison was supposed to be its customisable layout, a map ought to be redundant; but there it was, telling him that there was an interface panel at the opposite end of the chamber.

Gabriel reached the other side and saw the server interface sitting on a raised platform. There was also a backup generator, and switching it on was as simple as flipping the switch. There was a hum as the ceiling lights winked on again and the computer servers were restored to power. He switched off his gun's light and holstered it before turning around.

There was the warden, the shock-dart's effects having worn off. He had tried to sneak up on Gabriel whilst he was working on the backup generator. The surprised look on his face turned to anguished rage before exploding out of his mouth.

"Do you know what the fleek you've just done?!" he exclaimed.

"I shut down power to the entire facility in order to stop the computer trying to zap me," Gabriel replied unrepentantly.

"This prison contains over 20,000 convicts from thieves and smugglers to serial killers and rapists to terrorists!" the warden shouted, partly out of anger, partly out of horror, "and you just cut the power that enables this facility to keep them in line!"

"Can they get out?" Gabriel asked.

The warden's apoplectic rage deflated all of a sudden.

"Can they physically leave their cells during a shutdown?" Gabriel reiterated.

"Well…uh…" the warden struggled to answer, "the locks are electronic so…"

"So without power, they stay locked, correct?"

"…Correct," the warden replied sheepishly.

"Then there's no danger to the public," Gabriel replied.

He activated the server interface which informed him that power to 90% of the facility was still out, leaving only essential systems functioning. At least he could signal the outside world, but before that, he had to remove himself from the database.

Nearly all the prison's functions – including its vaunted ability to rearrange itself – were automated, leaving it up to the prison computer to physically keep unauthorised individuals away from control panels like this one. Now that Gabriel was here, however, all it took was his possession of the warden's wrist-top to bypass the security.

"What are you doing?" the warden demanded.

"I'm going to remove my name from the database," Gabriel explained as he accessed the prison register, "and then find out who added me in the first place."

"I'm guessing you think you're innocent?" the warden asked.

"I *am* innocent," Gabriel replied as he searched for his name.

"A lot of them say that," the warden said with a sneer.

"If I had been convicted of anything," Gabriel pointed out, "I would have arrived in manacles and not as part of an official delegation."

"Maybe you were trying to break someone out," the warden speculated.

"In which case I would have killed you as soon as you stepped out onto the landing terrace," Gabriel pointed out, "then taken your wrist-top and hijacked the prison."

He found his profile in the database and used the wrist-top to gain administrator access. Then he flagged his profile for deletion and used the wrist-top to authorise it.

'*Profile deleted.*'

An alarm chimed and the server interface flashed a message across the screen.

'*YOUR FATHER SENDS HIS REGARDS, GABRIEL.*'

Before he could react, a security turret appeared and fired.

The sting of the shock-dart piercing his flesh was nothing compared to the rush of fire he felt surge along his nerves. Gabriel felt every muscle in his body lock up completely, freezing him into a slightly hunched pose.

The shock-dart exclusively targeted the somatic nervous system, thereby paralysing the skeletal muscles and rendering the target incapable of voluntary movement. It left the rest of the nervous system untouched so that the target's heart would continue to beat and their lungs would continue to breathe.

Gabriel was frozen to the spot and could only watch through unblinkable eyes as the warden went through shock, then incredulity, then bemused schadenfreude at this turning of the tables. Having cautiously kept his distance, the warden approached without fear.

"Well," he said smugly, "you may be innocent of the things the database said you were convicted of, but now you're guilty of sabotage, criminal assault, and data tampering. All of which I would be more than happy to testify to."

The warden removed Gabriel's gun from its holster and weighed it in his hand.

"I guess it wouldn't hurt to pay you back for using me as a Human shield, though," he said vindictively, priming the gun and aiming at Gabriel's knee.

He pulled the trigger.

There was no gunshot. Instead, the warden jerked and dropped the weapon, clutching his hand in pain. He watched in horror as the veins in his palm turned black and spread across his hand and up his arm. His eyes bulged out of their sockets and he began to convulse as the nanotoxin took effect, spreading through his bloodstream and killing his vital organs.

Gabriel watched in grim satisfaction as the man who had tried to kneecap him collapsed, spasming and foaming at the mouth. The warden's loss of muscular control was the exact opposite of what he was experiencing and the ironic juxtaposition would have brought a smile to his face – if only he could move it.

* * *

A rapid response team deployed to investigate the shutdown found Gabriel along with the warden's body. Unable to twitch, let alone struggle, his paralysed limbs were bound before he was carried away. The warden was left where he was for the forensics team while Gabriel was brought aboard the response team's transport craft.

The transport took off and began flying back to Asgard City with the prime suspect manacled upside-down to the ceiling. The team leader plucked the shock-dart out of Gabriel's chest, then produced another device and pricked his flesh with it.

A jolt of electricity rushed through Gabriel's nerves, reversing the paralytic effect of the shock-dart. It felt like relief from a million pins and needles, and he gasped at the sensation.

"Do you know how much trouble you're in, Colonel Thorn?" the team leader asked.

"Are you going to tell me or do I have to guess?" Gabriel asked sarcastically.

"You were specifically ordered not to get involved in the investigation," the team leader continued, "and yet you disobeyed the director-general's orders and went on an unauthorised infiltration mission with comically disastrous results."

Only then did Gabriel realise that his captors weren't wearing Civil Security or Justice Ministry uniforms. He could guess which organisation they worked for.

"Do you have any leads?" Gabriel asked.

"None that we're authorised to share with you," was the curt reply.

"Well, it may interest you to know that when I removed my name from the prison database, a message from the saboteur appeared especially for me," Gabriel continued.

"And what did this message say?" the team leader asked.

"The instigator of the infiltration sends his regards," Gabriel answered.

"He sent his regards to you?" the team leader asked, raising a sceptical eyebrow.

"Yes," Gabriel responded, "the message named me specifically."

The other members of the response team exchanged confused looks.

"Do you have any other useful pieces of information to share?" the team leader asked.

"Yes, I do," Gabriel replied, "tell the delegation members not to take up the idea of the Bentham Prison and tell Asgard's planetary government to get a refund for the taxpayer."

"I take it you weren't impressed by the tour?" the team leader said, amused.

"The entire concept is stupid," Gabriel spat contemptuously, "a normal prison with normal security measures can securely house several times the number of convicts at the same cost, or the same number of convicts at a fraction of the cost."

The team leader nodded his head slowly.

"The idea of a shapeshifting prison may sound impressive," Gabriel continued, "but it does absolutely nothing to improve security. The designers were so wrapped up in the concept it never occurred to them that one person could shut it all down."

"How so," the team leader asked, barely able to contain his laughter.

"By confiscating the warden's wrist-top," Gabriel explained, "I gained total control over the entire prison. I could have incapacitated the warden as soon as he stepped out to greet us and wreaked whatever havoc I wanted to."

The team couldn't contain themselves any longer. They burst out laughing as Gabriel finished talking, leaving him hanging there bemused and upside down.

"Are you going to let me in on the joke?" he asked, annoyed.

"We were thinking the same thing when we were told about this incident," the team leader explained, struggling to stop laughing, "one guy managed to pose as a visiting dignitary and infiltrate the prison, and then shut it down from the inside."

"Which says a lot about how easy it was for the original saboteur to infiltrate the prison and arrange Jezebel Thorn's escape," Gabriel concluded.

The laughter died down all of a sudden.

"We're not discussing the investigation with you," the team leader said, stone-faced.

"You don't have to," Gabriel replied, "I went to all this trouble to get a face-to-face meeting with prisoner no. 11631, only to find that I'd been added to the prison roster before I arrived, and with the exact same prisoner number. My guess is that she was broken out of the facility some time ago with the help of the saboteur."

"Close enough," the team leader said, "and we would have liked to question the warden about it if only he hadn't tried to use your gun."

"So the warden was the saboteur?" Gabriel asked incredulously.

"I didn't say that," the team leader replied, "and if he were, do you think he would have been stupid enough to use a Directorate operative's own gun against him?"

"Maybe," Gabriel suggested.

"That's the most I can or will share with you," the team leader added.

"In that case, would you mind letting me down?" Gabriel asked.

"Not until we reach Asgard city," the team leader replied, taking a seat again.

85

"Is there a reason why I'm being strung upside-down like this?"

"Yes," the team leader replied, "as part of your punishment for disobeying the order not to get involved. The director-general herself told us to tell you that."

* * *

Mortimer found a breakroom where all the researchers could socialise. A dozen people were gathered there, chatting amongst themselves. They were dressed casually but still had the special tags singling them out as research staff.

Mortimer sat down beside two men and waited for a chance to introduce himself.

"You look new!" said one of the researchers with a beaming smile.

"Uh, that's right," Mortimer said hesitantly, "I'm Mortimer Shelton."

"I'm Jim and this is Frank," he said, pointing to his colleague.

Jim and Frank each had black hair with identical haircuts and looked like they were twins. Mortimer could only tell them apart by the nametags on their uniforms.

"So which project have you been assigned to?" Jim asked.

"Not any of the ones already underway," Mortimer responded, "the boss gave me my own lab for a separate project."

Jim and Frank became noticeably more serious.

"We won't ask," Frank said.

"You're not curious?" Mortimer asked them.

"When the boss gives someone their own lab for a 'separate project', it's probably not for sharing with other people," Frank explained.

"Were you the guy whose shuttle got hit by lightning on the way here?" Jim asked.

"That was me," Mortimer confirmed.

"Holy freaking Terra!" Frank exclaimed, "That must have been a rough arrival!"

"Is it true the boss himself took the Seraph out for a spin?"

"You mean the combat platform?" Mortimer asked.

"Yeah," Jim clarified, "we know Seraph's his call sign, but I think that's the nickname he gave his combat platform as well."

"Well, if it weren't for him, the natives would have torn us to shreds," Mortimer replied, "although it was pretty gory to watch."

"I bet," Frank remarked, "that pulse-cannon can—"

He stopped himself suddenly.

"Talking about the boss's toys is bad luck," Jim joked.

Mortimer decided to take the risk and ask the question.

"Why is there so much military hardware in this base?"

Jim and Frank looked at each other.

"You mean in the hangar?" Frank asked, "We almost never go back there."

"I saw the weapons when I first arrived," Mortimer told them, "the skimmer transport brought us here after the crash and then I was led through the hangar."

"We don't know, to be honest," Jim responded, keeping his voice low, "the boss keeps his cards flat against his chest most of the time, so we don't know much of anything about the Network's long-term plans."

"And it's best not to pry too deeply," Frank added seriously, "Hence the reason we're not interested in hearing about why the boss gave you a private lab."

Mortimer was left marvelling at Alexander's ability to grow and manage the Network without sharing his intentions for it with anyone. It also made him wonder if nosing around would get him killed as soon as Alexander no longer needed him.

"It's not all cloak and daggers around here, though," Jim said more cheerfully, "we're part of the team studying the natives' biology."

"After I arrived at the base for the first time," Mortimer said, "I saw some of the aliens who attacked us being thrown into the sinkhole."

"The aliens have been throwing sacrifices into the sinkhole for millennia as far as we can tell," Frank explained, "they believe that a sacrifice has to be thrown in alive and uninjured, which makes their superstition a perfect source of test subjects."

"Which is just as well, since we go through them so quickly," Jim added.

"And now, you're probably wondering what we do to them," Frank surmised.

"Someone told me you were doing toxicology tests on them," Mortimer said, hoping to glean more information but dreading what he might learn.

"That's the least of it," Frank replied excitedly, "the natives are born fighters. Not only are they resistant to all manner of diseases, toxins, and parasites, they heal rapidly."

"They reproduce at a phenomenal rate, too," Jim added no less enthusiastically, "the average female produces 30-40 spawn in one mating season, and of those about 10-20% survive to adulthood. That means populations are constantly outgrowing the resources required to sustain them, which leads to constant warfare."

"Just wait till they discover vaccinations and antibiotics," Frank said with a grin, "but all that warfare strengthens the entire stock of natives per natural selection, which makes this planet a perfect breeding ground."

"For what, exactly?" Mortimer asked.

"Fighters, obviously," Frank replied.

"So they're being bred to serve as soldiers?"

Jim and Frank snorted with laughter.

"They won't be using the weapons you saw in the hangar any time soon, I can assure you," Jim explained, "We can barely get them to stand still on command."

They were cagey about Alexander and the broader Network but were freely admitting that the aliens were being experimented on to serve as slave-soldiers.

"So what's your background?" Jim asked curiously.

"I was in the private sector," Mortimer lied, "I worked at a pharmaceutical boutique that did contract research for the bigger players until it got bought out by one of them."

"So you got bored with corporate life and took the Network's offer?"

"Basically," Mortimer replied, "so how about you guys?"

"We're both neurosurgeons by training," Jim answered, "but we also have expertise in cybernetics, which is why we were recruited."

"That and we bent the rules a bit in our research," Frank admitted.

"I've done it myself," Mortimer said, "after my old firm was bought out I was a medical doctor for a while, but I kept my skills sharp by practising botany."

"Botany?" Jim snorted with laughter, "Were you growing drugs or something?"

"Yes," Mortimer admitted, "but I never managed to make a finished product because the authorities raided my lab. I only escaped arrest thanks to the Network."

That was almost true, and Jim and Frank nodded with interest.

"We really are a motley band, aren't we?" Frank remarked.

"Pretty well-financed band, though," Mortimer observed.

"That's *definitely* not a topic any of us should delve into," Jim replied, getting up, "in fact, it's probably time to get back to work."

"Agreed," said Frank as he stood up.

"Well, it was nice to meet you two," Mortimer said amiably.

"Likewise," the two of them replied.

* * *

Gabriel was deposited at the intercity airport and ordered home. The indignity was a far cry from the punishment he was expecting, and he could hardly complain. His interference had resulted in the death of the warden, a person of interest to the investigation he had been ordered to stay away from. Red-eye would be furious.

He hadn't been the most reliable operative of late. Then again, she hadn't been the most trustworthy superior of late, either. First, there was the Loki mission, then she had had him interrogated as a possible traitor after the Nexus mission. Now, she was shutting him out of the investigation due to 'personal ties' to the mystery suspects.

'*YOUR FATHER SENDS HIS REGARDS, GABRIEL*,' the message had said.

Was his father actually alive? It could be part of a psychological operation or some other kind of ruse, but that still left the question of why it had been directed at him. Not to mention the original mole had named *him* as the principal orchestrator of the infiltration and the terrorist attacks.

When he got back to the apartment, Aster was still at work and the children were still in their learning pods, so Gabriel went to the master bedroom. Emerald was asleep in her crib, being watched over by one of the androids. He elbowed past the android and hovered over his infant daughter, the clouds in his mind clearing as he watched her sleep.

There was one cloud that wouldn't vanish: he knew all along that his children would inherit his enhancements, but the Directorate had never intimated any plans for them.

What were those plans? Aster had told him that Mortimer's message had speculated they were being groomed to form an elite social caste. Gabriel had served long enough to know what an idiotic theory that was. The DNI was a militarised intelligence agency, it couldn't care less about the social or political dynamics of any planet in Humanity's empire.

Civil matters and security matters don't mix. That was the 3rd Prime Law.

But then what did the Directorate want with his children or the children of the other voidstalkers? Gabriel was more disturbed by that question than by the message ostensibly from his father – a man he had never known.

The front door opened. Aster was home. He waited for her to come to the bedroom before turning around. She looked exhausted, too exhausted to do anything other than give him a curt nod to acknowledge his presence.

"How was work?" he asked her.

"Longer day than usual," Aster replied distractedly as she began to strip, "but not too bad. How was your debriefing?"

"Boring," Gabriel lied, "but not too bad."

Aster continued stripping as Gabriel watched.

"Android," Aster said commandingly, "run the bath."

"*Understood*," the household android replied before leaving the room.

* * *

Gabriel found himself in the bath with Aster lying back against his chest.

"How did I end up here?" he wondered aloud.

"Because I wanted you to join me," Aster replied, wrapping his arms around her naked body like a blanket, "and you did as you were told."

Aster's skin was soft and wet, and her feminine warmth aroused him.

"So how was your debriefing today?" she asked.

"I told you," Gabriel reiterated, "it was boring, but not too bad."

Aster reached down under the water, her fingers closing gently around Gabriel's crotch and causing him to stiffen up.

"Is that true?" Aster asked him.

"Do you think I'm lying?" Gabriel asked.

"The news was reporting an incident at that state-of-the-art prison outside the city," she replied, "and they had to shut it down. You're telling me you had nothing to do with that?"

"I haven't seen the news," Gabriel told her truthfully.

Aster's grip remained gentle but firm.

"Just making sure," she purred, resting her head against his shoulder, "although, it is weird that your mother is locked up in the same facility."

"Why is that weird?" Gabriel asked.

"I told you I spoke with your mother while you were away," Aster replied, "and the next day, that same prison had an unexplained security incident."

"You don't believe in coincidences?"

"I heard the first rule of spying is: 'there are no coincidences'," said Aster.

"The real first rule of intelligence is: 'facts first, conclusions later'," Gabriel answered, "Not that I'd call it a 'rule', more like professional common sense."

"Fair enough," Aster conceded, her fingers relaxing again.

They lay in the bath in silence for a while, quietly savouring the warmth of the water as well as one another's bodies.

"That's something we've never worked out, actually," Gabriel said.

"That covers a lot of things," Aster responded, "could you be more specific?"

"You know there are things I can't tell you about my work," Gabriel elaborated, "and I know you don't like it, but you've never told me which one you're least comfortable with: me lying to you, or me simply not telling you."

Aster was silent, and Gabriel waited patiently for her to finish thinking.

"You know," she said after a while, "the truth is I don't like that you're not entirely mine. The DNI controls what you do, where you go, how long you're away, and even the genes in your cells. Which means they also control the genes in our children's cells. I hate that."

Gabriel was silent, her words having new resonance in light of recent events.

"So I guess I hate the secrecy more than the lies," Aster concluded, "even though I understand why you can't tell me certain things. Then again, I probably don't want to know exactly what you get up to in your adventures in deep space."

A guilty shot of adrenaline rushed through Gabriel's heart as the unwelcome memory of his tryst with Aetherea rushed through his mind.

"What are you thinking about?" Aster asked him.

"How much I love you," Gabriel replied.

"That's reassuring to hear," she said, snuggling into his arms.

The sound of footsteps running on carpet and children's laughter reached their parents' ears, briefly puncturing their moment of marital bliss.

"Play nice!" Gabriel ordered.

"Yes, daddy!" the children chorused from the other side of the door.

"And no running!" Aster added.

"Yes, mommy!" the children chorused back.

They promptly resumed their play, running and laughing just like before.

"I can hardly ever get them to listen to me," Aster said with a sigh, "without the androids around the house it would be too much work."

"And yet you decided we should have five of them," Gabriel remarked.

"Is that a problem?" Aster asked, a note of tension entering her voice.

"No," Gabriel answered calmly, "I just don't understand why you wanted so many."

Now it was Aster's turn to be silent.

"It's hard to explain," Aster murmured after a while, "especially to you."

"Why?" Gabriel asked, "Because I'm a man?"

"Because you're *the* man," Aster replied.

"Now I'm really intrigued," said Gabriel.

"My family is all on the frontier world Sahara," Aster explained, "which means that I have no one on this planet except for you and the family we've built together."

"You miss your old home?"

"Fuck no," Aster snorted, "my home was a hot, sandy, dirty little outpost with a few thousand people on the edge of settled space. Asgard is paradise by comparison."

"So what do you mean?"

"I don't miss Sahara," Aster explained, "I miss you."

Gabriel tightened his embrace of Aster, hugging her close to his chest.

"Even if you never make it back," Aster said, a solitary tear rolling down her cheek, "I can see you every time I see their eyes."

There was a moment of morbid silence.

"Plus," Aster added more cheerfully, "I win hide-and-seek every time."

Gabriel snorted with laughter.

"Seriously," Aster said with her own laugh, "I'm the only member of this family who doesn't have glow-in-the-dark eyes. They're gorgeous and easy to spot."

"If you say so," Gabriel replied, smiling in spite of himself.

"So," Aster concluded sentimentally, "I guess I want as many smiling, happy versions of us running around as possible."

Gabriel's thoughts took a gloomy turn. The galaxy was full of awe-inspiring things, but mostly it was full of vicious marauders, sinister entities from bygone eras, greedy aliens who wanted to harness them, and the ruins of civilisations who had tried.

"What are you thinking about now?" Aster asked him.

"Are you sure you want to know?" Gabriel asked her.

"Yes, I am," Aster responded without hesitation.

It was easy enough to articulate, but Gabriel wasn't sure he wanted to tell her.

"The universe is a horrible place," he said gloomily, "every mission is like keeping a boulder from rolling down a hill and crushing something precious below. Every successful assignment feels like finishing a round of whack-an-alien. Sometimes I wonder if it's even fair to bring children into existence in such a miserable cosmos."

"That's very uplifting to hear," Aster remarked sarcastically.

"It's also true," Gabriel continued sombrely, "the cosmos is full of enemies that want to inflict death or worse on us. Killing them first is a Sisyphean task, and success isn't measured by good things happening, but by bad things *not* happening."

"Well, Humanity is still here," Aster pointed out, "and we've settled over a hundred worlds and built up a pretty nice civilisation for ourselves. So you and your fellow knights in spec-ops armour must be doing something right."

"Did I mention all of the dangerous and reckless schemes concocted by other Humans that I have to thwart?" Gabriel added.

"Of course not," Aster replied, "That would be classified."

She snuggled up closer into Gabriel's embrace.

"You don't need to tell me about man's inhumanity to man," she said at length, "Sahara once bought some groundwater extraction equipment on credit, and when we fell behind on the interest payments, the colonial vulture investors who made the loan sent a team of thugs to steal whatever wasn't bolted down as collateral."

"Did you fight back?" Gabriel asked.

"That's hard to do when the loan sharks have guns and the colonists don't," Aster shot back bitterly, "Sahara is a mining colony, not some frontier fort."

She squeezed Gabriel's wrists then relaxed.

"Even so," she added, "it seems like you keep the worst of them at bay, and from the sound of it the aliens are a hundred times worse."

"I hate to generalise, but they are," Gabriel replied, "I once interdicted an alien vessel on its way out of Human space."

"What was it doing in Human space in the first place?" Aster asked, fearing the answer.

"It was a corsair ship," Gabriel responded dryly, "fast-moving, powerful bombardment weaponry, moderate stealth capabilities, and large holding pens."

"Holding pens?" Aster asked, quivering in the water.

"It was a slave ship," Gabriel confirmed, cradling his wife, "they raided this mining station, kidnapped the work crew, and tried to make a break for it."

"You said you caught up with them, right?" Aster asked.

"We shot their engines and used a gravity well to hold it in place," Gabriel continued the story, "and then I boarded the ship alone and massacred its crew."

"Did any of them try to surrender?" Aster asked, disturbed by the story.

"Unlike them, we didn't take prisoners," Gabriel replied without pause, "the data in their computers is more useful than they are, and they deserved to die in a bad way, especially after we found out what they do to their prisoners."

"I'll take your word for," Aster interjected, "but I think you should stop there."

Gabriel held Aster in silence.

"When you have nightmares," Aster ventured, "are they ever about the missions you've been on? The people or aliens you've killed?"

"Most of them are," Gabriel admitted, "although I wouldn't call them nightmares. Just vivid recollections of the things I've done."

"So you're not haunted by the aliens you've killed?"

"No," Gabriel answered, "They're slavers and worse. I feel nothing when I pull the trigger, and I feel nothing when I wake up again."

Aster shifted uncomfortably in the water on hearing that, but she appreciated hearing the truth, however unpalatable it was.

"So riddle me this, Gabriel," said Aster, "what's the point in making the universe safer if you're not willing to fill it with new life to enjoy that safety?"

"...I guess that makes sense."

* * *

Red-eye surveyed the information on the screen in silence. The others present knew that she was angry. How angry was impossible to gauge, and they preferred not to find out.

"I never imagined that one voidstalker would prove to be such a maverick," she said at length, the lack of emotion in her voice belying her frustration.

"It seems the Bentham Prison computer system identified Colonel Thorn accurately," one person spoke up, "but wrongly believed that he was an inmate."

"Setting off events which resulted in the death of a valuable lead," Red-eye concluded.

"Be that as it may," someone else said, pulling up a video file on the main screen, "we do have the security footage from inside the server room."

The video was paused at the moment immediately after Colonel Thorn had removed his name from the system and a message had flashed across the screen:

'*YOUR FATHER SENDS HIS REGARDS, GABRIEL.*'

No one except Red-eye understood the significance of the message. She turned around and surveyed the room before speaking.

"You are all familiar with the Voidstalker Programme," she said to them, "how familiar are you with the zero generation test subjects?"

"As I understand it," answered someone, "they were 'pre-voidstalkers' who were given early iterations of the enhancements later given to the first and second generation voidstalkers. But I thought they were all reassigned or retired."

"Close enough," said Red-eye, "but out of several hundred first-generation voidstalkers, only one of them had a zero generation father."

One of those present looked at his flexi-tablet quizzically.

"Uh, Director-general?" he said, "according to the database, Colonel Thorn's father, zero generation voidstalker Colonel Alexander Thorn, has been dead for 45 years."

"But still sent his regards from beyond the grave," someone else pointed out.

"Alexander Thorn is not dead," Red-eye informed them, "and evidently he is no longer interested in convincing people otherwise."

Those assembled exchanged puzzled looks.

"Think about it," Red-eye commanded, "first they launch terror attacks right under the Directorate's nose and use the attacks as cover to exfiltrate a former Directorate scientist who led the Voidstalker Programme. Then the mole who made the exfiltration possible deliberately namedrops Gabriel Thorn, of all people, before self-terminating."

Red-eye paused to allow her words to sink in.

"Then at the same time," she continued, "Jezebel Thorn is secretly broken out of prison, and her son is added to the database with the same prison number, and when Gabriel Thorn removes his name from the database, that message appears on the screen in full view of a security camera which could easily have been disabled but wasn't."

"If he's been in hiding all this time, why would he suddenly go out of his way to break cover?" someone asked incredulously, "and why do it now?"

"That is what we need to find out," Red-eye replied, "in addition to where he is."

"We're still investigating how the original mole came to be recruited in the first place," the head of internal security said, "but the fact that we haven't already identified who recruited him makes his handler a threat to be reckoned with."

"Do you think his handler is still on Asgard?" the city intelligence chief asked.

"Almost certainly," the internal security chief replied, "and most likely continuing to influence events behind the scenes."

"What about the prison warden?" someone else asked.

"His path to being recruited was easier to trace," the city intelligence chief answered, "being the only person in the entire facility who isn't a prisoner is lonely and boring, even when the post is on a rotating basis."

He brought up another file on the screen.

"The warden didn't log any of these visits," he explained, "and for good reason."

The file was a set of video surveillance logs showing a different visitor each time being received by the warden. All of the visitors were female and provocatively dressed.

"Do we know the identity of the prostitutes yet?" someone asked.

"Yes," replied the city intelligence chief, "their bank accounts show that the warden didn't pay for their services directly. It was done through a third-party account."

"This may be how the warden was recruited by the Network," Red-eye said, "but if it were that simple, the civilian agencies would have flagged this up months ago."

"I already have teams on route to grab and question these ladies," the city intelligence chief said, "and to search their homes for anything suspicious."

"Good," said Red-eye, "anything else?"

"There was one other thing," the city intelligence chief noted.

The computer screen was zoomed in on the face of each woman. The city intelligence chief picked out the earliest video still and brought it to the centre of the screen, highlighting the woman's face. Everyone except Red-eye with her bionic eye squinted at the images to see what he was pointing to.

Then someone noticed it.

"What's that on the side of her head?"

THE TEST

IN spite of his situation, Mortimer found that he was getting a lot done. The prospect of death literally hanging around his neck was a powerful incentive. The medical records he had were a good enough start, but it had been decades since he had devised the original fix, and he would first need to reconstruct it from scratch.

Alexander still hadn't provided a time and place to observe one of his infamous 'rage episodes'. Also, the timer on his collar was down by nine hours. That still left just under 36 hours until the collar killed him, but that gave him two reasons to seek out Alexander directly.

Come to think of it, that must be part of the purpose of the collar. It was obvious he couldn't leave the facility – let alone the planet – but having to stay close to Alexander kept him on a leash. A physical collar and a metaphorical leash that made him a proverbial running dog for his boss and captor.

Alexander's sense of humour had turned very nasty indeed.

Mortimer had grown more accustomed to the layout of the facility, and he bypassed the cavernous hangar and intimidating armoury to reach Alexander's private quarters. He couldn't go inside, of course, but he had sent a direct message and received a response. Mortimer pressed the intercom button with a trembling finger.

"It's Mortimer," he said into the intercom, "I'm here."

Mortimer tugged nervously on the death collar around his neck, causing it to change black and become briefly visible again.

35:45:55

35:45:54

35:45:53

The fact that there was still plenty of time left did nothing to reassure him. In fact, it made him wonder if there was some countermeasure he could use to neutralise the collar, something Alexander might have overlooked.

There was no way that Alexander would tell him what the toxin was. Being a molecular geneticist, it would be child's play to cook up an antidote, even if it was something exotic or local to the planet. It might be a cocktail of various toxins. It might even be a nanotechnological toxin, in which case he was totally out of luck.

The door light flashed green and the door swung open. Alexander stepped out with a stern look crinkling his face. He really did look like an older and meaner version of his son.

"You spend a lot of time wandering about," he remarked as he approached Mortimer, "although, obviously I decided there was no need to restrict your access."

"I…was just wondering if we could set up a time for that test," Mortimer said nervously, "you know…the one that we…that I need to do…"

Alexander nodded his understanding.

"Your lab in five hours' time," he said perfunctorily, "there's a special chamber that's perfectly suited for the test. I'll take you there."

"Ok, I'll be ready when you…when you say."

"Was there anything else?" Alexander demanded.

"Yes, my…" Mortimer gestured to his neck.

Alexander grabbed Mortimer by the scruff of his jacket and dragged him away out of sight, forcing him against a wall before entering the reset code. The collar duly chimed and the timer returned to 45 hours before beginning the countdown all over again.

"I'll see you in five hours," Alexander said gruffly.

* * *

Jezebel woke up to find Alexander gone. She got up and searched for him, but he was nowhere to be found. She did find that the door to the control room had been left open. With nothing to do and no one to stop her, she snuck inside.

The centrepiece of the room was a concave holographic projector ringed with controls that pulsed gently in the dark. There wasn't much to see except for some furniture and a 3D chessboard. Jezebel tapped a few keys on the ring-projector experimentally and a simulation of the planet appeared.

Even in holographic form, it was a thing of beauty. The planet's surface was covered by irregular swaths of emerald vegetation stretching across whole continents and networks of inland azure seas. The pattern was broken only by strips of semi-arid desert in the subtropical latitudes and crowned at the north and south poles by caps of ice.

Adjusting another key swaddled the simulated planet in swirling clouds, depicting its entire weather system in real-time. Hundreds of storms were raging across the planet all at once, some of them with winds exceeding 300kph. The tail ends of their trailing winds spiralled out from their bodies as they spun across the planet.

Jezebel touched one of the hurricanes, and the simulation responded with a popup window detailing the coordinates, average wind speed, and trajectory of the storm. She touched another control and tried to bring up the main menu on the screen. The controls flashed red, demanding biometric authentication before reverting to the simulation.

That would have been too easy.

At the back of the room was another locked door. If it was locked, it was safe to assume that Alexander didn't want her going in there. Then again, she wasn't likely to find anything out until she forced the issue.

"What are you doing here?" asked a voice behind her.

Jezebel froze up.

"I was just exploring," she replied truthfully, turning around to see Alexander's shape towering over her in the dim light.

"Don't explore too much," Alexander warned her, "you may not like what you find."

"What's behind the door?" she asked.

"Nothing terribly special," Alexander said evasively, "maybe I'll show you when I have more time, but I wouldn't worry about it."

"Why don't you show me now?" Jezebel asked, pressing her luck.

"I'm busy right now," Alexander replied sharply.

He swiped his hand across the biometric pad, causing it to flash green and the door to open. Jezebel saw only darkness on the other side as Alexander stepped through.

* * *

The observation room was a dome-shaped chamber with a suite of cameras circling the inside, providing 360 degree coverage of the interior. Alexander had directed him here and told him to go on ahead. The entire wing was deserted when he got there, and Mortimer busied himself preparing the experiment.

He wasn't nervous. He was terrified. What kind of rage was Alexander holding in that came out every 24 hours? Even worse, what would happen if something went wrong? How would he explain such a medical emergency to his 'colleagues'?

He tugged at the collar, revealing that he had forty hours left on the clock.

The door opened and Alexander arrived, locking the door behind him.

"Everything's ready," Mortimer informed him.

"Good," Alexander said, stripping off his shirt, "so what do you need from me?"

"I need to observe your neurochemistry in real-time during one of these rage episodes," Mortimer explained, "how it's triggered, how it progresses, and how it resolves."

"Fine, then," Alexander said with a shrug.

He walked over to a secure cabinet and pulled out an injector along with a vial of misty-grey liquid. Then he inserted the nanoprobe vial into the injector and returned to the control panel, waving the vial over the reader.

A message appeared on the screen: '*Signal error: monitoring probes not activated.*'

"This contains 500 milligrams of medical nanobots," Alexander explained, "enough for you to monitor my vital signs at the biochemical and neurological level, although they're more invasive than the neural monitoring strips you used to make us wear."

"I'm ready whenever you are," Mortimer said apprehensively.

Alexander pressed the nozzle against his arm and pulled the trigger. There was a liquid hiss as the misty-grey solution was injected into his bloodstream. The error message vanished and was replaced by a representation of his body, highlighting his bioreadings in real-time.

"Once I'm inside the chamber," Alexander instructed Mortimer, "do *not* open the door until the episode has run its course."

"How will I know when it's over?" Mortimer asked with a gulp.

The readout chimed and flashed, registering a spike in certain neurochemical indicators. Alexander's eye was twitching in annoyance.

"Right…" Mortimer said nervously, "stupid question."

Alexander disposed of the injector and entered the observation chamber. Mortimer duly sealed the chamber behind him and the heavy door swung shut and locked.

The chamber was dark, only partially lit by the faint lighting strips around the edge. Alexander could feel the cold floor under his bare feet and could see the tapestry of claw marks all over the walls under the faint light.

"*Testing, testing, can you hear me?*" Mortimer's voice sounded from the speakers.

"Loud and clear," Alexander replied.

"*How exactly do we trigger one of these episodes?*" Mortimer asked.

"Press the secondary door lock indicator," Alexander ordered.

There was silence on the other end. Alexander could imagine Mortimer querying the instruction before holding his tongue and doing as he was told.

There was a metallic clang as another door opened. A stasis pod emerged from within, moving on automated rails as it slowed to halt. Visible inside was a leafy-skinned native.

"*What the frick is that?!*" Mortimer exclaimed through the speakers.

"The most reliable way to trigger an episode," Alexander replied gruffly, "now wake the creature up and don't do anything else until the episode has run its course."

The stasis pod cracked open and the native specimen keeled over and fell out of the pod. It landed on its claws and knees, taking in lungfuls of air as the last effects of its chemically induced hibernation wore off.

Alexander was alone with the creature. His muscles tensed up and he flexed his fingers before curling them into fists. This was one of the stronger specimens in the facility's inventory. The weaklings would never be thrown in – the natives didn't want to anger the Underworld with subpar sacrifices.

The creature looked up and saw him. Its flaming orange eyes narrowed and it peeled back its lips to reveal rows of spine-like teeth. It wasn't fear that welled up within Alexander as he faced this vicious carnivore. It was fury, and it was slowly clouding his mind, making him forget why he was there.

By this point, he would have reached for his inhaler, but he vaguely remembered that someone needed to see him in this state. All he was aware of was the threat before him, and he growled at the monster as the monster growled back. He felt nothing but black rage burning in his chest and desired nothing but to kill or be killed.

The creature squealed and lunged at Alexander, bounding towards him at high speed. Alexander snarled and charged.

* * *

The woman was wearing a completely see-through shirt under her jacket and a skirt that stopped less than halfway up her thighs. She had tattoos snaking up her neck and down between her cleavage. She also looked impatient rather than intimidated.

"When did you first meet Daniel Lawless?" the ACS officer asked.

"Who?" the courtesan asked.

The interrogation room's table had an interactive surface, and the officer selected a file and slid it across to her side.

"That's a video of you meeting with him at his workplace," the officer said.

"I go where my clients want me to go," the courtesan replied.

"So was this the first time you met him?" the officer asked again.

"I have hundreds of clients a year," the courtesan replied, "so I don't remember."

"You were contracted by a third party to visit Mr Lawless at the Bentham Penitentiary Facility where he works," the officer continued, "who paid your fee?"

"As long as the money arrives in full and on time, I don't ask those sorts of questions," the courtesan answered unhelpfully.

"Influencing a public official through inducements or threats is a criminal offence," the officer said threateningly, "and when the official in question ends up dead, criminal complicity in his death gets added to the charge sheet."

The courtesan's blasé demeanour dissolved. She began to scratch the side of her head nervously with nails painted jet black.

"So have I jogged your memory at all?" the officer asked.

"I didn't know his name before you told me," the courtesan explained, "but I remember being shuttled out to that weird puzzle-prison."

"Who booked the appointment?" the officer demanded.

"I don't know," the courtesan replied, "one morning I got the request and the money had already been wired to my account. I assumed he'd made the appointment himself."

"So you got on the shuttle, flew out to the prison, had your liaison, and left. Is that it?" the officer asked, unconvinced.

"Yes, that's what happened," the courtesan replied, scratching her temple again.

"You must have a terrible itch," the officer noted suspiciously.

"A little bit," the courtesan said, scratching the side of her head again, "what of it?"

"You've been scratching the side of your head every few minutes," the officer observed, "in fact, you were doing it a lot in the surveillance footage, as well."

"What fleeking difference does it make?" the courtesan retorted defensively.

"It's just strange that you and the other half dozen ladies of the night who visited him had the same itch in the same place in the surveillance footage," the officer noted, slipping a scanner glove over his hand and approaching her.

"Stay the fleek away from me, you fleeking pig!" the courtesan shrieked suddenly.

Her outburst took the officer by surprise, but as he stretched out his hand, she lashed out at him like a feral cat and scratched him across the face.

"I need some help in here!" the officer shouted.

Several other officers burst in with shock-sticks drawn, and one of them jabbed his weapon into her arm. The courtesan's muscles were paralysed and her thrashing stopped instantly. With his colleagues standing by, the interrogating officer extended his hand again and placed his palm against her temple.

The scanner node glowed and then flashed, highlighting a triangular shape the size of a fingernail planted on her temple. It was skin-coloured and as thin as a medical plaster, rendering it nearly invisible to the naked eye. The light from the scanner also illuminated a network of delicate circuitry.

"What's that fricking thing?" one of the other officers asked.

"Not a clue," the interrogating officer replied.

The courtesan snapped out of her paralysed state and lunged, shrieking like a demon as she knocked him to the floor. She made a rush for the door as the other officers swarmed over her, jabbing furiously with their shock-sticks until she stopped moving.

There was a trickle of blood coming from her nose, and her eyes were wide and empty. The little patch on the side of her head peeled off and curled up on the floor.

* * *

DNI operatives had been watching from the next room, and the courtesan's body was quickly removed from Asgard Civil Security's custody.

Her body was taken to a secure medical facility while the mysterious patch was sealed away in a sterile bag and sent to the nanoforensics wing of the same facility. Once the patch arrived, it was placed inside a spectroscopic chamber and subjected to a barrage of scans while two forensics technicians looked at the readings.

"The sample is too degraded," one of them complained.

"The analysis isn't even finished yet," his colleague replied.

"Just look at the readings," the first technician said, pointing to the readout, "the traces of nanocircuitry are gone, that means it's broken down already."

"No, it doesn't," the second technician answered irritably, "It means that the analysis isn't finished, now stop talking until it's done."

They watched tensely as the readings on the screen changed. After a while, the machine chimed, and the technicians rushed to start analysing the results.

"I told you," said the first technician, "less than 11% of the nanocircuitry is still intact."

Nanobots were supposed to be durable, but this sample had degraded so quickly that either the nanobots were poorly engineered or were designed to self-degrade.

"Good thing the machine was able to suspend the degradation," the first technician said, "but I don't think 11% is enough to go on."

The second technician initiated a second round of analysis while the first technician opened an internal communication line to the autopsy room.

"*Did you find any useable nanobot samples?*" the mortician asked.

"We did, but it's only a fraction of the original sample," the first technician responded, "we're running another round of tests now to see if we can work with it."

"*The cause of death was massive haemorrhaging in the brain,*" the mortician explained, "*but apart from degraded nanotechnological traces, we haven't determined what caused it.*"

"Where exactly did you find the traces?" the second technician asked.

"*On the side of her head where the patch was,*" the mortician replied, "*so the nanobots must have entered through the pores and then entered the capillaries.*"

"Any similarities with the way the mole died?" the first technician asked.

"*The mole died from nanotoxin-induced cellular necrotisation,*" the mortician replied, "*the hooker died from a simple brain haemorrhage.*"

"We also don't know if she intended to avoid capture or was killed before she could reveal anything," the second technician added.

"*I'll see what I can do on my end,*" the mortician concluded, "*but if you can get anything useful about the nature of the nanobots it would help enormously.*"

"We'll do our best," replied the first technician before terminating the link.

* * *

A forensics taskforce was already working on the investigation. Once they had finished analysing the nanobots and the autopsy results, the director-general arrived in the operations centre where the chief nanotechnologist was waiting.

"We have a preliminary idea of the nanobots' design," he informed her.

The man's stout frame and slightly pudgy face belied the fact that he was one of the planet's foremost nanoforensics experts.

"First of all, we know conclusively that the unusually rapid degradation of the nanobots was by design," the nanotechnologist explained, "evidently, whoever designed these particular nanobots didn't want their true function to be discovered."

He showed her an image on his flexi-tablet, depicting a reconstruction of one of the nanobots, including the web of nanocircuitry that permeated its body.

"The nanocircuitry is akin to an organic nervous system," the nanotechnologist added, "so based on its complexity, we can extrapolate the nanobots' capabilities."

"What have you extrapolated?" Red-eye asked.

"This module is unusually large for a peer-to-peer transmitter," the nanotechnologist answered, highlighting a specific component, "in fact, it's powerful enough to influence the surrounding neural tissue."

"You mean the subjects were brainwashed?" Red-eye asked.

"That appears to be the case," the nanotechnologist confirmed, "although we can't be totally certain until we see the original schematics or a live sample."

"Can you determine that based on the results you have?" the director-general asked.

"It will take a while," the nanotechnologist replied, then added, "we'll also be running the risk of re-triggering the self-degradation process of the suspended sample."

"Do what you can," Red-eye ordered.

He nodded and returned to work as the head of the neurological team approached.

"All of the surviving courtesans have unusual neural activity," he reported, "but it's subtle enough that it produces few behavioural symptoms. Our working theory is that these nanobots were designed to influence the subject to take certain actions."

He presented a flexi-tablet with the neural scan results displayed side by side.

"There may have been an initial infiltrator, himself possibly under the influence of the nanobots," the chief neurologist explained, "he then attached the patch to one or more of the courtesans, one of whom then used a similar patch to enthral the prison warden."

"And from there, they could gain access to highly placed individuals and enthral them to the will of whoever is behind this," Red-eye concluded.

There could be dozens of compromised individuals across the planet enthralled to the agenda of whoever designed the control-patch.

"Can you reliably detect the neurological effects of the control-patch?" Red-eye asked.

"We're already working on a wearable scanner to do exactly that," he confirmed.

"Good," said Red-eye, "have it ready for production as soon as possible."

* * *

The alien test subject was wide awake and struggling. It squealed at the top of its lungs, straining its vocal cords and thrashing all the way to the surgical booth.

The Human scientists stayed well back from the commotion, letting the androids handle the creature. The aliens possessed a superhuman strength belied by their sinewy physique. Their claws were deadly sharp as well, and the creature lashed out at the androids, leaving scratch marks across their faceplates.

The research team cast nervous glances at the nearest exit in case the creature broke free, but the androids were stronger than the terrified alien captive, and after several minutes of struggling, they forced the creature into the surgical booth.

The alien continued squealing, its fiery orange eyes bulging out of their sockets as the androids pinned it down, allowing the restraints to clamp down around its body and head.

Once they were confident that the test subject couldn't break free, the research team began the procedure. Microneedles injected the creature with a muscle relaxant. The alien's struggles became steadily weaker and before long it was lying limp.

"Ok, let's apply the cortical implant," said the research leader.

A robotic surgical arm extended from a slot in the wall, holding a claw-like device in its grip. The device's claws pricked the skin at the base of the skull, latching on like a parasite and pressing its body flat against the back of the head.

"The limbic control node is active and functional," one of the researchers announced, "all of the limbic implants are responding properly as well."

The effects of the muscle relaxant were already wearing off, but instead of thrashing about again, the test subject simply stood to attention. Its orange eyes blinked at exact intervals, but otherwise it didn't move a muscle.

"Looks obedient enough," remarked the research leader, "let's try making him move."

The rest of the research team looked at him and then each other, wondering if that was a good idea. The androids were still on standby, watching blankly for any sudden moves by the alien. Extending a nervous hand, one of the researchers pressed a button.

The restraints unlocked and retracted smoothly into their slots, releasing the alien and allowing it to stand up on its own. Its clawed feet scratched at the floor and its muscles twitched erratically, but otherwise it just stared ahead.

"Can it understand verbal commands?" someone asked.

"No," the research leader replied, "the control node takes commands from the control panel, or some portable equivalent, and makes the subject respond accordingly."

One of the technicians bravely approached the alien and waved his hand in front of its face. The alien's eyes followed his hand motions intently but otherwise didn't react.

"It's still aware of its surroundings and will still react out of instinct," the research leader explained, "but its critical faculties have been suppressed."

"So what do we do next?" one of the researchers asked.

"We see if it can still fight," the research leader replied.

He entered another set of commands and the hypnotised test subject began walking. There was something unnatural about the motion of its limbs. Instead of a smooth strutting gait, it jerked its limbs forward awkwardly like a puppet trying to walk without strings.

"Is it supposed to move like that?" one of the technicians asked.

"No," one of the researchers replied with a puzzled look.

"As I said, the control node suppresses critical faculties," the research leader explained, "and to some extent, walking in a particular direction requires conscious thought."

"But it shouldn't be interfering this much with the motor functions," someone else said.

"Everything that's wrong now can be corrected later on," the research leader pointed out, "that's what these tests are for."

The isolation pen was an improvised enclosure in the form of a curtain made of high-strength fabric, strong enough to resist slashing or tearing. The fabric was also smart-fabric, projecting an image of the interior onto the outside whilst staying opaque from the inside: people could see in but no one could see out.

After several minutes of awkward forward motion, the alien test subject made it all the way to the isolation pen unassisted and stood passively in front of the gate.

"If it can't even open a gate by itself, we've got a lot of work to do," snorted one of the researchers, stepping forward to do the honours.

He reached out a hand towards the enclosure gate and pulled it open, motioning to the alien to step inside. The alien stood rooted to the spot, gazing into the enclosure as if it were in a trance – which it technically was.

"Step inside," the researcher ordered the alien.

The alien stared blankly forward, ignoring or not hearing the instruction.

"Walk forward five steps," the researcher ordered.

The test subject did nothing.

"Didn't I say it can't understand verbal commands?" the research leader reminded him, "Besides, their spatial awareness under the control node's influence is still limited."

"That's an understatement," someone else said wryly, "not much point in a soldier that can't recognise the difference between an open door and a closed one."

"Let's see if a shove will work," the technician suggested, stepping forward again.

"No! Don't!" the research leader shouted.

Ignoring the warning, the man slammed his palm between the alien's shoulders.

The alien emitted a shrill squeal of atavistic rage and span around to maul its attacker. It raked a clawed hand across the man's face, then slashed his chest with its other clawed hand in quick succession before lunging at its reeling and bleeding prey.

The androids sprang into action, grabbing the vicious alien by its thrashing limbs and dragging it off the hapless technician. The other researchers looked on in horrified silence as more androids rushed forward to tend to their colleague.

He wasn't moving. His face was disfigured by three gory gashes across his face and his overalls had been slashed across the front. Blood was soaking his clothes as the medical androids worked to stop the bleeding.

The perpetrator was still venting its rage, emitting bloodthirsty squeals as it fought back ineffectually before the research leader snapped out of his shock and reset the control node.

The alien stopped moving as its rigid posture and blank stare returned. The team looked on warily, wondering if it might snap again, but its gaze was completely vacant.

"Does the boss seriously expect us to make soldiers out of these things?" one of the researchers asked, echoing the thoughts of the team.

"Yes," the research leader said resolutely, "and I've been told that the natives will be tossing more down pretty soon."

* * *

Jezebel was bored. Alexander came and went on whatever operations he was running, and had left her to her own devices in this luxury pseudo-prison. In the meantime, she had returned to the operations room and was playing a 3D chess game.

It was an order of magnitude more frustrating to play than its traditional 2D counterpart. The usual rules of movement still applied, but this time in three dimensions, meaning that the pieces could traverse the board diagonally up and down.

Jezebel wondered how Alexander managed to play this game without smashing it, given that he seemed to be trapped in a constant struggle not to lash out at the slightest irritation. She didn't remember him ever having such a temper when they were together.

Except once...

It had been half a lifetime since she had seen his face. That murderous face appearing in the doorway with rage burning in his eyes as she cowered in the corner with their son. Seven gunshots in the dark had stopped him.

Jezebel abruptly quit the game and stood up. It may have been nearly half a century ago, but it was still the worst memory she had.

There was still a whole facility to explore, so she left the operations room and went to the living room. She found the door through which she had arrived and was surprised to find it unlocked. Passing through, she followed a flight of steps down into another corridor before coming to another unlocked door.

The lack of security was puzzling. She was still trapped in the facility, but what kind of prison allowed the inmate to roam free?

After passing through the door, she emerged onto a viewing platform with a safety railing overlooking a processing area. It was much smaller than the hangar, but still a sizeable space. There was a loading cradle at one end and a cargo elevator at the other end, with an automated rack of machinery in the middle.

A team of Human technicians dressed in hazmat gear was overseeing everything. Under their watch, large armoured containers would arrive via the cargo elevator and be moved through the machinery to be scanned. Once the scan was complete, the container would be placed into the waiting loading cradle.

Each one was marked with the biohazard symbol.

Jezebel watched as the cargo elevator brought new containers up from below and the loading cradle carried each one away to the hangar. They were being taken out of the facility, not being delivered to the facility.

A klaxon sounded and orange warning lights began flashing around the periphery. Jezebel ducked behind the railing, then realised that the railing did nothing to conceal her from view. But there was nowhere else to hide and she couldn't risk making a run for it; all she could do was hope no one looked up.

A fault had been encountered and the machinery had shut down automatically. The Human technicians moved forward to investigate the cause of the fault, forcing the machine to spit out the container so they could examine it more closely.

The container resembled an iron sarcophagus; an oblong of dark metal with rounded edges and no visible hinges or interface. Using a pair of special tools, two of the technicians disabled the locks. The lid popped open, releasing a cool gush of condensation as the precious cargo was revealed.

The technicians crowded around the container, obscuring Jezebel's view of the interior and making her even more curious about what was inside.

She remembered Alexander intimating an interest in the pharmaceutical industry, but would pharmaceutical samples be considered biohazardous? The interior of the container was refrigerated and the biohazard symbol implied live samples. Was he smuggling xenobiological samples off of the planet?

Jezebel began to question the wisdom of snooping around. No one had noticed her, and the sooner she left, the less likely she was to be caught.

"Hey!" a voice shouted behind her, "what are you doing here?"

"I got lost," she responded, keeping her composure as she turned around.

The man who had challenged her was a foreman wearing blue engineers overalls with a backpack of tools slung over his shoulders.

"The exit is this way," the man said, gesturing for Jezebel to follow him.

As she followed the man to the exit, Jezebel took one more glance over her shoulder, wondering what was inside the containers.

Ignorance was probably safer.

* * *

Gabriel couldn't sleep. The events at the Bentham Prison wouldn't leave his mind. Neither would the mysterious 'Network' and the Directorate's attempts to flush it out, so now he was wandering through the darkened apartment. At least Aster wouldn't be kept awake by him, baby Emerald would handle that.

Gabriel peered into the children's bedroom. Orion, Rose, Violet, and Leonidas were all asleep in their beds. Their shared bedroom was big enough for a whole dormitory of siblings, and space had already been prepared for Emerald.

There was something soothing about watching them sleep. It reminded him that they were still largely oblivious to the dangers of the universe. Of course, that innocence was no longer intact. They knew they weren't normal children.

Gabriel had been disillusioned with the Directorate for a whole year now, but now a burning suspicion had been kindled in his mind. It had never occurred to him that his superiors would take a direct interest in his children. Mortimer had intimated just such an interest, but now he was either a fugitive or dead.

Of course, there was one other person who would know, but she wasn't going to tell. Not unless he forced the issue somehow.

It also occurred to Gabriel how precarious his own position was. His trust in the Directorate had been badly undermined, but their trust in him had no doubt been damaged as well. How much more slack would Red-eye cut him?

Gabriel ducked out of the children's bedroom and walked back down the hallway. There was no way he could get to sleep now, not after what he had just thought of. He wanted to keep his young family as far away from all of this as possible, but to do that there were preparations he needed to make.

He entered his personal gym, the equipment casting sinister shadows across the room under the faint light. In one corner was a closet, not as sophisticated as the one in the master bedroom. Gabriel swiped his thumb across the biometric pad and the doors popped open.

Inside the closet were seven sets of skin-tight suits, one his size, one for a woman, four child-sized, and one small enough for a baby.

At the back of the closet, obscured by the skin-suits, was a large plastic case secured by a biometric lock. Inside was an assault weapon, custom-made for Gabriel's use.

He hadn't told anyone about this closet, not even Aster. It wasn't strictly illegal for a military or intelligence operative to own weapons and armour, but it wasn't strictly authorised either. Notwithstanding the recent terror attacks, Asgard City was one of the safest places in the sector, obviating the need for a personal armoury.

The contents of this closet represented a substantial risk on his part. If his superiors found out, there would be no explaining away a set of custom-made personal protection skin-suits. There would certainly be no explaining away the assault weapon.

Hopefully, he wouldn't need to use it.

"What are you doing now?" asked a woman's voice.

Gabriel abruptly shut the closet and turned to face Aster.

"I was checking on something," he replied truthfully.

"And you had to do it in the middle of the night?" she asked suspiciously.

"Why did you leave Emerald alone?" Gabriel asked, changing the subject.

"Good point," Aster countered, "let's both go back and check on her."

Gabriel followed her back to the master bedroom, then stopped at the threshold.

"What is it now?" Aster demanded irritably, "if you've got something to do, you can do it in the morning, now come back to bed."

"How would you like to run away together?"

There was a shocked pause as Aster stood and stared at Gabriel.

"Are you serious?" she asked incredulously.

"Yes, I am," he replied firmly.

"Where is this coming from all of a sudden?" she asked.

Gabriel looked back over his shoulder. They couldn't see any little shadows peeking out from the children's room, but clearly this wasn't a conversation they should overhear. Aster beckoned him back inside the bedroom and he closed the door quietly behind him.

"I'm not sure I trust the Directorate anymore," Gabriel tried to explain.

That shocked Aster even more than his suggestion to run away. Being a colonial by birth, she was naturally suspicious of the government – despite now working for the Directorate. She had always taken it for granted that Gabriel, having served in the Directorate for decades, would hold ironclad loyalty to it.

"Is this about that message from Dr Mortimer Shelton?" Aster asked apprehensively.

"That's the least of it," Gabriel replied, unsettling her even more.

"I'm not sure I want to know what you mean," she said warily.

"You may still need to know it," he told her gravely.

They climbed back into bed and she entangled herself in his arms, snuggling close and running her hands across the sculpted muscles of his stomach and chest.

"Do you really not miss your home planet?" Gabriel asked Aster.

"I thought you were going to tell me why you want to run away," Aster replied.

"If we're going to leave, we'll need someplace to flee to," Gabriel explained.

"I can't believe you're serious about that," Aster said, keeping her voice low, "but to answer your question, no: the only living to be made on Sahara is digging ore out of the ground under the blazing hot sun."

Gabriel snorted.

"Do you find that funny?" Aster asked him.

"A little bit," he replied, "you look after the house and the children whilst I'm away, and you seem quite happy doing it."

"I'd be happier if the man of the house were around more often," Aster noted testily, "especially to help look after the brood."

"You're the one who wanted to make the brood so big," Gabriel reminded her.

Aster's hand slipped down between Gabriel's thighs and closed around his crotch.

"I don't like the way you said that," she growled.

"It's true, isn't it?" Gabriel said, shifting uncomfortably.

"Absolutely," Aster replied, fondling him below the waist, "but my point is that life is awful on a barren backwater like Sahara, especially for a family of young children. Asgard is paradise by comparison. I don't want to leave. Ever."

Gabriel was silent.

"Besides, I don't think running away would be very practical," Aster pointed out, "can you imagine trying to slip under the Directorate's nose with four young children and an infant?"

"It's possible," Gabriel insisted.

"And what about after our daring escape?" Aster added, "even if the DNI didn't object to one of their best operatives running away, what would we do for a living?"

"I can do more than kill things, you know," Gabriel said defensively.

"I'm sure that's true, sweetheart," Aster replied with a smile, "but even then, I reckon you'd go stir-crazy with a bunch of small children running around the house and without being able to go out and do what you do best."

Gabriel was silent again.

"Bottom line: I don't want to run away," Aster said emphatically, "and even if you did manage to convince me, we are NOT going back Sahara."

"Embarrassed to introduce me to my in-laws?" Gabriel asked.

"Now that you mention it, my father would be pretty angry to find out that a government operative got his daughter pregnant," Aster replied jokingly, "then again, he's probably drunk himself into an early grave by now."

"That's a flippant way of putting it," Gabriel noted.

Aster was silent for a moment.

"Asgard is my home now," she said eventually, evading the remark, "and it's the only home our children have ever known. For better or worse, we should stay here."

"If you say so," Gabriel conceded.

"I *do* say so," Aster reiterated, "no plotting to run away and no more sneaking off in the night to check on your equipment stash."

The couple lay together in the darkness, and Aster savoured the warmth of Gabriel's presence and the strength of his embrace. It wasn't long before drowsiness began to claim her again, the gentle drumbeat of Gabriel's heart sending her slowly to sleep.

Something buzzed on the bedside table. Gabriel retrieved his smartphone, finding an encrypted text message from a Directorate number.

'*Report to the Spire tomorrow morning at 9:00am*," the terse message read, "*you will be guided to your destination. Regards, the Directorate.*'

Presumably, he was being called in for some kind of formal disciplinary action, which ruled out running away. It was unlikely to be a new assignment, the last thing the DNI wanted was to give him a longer leash.

Either way, he had better not tell Aster.

THE TUNNELS

Nearly one thousand captives were thrown alive into the mouth of the underworld to propitiate the gods who dwelt below. The captives flailed and squealed all the way down, their warbling cries echoing all the way back up to the surface they would never see again. Caught by antigravity projectors, the captives were left suspended until the snatch teams could get to them and force each one into a casket.

The aliens squealed and struggled all the way from the capture net to their caskets. But once inside, their cries were muted and the snatch teams began the laborious task of carrying them back to the underground tram.

There wasn't enough space aboard the tram to carry all the caskets, so multiple round trips would be needed. Fortunately, there were plenty of spare caskets, and they were lined up by the hundreds all along the winding tunnel until they could be collected.

After loading the first batch of caskets onto the tram, the team climbed aboard. The whine of the tram's engine echoed down the tunnel, and its headlamps cut piercing swaths through the darkness as the snatch teams tried to relax.

"Hell of a catch," someone remarked.

"Hell of a victory party, too," someone else agreed, "parade your enemies through the streets, skin some alive, and toss the rest into the underworld."

There were nods of agreement. The description was brutally true.

"Do you reckon ancient Humans used to do things like that?" the second person mused.

"Probably," the first person agreed, "until we grew out of it."

"What kind of species that barbaric would just grow out of it, Dolan?" the second team member asked, "you know the expression about how people can't change their stripes?"

"I think you mean animals and spots, Triton," Dolan corrected him, "but are you saying our ancestors were peace-loving grass-munchers who all lived in harmony?"

"I'm not saying we were always nice to each other," Triton replied defensively, "I'm just saying they probably didn't go around torturing each other the way these primitives do."

"I've been meaning to ask you something," the third member of the team spoke up, "how come your parents named you 'Triton'?"

"Apparently, it's the name of some moon orbiting one of the gas giants in Sol," Triton explained, "in the great and clichéd tradition of spacers being named after spacey things."

"Back to the subject," Dolan said, "I've seen enough of the universe to know that under harsh conditions, only the harshest survive."

"So as conditions become less nasty, the creatures living in those conditions become less nasty as well?" Triton asked sceptically.

"That's my thesis," Dolan confirmed.

"Are you sure it's not ingrained in their genes?" Triton countered, "If they had to be nasty and vicious to survive in the first place, genetics had to be the key. Which means that even if they managed to create nicer and more civilised conditions, they'd still carry the genes that made their ancestors what they were down through the generations."

"Sweet Terra, not the fucking nature vs nurture argument," exclaimed the third person.

"What, you don't think it's worth debating?"

"I'm a biologist," the third person replied, "so I can tell you that the whole argument has been ongoing since science was invented. It's not worth wasting time on. Trust me."

The conversation petered out after that, and the members of the snatch team stared at the dull grey walls of the tram car. With so many life support pods stacked up against the walls, there was hardly any space to stand, let alone sit down, but it was an hour-long trip back to the facility, so they made do.

The passengers could hear the rattling of the wheels against the tracks, but the carriage itself was equipped with dampeners that minimised the vibrations. It was strange to hear so much shaking and rattling outside without feeling any of it inside.

"So how did you guys get recruited?" Triton asked.

"Got bored of being a grease monkey on a freight hauler and wound up here," Dolan summarised, "although, along the way, I may have helped the Network get their hands on some valuable machinery. What about you?"

"Born and raised on an asteroid mining colony," Triton replied, "got mixed up with the smugglers and ended up in a penal colony for a spell. Broke out of prison with some other guys and after many wonderful adventures, I got recruited by the Network."

"And what about you, Joseph?" Dolan asked, turning to their biologist team member, "did you get stripped of your doctor's license?"

"I'm not a medical doctor," the man replied, furrowing his brow in annoyance, "I'm a biologist. So just Joseph will do, thanks."

"Alright, Joseph," Dolan rephrased, "but you've still got an advanced enough education to call yourself 'doctor', don't you?"

"You could say that," Joseph replied with a shrug, "I never quite got the certificate, but the company trained me to be a marine biologist."

"Which company is this?"

"You won't have heard of it," Joseph answered, "it existed on one particular planet and catastrophic damage to their production plants forced them into administration years ago."

"When you say 'catastrophic damage'," Triton asked, "do you mean sabotage?"

"Indeed," Joseph confirmed, "and they had it coming. The whole colony was ruled by this one company as a de facto corporate holding. Half the population worked for the company and the other half were the local customer base."

"Where does marine biology come into this," Dolan asked.

"The main food staple are these giant eels that were bred to be nutritious and docile," Joseph responded, "They also had a biologically superfluous organ inserted through genetic engineering which could grow any drug the company wanted. Lower production volume than synthetic production methods, but vastly superior quality."

"And you blew up their production plants and fled?"

"Yes I did, and what a glorious comeuppance it was," Joseph confirmed unrepentantly, "although I did have some help. As a fugitive from justice, the Network picked me up, faked my death and brought me onboard."

There was more silence, broken only by the humming of the tram engine.

"No offence to those present," Dolan spoke up after a while, "but it seems the boss is mainly interested in recruiting crooks."

"None taken," Triton replied with an amused grin, "but I'm not sure he's got much of a talent pool to choose from. What with the government recruiting the best and the corporations snatching up the rest."

"What do you think he's planning down here?" Dolan wondered, touching a tripwire.

"I'd rather not find out," said Joseph, averting his gaze.

"Really?" Dolan asked, "You're not curious at all?"

"No, I am not," Joseph replied emphatically, "and neither should you."

"Curiosity killed the mouse," Triton reminded him.

"You mean the cat," Dolan corrected him.

"For someone who knows so much about classical idioms, you have a remarkable lack of common sense," Triton retorted, but with an edge of seriousness, "the point is: don't go poking your nose in the boss's business if you want to stay on his good side."

"I second that," Joseph added.

An alarm began to beep and the tram decelerated as the engine fell silent. Dolan went to the front of the carriage and opened the interface panel.

"What the fuck's going on?" Triton demanded.

"The engine's shut down," Dolan replied, "someone's gonna have to take a look."

The crew grumbled, but they weren't going anywhere until the problem was fixed, so Triton retrieved a toolkit and climbed out. He trudged to the front of the tram, followed by Dolan and several others. Once he reached the front, he opened the maintenance panel and shone a light over the machinery.

"So what's wrong with it?" one of the men asked impatiently.

"Looks like one of the power cells has come loose," Triton concluded.

"How does that happen?" Dolan asked.

"Someone didn't lock it in place properly when they were swapping out the old one," Triton explained, "and the vibrations did the rest."

He undid the fastenings securing the power cell, pulled the cell out of its slot then pushed it back in again, locking the fasteners into place properly.

"Should be alright now!" Triton announced, "All aboard!"

"Uh, guys?" someone else spoke up, "you might want to take a look at this."

Puzzled, the group of men went further down the tunnel to investigate. On the outer edge of the bend in the track was a slope leading down into a separate cave. The man who had called his fellows over shone a light down into the cave, illuminating the foot of the slope where the rocky floor became smooth and level.

Someone kicked a stone down and they watched it bounce down until it hit the smooth floor at the foot of the slope. From there, it kept on rolling across the floor before hitting the far wall with a hollow thud.

"I don't know about you," the man said, "but that looks artificial to me."

At the end of the cave, the floor ended at a vertical wall of rock. The rock wall was as smooth as the floor, so smooth it looked machine-polished.

"How well have these tunnels been mapped?" Triton asked.

"Well enough for this segment to be on the map," Dolan responded, "but I don't think anyone's explored this particular fork. It's certainly not part of the facility."

The men looked at each other, wondering at this discovery.

"It looks almost like it was going to be part of the facility, but then got sealed off," Dolan surmised as the others nodded in agreement.

"What's going on over there?!" someone shouted from aboard the tram.

"We fixed the engine!" one of the party shouted back, "we're coming back now!"

The group of men trudged back to the tram and climbed back aboard. Once the doors were sealed, the engine was reactivated and the tram began to trundle forward again.

"Do you think the boss knows about it?" Triton wondered aloud.

"Knows about what?" someone else asked, "did you guys find something?"

"Yeah," Dolan replied cryptically, "you could say that."

* * *

Alexander awoke face down on the cold floor. He recalled walking into the chamber and nothing after that. His mind was completely clear, but his body was immobilised by pain. He felt the sting of countless wounds across his torso and his muscles were aching from superhuman exertions that he couldn't remember.

He turned his head, his neck straining to obey, and saw another body lying next to him. The body had viridian skin and wiry limbs with taut muscles, and its hands and feet ended in vicious claws. Even from this awkward floor angle, he could see that the alien's body was covered in a bloody patchwork of bruises and other wounds.

The door to the chamber unlocked and creaked open. He heard footsteps come rushing over and a pair of hands grab his ankles as someone struggled to drag him away. His muscles were too sore to move, so he let Mortimer – presumably it was Mortimer – rely on his own efforts to haul him out of the chamber.

Impressively, Mortimer was able to drag him all the way out of the chamber before shutting the door behind them. He then lifted Alexander's torso up again and lay him against the wall before checking his eyes with a pencil-torch.

Alexander squinted at the bright light but kept his eyes open.

"How do you feel?" Mortimer asked, putting the pencil-torch away.

"Like I have a horrible hangover," Alexander replied groggily.

"I made you immune to the aftereffects of intoxication," Mortimer pointed out.

"Don't get pedantic with me," Alexander countered testily, "I have a huge headache, my muscles feel like they're on fire, and I have no memory between the door shutting and now. In fact, I can barely move my limbs."

"Judging by the data gathered by the nanobots, that's not surprising," Mortimer said, "but your muscles should recover within the hour."

"So, did you get anything useful?" Alexander asked.

"I've now got plenty of raw data," Mortimer answered, "but it will take some time to analyse it all before I can create a treatment."

Having just experienced a complete rage episode, Alexander's temper was enormously dampened, and he calmly accepted Mortimer's explanation.

Mortimer handed Alexander a nutrient drink to replenish his strength and rebuild his muscles. Alexander took it and drained it in one go before tossing it to one side.

"I guess I should re-enter the reset code," he said.

He tried to lift his arm, but winced as the muscle pain thwarted his movements.

"That would be greatly appreciated," Mortimer answered, "but your muscles need to recover before you can do that."

"I guess you'll have to be patient, then," Alexander remarked with a sardonic sneer, "so, were you impressed by the show?"

Mortimer didn't respond. The sight of a mostly-normal Human transforming into an enraged beast, going hand-to-claw with a predatory alien, and beating it to death wasn't the sort of thing he could enjoy watching.

"Aren't you proud of what you've accomplished?" Alexander followed up.

Proud? Throughout his career, Mortimer had never once felt proud of his work for the Directorate. He wasn't exactly ashamed of it, either. He understood the threats Humanity faced, but the botched enhancement that had caused Alexander's rage episodes was certainly not a source of pride.

"I don't know what word I'd use to describe it," Mortimer answered eventually, "but 'proud' is definitely not on the shortlist."

"So you never felt any sense of accomplishment knowing that voidstalkers like my son roam the galaxy fighting the enemies of Humanity?" Alexander asked.

The way he asked the question didn't sound very curious, more like an interrogation with a veiled accusation buried inside. Mortimer knew what he was hinting at, and despite his patient's comparatively mellow mood, he stayed cautious.

"I followed orders exactly the way you did," Mortimer responded simply, "and exactly the way Gabriel does now."

"I'm not sure I like my son being a faithful pawn of that bioniceyed bitch," he remarked, "but at least I'm not one anymore."

"I'm not sure it's a good idea to call her that," Mortimer said.

"I don't care, and neither would she," Alexander retorted.

There was a round of silence.

"You've got quite a stable of pawns of your own," Mortimer pointed out bravely.

"Yes, I do," Alexander answered with a cynical sneer, "scrape away enough layers of high-minded civilisational accomplishment and you're bound to find plenty of lost souls who'll follow you for profit or purpose."

"I've heard that everyone here is an 'equity partner' of sorts," Mortimer said.

"You should mind your choice of subject," Alexander replied through gritted teeth.

"How carefully?" Mortimer asked, his resolve holding, "You still need me to devise a cure for your condition. If you kill me, then the search for a cure will be moot."

Alexander snorted with laughter before grimacing in pain at his still sore muscles.

"Very true," he conceded with a smile, then his expression turned serious again, "but that doesn't mean I'm going to tell you my plans."

"You'll have to tell someone your plans sooner or later if you want them to succeed," Mortimer pointed out, hoping to pry a little further while it was safe to do so.

Alexander laughed again, ignoring the pain to force the amusement out. Then a serious expression returned, sharpened by a lethal stare.

"I've survived and done pretty well for the past half century," was his steely reply, "and I did so without pouring my heart out."

"I'm the one who enhanced that heart of yours," Mortimer reminded him.

"And if you pry any deeper into my plans, I'll rip yours out and feed it to one of those aliens," Alexander retorted menacingly.

Mortimer gulped, knowing full well that he wasn't joking.

* * *

There were any number of reasons why Red-eye would call him in, and Gabriel couldn't help the feeling that she wanted to lock him up to keep him out of the way. An armoured sky-car had come to the apartment tower's landing pad to pick him up and neither of the agents had said a word to him for the whole journey; not that they were likely to know much.

Gabriel sat in silence, staring at the partition. The vehicle weaved through the air, its aerial movements minimised by the motion dampeners. The journey was only half an hour by mag-train, less than that by sky-car, so they should arrive fairly soon.

He activated the viewing screen in the back of the partition, switching to the live camera feed. Windows were a frivolous luxury and a structural weakness to boot; few modern vehicles came installed with them, and certainly not government vehicles. High quality video cameras were a more versatile alternative for viewing pleasure.

The view was impressive as always. The sky-car manoeuvred gracefully between the towers, the scale akin to an insect flying through a forest as hundreds of other airborne vehicles wove in between the towers in concentrated streams.

Gabriel angled the camera downwards, catching a glimpse of the Undercity far below, obscured by the glare of the morning sun and the shadows cast by the skyscrapers. The people who lived down there were mostly out of sight, but never completely out of mind.

The sky-car touched down on one of the Spire's landing pads and Gabriel disembarked. He walked towards the blast door as the sky-car took to the air again. The biometric sensor flash-scanned Gabriel's eyes and the blast door opened. He entered and proceeded down the corridor as the blast door sealed shut behind him.

The corridors were plain and perpendicular, though not quite as dark as the exterior and certainly better lit. Operatives and analysts flitted from office to office, conversing quietly and giving the green-eyed, dour-looking operative a quick salute and a wide berth.

Gabriel didn't know where he was going. The message had told him to come to the Spire and that he was going to be guided to his destination.

"Colonel Thorn!" someone called from behind him.

Gabriel turned around and saw an operative approaching. He had a virtual map on his wrist-top with a flashing dot on the screen marked with Gabriel's name.

"Your biometrics getting logged by the cameras enabled me to find you," the operative explained, "in case you were wondering."

"Actually, I'm wondering where I'm supposed to go," Gabriel replied less than coolly, "I'm assuming that you would know."

"Yes, I was sent to guide you to the operations centre," the operative replied.

"Well, lead the way," Gabriel ordered.

The operative nodded and turned around. Gabriel followed him through the corridors until they reached the elevators and boarded one of them. The operative selected one of the sublevels and the elevator began to move.

Gabriel watched the numbers tick downwards. There were all sorts of mysterious facilities down here serving various esoteric purposes, most of which he had never visited. In fact, it was doubtful if anyone other than Red-eye had ever toured the entire Spire.

After several minutes, the elevator decelerated and came to a halt before the doors opened. The operative stepped out and Gabriel followed him. The fact that they were this far down meant they were in the Rand Block: the research and development block where the Directorate's in-house scientific empire was housed.

Gabriel had been down to the Rand Block before, but only for routine medical tests or to be equipped for his next assignment. No doubt his many physical and genetic enhancements had been designed here, as had the weapons and armour he used.

The operative guiding him was relying on his wrist-top map. He had probably never been down here before and may never come down here again. Eventually, they came to a set of doors marked by an alphanumeric code and marked on the map as the destination.

"This is where I'm supposed to take you, Colonel," the operative said with a salute.

"Thank you and good day," said Gabriel, returning the salute.

As the operative went back the way they had come, Gabriel approached the biometric sensor and allowed it to flash-scan his eyes. The red light flashed green and the doors slid open. He walked into an operations centre with a dozen people working on various simulations. None of them turned to acknowledge him as the doors shut behind him.

Like so much of the Rand Block, the operations centre was dark, with much of the light coming from the glowing simulations. Some of them featured nanotechnology schematics while others looked like computerised neural images.

"Colonel Thorn," a researcher called to him, "over here, please."

Gabriel duly approached and entered a side booth adjacent to the main chamber. The door shut behind him, silencing the din of activity on the other side.

Besides the researcher, there was a third person in the booth: a woman in a midnight black uniform with an admiral's insignia on her lapel. She had light skin, jet black hair tied back in a bun, and a bionic right eye with a laser-red iris.

"Director-general," Gabriel said, saluting out of disciplined habit.

"Colonel Thorn," replied Red-eye, acknowledging him with a nod.

Gabriel was anything but pleased to see Red-eye, but he kept his feelings to himself as the researcher pulled up a simulation for him to look at.

"This is Dr Benjamin Solaris," Red-eye said, introducing the researcher, "his team has been studying how the Network controls its agents."

"The nature of the threat is nanotechnological," Dr Solaris explained, "the Bentham Prison warden was visited by a string of courtesans, each one showing signs that their neural pathways had been altered by custom-designed nanoprobes."

"Was that how the prison warden was turned," Gabriel asked.

"We don't know if the prison warden was affected or simply being manipulated by the Network to further its agenda," Red-eye remarked, "and because he died before we could interrogate him, we will likely never find out."

The prison warden would be alive if it weren't for Gabriel's ill-considered break-in mission. Red-eye's remark was a veiled rebuke for his ears alone.

"However," Dr Solaris added, the rebuke passing straight over his head, "the warden was visited at the prison by a number of courtesans over the past few months. Under medical examination, each of them showed signs of exposure to nanoprobes and that their neurologies had been noticeably altered as a result."

Gabriel hadn't been debriefed after the incident at the prison, so this was news to him.

"One of the courtesans that visited the warden had a nanopatch on her temple," Dr Solaris continued explaining, "The nanobots inside were insinuated into her body through the pores, then into the capillaries, and from there into the brain."

The main screen depicted one of the nanobots shaped like a tadpole with a bulbous head and a flagellum moving in a corkscrewing motion.

"The nanocircuitry is a lot more complex than one would expect," Dr Solaris continued, "and the peer-to-peer transmitter is several orders of magnitude more powerful than–"

"I can guess what the term means, but I'm not a nanotechnologist," Gabriel cut in.

"Of course," Dr Solaris said, "peer-to-peer transmitters link the nanobots together in a swarm network that enables them to exchange information and work in concert. Usually, the transmitter's range only extends a few hundred micrometres."

"But this one is unusually powerful?"

"Powerful enough to influence the surrounding neural tissue," Dr Solaris continued, "especially when acting in concert with the other nanobots in the solution. The signal can be amplified enough to influence the neurotransmitters within the synapses of the brain."

"So the Network's infiltrators are brainwashed?" Gabriel asked.

"With all due respect, Colonel," Dr Solaris replied, "that layman's term is woefully inadequate. There is a spectrum of neurological manipulation that affects a subject's behaviour to varying degrees. We don't yet know if the subjects have been affected to the extent that they could be considered 'brainwashed'."

"Be that as it may," Red-eye cut in, "we still don't know how widespread the infiltration is or if there is a single agent or a group of agents facilitating it."

"Although, we have managed to devise a way to reliably detect the neural alteration," Dr Solaris added, "which means we can detect someone who is enthralled."

He picked a device off the worktop and held it up for Gabriel to examine. It was shaped like a glove, but with a disc-shaped component in the middle of the palm.

"Do I just press that against the side of someone's head?" Gabriel guessed.

"Correct," Dr Solaris replied, "and the display on the back of the glove will tell you whether the results are positive or negative."

Gabriel accepted the device and slipped it over his hand.

"One other thing," Gabriel asked as he examined the scanner device, "is there any sort of countermeasure against these nanobots?"

"Indeed, there is," Dr Solaris responded, picking up an injector gun, "this serum will destroy any nanotechnological intrusions into your system."

"Including those found in the nanopatch?" Gabriel asked.

"Yes," Dr Solaris answered.

Gabriel nodded and rolled up his sleeve. Dr Solaris pressed the nozzle against one of the blood vessels and pulled the trigger. Gabriel felt the cool liquid flow into his bloodstream before dissipating through his arm.

"You're dismissed, doctor," Red-eye ordered.

Dr Solaris nodded and departed, taking the injector gun with him.

"Evidently, you need to be kept occupied in order to stay out of trouble," Red-eye noted, "so this is your newest assignment."

There was something different about Red-eye's demeanour. She was infamous for being implacably cool and devoid of emotion, but as she looked at him and spoke to him there was an unmistakeable undercurrent of displeasure.

"Who is your prime suspect?" Gabriel asked.

"We don't have one yet," Red-eye replied.

"Not even from the Bentham Prison's computer systems?" Gabriel demanded.

Red-eye's eyes narrowed slightly, catching his reference to the mysterious message.

"The message could have been a false flag," she replied, "but the mere fact that it named you is precisely why I wanted to keep you away from this investigation."

"Is my father alive?" Gabriel asked.

"Who knows?" Red-eye answered flatly, "The real concern for me is why this Network takes such an inordinate interest in you."

"Is my father the prime suspect?" Gabriel demanded, barely keeping his composure.

"As I said, the salient question here is why the Network is taking such an interest in you personally," Red-eye replied, unsubtly evading the question, "the whole purpose of implicating you in the first place might be to undermine your faith in the organisation you've served so faithfully for so many years, maybe even enough to motivate you to run away."

Gabriel managed not to flinch, but he could guess what she was talking about.

"Skin-suit body armour is a strange thing for anyone to purchase," Red-eye continued, "especially models that come in children's sizes."

"It's no different from the maganiel android," Gabriel tried to argue.

"The maganiel android is Directorate property and intended to protect your family," Red-eye pointed out coolly, "You have no need for those protective skin-suits, just as you have no need for that custom assault weapon you acquired."

"Do you seriously think I'm plotting to go AWOL with my family?" Gabriel demanded.

"It's also possible that you expect someone to lay siege to your family apartment," Red-eye remarked with an uncharacteristic dose of sarcasm, "but somehow I find that unlikely."

Gabriel had nothing else to say. Of course it was foolish to think that his preparations would escape the notice of the Directorate. They had an enormous vested interest in him and his family, a fact which made him even more distrustful of Red-eye.

"We never had a proper debriefing for the Nexus mission," Gabriel remarked, changing the subject, "you were too busy interrogating me about my alleged treachery."

"This is neither the time nor the place," said Red-eye perfunctorily.

"Of course, not," Gabriel said with his own dose of sarcasm, "we don't want people finding out about our backchannel with aliens, do we?"

Red-eye took a step towards Gabriel and looked up at him, the corners of her eyes crinkled into a glare. Gabriel stood a head taller than her, but there was something undeniably chilling about that glare. The bionic red eye regarded him with the cold interest of a targeting laser whilst her hazel organic eye simply stared him down.

Gabriel stared back, holding his composure and her gaze whilst being made acutely aware that he was skating on thin ice.

"Unauthorised contact with alien species is strictly forbidden by the 2nd Prime Law," Red-eye said, "I'm sure you are aware of that."

"The key word is 'unauthorised'," Gabriel remarked.

"A fact which undermines the implicit point you were making," Red-eye pointed out, "especially since the 'contacts' in question reached out to *you*."

"Using one of *our* authorisation codes to do so," Gabriel replied.

"As I said, this is neither the time nor the place," Red-eye answered, breaking off the staring match, "we have a counterintelligence investigation to pursue."

Gabriel ground his teeth in frustration. If the Network really was trying to undermine his trust in the Directorate, the director-general herself was doing a fine job of that all by herself. However, it was clear he wasn't going to get any answers out of her.

"In that case," he said, swallowing his frustration, "what exactly is my assignment?"

"To identify the 'influencer'," Red-eye responded, "that's the codename we've given to the individual who we believe is the Network's principle operative on Asgard."

"As in the one influencing the rest of them to do the Network's bidding," said Gabriel, "how do we know there aren't multiple influencers?"

"We don't," Red-eye conceded, "but so far, the evidence of infiltration and Network activity is such that we can reasonably assume that only one influencer exists."

"Does that mean you've already narrowed down the pool of suspects?"

"Up to a point, yes," Red-eye replied, "the courtesans' movements have been tracked and cross-referenced, and your task is to narrow down the pool of suspects by scanning their neural pathways using that device."

"It's either a small list of names or you're expecting them to show up in one place," Gabriel surmised, unless Red-eye was planning to make him go door to door.

"The latter," Red-eye answered, "you'll be going to an event tonight along with the rest of high society. Stationary versions of the hand-scanner will be installed at the entrances, so it should be easy to identify which guests, if any, are enthralled."

"Then what do I do," Gabriel asked, "Just mingle with the crowd?"

"The influencer will need to remain close by for the enthralled individuals to remain useful," Red-eye explained, "so they will almost certainly turn up to this event."

Gabriel failed to see why a conventional team couldn't handle that, but he wasn't in much of a position to complain.

"In that case," he asked, "what kind of event is this?"

* * *

After his muscles had recovered enough to move, Alexander entered the reset code on Mortimer's collar and sent him on his way. He made his own way back to the living quarters only to find one of the foremen waiting for him with Jezebel.

"I'm sorry to bother you, sir," the foreman said hesitantly, "but I caught her wandering around one of the processing areas."

"Good catch," Alexander replied, not quite sarcastically, "return to your tasks."

"Yes sir," the foreman answered with a salute before departing.

"You've got some explaining to do," Alexander said.

"That's funny," Jezebel replied, "I was about to tell you the same thing."

Alexander glared and motioned for her to follow him. She obeyed, wondering if he was going to punish her or if he was finally going to tell her what was going on.

When they reached the living quarters, she noticed that the locks were on the outside. Anyone already inside could leave at will, but only authorised individuals could re-enter.

She followed Alexander back into the living quarters and through to the living room as the door swung shut behind them. He sat down on the plush furniture and she took a seat opposite him, keeping her distance.

"So, what did you want to confront me about?" Alexander asked, the calmness of his voice clashing with the glare in his glowing green eyes.

"Those containers," Jezebel said, returning his gaze with a hard stare of her own, "the ones marked as biohazardous. What are they for?"

"It's a long story," Alexander replied.

"Well I've got plenty of time to hear you out!" Jezebel snapped, "so treat me to a long story about what those containers were and what you're doing out here on the frontier. In fact, why don't you also treat me to an explanation about where you were for half a century and why you brought me all the way out here? Because I still have no fleeking idea!"

If Alexander was taken aback by the outburst, he didn't show it.

"The natives make excellent test subjects," he answered coolly, "and if they can be tamed sufficiently, they also make excellent shock troops."

"That's it? That's your business plan?" Jezebel exclaimed, "Rent out alien mercenaries so they can be used to keep uppity colonials or business rivals in line?"

"I'm sorry it's not grandiose enough for your tastes," Alexander replied, "but it's one of several projects I have running that involve the locals."

"Grandiosity isn't the issue," Jezebel shot back, "I never went into the private security end of the colonial venture capital business because of the unwanted attention it garners. Using aliens for that purpose is guaranteed to foster the wrong kind of attention."

"Well, there's also the potential killing to be made in the pharmaceutical industry," Alexander added, "Although, I think I may have mentioned that earlier."

"I find it hard to believe that you would go to all this trouble just to get rich," Jezebel continued, "for one thing, it's clear you're already rich, judging by the size of this complex, and for another you've never had your eye on anything as simple as wealth."

Jezebel sat there glowering at him, waiting for an answer.

"You know me so well," Alexander answered, "far too well, I think."

"This is the part where you tell me the full story," Jezebel ordered him.

"You won't like what you hear," Alexander warned her.

"I don't fleeking care," Jezebel snapped back, "I'm sick of being kept in the dark, both figuratively and literally in this cushy prison."

"It's not a prison," Alexander replied, "not for you, at least."

Jezebel launched herself out of her seat and closed the distance to where Alexander was sitting, grabbing him by the scruff of his shirt.

"Fleeking tell me already!" she growled.

Alexander looked surprised for a moment, then a flash of anger passed across his face. He gave Jezebel a shove, pushing her backwards onto the couch.

She landed unharmed on the cushions and sat up again, glaring back defiantly as he towered over her, eyes narrowed and fists clenched.

"Fine," Alexander said with a growl, "I'll tell you."

* * *

Mortimer took a long time to mentally process what he had just witnessed.

Aggression was a vital part of producing effective soldiers, but what Alexander had displayed far exceeded that. He had been reduced to a mindless animal, completely ignoring serious physical injuries from the alien's claws as he beat it to death with his bare fists.

Mortimer activated a screen and brought up footage of the fight. Alongside it, he brought up the recorded data from Alexander's neurochemical readings and pressed play. The footage and the data readings began to play in sequence.

He watched as the enhanced and bare-chested Human squared off against the green-skinned alien. On the display, Alexander's heartrate accelerated while his breathing became deeper. The display also registered a dramatic shift in activity from Alexander's prefrontal cortex to his limbic system.

The neurochemical shift was the important part. Fear and aggression were difficult to disentangle because each was integral to the Human body's response to danger. Nonetheless, creating better soldiers required that they be disentangled so that fear could be suppressed in favour of aggression.

With Alexander, there was no fear to suppress, but the aggression was definitely there. In fact, the neurotransmitters responsible had gone into a runaway positive feedback loop that had continued until Alexander had passed out from sheer exhaustion.

The results represented only a small fraction of the data collected, and it would take a day to crunch through it all. Mortimer set about preparing the tests and running them through the quantum computers. The sooner he got started, the sooner he could devise a cure.

Could he devise a cure? Mortimer tugged at the deadly elastic collar around his neck, his throat feeling suddenly dry. Failure to devise a satisfactory treatment would mean certain death. The collar wasn't just there to keep him from escaping, it was meant to keep him motivated in his search for a cure.

What if his efforts proved fruitless? It was possible that the mechanism behind the positive feedback loop was baked permanently into Alexander's neurology. If that was the case, there would be no way to reverse it without causing other undesired side effects, maybe even permanent damage.

For Alexander, that would mean enduring the rage episodes for the rest of his natural life. For Mortimer, it would mean a very unnatural end to his own life. Either Alexander would be too impaired to remember the reset code, or he would let the countdown reach zero.

Mortimer took a deep breath, exhaled, and continued working on the analyses. Both of those depressing outcomes were possible, but neither were certain. Besides, he was a first-rate scientist with decades of experience in this field. The best way to survive this was to think of it like a thorny scientific challenge, which it most definitely was.

It occurred to him to wonder what use Alexander would still have for him if he actually succeeded. But then it also occurred to him that Alexander's reaction to success couldn't be any worse than his reaction to failure. He had nothing to gain by giving up and nothing to lose by persevering.

* * *

After explaining his plans to Jezebel – the parts he had decided to tell her – Alexander returned to the operations room. She was certain to discover that there was more to all of this than semi-legal xenobiology experiments, but for now, his estranged wife and sort-of business partner could be left to her own devices.

Keeping her under control posed a serious dilemma. One the one hand, he couldn't let her poke around too much, but on the other hand, confining her to the living quarters would undermine her already minimal trust. She *was* technically a prisoner here – albeit a very well cared for prisoner – there was no need to rub it in.

Besides, both Jezebel and Mortimer were fugitives from justice, not to mention the Directorate. If they did escape, to what refuge could they flee and to whom could they disclose his secrets? Their respective leashes were long but strong, so it wouldn't hurt to tell them a little bit from time to time.

In the operations room, Alexander found several messages waiting for him, one of them was flagged as urgent and tagged with the label 'Asgard'. Apparently, the prison warden was dead after an incident at Bentham Prison, and the various courtesans used as go-betweens were in the custody of Asgard Civil Security.

Asgard was home to the DNI's sector headquarters, a fact which made discovery of the infiltration inevitable. Since the courtesans had been discovered, it wasn't a surprise that the prison warden had been found out as well. That didn't explain how he had ended up dead, but it did mean that the bait had been taken.

It was hard to calculate how things would play out, especially when he was dozens of lightyears away from the action. For all he knew the whole plan had already succeeded or long since failed. Whichever was the case, the drip feed of reports was his only indication of progress; but it was still better than nothing.

Despite the brief twitch of anger with Jezebel, his mind was clear. Sheer force of will had kept his rage in check better than any of the partial treatments he had found. Even so, he could still feel the fury buried below, burning at the back of his mind and flaring up whenever the slightest frustration appeared.

The other messages were mostly non-essential progress reports, but there was another notification: an automated planet-side alert flagged as urgent.

Alexander shut down the display and turned to the backdoor, swiping his thumb across the biometric pad and entering. Once inside, he made sure that the door was locked before turning his attention to the room. He didn't mind Jezebel wandering around the living quarters, but he would never allow her in here.

In the centre was an immersive computer interface, much more elaborate than the one in the operations room, and featuring an all-encompassing display with a 150 degree viewing arc. The interface activated as he sat down, lighting up with readings and controls. There on the display was the urgent notification.

The underground tunnel network permeated the mountain like a web of subterranean capillaries, with the facility itself occupying a tiny fraction of them. From this room he could monitor the entire facility and everything below it thanks to a web of sensors criss-crossing the tunnels – one of which had been tripped.

The snatch squads were busy transporting hundreds of alien captives from the sinkhole to the research labs. Apparently, one of them had stumbled onto one of the entrances to the deeper tunnels. The protective wall was over a foot thick and couldn't be breached, but it hadn't been disguised properly.

Alexander's face twitched with irritation. There was nothing to suggest his underlings suspected anything about the deeper tunnels, nor had they tried to break into them. Even so, it was yet another potential complication to keep an eye on.

It was amazing how he had managed to recruit so many people and keep them all more or less in line. Vague promises and a chance to escape justice or drudgery or both had brought most of them on board. Remuneration, adventure, and sheer force of personality kept them on board – that and the aura of menace that he projected.

If and when that failed – the deeper tunnels contained his backup plan.

THE KIDNAPPING

THE tallest skyscraper in Asgard City was Ellipsis Tower. It was a magnificent monument stretching high into the clouds with foundations extending a kilometre below ground. It was larger even than the Spire, and its gleaming image stood in stark contrast to the surly exterior of the DNI headquarters.

Gabriel arrived by mag-train and followed the better-dressed parts of the crowd to the Ellipsis Performance Hall. Android security guards stood unblinkingly watchful as robotic ushers in crisp uniforms greeted the attendees and directed them through the temple-like doors into the auditorium.

The great and the good of Asgard City were present, and they were dressed for the occasion. The men wore dark suits with white frilled collars, while the women were dressed in flowing gowns in various colours with shimmering patterns woven into the fabric. Some of the dresses revealed a little more than they should.

Gabriel was conspicuous by his height and dour expression, wearing a dark uniform with an open collar that allowed him to breathe. People cast bewildered glances at him as he passed, even more so when the ushers directed him to the premium box while everyone else queued for the regular seats.

The auditorium was a near-perfect sphere, ensuring that the sound washed over the audience before rippling back and returning to the stage. The other concertgoers gawped before breaking into excited chattering as they took their seats. Gabriel had a seat to himself and was the only one who hadn't brought a companion.

Apart from the need to look after five children, he couldn't bring Aster along on anything work-related. Besides, this wasn't her scene. The combined net worth of the audience was enough to buy half the planet. Aster might have learned to love Asgard, but as a colonial, she loathed its high society, and the feeling was mutual.

"*Colonel Thorn*," said a voice in his ear.

"Yes," Gabriel muttered, as if to himself.

"*One of the guests has been flagged as a match*," his handler informed him, "*Byron Sade. His companion came up clean.*"

Gabriel grunted his acknowledgement. Talking to himself in public would look strange at best and suspicious at worst.

His comm. piece was a strip of skin-coloured electronic film attached to the inside of his ear. A similar device was attached to his throat as a microphone, allowing him to murmur into it without being overheard.

"*He's sitting to your left*," his handler added.

That was quite a coincidence. Gabriel glanced to his left and saw a slender man with gaunt features and dark, slicked back hair streaked with silver dye. It was indeed Byron Sade, a bioengineering magnate whose fortune made him one of the richest people on the planet. The fact that someone so highly placed had been turned was quite an espionage coup.

Byron Sade's companion wore a glittering silver dress with a thigh split all the way up to her hip. She had flowing golden hair braided at the back and diamond studded earrings to complement her look. She also looked less serious than the stern, aristocratic man she was accompanying, watching the empty stage in reserved anticipation.

"*Once the performance is over, follow him back to his penthouse and subdue him*," Gabriel's handler instructed.

Now that Byron Sade had been identified as a thrall, there was no need to follow him around the old-fashioned way. Why not just snatch the man right now and grab the intelligence from his penthouse later?

Gabriel was in no position to argue. Having made a nuisance of himself by refusing to stay out of the investigation, Red-eye had brought him on board on a short leash rather than shut him out altogether. It was better than being singled out as a suspect.

The lights dimmed and the audience fell silent. A hatch in the floor of the stage retracted and a platform was elevated from below. On the platform was a grand piano – an instrument invented a thousand years ago – and a single player seated in front of it. A wave of applause swept through the audience, echoing back to the stage as the pianist prepared to play.

Every concertgoer's seat had a personal interface with a choice of live camera feeds from various angles. It also provided details of the evening's programme, biographies of the performers, as well as technical commentary for those interested in the music theory. Once the applause had subsided, the pianist began to play.

What emerged from under her fingers was difficult for the untrained ear to follow. There was no doubt, however, that no one in the audience could have reproduced it.

The notes trilled and chimed in rapid succession, following a melody that meandered up and down the scale at high speed, each chord overtaking the other before it could reach a cadence. Gabriel could vaguely make out the four-bar phrase structure in the mellifluous blizzard of sound, but the melody was too complicated to follow.

The fact that he could make out the chords at all was impressive. The acoustics of the auditorium were such that each successive series of notes melted into the echo of the previous series of notes. Without the interface showing him what was going on, he wouldn't have been able to make it out at all.

Perhaps he was overthinking it, everybody else just sat there in rapt awe as the music drowned their senses. Hardly anyone else was trying to parse the harmonics of the piece. It was hard to analyse something that was holding them spellbound.

One of the cameras was focused on the pianist's fingers as they raced back and forth. She must have undergone augmentative surgery to enhance her reflexes and dexterity. Even so, it was still impressive how fast she could play without muddling the tune.

Her technique was perfect. The computers analysing the tune in real-time said so. Not a single note was missed, not a single chord was out of place, and everything was perfectly spaced without any embellishments. That type of mastery could only be achieved with years or decades of daily practice.

And yet, Gabriel couldn't bring himself to fully enjoy the music. He could appreciate in an abstract way the effort and sacrifice required to reach such a level of skill, but the music didn't really speak to him. It simply immersed him in sound, no more explicable to him than the chemical composition of water to a fish.

It occurred to him that some of the other concertgoers secretly felt the same way. The event organisers raked in vast profits from ticket sales alone, but how many people here professed to understand the music for the sake of keeping up a cultured appearance?

"Maybe I'm just not smart enough," Gabriel mused to himself.

"*Come again, Colonel?*" said his handler, "*I didn't copy.*"

"Nothing," he replied, remembering how sensitive his throat mic was.

The pianist was only halfway through the piece and literally hadn't missed a beat. She was completely absorbed by the music. Her fingers danced across the keys in a blur of motion that even the camera struggled to capture, all without even looking up at the score. She had the audience under her complete control – most of it.

The composition was beyond Gabriel's understanding. He could see that the audience was captivated, but he couldn't hear what it was that held their undivided attention in its grip. Frankly he would rather be spending the evening with his young family.

* * *

When the intermission arrived, the doors opened and the concertgoers spilled out into the foyer. They were greeted by a feast prepared for them during the performance. Ushers stood politely to the side as the guests swarmed over the food. Gabriel queued up with everyone else as Byron Sade and his companion helped themselves.

"You seemed rather distracted during the performance," noted a deep voice.

Gabriel turned his head and saw the mark looking at him with jet black eyes, his features looking even gaunter up close with the skin tightly drawn across his skull.

"How so?" he asked.

"You muttered something to yourself," Byron Sade remarked, "something about 'not being smart enough'. It was rather distracting."

It was hard not to scowl back at the disdainful look on the man's face.

"Perhaps you misheard," Gabriel suggested.

"I have undergone auditory augmentation to better appreciate performances such as these," Byron Sade answered, "I most certainly did not mishear."

Gabriel said nothing. Byron Sade's companion gave the two men a disinterested glance while the man himself took a step closer, glaring into Gabriel's glowing emerald eyes.

"If this sort of event is not to your liking," Byron Sade said imperiously, "one has to wonder why you are here in the first place."

"You're standing much too close for your own good," Gabriel replied menacingly.

Byron Sade continued glaring at him with deep suspicion and disdain. His companion cast another sideways glance at the two men, this time with an amused smile on her face. Some other concertgoers had noticed the staring match.

Byron Sade turned away and returned to the auditorium with his companion, leaving Gabriel wondering if his cover had just been blown.

"*If he suspected you, he would have tried to leave,*" said his handler, pre-empting his concern, "*and we have operatives ready in case he tries.*"

"What exactly am I supposed to do?" Gabriel demanded under his breath, "Why don't we send in a snatch team to grab him and another team to search his home?"

"*A backup team is on standby in case you need it,*" the handler explained calmly, "*but the director-general wants this completed with minimal publicity, something a full team of operatives would have difficulty accomplishing.*"

"That doesn't answer my question," Gabriel said impatiently, "why am I doing this mission solo in the first place, and why would it be so hard for a full team of operatives to finish this mission with 'minimal publicity'?"

"*Those are the director-general's orders,*" the handler answered, "*I'm sure she will explain everything when the time comes.*"

Gabriel was pretty sure she wouldn't.

"Understood," he replied, barely convinced.

* * *

Two more intermissions passed, and when the performance was over the audience gave a standing ovation for ten whole minutes. Gabriel applauded along with everyone else until his hands were stinging, but it was a relief when people began to leave. Once he was outside, he split off from the crowd and boarded a Directorate stealth pod.

Byron Sade didn't live in Ellipsis Tower. His penthouse was in a tower in the industrial suburbs where his company's headquarters was located. The stealth pod followed the mark's sky-car, flitting in between the skyscrapers, and deftly avoiding the aerial traffic.

Gabriel watched the sky-car's progress from the backseat while another operative piloted the pod. The camera feed highlighted the sky-car through the darkness, estimating its speed and trajectory in real-time.

He still wanted to know why he was the one following Byron Sade. A snatch team ought to be sent in to subdue him and his companion. After that, it would be easy to sweep his penthouse for evidence of the influencer. Why were both jobs being left to him?

That was an ironic complaint for him to have. The whole point of voidstalkers was to operate alone in hostile territory for extended periods of time. With more information, he could certainly handle this mission on his own. Even so, if this was Redeye's way of throwing him a conciliatory bone, it was a strange bone indeed.

Rather than make him carry out a daring climb up the side of the skyscraper, the pilot used the stealth pod's cyberwarfare module to override the cargo delivery hatch. The security cameras were also overridden so that no one would notice the hatch open or Gabriel emerging seemingly from thin air.

Under his evening uniform, Gabriel was wearing a lightweight suit of personal armour. He had also retrieved a high-powered pistol and a stun-gun from the arms cache.

"*We'll be following your progress as you proceed,*" his handler informed him.

"Acknowledged," Gabriel replied gruffly.

At the end of the corridor was a locked door. Gabriel was still wearing the scanner glove on one hand but had another device on his other palm which he waved over the lock, bypassing the security. If the rich and powerful knew how insecure their properties really were, they would be horrified – or furious.

The room he entered had a carpeted floor and ornate furniture. In each corner stood a humanoid statuette enshrined in an alcove. The statuettes were animatronic, judging by the slow dancing moves they made, but they had the aesthetic look of exquisitely carved stone.

Gabriel trod carefully across the carpet, its soft fabric absorbing the sound of his footsteps. The door on the other side was already ajar, and he gripped the handle and opened it carefully. It moved easily enough and he squeezed through the gap.

Beyond was a spacious living room with similar decor. The wall was lined with a single gigantic fresco that ringed the entire room, depicting a menagerie of mythological creatures frolicking and fighting. The images were moving slowly and subtly just like the statuettes.

The living room had several doors leading off from it. It was like a mini-maze, and it was impossible to tell which door led where. One door must lead to Byron Sade's bedroom, which was where he and his companion presumably were. It wouldn't be very helpful if two valuable intelligence leads ended up dead, so Gabriel drew the stun-gun.

The floor was carpeted with bioengineered fur. There was something grotesque about growing hundreds of square feet of organic fur in a lab for the sake of home decoration. Then again, that was a lot less barbaric than skinning dozens of live animals for the purpose.

Gabriel crossed the room to one of the doors and stood at the threshold, then yanked it open and stormed in, shooting each figure he saw with a shock-dart. Two androids crumpled to the floor as the shock-darts pierced their synthetic skin.

He spun around in time to be hit in the chest by something. The projectile wrapped itself around his torso like a super-elastic web, instantly entangling his limbs and forcing him to relinquish the stun-gun. He tumbled to the floor, unable to move a muscle.

Byron Sade himself approached the immobilised Gabriel. He put the web-gun to one side and stood over Gabriel, looking down with gaunt features twisted into a grotesque smirk.

Another figure appeared, her flowing blonde hair tied back into a bun, and wearing a tactical suit with a protective body armour shirt.

"Good night," she said with a smile.

Gabriel thought her voice sounded familiar, but he couldn't think about it because the woman sprayed something in his face. An overwhelming feeling of drowsiness bore down on his senses like a weighted cloth until he passed out.

* * *

The two conspirators watched the intruder slowly lose consciousness. His body was completely trussed up by the synthetic restraints, tightening in response to the slightest twitch with strands as thick as a finger.

"That was easier than I thought," Byron Sade remarked with satisfaction, "and a pretty poor assassination attempt. Not that I'm complaining."

"We need to move him quickly," his co-conspirator said, "get the door for me."

Byron Sade wrinkled his nose at being given an order, but complied nonetheless. As she dragged the unconscious captive across the bedroom, he opened up a door concealed in the wall, enabling her to haul the intruder into the hidden space beyond.

"Where are you taking him?" Byron Sade asked.

"That's what the spooks call 'need-to-know'," the woman replied as she shut the door.

"I *want* to know," Byron Sade said irritably, "especially since I still don't know very much about who you work for."

"You may want to know," the woman rebuffed him a second time, "but you don't need to know, and that's what counts here."

"What I really want to know is who sent an assassin after me," Byron Sade said icily.

"How many investors have you defrauded? How many courtesans have you raped?" she asked sardonically, "And how many people would gain from your death?"

"I have many enemies," Byron Sade replied, "and they're all dead."

"I like the turn of phrase," she smirked.

"I still want answers," he demanded.

"What makes you think I have any to give?" she asked.

"The mere fact that your people are taking the assassin away means that you have an idea of who tried to kill me," he pointed out.

"As long you continue to cooperate with the Network, no one will succeed."

"How do I know you didn't send the assassin?" Byron Sade said accusingly.

"Has it occurred to you that if we had sent the assassin you would be dead?" the woman replied with a succubus-like smile.

Byron Sade grabbed her in a fit of rage and tossed her onto the king-sized bed, pouncing on top of her as she laughed at him.

"You're a sly little bitch, aren't you?" he snarled.

She responded by smacking him across the face. It was just a slap, but the blow knocked him over sideways, enabling her to get off the bed again.

He looked up at her, clutching the red welt on his gaunt cheek. He was livid, and showed it in the rage burning in his eyes. By contrast, she just stood there clutching her palm.

"Do you have a metal plate in your jaw?" she asked in bewilderment.

"Augmented mineralisation surgery produces stronger bones," Byron Sade growled, "so that probably hurt you more than me."

"If we're talking about egos I'd have to disagree," she quipped cuttingly.

Byron Sade's face twitched, but he held his temper under control.

"You've been an invaluable asset to the Network thus far," the woman said, "especially regarding the 'scientific' support you've provided."

"I'm not complaining about the terms of the deal," Byron Sade answered.

"That's good to know," she replied, "because they're not up for renegotiation. In any case, the DNI knows about the nanopatch."

"How do you know that?" Byron Sade asked, his voice quivering slightly.

"We have our sources," the woman answered simply, "which means that if I were you I'd worry more about the DNI than some incompetent assassin."

"What about the courtesans?" Byron Sade asked.

"Your concern for their safety is touching," the woman said wryly.

"Have they been compromised?" he demanded, "did any of them give me up?"

"Six of them were arrested in connection with the Bentham Prison incident," the woman explained, "It doesn't mean the authorities know what you did to them."

"If all six of them have been caught, it's only a matter of time before they give me up!" he exclaimed in a panic.

"Calm down and man up, will you?" the woman replied dismissively.

The emasculating comment caused another flash of anger to pass across Byron Sade's face, but it passed quickly.

"The only connection you have with the Bentham Prison investigation is that you and the warden both like whores," the woman explained, "and there is nothing connecting you or your company to the nanopatch."

Byron Sade was silent, but her explanation made sense to him.

"The point being that there's no reason to panic," the woman concluded, "besides, I'm sure there are plenty more holes for you to stick your dick in."

She turned to leave, but Byron Sade grabbed her by the wrist.

"I think I've already found one," he said in a low growl.

"Just because I posed as your companion, doesn't mean I'm going to act out the role," the woman replied, deftly twisting her wrist free of his grip.

"You seem to like playing rough," Byron Sade said lecherously.

"I love playing rough," the woman replied, "but you are definitely not my type."

"Will you at least tell me your name before you vanish?" Byron Sade asked.

"It starts with an 'A'," she told him.

"I guess that's all I'm getting out of you," Byron Sade said with a shrug.

"You can proposition me all you want," 'A' answered, "but if you ever try to force the issue, I'll cut your balls off."

"Did I mention that I run a bioengineering company?" Byron Sade pointed out with a chuckle, "I can always have another pair grown to replace them."

"Ugh," 'A' remarked in disgust.

* * *

None of the operations chiefs could understand why Red-eye was so calm.

"Director-general," one of them ventured, "The kidnapping of a voidstalker is an unprecedented emergency. With all due respect, if there's something you haven't told us—"

"Not yet," Red-eye cut him off calmly.

She turned to the console in front of her and activated a holographic simulation. A fully rendered 3D image of the planet Asgard circled slowly, casting a cool digital glow across the room. The image was crisscrossed by hundreds of dots travelling to and from the planet, or orbiting in tight geosynchronous circles.

It was the orbital traffic around Asgard and the immediate space beyond. Red-eye watched the hologram intently – and sure enough, an icon appeared. An orbital beacon was highlighted on the hologram with the words 'signal acquired' displayed in bold.

"This was all an elaborate sting," Red-eye explained, "The Network has an unusual interest in Colonel Thorn, which makes him the best possible bait to flush them out."

"What about the brainwashed infiltrators?" one of the operations chiefs asked.

"Dr Benjamin Solaris here can explain that," Red-eye answered, pointing to the only non-intelligence official in the room.

"The nanobots we found in the nanopatch cannot 'brainwash' an individual," Dr Solaris explained, "to truly turn someone in that way requires a long period of mental conditioning in a controlled environment, which explains the neural alteration we found."

"So what were the nanobots for?" one of the operations chiefs asked.

"The nanobots do little more than track an individual's location and provide a failsafe to terminate a compromised agent," Dr Solaris answered, "the former explains the unusually powerful peer-to-peer transmitters in the nanobots themselves."

"If this is true," said another operations chief, "then the 'influencer' may not even exist. These infiltrators could have been turned into cat's-paws off-world and then sent to Asgard on commercial transportation without arousing suspicion."

"What about Byron Sade?" someone else asked.

"The courtesans were mentally conditioned at his company's laboratories," said Red-eye, "but neither Byron Sade nor his companion showed signs of mental conditioning."

Her revelation elicited a long period of surprised silence.

"But…that means Colonel Thorn was lied to about Byron Sade being enthralled," one of the operations chiefs said in disbelief.

"As I said," explained Red-eye, "the objective is to track down the Network's leader, who seems to have an inordinate interest in Colonel Thorn personally. Colonel Thorn himself could not be told the true purpose of the operation."

"Was the counteragent given to Colonel Thorn just another part of this deception?" one of the operations chiefs asked.

"The counteragent does exactly what we told Colonel Thorn it would do," Dr Solaris replied, "just in case he was exposed to the Network's nanobots."

Of course the director-general had had a plan this whole time, she always did.

"In the meantime the nature of Byron Sade's ties to the Network still needs to be investigated," one of the operations chiefs pointed out.

"We already have an asset in place," the Asgard City counterintelligence chief replied, "but we can't afford to tip our hand until the Network's leader has been located."

"Don't we already have intelligence on Byron Sade?" someone asked.

"Him and everyone else of importance on the planet," the counterintelligence chief answered, "Sheraton Biopharma routinely bends the regulations governing life sciences, and the man himself is slightly more of a pervert than the other sybarites in this city."

"Information which is only relevant now that his actions potential endanger Humanity's security," Red-eye made clear, "civic matters and security matters do not mix."

They all knew the 3rd Prime Law as well as they knew the first two.

"No active measures are to be taken against Byron Sade or his associates," Red-eye ordered, "not until we have tracked down the Network's leader."

The simulation of Asgard's space traffic was still running, and the red dot the director-general had pointed to was speeding away towards the edge of the system.

"How exactly is Colonel Thorn being tracked?" someone asked.

"That is not to be discussed any further," Red-eye said with a soft tone and a sharp glare, "not until this matter has been successfully concluded."

* * *

Gabriel wasn't home yet.

Aster had been waiting up for him for the past few hours. She knew he had an official function tonight, but it was past midnight now. He couldn't be gone this long unless he had been called in for another mission.

That couldn't be possible. He'd only been home for a few days, and he always had at least a month of leave between deployments, not to mention there would always be a scheduled face-to-face call before he departed. Gabriel hadn't contacted her at all. She had left him several text messages and tried to call him. Nothing.

At least Emerald was asleep, and the rest of the children were in bed. But when they woke up in the morning and discovered that their father wasn't home…

Aster suddenly feared the worst. She approached the armoured closet on Gabriel's side of the bed and swiped her thumb across the touchpad, causing the doors to open up. Inside stood the dormant maganiel android, its featureless face consisting only of two eye slits and a vocaliser under its chin.

Aster rapped the maganiel on the forehead with her knuckles. The android's eyes lit up with an electric blue glow and it inclined its head towards Aster, flash-scanning her own eyes to confirm her identity.

"*Good evening, Aster Thorn,*" said the maganiel in an electronic voice, "*Maganiel Mark V online. How may I be of service?*"

"Personal protection for the family," Aster ordered the android, trying to remain calm as she spoke, "lethal force authorised."

"*Understood,*" the maganiel replied, "*Seven protectees. Lethal force authorised.*"

The maganiel reached back into the closet and drew a large sidearm. Aster stepped aside as the maganiel stepped forward and exited the closet, leaving the bedroom to stand guard in the front hall. She quickly checked on baby Emerald sleeping peacefully in her cot before rushing to the children's bedroom to check on them.

They were sleeping peacefully in their beds, oblivious to their mother's troubles or their father's absence. She returned to the master bedroom and crawled under the covers.

Emerald began to cry, demanding to be fed. The household android moved into action, lifting the baby out of her cot and bringing a bottle of formula to her mouth. The infant's cries subsided as she began to feed.

"Bring her to me," Aster ordered, sitting up in bed.

The android brought Emerald over as Aster pulled down the front of her nightshirt. The android carefully handed the infant over and Aster let Emerald feed.

The android stood obediently to one side, waiting for follow-up instructions. It was humanoid in design without a real face, but that was better than the rubbery-skinned models whose resemblance to actual Humans was uncanny to the point of creepy.

Aster wondered if the household androids could be used by the Directorate to spy on them. That was almost too creepy to contemplate. Every personal moment with the family, every conversation with Gabriel, every time they made love…even though the androids were dismissed from the room, they could still hear.

It wasn't the first time she had wondered such a thing, but the paranoia had new resonance with the man of the house missing in action.

And then there was the maganiel android, a military-grade home defence robot supplied by the Directorate to protect the family. At least it had proven its worth on that front. It mostly just sat in its armoured cradle waiting to be called upon, but it could theoretically be used to monitor them as well.

In the past, she would have wondered what reason the DNI had to spy on them in the first place, but now she could guess it had to do with protecting their 'investments'. It was too late to worry about the DNI watching them now, and it was really a distraction from the more immediate concern that Gabriel wasn't home.

Emerald finished feeding and licked her lips contentedly, her bright green eyes glowing in the dark. It was nice that the children had their father's eyes, although it would have been nicer if they had inherited more of their mother's features.

"Take her back to her cot," Aster ordered the household android.

The android gingerly collected the infant from Aster's arms, returning her to her cot and draping the covers over her. Aster rolled over and tried to get some sleep. If Gabriel still wasn't back by morning, she would have to call the DNI and demand answers.

Whether she would get any was another matter.

* * *

Alexander and Jezebel were bonding – after a fashion. A game of 3D chess usually frustrated people even more than the traditional variant, but with little else to keep her occupied, Jezebel had challenged her estranged husband to a match. To her surprise, he had accepted, and now here they were.

He seemed entirely focused on the game, glaring at the grid as he pondered his next move. Jezebel divided her attention between the game and her opponent, watching for twitches of displeasure under his stony expression.

"How long have you been practising chess?" she asked.

"A few decades," Alexander replied, "activities requiring concentration and deferred gratification help me suppress the rage episodes better than drugs."

"I can see the practice has paid off," Jezebel remarked.

"Raging at the computer opponent achieves nothing," Alexander pointed out, "the game forces you to think in order to win, and what I want is to win."

"Is that all you want?" Jezebel asked, moving one of her pieces.

Alexander stared at the grid in silence. His expression looked contemplative rather than like a mask of suppressed rage, but it was hard to tell.

"No," Alexander answered, reaching towards one of the chess pieces, "it's not."

"Revenge against the DNI?" Jezebel suggested, taking a risk.

Alexander's hand froze in the air on its way to the piece and his expression hardened. Jezebel watched him warily as his outstretched hand tightened into a fist.

"Most definitely," Alexander confirmed with a growl, "they made me what I am now, and almost caused me to murder my own family."

His clenched fist began to shake in the air, and his eyes narrowed and darkened as Jezebel regretted asking the question.

"I lost almost five decades of my life because of what the DNI did to me," Alexander said, his voice quivering with rage, "revenge is the least I'm entitled to."

Jezebel edged away from the chess board, watching Alexander's whole body tremble with fury as he tried to suppress another reflexive outburst of violence.

As he squeezed his eyes shut, desperately trying to hold his volcanic temper in check, Jezebel's eyes darted towards the door. Could she outrun him? There was no gun lying around this time. If he caught her, he would kill her.

Alexander spun around and grabbed something from the table behind him. He pressed it against his nose and pressed the trigger, inhaling a lungful of the drug. He shut his eyes and scrunched up his face as if the act of holding in his rage were physically painful.

Jezebel sat frozen in her seat, watching and waiting.

Slowly but surely the fury dissipated from his face and he relaxed his grip on the inhaler, letting it slide out of his hand and onto the floor.

"And then, of course, there are the rage episodes," Alexander added, more calmly but no less resentfully, "so excuse me for wanting the DNI to burn."

Jezebel decided to leave the subject alone. Once Alexander had calmed down, he tried to make his next move. Before he could do so, a message alert chimed on the console.

A flash of annoyance passed across his face, but the drug he had just inhaled blunted the edge of his temper. Besides, he still had an information network to run, so he tapped the notification to read its contents.

He grinned at what he read.

"What's the good news?" Jezebel asked him.

"Our son is coming home," Alexander replied.

* * *

In one of Asgard City's smaller towers, the ten uppermost storeys were taken up by the headquarters of Sheraton Biopharma. A group of smartly dressed men and women arrived at a private landing pad and were escorted indoors. Once inside, they were guided through the security screening to the entrance.

Their host, the company's founder and owner, was a slender man with slightly gaunt features. He had black hair with silver streaks running through it and was wearing a simple business uniform without any finery.

"Greetings, ladies and gentlemen," Byron Sade announced to the delegation, "If you'll follow me, we can start the tour."

The delegation entered Sheraton Biopharma's headquarters and followed their host into the research wing. It was an open hall with several work levels, filled with equipment and teams of researchers. Bioreactors two storeys high lined the walls, connected to the surrounding equipment by tangled webs of cables and flexible piping.

"This is the main development facility that Sheraton operates," Byron Sade explained, "we can synthesise tens of billions of custom enzymes using the equipment here."

The delegates looked up at the impressive array of equipment, nodding politely without looking overawed. They were all experienced investors who specialised in the biomedical industry, so what they were seeing was standard fare. Their host knew that too, of course.

The next section was a smaller chamber with a low roof, dim lighting, and walls lined with computers and work stations. The floor was a single pane of ultra-strong glass running the length of the room, through which the delegates could see a seething mass of crystal-clear water and the silhouettes of long eel-like creatures swimming back and forth.

"It's one thing to synthesise new enzymes artificially," Byron Sade said, pointing to the creatures, "but as you all know, it's often better to take advantage of the fruits of evolution's own trial-and-error experiments over millions of years."

Each of the creatures was several metres long and as thick as a bundle of power cables. Their snouts were long and thin, and they had large compound eyes recessed into their skulls. Their skin was smooth and slippery, and it flickered fluorescently under the dim light as they slithered gracefully through the water.

"These creatures are native to a planet with an extensive network of inland seas," Byron Sade continued, "They have an incredibly rich biochemistry and secrete a rich array of enzymes, a small fraction of which hold promise for drug development. The others may prove promising in the years and decades to come."

"Are these creatures live captures or clones?" one of the delegates asked.

"Clones," Byron Sade replied, "live captures of creatures like these would have been difficult. However, these clones have been rendered docile by a neurochemical patch, so we can observe them and take samples without them tearing each other apart."

The delegates watched the creatures swimming sedately back and forth, exhibiting no interest in each other or the onlookers. Most of the delegates had seen stranger creatures.

Byron Sade continued the tour, leading the delegation to another laboratory, this time dedicated to drug synthesis. Robotic arms moved samples from one machine to another as a handful of technicians looked on.

"And this is where final synthesis takes place," Byron Sade said, "We also use labs like this one to conduct chemical analyses on samples we receive."

The delegation toured the laboratory for a few minutes, examining the machinery whilst keeping out of the way of the technicians. So far, they were impressed: a complete R&D facility that carried out the full range of biomedical research. They were ready to be presented with a business proposition.

Byron Sade led them through the rest of the facility to an elevator which took them up to the administrative floor. They were brought to a conference room dominated by a table made from bioengineered wood and lined with ergonomic chairs. One wall was dominated by a giant window which provided a panoramic view of Asgard City.

The still-rising sun was visible as a white orb casting an orange hue across the dawn horizon. The blue gas giant Odin was also visible, its silhouette blurred by the artificial ozone in the atmosphere. The centre of the city was also visible in the distance, a cluster of kilometre-high towers huddled together like a grove of artificial trees.

Upon closer inspection, the 'window' turned out to be a high-resolution viewing screen. Despite the strides made in materials science, windows were still a structural weakness frowned upon by most architects; plus they were expensive to install in a building this large. Why use an actual glass window when a live camera feed would accomplish the same effect?

After pausing to admire the view, the delegates took their seats.

"There is only one thing missing from Sheraton Biopharma's existing business model," Byron Sade informed his guests, "mass production capabilities."

"So you want money from us to vertically integrate your business?" one of the delegates surmised, speaking with a fluty Clouds accent.

"Yes," Byron Sade responded, "two billion credits to be precise."

"I take it you already have a facility in mind?" another delegate asked.

"Correct, again," Byron Sade replied, "it's a facility on the outskirts of Haven City. Its current owners are looking to hive off part of their business and I made them an offer."

"No one charges two billion credits for a drug manufacturing plant," a third delegate said sceptically, "you could build one yourself for a fraction of the cost."

"This facility is located next to the Haven City atmospheric transport terminal," Byron Sade answered smoothly, "but you are correct that most of the money is not for purchasing the facility. The rest will be needed to refurbish and upgrade the plant and to rent a private section of the terminal for the company's exclusive use."

"In that case, the investment you're looking for will have to be in stages," the first delegate said, "half to finance the purchase itself, and then the rest in instalments."

"I'm happy to accept an arrangement of that sort," Byron Sade answered, "but for now, can I assume that you all agree in principle to my proposal, notwithstanding the fact that an unwritten contract is not legally binding?"

There was a silent raising of hands as everyone assented.

"Ladies and gentlemen," Byron Sade announced, "thank you very much for your time and I look forward to thrashing out the details with you at some future date."

* * *

Once the delegates had gone, Byron Sade returned to his penthouse and went to the living room. The service entrance through which last night's would-be assassin had infiltrated had been sealed. The penthouse was now as secure as a bunker.

Suspended from the living room ceiling was a chandelier made of countless artificially forged diamonds. Each diamond was perfectly smooth and refracted the light across the room in a kaleidoscope of colours, casting a rainbow-like glow over the fresco.

The fresco that ringed the living room was a thing of beauty – he would know, having designed it himself. Countless animated figures, male and female, Human and mythological, wrestled and cavorted together in exquisitely slow motion.

The detail was extraordinary, right down to the curvature of the muscles and the hair on their bodies. One could make out the subtle changes in the creatures' positions as they rocked and thrusted in violent, orgiastic union. It was a poor substitute for the real thing, but the delicious debauchery was still satisfying to behold.

The service chute opened and a small creature with fluffy white fur appeared, pausing to sniff at the carpet. The furry animal had short legs and a small face with big black eyes atop a narrow snout, and a fluffy tail sticking up in the air like a plume.

It was a dog, albeit one with a custom genome tailored to its owner's specifications. Byron Sade snapped his fingers and the creature came bounding over. It jumped onto the couch and climbed onto his lap, curling up into a contented ball as its owner stroked its fur.

The geneticists had produced an animal that displayed perfect docility and obedience. The fur colouring was especially difficult to control, and yet the team had managed to suppress any pigmentation in the hair follicles, achieving a snowy white colour.

Byron Sade smiled, admiring the handiwork of his employees as if it were his own. Then he noticed something. Digging his fingers into the dog's fur, he exposed part of the skin and saw a mottled pink blotch splashed across the dark flesh beneath. He ran his fingers through its beautifully soft fur, scratching it behind the ears and holding its head in his hands.

Then he snapped its neck.

A single violent twist of his hands was enough to end its life after less than an hour of existence. He stood up abruptly, letting the furry animal's still warm corpse roll off his lap and onto the floor. Then he activated the intercom panel.

"*Mr Sade?*" said a voice, sounding both hopeful and fearful.

"There was a blotch of discolouration on its back, beneath the fur," Byron Sade said sharply, "and if you had conducted a simple visual inspection, you would have spotted it."

He terminated the link, then summoned a service android to collect the dead pet. He scowled at the room, his mood befouled and his gaunt features contorted with rage.

Growing an animal with pure dark flesh and pure white fur was certainly challenging, but checking its skin and fur should be easy enough. Was the team so lazy that they skipped that part of the process, or were they too squeamish to dispose of the failed specimen after discovering their mistake?

Byron Sade stormed out of the living room towards the other side of the penthouse, passing down an ornately decorated corridor. Androgynous statuettes in scandalous poses lined the walls, moving in animatronic slow motion. He turned a corner and swiped his thumb across a biometric pad to open the door.

The chamber he entered was a dungeon, albeit a very well furnished one. Like the living room, the floor had a carpet made of bioengineered fur, but this room was dominated by a deep red mattress that stood at waist height. The lighting cast an erotic ambience across the room – rather fitting, given its purpose.

The room's occupant lay sprawled across the giant mattress, naked and clueless. Her skin was ivory pale, the signature trait of an Undercity dweller, although she hadn't lived there for years. She had flowing black hair with gossamer locks that reached down to her waist, and her fingernails and toenails were painted blood red like the mattress.

A regimen of drugs and mental conditioning – none of it legal to use on Humans – had reduced her to a docile state, only dimly aware of the fact that she was a prisoner.

"Spray your hair blonde," Byron Sade ordered, undressing in front of her.

She obediently picked up an aerosol bottle and sprayed it over her hair. Her black locks slowly lightened in colour, turning chestnut brown, then light brown, and finally golden blonde.

Byron Sade finished undressing and reached for the dispenser on the wall. He collected a single blue pill and swallowed it whole, waiting for it to take effect.

It didn't take long. His head started to feel buoyant and his peripheral vision blurred. A potent feeling of arousal flowed through him, energising his whole body from head to toe. Before long, he was painfully hard, and a powerful urge numbed his critical faculties until he was barely coherent.

He turned his attention to the sex toy, watching with a wolf-like leer before approaching. She was oblivious to what was about to happen, and would barely remember it afterwards. She looked just like that little Network bitch, only without the smirk.

"For the next hour," Byron Sade growled with sadistic menace, "your name is 'A'."

* * *

Something was stuck down his throat. His gag reflex was being triggered and blocked by a rubber pipe blasting fresh air into his lungs. He wanted to struggle, but his limbs were trussed up tight against his body. Worst of all, it was pitch black, as dark as a Directorate holding cell, but with less space and even less hope of freedom.

He was trapped in a space barely wider than his shoulders, and he couldn't even struggle or cry for help. He tried anyway, bucking and thrashing from side to side only for the restraints to tighten in response. It was like being trapped in the embrace of a constrictor serpent, but one that relaxed as soon as he stopped struggling.

The lid opened abruptly and the ceiling lights blinded him.

"Holy Terra, will you give it a rest?" demanded a voice.

Gabriel flinched in recognition, provoking the restraints into tightening again.

A woman with blonde hair tied back in a bun peered over the lip of the container with a smirk on her face. Her irises glowed just like Gabriel's eyes, but they glowed a shimmering sapphire colour in contrast to the bright emerald of his own irises.

"Comfortable?" Aetherea Starborn asked.

Gabriel didn't reply.

"Right, stupid question," Aetherea remarked.

Gabriel tried to free himself one last time, only for his restraints to constrict violently, tightening painfully against his chest and limbs, and forcing him back down again.

"You know, I could stand here and watch you struggle help-lessly for hours," Aetherea said, relishing his predicament, "but we don't have much time before you get taken away."

Countless questions were swirling around Gabriel's mind. What was Aetherea doing here? Had she been the one accompa-nying Byron Sade to the concert? Had she somehow been turned by the Network or was this all part of some elaborate Directorate plot?

"The good news is that everything is going according to plan," Aetherea continued, "but I can't tell you whose plan it is yet, and the bad news – for you, anyway – is that you're going to be stuck in there for a while."

Volcanic rage burned within Gabriel's chest, made all the more potent by the fact that he was completely helpless to Aetherea's manipulations.

"Of course," Aetherea added, "I'm still kind of hurt by how you were so cold to me after…you know what. So I don't feel *too* bad about your situation."

A spike of guilty rage pierced Gabriel's heart.

"Well, goodbye for now," Aetherea said with a smile, "enjoy the trip!"

The lid closed and locked once again, sealing Gabriel inside like a corpse in a tomb.

THE SPECIMENS

H E still wasn't home. Aster's head swirled with dire scenarios about what might have happened to Gabriel; as a result she hardly got any sleep. Morning was no relief, but she got out of bed to greet it anyway, checking on baby Emerald before taking a shower and getting ready for the day.

She would have to call the Directorate for answers, but if Gabriel was on assignment, there was no way they would tell her. Aster dismissed the household android before opening the maganiel's armoured closet. Nestled in the corner was a secure communication box for emergency use. She initiated the connection and waited for a response.

"Please state your name and the emergency," said a voice.

"This is Aster Thorn," Aster replied, "my husband, Colonel Gabriel Thorn, is missing. I haven't seen him since yesterday evening."

"I'm afraid we cannot discuss active deployments–" the operator began.

"He's not supposed to be on fucking deployment!" Aster snapped, "He just went out to a music concert at the Ellipsis Auditorium last night and never came home!"

There was silence on the line.

"You know as well as I do that it's standard procedure for operatives to have a final call with their loved ones before they deploy," Aster kept arguing, "and no such call took place, especially since he just got back from deployment a few days ago."

"*Did he say when he would be returning?*" the operator asked.

"Yes!" exclaimed Aster, "Last night! And he hasn't returned!"

"*One moment, please,*" the operator said.

Aster was put on hold and left waiting, nursing a horrible feeling in her stomach.

"*Dr Thorn,*" said the operator after a tense minute, "*I'm afraid your husband was called in for an emergency assignment of some kind. There was no time to arrange the usual farewell call or to inform you until now. That's all the information I have, I'm sorry.*"

Aster's blood ran cold.

"Ok," she said with a dry mouth, "thank you for letting me know."

"*Is there anything else I can help you with?*" the operator asked.

"No," Aster replied, "thank you and have a nice day."

"*You too, goodbye,*" said the operator before disconnecting.

Aster steadied herself against the armoured closet.

"Android!" she called, louder than intended, "keep an eye on the baby."

"*Yes, Mrs Thorn,*" said the household android in a digitised voice.

Aster went to the children's bedroom to check in on them. They were still waking up, cocooning themselves defensively under the covers. She felt terrible. Once they realised that daddy had disappeared, she wouldn't have any concrete answers for them.

Aster went to Gabriel's gym and the lights flickered on as she entered. She went to the closet on the other side of the room – another of his work-related secrets.

She swiped her thumb across the biometric pad and, to her surprise, the doors popped open. Aster had always disliked guns, and the sight of the assault rifle sitting in a plastic case at the back made her shudder.

The closet also had seven sets of skinsuits, one Gabriel's size, one her size, four child-sized, and one for an infant. She could guess that they were flexible body armour suits. The fact that Gabriel had taken such precautions meant he must have been serious about running away. Whether the DNI knew about it was another question.

* * *

Jezebel stared at Alexander, trying and failing to believe that she had misheard.

"What do you mean 'our son is coming home'?" she asked.

"You're a smart woman," Alexander replied, "I'm sure you can figure it out."

Jezebel didn't answer. The blank stare on her face turned to horror.

"You kidnapped a DNI agent?" she exclaimed.

"That would be the technical way of describing it," Alexander said casually, "but it could also be described as acquiring a valuable new asset."

"But you kidnapped a DNI operative!" Jezebel shouted at him furiously, "never mind that he's our son, the DNI will be after us now!"

"The DNI has been after me since I had you whisked off of Asgard," Alexander replied, unmoved by her outburst, "besides, I'd like the family back together again."

"So that's your real plan," Jezebel murmured, "I wondered what possible use you could have for me. Now I see you just want to play house and make up for lost time."

"That time was stolen from me," Alexander reminded her, bearing his teeth in anger, "and all I've ever wanted was to restore things back to the way they were."

"Will you try to make use of Gabriel's 'contacts' as well?" she asked sharply, "Or will you be content just to have him around?"

"The former would be nice," Alexander replied, "but the latter will do."

"Did you consider our grandchildren at all?" Jezebel asked, "I hope there's more to this plan of yours than separating one family to reunite another."

"Well, it would be nice to have the whole clan together," Alexander responded, getting up from the table, "but bringing everyone else over will have to wait."

"What the fleek does that mean?" Jezebel demanded.

"It means that we can't make another move until the previous one has run its course," Alexander explained, "which, in this case, means that we have to wait until Gabriel arrives before trying to get Aster and the children over here."

Jezebel was speechless.

"What's wrong?" Alexander asked, "I know you're not very fond of our daughter-in-law, but don't you want to see our grandchildren again?"

"It's bad enough that you've kidnapped their father," Jezebel countered angrily, "now you want to uproot them from their home so you can 'reunite' the family?"

"Would you rather I leave them with a single mother and no father at all?"

The question was calculated to provoke and Jezebel swung her hand, slapping him across the cheek. She winced in pain and rubbed her hand.

"What the fleek is your cheekbone made of?" Jezebel exclaimed.

"Something an order of magnitude stronger than regular bone," Alexander answered, "plus nanofibre threading which adds another order of magnitude worth of strength."

"Well...you still deserved that slap," Jezebel said, keeping her resolve.

"Fine by me," Alexander said with an amused smile, "besides my ribcage could stop a bullet – as long as you're not the one pulling the trigger."

He added that last point with a laugh that gave Jezebel chills. Somehow he was a lot more frightening when he was in a good mood.

* * *

At long last, the equipment Mortimer needed arrived. Androids came to his lab with crates and began unpacking them, removing their contents and assembling the machines. Once the machinery was ready, he would have a state-of-the-art operating surgery complete with neurochemical and nanosurgical equipment.

Mortimer's thoughts returned to what he would do afterwards. He had been assuming that Alexander would simply dispose of him. Could he convince Alexander to remove the poison collar once he had completed his task? Now that he had the equipment he needed, it was only a matter of time before he found out.

Mortimer left the androids to their own devices and retraced his steps back towards Alexander's private quarters. He was dreading even raising this topic, but he had to use what little leverage he had while he still had the chance.

He found the reinforced entrance again without much difficulty, but before he could use the intercom, the red door light flashed green and the door swung open. Alexander appeared, accompanied by an older woman with black and gold hair styled into a cornbraid.

"Ah," Alexander said, looking pleasantly surprised, "I was just looking for you."

"So was I," Mortimer responded.

"Any problems with the equipment?" Alexander asked, looking more serious.

"No, the androids are busy unpacking and assembling everything," Mortimer answered, "but it will take a while for them to finish."

"Well, in the meantime, let's take a walk," Alexander suggested.

"Where to?" asked the woman.

"Part of the research facilities we've got here," Alexander replied, "unless you'd rather stay cooped up in the living quarters?"

The woman opened her mouth to say something but no sound came out.

"That's what I thought," said Alexander, motioning for them to follow.

Confused by his sudden eagerness, Mortimer followed Alexander with his female guest in tow. She was dressed in a white business suit with nice shoes that made her look like she had wandered out of a board meeting. Mortimer avoided meeting her gaze as they followed Alexander to the research wing.

The doors opened for Alexander everywhere he went, and the pair did their best to keep up. The people they encountered either saluted or acknowledged their leader, but paid no heed to either of them. Somehow, it didn't seem strange that the boss was being followed around by a scientist and a business executive.

Mortimer realised that they weren't following the route back to his private laboratory. That made sense; whoever this woman was, Alexander probably didn't want her finding about his rage episodes. In that case, where were they being taken?

His question was answered when Alexander led them through one more biometrically-secured blast door into a new section of the research wing – new to them, at least.

They entered a cylindrical chamber that stretched up several levels. The chamber was dominated by a central column with stasis pods slotted into alcoves in its surface. The inner wall of the chamber was lined with work stations facing in towards the central column.

The chamber was abuzz with activity. Robotic manipulator arms would remove pods from the central column and place them inside a testing frame. Once the tests were completed, the robotic arm would pick the pod up again and place it back in its alcove.

"This is where most of the research takes place," Alexander explained, "focusing on the natives' biology and biochemistry."

"What exactly are you doing with them?" Mortimer asked.

"And who are you?" the woman demanded, looking at Mortimer suspiciously.

"Oh, I forgot to introduce you," Alexander said, taking them to one side, "Mortimer, this is Jezebel Thorn, the woman who shot me. Jezebel, this is Dr Mortimer Shelton, the man who made you have to shoot me."

Mortimer and Jezebel eyed each other awkwardly, unable even to shake hands.

"Shall we continue with the tour?" their host asked.

Alexander led them around the central column where they stopped to peer inside the stasis pods. They could see each native specimen trapped inside, their leafy green skin kept moist by the pod's atmospheric controls and their eyes closed in chemically-induced sleep.

"How many of these aliens do you have in here?" Jezebel asked.

"I don't have the exact number to hand," Alexander replied as he led them to another door, "but it must be over a thousand at this point."

"And what exactly are you doing with them?" Mortimer asked apprehensively.

"Through here," Alexander said, opening up another blast door.

He ushered his two bewildered guests down a connecting corridor until they reached another blast door requiring his biometric credentials.

The next chamber was larger and longer than the stasis pod chamber as well as noisier. The space echoed with the sound of robotic arms moving, the thrashing and squealing of captive aliens, and the crack-and-bang of guns being fired.

All along the right-hand wall were dozens of booths equipped with robotic machinery, each one manned by several technicians. The left-hand wall was dominated by a shooting range and a set of fighting pens watched over by teams of researchers.

Each booth had a specimen held securely within while the robotic arms implanted devices into their skin. The aliens' bright orange eyes were wide and unblinking, as if entranced, and they didn't flinch as the devices were attached to their flesh.

Once their cybernetic modifications were complete, each native warrior was sent to the testing ranges. They were then given a firearm – mounted on a swivel with restricted motion – and made to fire at targets on the opposite wall. Those in the fighting pens went claw-to-claw for a few seconds at a time before a switch was flipped, causing the fighting to cease.

"This is the core of the Network's experiments with the natives," Alexander explained, looking and sounding proud of himself.

"You mean *on* the natives, don't you?" said Jezebel, displaying her lack of approval.

"If you want to be pedantic, yes," said Alexander, annoyed, "in any case, the point is we're building a battalion of controllable shock troops out of the aliens we capture."

"Why are you showing us this now?" Mortimer asked, his stomach churning.

"Because everything is pretty much ready," Alexander replied, "Jezebel, you wanted to be more involved in what I'm building here; and Mortimer, you wanted to know why we've been experimenting *on* the natives."

"This isn't what I had in mind," Jezebel answered.

"Nor me," Mortimer added, knowing that his own leverage was weak.

"It wasn't what I had in mind either," Alexander responded, "at least, not at first. But even though the initial experiments to mitigate my own anger didn't go anywhere, they did produce a body of research that we've been able to put to other uses."

"Like turning these aliens into a private army?" Jezebel guessed.

"More or less," Alexander confirmed.

"I don't like this plan of yours," Mortimer said, instantly regretting the words.

Alexander transfixed Mortimer with a deadly green-eyed glare. Jezebel quietly stepped aside as Mortimer remained rooted to the spot, not daring to move as Alexander grabbed him by the scruff of his shirt and yanked him to one side.

"I thought you might say that," he growled menacingly, entering the reset code for the collar, "but I think you also realise that you don't have a say."

* * *

The chamber was dark. Byron Sade preferred it dark. Thanks to his enhanced eyesight, he could make out the shapes moving inside the observation tank. They were the sea eels he had shown to the delegation, constantly drawn back to the dim light on the other side of the glass as they circumnavigated the tank.

Their brains were the size of a fist but with only a fraction of the encephalisation of a Human brain. They spent their lifespans swimming through the inland seas of their homeworld. Inside the tank, they were content to swim back and forth in a space no bigger than this room.

Swimming in circles from birth till death – a fitting metaphor for most people's lives.

He heard footsteps from the far end of the chamber. Without his augmented hearing, he wouldn't have heard the person approach.

"Quite a menagerie you've got in this place," said 'A', standing beside him.

He was surprised to see her wearing a set of Sheraton Biopharma technician's overalls. Perhaps it shouldn't be surprising. Evidently, she came and went as she pleased, and disguise must be part of how she did it.

"You should know," he replied, "your Network supplied the original specimens."

"I always thought that was a violation of the 2nd Prime Law," she mused.

"It's a fascinating grey area of law, actually," Byron Sade noted, "the 2nd Prime Law prohibits unauthorised contact with alien species, but the regulations do permit experimentation on non-intelligent alien life. The grey area is what constitutes 'intelligent' life."

"So if the creature can obey commands, it's not okay to experiment on it?" she asked.

"Technically, yes," he responded.

"But it is okay to snap its neck on a whim?"

Byron Sade had to assume that she had been snooping around the labs, a fact which irked him far more than the question.

"Its life began at the whim of its creator," he remarked loftily, "it can be ended at the whim of its creator as well."

There was something bizarre about watching the two pairs of compound eyes circling the tank in the dark. The reflected light from the lenses made them look almost ghostly.

"Have you found any military uses for the specimens?" she asked.

"You assume that I've been looking for one in the first place," he answered, "besides, what possible military use could these creatures have?"

"Maybe not these particular creatures, unless you had a private pool of some kind you wanted to keep intruders out of," his mercurial intermediary mused.

"Doesn't your leader have an interest in those tree-hugging creatures you're sending to me?" Byron Sade pointed out, "If there are any military applications, I would have thought he or she or they would know more than me."

He turned to her with a suspicious glare.

"I would also have thought that such a capable spy would know more about her master's long term plans," he added accusingly.

"As I explained last night, the Network only divulges information on a need-to-know basis," she answered, "and that rule applies as much to me as to you."

Byron Sade continued to glare at her, far from mollified.

"I understand that you want to know who broke into your penthouse," 'A' replied calmly, "but the Network is *not* going to let you interrogate him."

"So you're just going to send me exotic new samples to experiment on," Byron Sade continued, stepping into her personal space, "and in return for helping me make a new fortune, all you want in return is me not to question your broader motives?"

"That's a good summary, yes," said 'A', unperturbed by his display, "and I remember you saying you didn't have a problem with that."

"No one wants something for nothing," Byron Sade pointed out, then added menacingly, "and I don't like being kept in the dark."

"Then turn up the lights," 'A' quipped with a smirk.

Byron Sade lunged at her, but she sidestepped him easily and tripped him up on his way past. He broke his fall as he fell towards the floor and scrambled back to his feet, looking at her with a face crinkled with rage.

"I'm not one of your sex captives," 'A' informed him, "so if you want to find out what the Network wants from you, you'll have to keep your temper in check."

* * *

Q-flight suffered from a trade-off between speed and capacity. The faster the ship needed to go, the bigger the Q-engine required, the bigger the power plant needed, and the less space aboard for anything else. Building very large or very fast FTL-capable spaceships was an enormous engineering challenge, and for the most part prohibitively expensive.

Q-couriers were ultra-fast cargo ships with Q-engines and fusion plants much larger than normal, sacrificing capacity and crew comfort for extra speed. The fusion reactor and Q-engine were housed in a bulbous module with the much smaller crew module and cargo hold extending from the front and the conventional engines mounted on the back.

The lack of space aboard a Q-courier meant that they had to operate with minimal crew. In fact, there were only three people aboard this vessel – four, counting the man in the stasis pod – and they were all gathered together in the cargo hold.

"How long before we arrive?" someone demanded of the man next to him.

"How should I know?" was the gruff reply.

"Because you're the pilot," his co-pilot pointed out.

"Who is accompanied by a perfectly capable co-pilot and Q-flight engineer," the pilot countered, "so you can both check the readings for yourselves."

"As long as we don't take any detours – or suffer any technical problems – the journey will last less than two days," said the Q-flight engineer.

"There you go," said the pilot.

"Less than two days from the moment we departed," the engineer clarified.

"Much less than two days, then," the pilot added, "even better."

Silence prevailed as they played a game in a corner of the cargo hold. Tubes and power cables criss-crossed the floor, connecting the container's systems to those of the ship. The container itself resembled an armoured sarcophagus held in place by motion-dampening clamps on the ceiling and floor.

"Why do you think the boss wants this guy?" the co-pilot wondered.

"You're asking us like we would know," the pilot pointed out.

"We can speculate all we want," the engineer agreed, "but that's all we can do."

"Ignorance is safety as well as bliss," the pilot added.

Rather than object to the non-answer, the co-pilot cast a wary eye at the black container, as if it were the tomb of some cosmic monster.

"You're not getting superstitious, are you?" the pilot asked with a wry smile.

"About what?" the co-pilot demanded defensively.

"You keep looking at the container," the pilot pointed out.

"That doesn't mean I'm superstitious about it," the co-pilot replied.

"I thought spacers were more afraid of pirates or accidents than space demons," the Q-flight engineer said with amusement.

"Aren't you a spacer as well, you smug hypocrite?" the co-pilot shot back.

"I've never spent more than a month at a time in space," the engineer replied.

More silence followed, broken only by the background hum of machinery.

"The blonde was smoking hot," the co-pilot remarked as he finally moved a piece.

"Our contact at the spaceport?" the engineer asked.

"Yeah, her," the co-pilot said, "The one with the weird blue eyes."

Before anyone could reply, an alarm chimed.

"What's that?!" the co-pilot demanded in a panic.

"Relax," said the Q-flight engineer, climbing leisurely to his feet, "it's a low priority alert, otherwise the lights would have turned red."

The pilot and co-pilot still looked worried. They paused the game and followed the engineer to the back of the ship where the Q-engine was housed.

"Don't touch anything, or we'll all be vaporised," the engineer warned jokingly.

As they entered the engineering room, the low hum of machinery became a loud din. The engineer grabbed a set of earmuffs and put them on. The pilot and co-pilot each grabbed a spare set for themselves as they followed him.

They came to the interface panel and the engineer approached it. There was a single yellow icon flashing on the panel. The engineer tapped the icon and expanded it, reading through the data as the pilot and co-pilot waited nervously for his verdict.

"There's a distortion," the engineer said, furrowing his brow.

"What kind of 'distortion'?" the pilot asked.

"Something is causing a minute but detectable distortion in our quantum wavefront," the engineer replied, "enough to trip the least important of the alarms."

"But why would it be doing that?" the co-pilot asked.

"Probably just a glitch in one of the emitters," the engineer suggested.

"Doesn't that mean the Q-engine is damaged?!" the co-pilot exclaimed.

"If the Q-engine were damaged, our quantum wavefront would break down and we'd be forced back into normal space," the engineer explained calmly, "like holding an inflated ball underwater and letting go."

"But then we'd be stranded in the middle of interstellar space!" the co-pilot pointed out.

"Get a fucking grip, will you?" said the pilot, cuffing him across the back of his head, "he said it's nothing to worry about."

"Well in that case," the co-pilot suggested peevishly, "what if that distortion is actually some kind of signal being used to track us?"

"That's paranoid nonsense," the engineer snorted, "unless you're telling me someone is manipulating our quantum wave-front in such a way as to signal our location."

"It's technically possible, isn't it?" the co-pilot insisted.

"No it isn't," the engineer replied, "let's get back to the game."

* * *

Byron Sade was fuming as he walked. 'A' infuriated him, no doubt deliberately, and there was only so much he could do to vent his frustration. It was nothing another session with his sex toy couldn't relieve, but he hated the smug and irreverent way 'A' carried herself, especially the way she addressed him.

That was all personal. Of much more immediate concern was her propensity to nose around. The Network's reach was clearly extensive, but the fact that she was able to come and go as she pleased meant that some of his most precious secrets were at risk.

This wing of the facility was off limits to most of his staff. Only he and a trusted team of research personnel were permitted here. It was also conveniently next to the detention block, a place he would love to throw 'A' if he ever got his hands on her. He stood before the vault-like blast door and stared into the biometric scanner.

The sensor flash-scanned his eyes and the mighty door unlocked, heaving open inch by inch to allow him entrance. Byron Sade stepped through and waited for the blast door to seal itself again before proceeding further.

The laboratory he entered was shaped like a fishbowl. The ceiling lights were turned down and the floor absorbed the sound of his footsteps. Half a dozen researchers were gathered around a life support tank, observing the thing growing inside. Tangled bundles of translucent tubing were connected to the thing in the tank, feeding it nutrients as it grew.

The thing in the tank had nothing to do with the Network's two-faced generosity; this was entirely a creation of his own company's research efforts.

It had nearly twice the body mass of a Human. At the moment it looked more like an inflated jumpsuit, with fleshy pink limbs and a torso that were comically distended in the liquid solution. The head – if one could call it a head – was stunted, looking more like an outgrowth from the shoulders than an actual head.

"Progress?" Byron Sade demanded as he approached.

"Excellent," the research leader reported, "the musculature is now fully developed, we were about ready to apply the dermal infusion solution."

"What about the underlying systems?" Byron Sade asked.

"All fully functional and perfectly integrated into the sur-rounding tissue," the research leader responded confidently, "all that remains is to apply the dermal infusion solution and we can begin live testing."

"Proceed," Byron Sade commanded, a pleased smile curling his lips.

The research leader adjusted a set of controls before initiating the procedure.

Dark fluid began to flow through the translucent tubing, en-tering the specimen and spreading like so many inkblots across its surface. The fluid slowly saturated the flesh, causing the pale pink colour to darken until it was glossy black.

The physical look of the specimen began to change as well. The bloated limbs shrank and tightened into things vaguely re-sembling arms and legs. The torso also became more defined as the distended fleshy material congealed and hardened.

"The entire process will take an hour to complete," the research leader informed Byron Sade, "once it's done, we'll begin pilot testing."

"I will be the one conducting the pilot testing," Byron Sade made sharply clear, "no one else. That includes all live-testing."

"Of course, Mr Sade," the research leader replied.

"I must say, however, that this is genuinely impressive work," Byron Sade added.

"Thank you, sir," the research leader said with an appreciative nod.

Byron Sade turned his attention back to the specimen. Its 'flesh' was now completely black, as if it had been immersed in tar, and its shape was more clearly defined. It still looked some-what bloated, but visual aesthetics were not a priority.

He turned and departed the laboratory with a smile on his face, content in the knowledge that his ace in the hole was almost ready.

* * *

A dozen cargo containers arrived at Asgard Spaceport early in the morning. They were taken by freight hauler to the landing pad on top of Sheraton Biopharma's headquarters, then transported by cargo elevator down into the labs. The technicians watched the elevator descend, noting the biohazard symbol on the side of each container.

"When can we start analysing the cell cultures?" asked a female technician.

"Cell cultures?" said the research leader, "these are fully grown specimens; we're way past the point of using cell cultures. I don't know what kind of connections Mr Sade has, but we're lucky to have samples like these."

The cargo elevator reached the bottom and a team of androids moved forward to begin loading the containers onto the waiting transport sleds.

The research leader turned to leave and gestured for everyone to follow him. The team departed the area, heading to the other side of the facility. The woman trailed behind them for a while before ducking into a stairwell.

It took several round trips, but the androids worked more diligently than any Human workers could. Their sensors were blind to everything except the task before them, including the flicker of distorted light watching them from the shadows.

One of the containers was loaded onto a trolley and a pair of handles were physically turned in order to unlock it. The container cracked open and the panels retracted, releasing a gush of icy cold air from within.

Inside was a creature with wiry limbs, clawed hands, and a bony ridge on its forehead. It looked like an amphibian, but with a lizard-like snout and bulging eyes closed in cryogenic sleep. Its skin was a lush green colour, but covered in a fine layer of icy condensation.

It was an alien – a live alien, no less – a fact both extremely obvious and completely unmentionable. The group of researchers who were watching were certain they had just broken several laws. So too was the invisible figure observing from the floor.

The reversal of the stasis procedures would take a while to complete, but the figure had seen all she needed to see. She departed and navigated her way through the service corridors until she had left the research labs.

In the lobby of Sheraton Biopharma, several smartly dressed attendants were manning the front desk. A woman emerged from a backroom, dressed in the same attendant's uniform with a floppy bow tie. She smiled and waved at her colleagues before departing, hailing a sky-taxi for the ride home.

Alone in the privacy of the sky-taxi's cabin, Aetherea deactivated the masking device. The scientists in the Rand Block had outdone themselves, even more so than with the cloaking field generator. The masking device enabled her to take on a hundred different appearances, and could even fake her voice and accent.

Technological disguises were always risky. In principle, anything with a power source could be detected, no matter how sophisticated the deception. Nonetheless, it had worked so far, and had helped her to gather valuable intelligence.

Aetherea removed her hair clasp and let her blonde locks free. Then she opened up her wrist-top computer and uploaded the information she had collected.

"*Where would you like to go, Madam?*" asked the digitised voice of the sky-taxi AI.

"Ellipsis Tower, the mag-train station," Aetherea instructed.

It was a strange double act to pull off: impersonating an agent of the very organisation she was trying to collect intelligence on. She had succeeded thus far, and Byron Sade seemed more like a pawn than a player. As long as there were no other Network agents nearby, it should be easy to maintain the deception.

* * *

Aster had gone to work and completed all the tasks in her work inbox as if nothing was wrong. It was hard to concentrate when she was working for the same organisation that wouldn't tell her where her husband was. Nonetheless, she had made it through the day and was on her way home via mag-train.

The view from the mag-train window was uninteresting to most of the passengers; they had grown up with it, after all. Aster, however, could never take her eyes off the shining forest of metal and glass stretching up to cloud level. The sun was already setting, and the light from the oncoming dusk was smeared across the horizon as an orange glow.

It was a sight that the native-born residents of Asgard City took for granted, and one that had filled Aster with awe when she had first arrived at the spaceport. More than a decade later, the feeling of awe had never quite gone away.

Mixed in with the awe was a dash of resentment. The construction of this artificial paradise had required millions of tonnes of metal ore dug up from colony worlds like Sahara, scraping by while contributing to the unfathomable wealth before her eyes. Gabriel had wanted to ditch it all just to escape the gaze and grasp of the DNI.

And then he had disappeared.

It may be paradise, but this paradise had a nasty habit of swallowing people whole. Gabriel understood better than anyone what kind of place Asgard was – not to mention the machinations of their mutual employer. Had he found out something he shouldn't have? Was that why he had vanished?

The thought made Aster's heart leap and her breath began to shorten. It was hot inside the carriage. How had she not noticed before? All of a sudden she could hardly breathe. Her head suddenly felt light and she began to sway drunkenly. Were it not for the crowd of people around her, she would have keeled over.

The mag-train decelerated as it approached the station, and she pushed herself away from the window towards the doors, hyperventilating as she stumbled forward. The other passengers caught her and helped her towards the doors.

Once the doors opened, Aster was carried by her fellow passengers onto the platform. The cool air from the air conditioning washed over her, calming her down.

"Are you alright?" someone asked, planting a reassuring hand on her shoulder.

"I'm fine, thank you," Aster said weakly.

Slowly and groggily, she stood up and looked around. There was a crowd gathered around her, watching with concern to see if she would keel over again.

"Should we call the paramedics?" someone asked.

"No, I'm fine thanks, I just got lightheaded," Aster replied hastily, not wanting to cause any more of a scene, "I'll just take a sky-taxi home."

* * *

The surveillance pod was latched onto the underside of one of the mag-train rails like a tick. Its presence was concealed by stealth technology while its surveillance array enabled it to monitor all nearby electronic communications.

The two operatives sat side by side, looking at data feeds from the public surveillance cameras. There was no need for them to manually flick through the feeds, the pod's AI followed the mark for them, displaying the relevant camera feed front-and-centre wherever she went.

One of the operatives squinted at the screen as the mark suddenly looked unwell. The camera feed warned of an elevated pulse and faster breathing rate as she tried to get away from the window and stumbled towards the carriage doors.

"Big Brother, this is Watchdog-three-nine," said one of the operatives over the comm., "the mark is having some kind of panic attack."

"*Affirmative, Watchdog-three-nine,*" said their handler, "*we see it as well.*"

They watched as the passengers spilled out of the carriage with several of them guiding Aster Thorn to a corner and helping her recover.

The screen threw up dozens of personal profiles as it automatically identified everyone who walked past the camera. It was just as well that everything was being recorded; the two operatives could hardly see the mark through the crowd.

One particular profile was flagged up in orange. It was a man's face – an Undercity dweller, judging by the pale skin and dark eyes – but belonging to someone who apparently didn't exist in the database. Stranger still, by the time the person had passed within range of the next camera, he was gone.

"Who the frick was that?" asked the second operative.

"No idea," the first operative responded, puzzling at the profile, "it's possible there's an operative on the ground with a masking device."

"But shouldn't we be the only assets tailing the mark?" the second operative asked.

"Big Brother, this is Watchdog-three-nine," the first operative said, "Aster Thorn is recovering and is on her way home, but we just flagged a surveillance profile for someone who apparently doesn't exist. Are there any other surveillance assets in the vicinity?"

"*Affirmative, Watchdog-three-nine,*" came the response, "*we have one other operative on route to the station via sky-taxi now.*"

"Big Brother, the flagged profile belongs to someone who was already on the platform," the first operative explained, "they literally just walked past the mark as she was crouched on the floor, and now they've disappeared from the cameras."

"*Acknowledged, Watchdog-three-nine,*" their handler replied, "*but I'm telling you there are no other Directorate assets in the vicinity.*"

The two operatives looked at each other in confusion.

"Big Brother," said the first operative, "we may have a third party involved."

"*Understood, Watchdog-three-nine,*" their handler responded, "*keep an eye on the mark. We'll investigate further on our end.*"

"Acknowledged, Big Brother," the operative replied before terminating the link.

"Could that have been the influencer?" the second operative asked.

"I thought they'd ruled out that theory?" the first operative said.

"Prematurely, if you ask me," the second operative responded, "unless we're going with the working theory that it's just another glitch in the system."

* * *

Even though they had only just met, there was an instant cloud of ill feeling between Mortimer and Jezebel. Mortimer felt the ill feeling to be intensely one-way, and it was obvious that Alexander wanted it that way. They kept a suspicious distance between themselves as their host showed them around, and it was a relief when the tour was over.

After seeing the research facilities, the pair were shepherded back to the living quarters. Jezebel was ushered inside before Alexander accompanied Mortimer back to his lab.

By the time they arrived, the androids had finished assembling the machinery and were clearing up. The space had been transformed into a state-of-the-art operating theatre.

"Nice," Alexander remarked, "now you can start working on a proper cure."

"Will you take this collar off once I succeed?" Mortimer asked suddenly.

Alexander looked at him with a dangerous glare without answering immediately, but slowly the glare dissolved into a pensive grimace.

"Depends how permanent the cure is and how few side effects there are," he replied, "but in principle, I don't see why not."

"I'll start looking at the results of my analyses," Mortimer said, "once I've devised a treatment, I'll let you know so I can talk you through it."

"Will you need anything else?" Alexander asked.

"Hopefully not," Mortimer replied, "it's the equipment here that's most important."

"There is one other thing," Alexander said, taking a step towards Mortimer, "how do you feel about me experimenting on the natives?"

"Very uncomfortable, if I'm being honest," Mortimer answered truthfully, "they may be aliens, but it's not that far removed from what I was tasked with doing to you."

Alexander closed the distance and grabbed Mortimer by his shirt again.

"They already had uncontrollable tempers," Alexander snarled menacingly, "mine was an unintended consequence of the DNI's meddling. *Your* meddling."

"'Meddling' for which you volunteered," Mortimer pointed out boldly, "just like every other zero-generation voidstalker and every single one of the first generation voidstalkers who came after them – including Gabriel."

Alexander released Mortimer's shirt and grabbed his throat instead.

"Since when did you grow such a pair?" Alexander growled through gritted teeth, his shining green eyes boring into Mortimer's soul.

"I didn't need to," Mortimer replied, barely keeping his nerve, "if you kill me, you won't have anyone to cure your temper."

The truth of the remark punctured the furious look on Alexander's face. A tense silence reigned as Alexander's anger and grip slowly relaxed.

"I've been wondering how much of that bionic-eyed bitch's craftiness rubbed off on you," he remarked with a wry smirk.

"You really shouldn't call her that," Mortimer said.

"Why not?" Alexander demanded, "She's lightyears away, and since she orchestrated the whole thing, it's the least I'm entitled to."

"She was always an unflinching taskmistress," Mortimer remarked.

"Well to be fair, I can be a taskmaster as well," Alexander replied.

"Are you seriously planning on creating an army out of those things?" Mortimer asked, shifting the subject back again.

"Of course not," Alexander retorted sarcastically, "I'm just kidnapping random aliens and fitting them with cybernetics out of sheer boredom."

He laughed. The laugh chilled Mortimer's blood.

"I hope you're not planning on attacking any colonies," Mortimer said.

"Don't be ridiculous," Alexander retorted more seriously, "that would be tantamount to declaring war on Humanity, and it's a war I'd lose."

"But then what will you do with this private army of yours?" Mortimer asked.

Alexander didn't answer immediately, but he did ultimately answer.

"Whatever I want."

THE CURE

Exactly what was her role in Alexander's plans supposed to be? As far as Jezebel could tell it had all been a charade, a bizarre family reunion scheme. Kidnapping Gabriel was bad enough, but apparently he also wanted to bring their daughter-in-law and grandchildren over as well.

On top of that, he was manufacturing an army of alien soldiers and expected her to go along with it. From self-made spymaster to amateur business magnate to petty warlord – or perhaps some ad hoc combination of all three. It was impossible to tell what he was now, or what he was trying to be, but the less involved she was, the better.

The door to the living quarters opened and the man himself appeared.

"What exactly are you planning?" Jezebel demanded, blocking his path.

"In general or with the specimens?" Alexander asked, unperturbed by her tone.

"Both!" Jezebel snapped, "And who was that guy you brought along?"

"Dr Mortimer Shelton," Alexander replied, "a former DNI scientist who served as head of research for the Voidstalker Programme until he resigned a decade ago."

"You kidnapped a DNI scientist?!" Jezebel exclaimed in disbelief.

"*Former* DNI scientist," Alexander corrected her, "and I didn't kidnap him, he was brought here willingly, and now he works for me."

"Is he helping you build your little private army?" Jezebel interrogated.

"If he were, do you think he would need a tour of the facility where the research is taking place?" Alexander pointed out.

"Then what is he here for?" Jezebel demanded.

"That's not up for discussion," Alexander replied, his tone hardening.

"Then what am *I* doing here?" Jezebel demanded, more angrily this time, "Or is that not up for discussion either? And don't give me any more fleeking lies about needing my contacts. With the resources you have, you clearly don't need them."

Volcanic rage began to bubble up in Alexander's mind.

"I have a facility to manage," Alexander said, trying to bypass Jezebel.

She stood in his way, glaring up at him.

"Don't make me angry again," Alexander warned her dangerously.

"So lose your temper then," Jezebel challenged him, "you can finish what you couldn't do the last time we had an argument."

Alexander was trembling. His fingers curled slowly into fists and his facial muscles tightened as the rage fought to be free.

Jezebel was also trembling, partly in anger as well, but also with fear. She was terrified that he might actually attack her.

Finally, he shoved her aside and stormed away.

* * *

Alexander locked himself in the operations room and fumed. Jezebel had sorely tested the limits of his self-restraint, and he had barely pulled through. After a moment of fuming, his head cleared up enough to get back to work.

There was a new message waiting for him on the terminal. It informed him that the specimens had arrived safely at Asgard Spaceport. 'Safely' meant that they had passed – or bypassed – the customs checks, so by now they would be in the care of Sheraton Biopharma. Another piece of the plan was unfolding.

Byron Sade had proven indispensable to the Network on Asgard. Alexander was quite prepared to sacrifice it all to see his son and grandchildren again, but he didn't really know what to do with Byron Sade.

Alexander pulled up his profile and glared at the man's image. Even in digital format it looked slightly off, especially the way his skin was stretched taut over his skull. The rich and powerful on every planet spent fortunes trying to keep up appearances; literally, in the case of Byron Sade, and the traces of it were all over his face.

His company was still useful, at least for the research capabilities and other resources at its disposal, more useful than the man himself.

Alexander had considered getting rid of Byron Sade and replacing him with some kind of imposter he could control. By all accounts, including those of his operatives, the man was a pretentious sybarite in public and a grotesque pervert in private. For the time being, however, he was more useful alive than dead.

Alexander dismissed Byron Sade's profile and opened another profile. The image was Jezebel's mugshot from when she had been arrested for murder. She was dressed in her usual business suit and had her hair done up in her trademark cornbraid, but the look on her face resembled that of a peeved teenager arrested for petty vandalism.

What to do with her? His estranged wife was right about him wanting to recreate the life they use to have, but she didn't seem very happy about it.

Why would she be? She had done just fine without him. It was hard to bring himself to contemplate it, but she didn't really need him.

It was less difficult to believe what a criminal career she had built for herself in the meantime. Not that it was strictly illegal to prey on financially vulnerable colony worlds. But it *was* strictly illegal to engage in corporate espionage, blackmail, and murder, the latter of which she didn't have the stomach to do without android assistance.

So what was he supposed to do with her? Locking her up would defeat the point of bringing her here, especially after he'd broken her out of prison. Even so, he couldn't risk her running away, not that there was anywhere she could flee to.

He dismissed Jezebel's profile and brought up Mortimer's profile. The man he had forced to become his personal doctor was the biggest potential liability. The collar was there to ensure that he survived the final treatment.

Should he take the collar off afterwards? It was tempting not to, not just out of spite but also given how useful his talents were. Plus, if he did take the collar off, he would have to keep Mortimer around some other way.

In particular, he had to be kept in the dark. He had synthesised the poison used in the attacks on Asgard City, having been told it was just a precaution, and Alexander's operatives had smuggled him off the planet before the attacks.

He still had no idea that he was wanted for terrorism and the murder of sixty people.

* * *

The sky-taxi touched down on the landing pad and Aster climbed out. She made it back to the apartment without any more panic attacks, slamming the front door shut behind her and feeling a profound relief to be home.

The maganiel android was still standing guard in the hallway, silently watching through electric blue slits for eyes. The sight of the oversized handgun attached to its thigh made her nervous, but at least she could be certain that the house was safe. Aster took her coat off and was about to hang it up when she saw something.

Stuck to the right shoulder was a patch of fabric shifting in colour under the light. She vaguely remembered someone planting their hand on her shoulder at the station before walking off, and now this patch was here. She scraped at it, peeling it off in one go.

It was a piece of smart fabric, judging by the flickering circuitry on the underside, and it began to warm up in her hand. As it warmed up, the underside began to glow.

The doorbell rang.

Aster spun around like a thief caught red-handed, scrunching the smart fabric up in her hand as the maganiel stepped forward to answer the door.

"*This is the Thorn residence*," the maganiel announced in a digitised voice, "*please identify yourselves and state the purpose of your visit.*"

"*Hello*," said a voice through the intercom, "*I'm Agent Blake accompanied by Agent Gibson. We're here to check in with Dr Aster Thorn after her emergency call.*"

"*Please present your biometrics*," the maganiel requested.

Two pictures appeared on the security screen showing two men's faces along with their names and Directorate affiliation. The fact that they were with the DNI didn't make Aster feel at ease, but the maganiel was satisfied and it opened the door.

The two agents were dressed in dark uniforms and had sidearms holstered at their thighs. The maganiel spotted the weapons and positioned itself between them and Aster.

"Dr Thorn," said one of the agents, "we understand you had some kind of panic attack on the mag-train earlier, we just came to check up on you."

"I'm fine," Aster assured them, "thank you."

"Did you notice anything suspicious immediately before the incident," the other agent asked, "or whilst you were recovering on the platform?"

"No," Aster partially lied, "why do you ask?"

"Well, you don't have a history of illness as far as we know," the second agent added, "it's kind of odd that you would have a fainting episode out of the blue."

"Like I said, I'm fine," Aster insisted, "but thank you again."

"Ok, that's all we wanted to know," the first agent said, "have a good evening."

The two agents departed and the maganiel closed the door.

Aster went to the master bedroom and dismissed the household android. Then she sat down on the bed and unscrunched the piece of smart fabric, smoothing it against her palm.

It warmed up again, and as it brightened, a message appeared. *'We know where Gabriel is. Wait for instructions.'*

The smart fabric continued to warm up in her hand, becoming hot to the touch. Aster ran to the bathroom and dumped it in the sink where it fizzled and crackled. Before long, it had shrivelled up like a dead leaf, releasing a thin wisp of smoke.

Evidently, the Directorate weren't the only ones watching her and the family.

* * *

The entire building was connected, including the security system. The more complex the system, the more security weaknesses there were, and it hadn't taken long to find one.

He swiped through the camera feeds with a gloved finger until he was looking at the Thorn's front door. The two agents had appeared seemingly from nowhere, no doubt using one of the DNI's stealth pods to get around. There was no audio, so he could only guess what they might be saying to her.

He waited until the agents had left, then folded the screen away, and exited his hiding spot, striding down the corridor as though he lived there. An elderly man appeared from around the corner, giving a wide berth to the stern-looking teenager covered in tattoos. It was one of hundreds of possible disguises the masking device gave him.

That was how he had always lived: as a shadow unnoticed by anyone. The Undercity was where most of Asgard City's population dwelt: near or beneath the surface of the planet, living and dying in the shadow of the city's great towers. The better off residents who lived this high up knew little about the Undercity and cared even less.

It was his biggest advantage. The masking device just made it easier.

He took the stairwell up to the nearest landing pad where he summoned a sky-taxi. It arrived a few minutes later, alighting gently on the pad. Once he was aboard, he used the control for his masking device to alter his appearance once more.

He didn't dare change his disguise anywhere where there might be cameras. He knew Aster Thorn had received his message, but she was still a DNI employee, so he couldn't risk getting too close. Besides, there were other preparations to be made.

He selected a business park on the other side of the city as his destination, then activated the viewing screen as the sky-taxi took to the air again. As it cruised past the city centre, he got a clear view of Ellipsis Tower and the other high-rises it dwarfed.

He used to gawp at this sight, unable to believe it was possible to build such structures, let alone that they had existed on top of his own home for almost a century. Since then, he had passed through each tower countless times and had seen the rot within.

He couldn't fathom the master's plans or his interest in the Thorn family, but he had an idea of why he wanted them away from Asgard. Beneath the glittering glass and polished metal of the city was all manner of corruption, fed and financed by the wealth that poured in from the colonies and bubbled up from below.

The master had orchestrated the first blow against the debauched parasites who resided in the Clouds. It had taken months of preparation, but the panic and fear that the gas attacks had caused amongst the fleeksters still filled him with vindictive satisfaction.

He hoped the master's latest instructions hinted at future attacks and that the master's parallel interest in Byron Sade would help bring them about. Manipulating that corporate tyrant into bringing about the downfall of his fellow fleeksters would also be deeply satisfying.

As the sky-taxi sped towards the outer districts, he switched the camera angle to keep watching the city centre as it receded slowly into the distance.

What a pleasure it would be to watch those towers burn.

* * *

The elevator doors opened and Byron Sade stepped out into a sanitised space with bright lighting and a bank of computers along one wall.

A dozen scientists were present, preparing for the first round of tests. When they saw their employer, they nodded respectfully. Byron Sade gestured for them to keep working and they returned to their preparations as the research leader approached.

"We were about to start the first round of genetic screening," he said.

Along the opposite wall were a dozen life support tanks standing in a row with one specimen inside each tank. They were visible through the glass casing, suspended in fluid and held in place by restraints made of translucent cord. Breathing masks covered their snouts and their eyes were closed in slumber.

Byron Sade approached the tanks, and the research leader followed him. Through their oxygen masks, the specimens could be seen reflexively baring mouthfuls of carnivorous teeth as if confronting some invisible opponent in their dreams.

"Preliminary medical examinations revealed traces of extensive surgery," the research leader explained, "there's also a network of cybernetic implants under the skin."

"So someone else experimented on them before shipping them to us," Byron Sade concluded without sounding surprised.

"Indeed," the research leader said, "although, why someone would take the trouble to modify these creatures before sending them to a rival firm is beyond me."

"It's also beyond the scope of your concerns," Byron Sade told the man sharply.

"Yes sir," the man replied nervously before continuing, "The specimens possess an overdeveloped limbic system, making them prone to extreme aggression."

"Which would mean the cybernetics are meant to control them," Byron Sade surmised.

"This seems rather outside the remit of the company's usual line of business," the team leader said apprehensively, "would you like us to explore their fighting potential?"

"Yes," Byron Sade ordered, "not that we're planning to get into the arms industry."

"That's something else, sir…" the research leader ventured to say.

"If you have qualms about the legality of this research, you should have disembarked before the ship left the port," Byron Sade answered, "experimenting on these creatures will be no different than experimenting on any other species, so don't get squeamish just because these ones can count to ten."

"Of course, sir," the research leader replied before returning to his team.

Byron Sade saw the faint patterns made by the cybernetic circuitry under the creatures' skin, like traces of a full body tattoo. He was more impressed by the wiry musculature which implied an evolved strength that science still found difficult to replicate.

It would be a shame to waste them as mere gladiatorial fighters or glorified guard dogs, not to mention conspicuously illegal. In fact, the mere act of smuggling them in and bringing them to a research lab was flagrantly illegal.

Was the Network *trying* to entrap him?

Byron Sade's patience with the Network was wearing thin. He needed to speak to 'A' again and get some answers out of her. But, of course, she came and went as she pleased, and wouldn't just show up whenever he summoned her.

He clenched his fists and bared his teeth in unconscious emulation of the specimens. That smug little bitch was infuriating, the way she swanned around the place, appearing and disappearing without explanation. He hated being a pawn of this so-called Network – no one manipulated Byron Sade into doing anything.

* * *

Alexander received a message from Mortimer and returned to the lab, using a separate route to bypass Jezebel. He found Mortimer making final adjustments to one of the machines.

"I presume you've devised a cure," Alexander asked, locking the door behind him.

"I've prepared a neurochemical solution deliverable by nanobots," Mortimer explained, "everything's ready to go when you are."

"That was fast," Alexander noted, "so what do I have to do?"

"First of all, sit in the chair," Mortimer said, pointing to the patient's chair.

"How long will this take?" he asked.

"The procedure itself will take a few hours," Mortimer explained, "but the effects will take up to 24 hours to manifest fully, or so the simulations say."

"In that case," Alexander said, "I should probably give you another reset."

Mortimer nodded and turned his back to Alexander, allowing him to enter the reset code. The collar chimed in response and the countdown returned to its starting point.

45:00:00
44:59:59
44:59:58

"Will you take the collar off once the treatment is successful?" Mortimer asked.

"You've already asked me that," Alexander reminded him irritably, reclining on the chair, "and the answer is the same: as long the treatment is successful and there are no unwanted side effects, I don't see why not."

Mortimer nodded.

"So what role will I have in your grand design after your condition has been cured?" Mortimer asked, "Will you put me to work on those captive aliens?"

"Considering that you're a fugitive from the DNI, I don't think you have many options other than to stay here," Alexander pointed out, "although, if you insist, you don't have to be involved in any live experiments on the natives."

"I'm genuinely relieved to hear that," Mortimer replied.

"Maybe you could stay on as my personal physician," Alexander suggested.

"Now that you mention it, I did quite like being the neighbourhood doctor after retiring from the Directorate," Mortimer said.

He paused his preparations, staring pensively at the wall.

"Are we getting started or not?" Alexander demanded impatiently.

"Of course," Mortimer replied, snapping back to attention.

He tapped a sequence of keys and one of the robotic arms overhead descended. It was equipped with a vial filled with a misty serum and tipped with an injector needle. Alexander eyed the needle warily but didn't flinch.

"Well," said Mortimer, "as the closest thing you have to a personal physician, I am obligated to inform you that I cannot guarantee that this treatment will work, or that there won't be any side effects, and the threat of death by poison collar won't change that."

"Understood, doctor," Alexander replied, sounding resigned.

"You'll also need to be in medical restraints," Mortimer added, "just in case."

"Just in case what?" Alexander asked, his eyes narrowing.

"In case you struggle," Mortimer replied.

Alexander scowled at Mortimer, then nodded his assent. Mortimer pressed another button and a set of medical restraints wrapped themselves around Alexander's body. He looked like an inmate in an asylum as he stared up at the ceiling, waiting for the procedure to start.

One final button press, and the robotic injector arm closed in on Alexander's carotid artery. The pinprick barely hurt as the nanoserum entered his bloodstream. His vision darkened as the tranquiliser took effect. Mortimer was already an indistinct shadow in the distance as his mind began to slide into a black hole.

"Thank you…Mortimer…" he murmured as the waking world receded.

* * *

Mortimer watched as the sensory apparatus closed in around Alexander's head and the screens came alive with data displayed in real-time. The procedure was automated and the sophisticated medical AI could handle any complications.

Mortimer became filled with foreboding. He had worked his brain to the limit to prepare for anything that might go wrong, so it wasn't failure that he was afraid of.

'Whatever I want.' The image of Alexander jumping from planet to planet like some pirate king or interstellar warlord at the head of a private army formed in his mind. It would be comical if it weren't so disturbing, and not just because this private army would consist of alien soldiers created through unethical experiments.

A previously unthinkable thought entered Mortimer's head.

Alexander was completely unconscious and would never be more vulnerable than he was right now. If he prepared some kind of toxic serum and inserted it into the injector...

Mortimer blanched at the idea of killing his patient, despite the fact that Alexander had no reciprocal qualms about killing him.

Moreover, it wouldn't work. Only about 30% of the Voidstalker Programme's genetic enhancements contributed to physically superiority. Most of the rest produced immunity to every conceivable disease and toxin. Mortimer knew more than anyone else about genetic immunology – he had been the DNI's leading authority on the subject.

He headed for the exit. It would take a while for the nanoserum to finish its work, and he didn't need to stand around and wait. He paused at the door, turning around for another look at Alexander lying unconscious.

What an arrogant notion: to think he might be changing the course of history – let alone for the better – by poisoning a man in his sleep. It was actually a relief to know that his idea would likely fail. He didn't know if he had the will to do something that cowardly, and since it probably wouldn't work, he didn't have to find out.

"You're welcome," he murmured before departing the room.

* * *

At the edge of the system, a black clump appeared, blotting out the starlight around it as a bulbous-looking vessel emerged. Most of its hull consisted of an oversized Q-engine and a massive fusion plant to power it. The cockpit and crew compartment extended from the front and the regular engines from the rear like outgrowths rather than standalone modules.

The Q-courier was exceptionally fast when travelling through Q-space, but painfully slow using conventional propulsion, and it took several more hours to reach the planet. Once it arrived, it waited in geosynchronous orbit as a shuttlecraft from the planet flew towards it.

The shuttle was equipped with a set of gripper claws, and performed a barrel roll until its underside was facing the Q-courier's cargo hatch. The hatch opened and a cargo container was ejected into the shuttle's waiting claws. The claws took hold of the container and hugged it close, then the shuttle gunned its engines, speeding back towards the planet.

The weather was clear all the way down with minimal turbulence while a stealth field obscured the shuttle's visual profile. If any of the natives cared to glance skyward, they might have seen a speck of cloud moving at unusually high speed and nothing more.

Carrying the container in its grappling claws like a bug clutching a larva, the shuttle circled around the mountain. The hidden entrance in the mountain's flank opened up, and the shuttle swooped down low and flew straight into the open hangar entrance. As soon as the shuttle was inside, the hangar door sealed up again.

Inside the hangar, the shuttle slowed to a hovering halt, allowing the docking arms to pluck it from the air and lift it into a docking cradle. Once the engines had been powered down, a separate set of robotic arms plucked the container out of the shuttle's claws.

The container was driven to the other end of the hangar bay and received by a team of technicians. They watched expectantly as the container was lifted onto a cargo cradle before being manoeuvred into position.

"Another special delivery for the boss," someone mused aloud.

"We need to be extra careful with this one," the line manager announced, "it's a live specimen, but not one of the natives."

No one inquired further. If the man who ran the Network wanted it delivered, it was certain to be important, and that was all they needed to know.

Once the container was in the unloading cradle, the team approached. The first step was to release the manual locks. Once done, the top of the container cracked open and the two wing-like hatches opened up and unfolded like the lid of an ancient tomb.

The container was several inches thick and reinforced with a shockproof cradle. Inside was another package, the same shape as the larger container but smaller and housed inside a sterile plastic casing. Someone reached in and opened up the casing, revealing another secure container inside, like a coffin within a coffin.

"Alright," someone said, "let's reverse the stasis protocols first."

A click arrested everyone's attention, followed by a whining noise that steadily grew in pitch until it was cut off by another click.

* * *

The technicians died instantly. The explosion that erupted from the container ripped through the processing chamber before continuing into the hangar in the form of a fast-moving tongue of flame that scorched the walls and floor. With complete freedom of movement, the blast front travelled down the hangar, destroying everything it touched.

The incendiary blast was followed by a rumbling boom as the shockwave violently compressed the air in the tunnel. The sound of the explosion raced down the length of the hangar, resembling the roar of a subterranean monster waking from a deep slumber as it echoed back and forth through the cavern.

Warning lights flickered on and klaxons began to blare, prompting the Humans to flee the scene while teams of androids scrambled to put out the flames.

The cargo processing chamber was little more than a spherical crater. Pieces of girder melted and twisted out of shape dangled from the ceiling and walls, still glowing a soft red.

At the epicentre sat the inner container, seemingly intact. The shaped charges had been built into the wall of the outer container, directing the explosion outwards while protecting the inner container from damage.

No one was left alive nearby to witness the container open, or the figure emerge from within. The container's occupant sat up and surveyed the devastation. Then it retrieved something from inside the container and climbed out.

The figure was humanoid, but taller than usual and with a physique to match. He was dressed in black combat overalls with armoured layers woven into the fabric and wore a combat helmet with a trio of glowing green visual sensors. The object he had retrieved was an assault weapon, too large for a normal Human but large enough for him.

The figure traversed the chamber and climbed over the wreckage up to the next level. Once he reached the blast door at the top, a sharp twist of the handle was all it took to unlock it. The door opened with a pained metallic squeal and the infiltrator stepped through, not even bothering to close it behind him.

* * *

Jezebel heard the distant boom and rumble. Then she felt it. The tremor shook her off the couch and rattled the cups on the table. She had never been in combat, but she knew what an explosion sounded like. The lights in the living room turned a dangerous red and the sound of a klaxon could be faintly heard.

Once the tremors had stopped, she stood up and looked around in a panic. The common-sense thing to do was wait for more information, but none seemed to be forthcoming. Should she start wandering around looking for someone in charge?

Come to think of it, where had Alexander disappeared to?

Jezebel raced to the operations room but the door was locked. With a biometric lock on the door, if Alexander was inside then there was no way she could enter. Maybe he was already busy coordinating the response, in which case it was better to stay put.

She returned to the living room and sat down on the couch again, trying to get comfortable – as comfortable as it was possible to get with blood red lighting and the distant wail of alarms. Then she heard the door to the living quarters open and felt a wave of relief wash over her. Alexander had returned to explain what was going on.

The figure who walked in was not Alexander.

Jezebel jumped off the couch when she saw the figure dressed in black combat overalls and a sinister combat mask. The mask was watching her, pinning her down with three optical sensors. The giant assault weapon the figure was carrying was even more frightening. It wasn't pointed at her, but that didn't make her feel at ease.

The figure approached. Jezebel scrambled to get away, but he caught up to her and grabbed her before forcing her to turn around. Jezebel's heart froze up as the figure held her by the chin while glaring into her eyes.

"*Jezebel Thorn*," said the figure in a Human voice through an electronic filter.

Jezebel's eyes widened in incomprehension at being identified by name.

"*Where is Alexander Thorn?*" the figure demanded, still gripping her chin.

"I don't know," she replied, struggling ineffectually.

"*Where is Mortimer Shelton?*" the figure demanded.

"I don't know," she replied.

Without another word, the figure released her and headed towards the operations room.

"Who are you?" Jezebel demanded.

The figure ignored her.

"Hey!" Jezebel shouted, running and blocking the figure's path, "who are you?!"

The figure shoved her aside and kept walking, assault weapon in hand. She watched as the figure pressed a hand against the biometric lock. The light flickered before flashing green, then the figure opened the door and entered.

The infiltrator's appearance minutes after the explosion couldn't be a coincidence, and he definitely wasn't a member of the Network. But he was obviously looking for Alexander, and his weapon gave a clue as to why.

Jezebel turned and fled.

* * *

Asgard had no tectonic activity, so Mortimer didn't know what an earthquake was like. When the shockwave struck, he was shaken off his feet. The sonic rumble roared after it through the rock, more like an explosion than an earthquake. All along the corridor, red danger lights flashed on and a klaxon sounded a shrill note of alarm.

Mortimer scrambled to his feet and raced back to the lab to check on Alexander. He was almost out of breath by the time he was back inside.

His patient was still there resting in blissful unconsciousness, the medical restraints wrapped around his body keeping him where he was. A quick check of the medical equipment showed that it was undamaged and still functioning properly.

Mortimer breathed a small sigh of relief. There were no sirens here, creating an eerie silence even as the warning lights cast a bloody glow over the room.

Alexander couldn't have picked a worse time to go under. Who was his second-in-command? Did he even have a second-in-command? Who was meant to be in charge when he wasn't available? Were there any emergency protocols in place?

Mortimer accessed the computer terminal, but the features on the terminal were limited by security considerations and the intra-facility messaging system was down. Even if it was functioning, he had no idea who to contact.

A chiming sound from the other side of the room caught his attention. There were two doors into his lab, and the intercom for one of them was beeping. He walked over to the other door and activated the intercom.

"*Hello!*" said a panicked voice on the other side, "*do you know what's going on?*"

"I was hoping you could tell me that," Mortimer replied.

"*We were expecting a cargo delivery today,*" the man explained, "*but there was an explosion when the unloading crew tried to open it. That's all I know, I was hoping someone more senior might know more.*"

"I'm not very senior," Mortimer admitted, "so I can't help you there."

"*The boss would know what to do,*" the man said, "*but we don't know where he is right now. Someone said he comes down to this part of the lab sometimes.*"

There was absolutely no way he was going to wake Alexander up before the procedure was complete, no matter what might be happening outside. If he interrupted the procedure, it could inflict permanent damage, in which case Alexander wouldn't be much use as a leader.

"I haven't seen him either," Mortimer lied, "I thought he was down in the tunnels."

"*Are you sure?*" the man asked, "*The androids can handle the automated emergency protocols, but anything involving personnel is up to the boss.*"

Did the Network have *any* hierarchy below Alexander himself?

"*Open the door and let me in,*" the man suggested.

"I'm afraid I can't do that," Mortimer responded, "I've got a very sensitive experiment running and it can't be interrupted."

"*This is an emergency for fuck's sake!*" the man shouted back, "*I'm not going to touch any of the equipment, just open the fucking door!*"

"The answer is no," Mortimer replied firmly, "sorry."

* * *

Very little escaped the notice of Sheraton Biopharma's security, and now that they had identified the abnormal thermal signature, 'A' was no longer an exception. Byron Sade knew she had seen the alien specimens arrive and that she was using personal cloaking technology. What he didn't know was why she was back so soon after departing.

He was sitting in the living room with a portable projector on the table in front of him, displaying a fully rendered model of the building. He watched the red dot representing the anomalous thermal signature emerge from the sky-taxi before making its way across the roof and down into the service tunnels.

Byron Sade stroked the animal sleeping on the couch beside him. At last, the genetics team had managed to get the pigmentation correct, pure white fur with pure black skin beneath and not a single blotch or blemish to be found. Right now, he was more concerned about the Network's agent coming back.

The red dot was slowly making its way through the building, taking a circuitous route towards his penthouse. One press of a button would designate her as hostile and the defence systems would tear her apart. However, that wouldn't exactly endear him to the Network.

He watched as the red dot moved through the service corridors – supposedly a blind spot in the penthouse's defences – and sure enough, the door at the far end opened. A distorted outline appeared in the doorway, stopping in the centre of the room. Byron Sade puzzled at the respectful distance the figure was keeping as she deactivated her cloaking field.

His cloaking field.

The figure standing in his living room was not female and was definitely not 'A'. The security sensors told him that the figure was wearing a masking device, but it wasn't covering his physical build. This was someone completely different.

"I am with the Network," the figure announced in an unmistakeably male voice, "and I need to speak with you urgently."

"If the Network needs something else from me, then your fellow agent could have told me earlier," Byron Sade said acidly.

The masking device made it difficult to be certain, but he thought he detected a flicker of confusion pass across the man's face.

"Fellow agent?" the figure asked.

"Yes, the blonde who calls herself 'A'," Byron Sade elaborated, "she was just here snooping around the building before taking a sky-taxi away from here."

The figure looked at him blankly before speaking.

"If that is true, then I believe you have suffered a serious security breach," the figure informed him, "I know of no fellow agents who go by that name."

Byron Sade's already taut skin tightened as the figure's words sank in.

"But she accompanied me to the concert the night the assassin was snatched," he said, his voice wavering, "she assisted in capturing the assassin. She also observed the specimens being delivered to this building."

"If that is true," the figure replied coolly, "then the security breach is even more serious, since it jeopardises the Network's own plans, not to mention my own cover. This 'A' person that you speak of is almost certainly a DNI operative."

Byron Sade inhaled sharply.

"The matter I came to discuss is now a moot point," the figure concluded, reactivating his cloaking field and becoming a disembodied voice, "if the DNI has inserted an operative into your circle posing as an operative of the Network, then the DNI is coming for you."

"Wait!" Byron Sade called after him, "if this person really is a DNI operative, maybe we can work together to catch and eliminate her."

"And endanger the Network's activities on Asgard even further?" the disembodied voice asked, "I will be going to ground, and I suggest you do the same."

The still-open door shut seemingly of its own accord and Byron Sade watched as the figure's thermal signature went back the way he had come. He scowled furiously, his fists clenching and his knuckles turning white with rage.

Despite the volcanic anger boiling over in his mind, he couldn't suppress a modicum of grudging admiration for the duplicitous 'A'. Perhaps he should have been more paranoid, but then again posing as an agent of the very faction she was collecting information on was not something a common liar could pull off.

Evidently, the Network was nowhere near as competent or organised as he had thought. Or perhaps they had underestimated the DNI's cunning and resourcefulness. Either way, he had to assume that the DNI knew all of his dirty secrets.

He activated the intercom.

"Send everyone home early, now," he ordered, "no exceptions, no excuses."

"*Uh…yes sir, right away,*" replied the voice on the other end hesitantly.

Anyone who stayed behind would be killed.

* * *

Terrestrial counterintelligence was usually not a priority for the Directorate, but events had forced the Directorate to shift its priorities dramatically.

"The influencer definitely exists," the counterintelligence chief said stoically.

"So we have yet to roll up the rest of the Network's agents," Red-eye mused coolly.

"The Network only ever had two agents on Asgard," he added, "one was the mole who enabled Mortimer Shelton's escape and the other was the influencer himself."

"Go on," said Red-eye with a raised eyebrow.

"The mole was disaffected and joined the Network willingly," the counterintelligence chief explained, "he was cunning enough to manipulate someone into doing the more technical sabotage. Apart from that, there's no evidence that he had more of an impact than that."

Red-eye nodded, having come to a similar conclusion herself.

"As for the influencer," the counterintelligence chief continued, "he or she operates through a network of patsies rather than fellow agents. The courtesans and the prison warden, for example, were simply pawns."

"I take it Colonel Starborn has concluded the same thing?" Red-eye inquired.

"Indeed she has," the counterintelligence chief confirmed, "the rest of the Network's agents on Asgard, particularly those at the spaceport, and even Byron Sade himself, all appear to be catspaws. We can seize them and wrap up the ring at a moment's notice."

"What about Byron Sade?" Red-eye asked.

"There's no evidence that Byron Sade is an active member of the Network, more like a highly placed pawn," the counterintelligence chief answered, "but we have several teams on standby to raid his company's headquarters as soon as you give the word."

"Not yet," Red-eye ordered, "there are several other ongoing operations which could be affected if we move too soon."

"Understood," the counterintelligence chief replied, "there's one other thing: someone, almost certainly the influencer, placed a strip of smart fabric on Dr Aster Thorn's jacket while she was having a panic attack at the station. Two operatives went to see her and she lied to them about nothing being wrong."

"Do you think that she might be compromised?" Red-eye asked.

"She reported Colonel Gabriel Thorn missing," the counterintelligence chief replied, "but up until now she has shown no signs of disloyalty or suspicious behaviour."

"Then the influencer is probably trying to gain her trust by sending her a message," Red-eye concluded, "keep the family under the usual surveillance, but we don't need to treat her like a mole without evidence that she is one."

"What about her husband?"

"Colonel Thorn is on special assignment," Red-eye replied, "and being at short-notice, we couldn't arrange the usual family call."

"Is Colonel Thorn's assignment related to ongoing operations against the Network?" the counterintelligence chief asked.

"Yes," Red-eye replied, "and for now, that is all you need to know."

THE NIGHTMARE

VERGING on blind panic, Jezebel fled the living quarters and kept on running, the crimson warning lights illuminating her way. She reached the entrance and saw that the door was open, presenting a path to freedom. No doubt this was the way the infiltrator had come, and she ran towards it.

The heat slapped her in the face as she approached. Squinting through the open door, she saw the aftermath of the explosion. Teams of robots were rolling towards the blast site, spraying jets of water at the blackened walls and floor, sending up a hissing cloud of steam as the water soaked the superhot metal.

The firefighting robots wheeled forwards, sweeping their turrets from side to side. The air still felt like a sauna, but now it was bearable, and Jezebel approached the threshold.

The shockwave from the explosion had flattened the metal walkway against the wall. The rapidly condensing steam was forming a layer of moisture on the walls and floor, and she almost slipped as a result. The mangled safety railing was still hot to the touch, but she was still able to navigate her way down to the floor.

The firefighting robots ignored Jezebel, fixing their attention on an object in the centre of the chamber. It was an open container sitting right at the epicentre of the blast, its exterior scorched black and its interior completely untouched. Jezebel saw the casket, remembered the infiltrator, and put two and two together.

She couldn't fathom how the explosives could have destroyed the chamber and left the container intact, let alone left the infiltrator unharmed. However, the facility was clearly under attack, maybe even by the DNI. How else would the infiltrator have known her name or asked about Alexander and that Mortimer Shelton person?

If the DNI or the Navy had discovered the Network's headquarters, they must be in orbit right now or soon would be, with the infiltrator deployed to sow chaos ahead of time. If that was the case, then the facility would soon be overrun and she would be rearrested and sent back to prison – or killed in the crossfire.

Alternatively, she could escape the facility and surrender to the authorities. Prison was preferable to dying on this forsaken planet.

Jezebel navigated the obstacle course of robots, wreckage, and puddles of condensation, finding herself standing at the outer corner of the L-shaped hangar. Ahead of her, the hangar continued deeper into the mountain. To the right, the walls were lined with shuttles and other vehicles. She could also see the blast doors at the far end of the tunnel.

She turned right and raced down the hallway, leaving herself almost out of breath by the time she got to the other end.

As luck would have it, there was a cargo shuttle already sitting in the docking cradle. A team of androids was working on the shuttle, sublimely indifferent to the chaos. They ignored Jezebel as she climbed up and paid no attention as she nosed around the docking controls.

The shuttle was in perfect working order and the androids had almost finished refuelling it. The only problem was the docking clamps. There was a biometric pad on the control panel which would unlock the clamps and initiate the launch sequence. The androids couldn't use it, and even if they could it was unlikely they would follow her instructions.

"Who are you?" someone behind her demanded, panting heavily as he spoke.

Jezebel turned around, trying not to look guilty.

"Don't you know about the fire?" the technician asked, his cheeks red and his breath short, "you're supposed to evacuate until the emergency is over."

"Evacuate to where?" Jezebel asked, noticing a hefty tool lying to one side.

"Just come with me and I'll show you," the technician replied in exasperation.

As he turned around, Jezebel picked up the tool and swung it as hard as she could. The improvised weapon was a lot heavier than it looked, and she ended up hitting him in the back of his knees. The man yelled in surprise as his legs were knocked out from under him. She swung again and hit him in the gut, knocking the air out of his lungs.

The androids didn't react at all to a man being assaulted right in front of them. Jezebel dropped the tool and grabbed the man's wrist, forcing his hand onto the biometric pad.

The red light flashed green and a klaxon sounded. Jezebel scrambled to get to the still-open shuttle door, squeezing inside just before it closed. The hatch shut with a clang and a hissing sound as the interior was repressurised. The docking clamps relaxed their grip on the shuttlecraft, leaving it to hover under its own power.

The interior was cramped and she had to duck to enter the cockpit. The launch sequence was automated, all she had to do was confirm the selections on the control panel and strap in. The pilot's HUD showed her the previous flightpath from orbit – that would do.

Jezebel strapped herself in as the display prompted her to confirm that she wanted to take off. She extended her arm, her hand trembling as she worried suddenly about what could go wrong – then she pressed the button.

The launch sequence began and the shuttle edged out of the docking cradle, turning around in the air until it was facing the hangar entrance.

As the multi-tonne blast door inched open, the sunlight shone through, its intensity mitigated by the filtering in the shuttle's cockpit window. She could see the jungle spread out below, carpeting the landscape around the foot of the mountain. The sky above was clear and cloudless, so hopefully it would be a smooth flight.

A countdown appeared on the screen. Orange lights flashed around the edge of the open blast door, and maintenance androids scurried to safety.

"Sorry Alex," Jezebel said, feeling a pang of genuine regret as the engines ignited.

* * *

The research chamber was a riot of activity as scientists and technicians scrambled to secure the equipment. They had no idea what was going on, only that there was an emergency of some kind and that everything had to be locked down until further notice.

There was so much noise in the lab that few people noticed the door open. An imposing figure carrying a modified assault weapon and dressed in dark combat fatigues and a combat mask entered the chamber. He closed the door and locked it behind him.

Then he opened fire.

The rattling drumbeat of automatic gunfire was followed by screams as people saw a dozen of their colleagues mowed down in an instant. Bullets punched through flesh and ricocheted off walls. Bodies piled up as a mass of terrified people made a mad dash for the exit at the far end.

The infiltrator continued firing without missing a target, directing each burst with lethal precision into the fleeing mass. The central column proved to be a lifesaving obstacle, allowing the survivors to pile through the far door and escape. The infiltrator continued firing until the last person had slammed the door shut behind them.

The floor was covered in corpses. Men and women dressed in lab overalls spattered with their own and each other's blood. The infiltrator surveyed the carnage without feeling, the trio of green optical sensors on his helmet coolly scanning for survivors.

Several bodies stirred, injured by not quite dead. Several shots shattered the eerie silence as the infiltrator finished the job.

Stepping over the bodies, the infiltrator made his way to the opposite door. It was locked from the other side, so he placed his hand on the security pad. After a moment, the light flashed green and he opened the door, advancing down the corridor.

The next laboratory was a long, wide space with a firing range and fighting pens on the left and robotic equipment booths on the right. The infiltrator saw people at the far end, including survivors from earlier, and he raised his weapon and fired.

They screamed and scattered, tripping over bodies and fleeing for cover as the infiltrator fired with deadly accuracy. Someone took cover behind a control panel and slammed their hand against the release button.

The booths along the right wall unlocked. Each one contained a cybernetically modified alien, its body semi-armoured and its green skin covered with faintly glowing circuitry. One by one they awoke and were freed from their restraints. They appeared groggy and disoriented, struggling to get their bearings.

The infiltrator decided that the aliens were a more immediate threat and turned his fire on them. One of them staggered back as the rounds struck its armour, the sound and force of the shots snapping it out of its dazed state. The rest of the creatures snapped to attention as well, focusing their fiery gazes on the infiltrator.

They let out a discordant squeal and charged, bounding forward on sinewy limbs. The infiltrator opened fire again, blowing the head off of one and hitting others, but there were too many and they moved too quickly. The aliens closed the distance and bowled him to the ground, knocking his gun out of his hands.

They screamed and raged and slashed at him with metal-coated claws. Although they failed to damage his armour, his combat overalls were shredded. He kicked at the aliens, hitting one in the gut before lashing out with a gauntleted punch, the knuckles becoming electrically active as he clenched his fist.

The punch connected with the jaw of another alien, delivering a concentrated spike of energy and artificial gravity to the jaw-bone. The blow cracked the creature's jaw, and broke its neck, sending it flying across the room like a ragdoll.

Its comrades continued thrashing and slashing, squealing at the top of their high-pitched vocal cords as they attacked. The infiltrator fought back without making a sound, his shock-fists connecting with the jaws and ribcages of his attackers, breaking bones and pulping internal organs. After a vicious struggle he managed to fight his way out.

In a split-second reprieve, the infiltrator drew a sidearm from his thigh holster and fired. The bang of each gunshot echoed down the hallway, each shot punching through the skull of a target or the unprotected gaps in their armour. He discharged each shot faster than any Human could have done, killing or maiming each of his targets in short order.

Before long the aliens lay dead, their bright crimson blood spreading and congealing on the floor. Their flaming eyes stared vacantly up at the ceiling, and their limbs twitched as their nervous systems caught up with the fact of death.

Holstering his sidearm, the infiltrator retrieved his primary weapon and continued on. When he reached the other side of the test range, he found that the survivors had used the distraction to escape. The door had been sealed and the electronic lock had been deactivated, making it impossible to open.

The intercom was still functioning.

* * *

After retrieving some equipment, Aetherea returned to Sheraton Biopharma through a delivery entrance instead of via skytaxi. The 2nd Prime Law prohibited unauthorised contact with alien species; possession of sentient aliens, even as prisoners, most definitely counted as 'unauthorised contact'.

Byron Sade would never surrender to the authorities. For him, facing decades in prison and the end of his business empire – not to mention his professional and social reputation – would be worse than death. To have a chance of capturing him, the groundwork for the raid had to be prepared in advance.

Aetherea moved through the facility with ease. She was using her stealth field to mask her presence, but hiding in the shadows was as natural to her as walking.

The facility was deserted. The working day was coming to an end, so the building should be full of people preparing to head home; but there was no one around. Not only that, but the lights were off and the equipment had been shut down.

Aetherea came to the cargo processing chamber, a wide open space several storeys tall that had been completely cleared out. It was as dark and deserted here as everywhere else in the building. Something wasn't right.

The lights flashed on suddenly, illuminating the empty chamber like a sports stadium. Her stealth field was still functioning but she raced for cover anyway.

Something whizzed out of the darkness and struck her in the back. The projectile ensnared her limbs, causing her to topple over. She struggled furiously against the restraints, but her superhuman strength wasn't enough. She couldn't reach her equipment even as her stealth field flickered and failed.

Footsteps echoed through the chamber as someone approached. Rolling over, Aetherea saw a pair of armed androids flanking a man in combat boots and what looked like a pilot's bodysuit walking towards her.

"Snooping around private property is illegal," said Byron Sade.

"So you finally caught me," Aetherea hissed, "congratulations, now let me go."

"Why?" he asked, crouching down to her level, "So you can sabotage this building's security and let the DNI arrest me?"

"Why would I assist the DNI in arresting one of the Network's most valuable assets?" she demanded, doubting whether she could lie her way out of this.

"Because you work with the DNI," Byron Sade replied, "not this so-called Network, who evidently can't find their own face in the dark when it comes to espionage."

"What are you talking about? I *am* with the Network!" Aetherea insisted, "Now let me out of these fucking restraints!"

Byron Sade pulled a device out of his pocket and knelt down beside Aetherea. He held her head still with his free hand while rolling the device over her eyelids. She felt an itchy tingling sensation on her eyes which made her tear up.

"What lovely eyes you have, 'A'," Byron Sade said menacingly, "they glow blue just like the man who tried to kill me had eyes that glowed green."

Aetherea had nothing more to say.

"It seems your flow of lies has run dry," he said with satisfaction.

"If I were with the DNI then your illegal experiments would have been exposed and the authorities would be raiding your labs now," Aetherea said coolly.

"Why do you think I sent everyone home early?" Byron Sade pointed out, "I can't guess what the DNI will do to me once they capture me, but I can guess that they're on their way. So I may as well prepare to go down on my own terms."

"And what would that entail?" she asked.

Byron Sade glared into her shimmering sapphire eyes.

"I'm going to fuck you," he said with a sadistic sneer, "and then I'm going to kill you."

* * *

He never took the same route twice. If he had, he would have been caught by now. This time, he rode one of the lower level mag-trains to a nearby station, then made his way through the service tunnels. It added an hour to his journey, but he made it back to the Thorn family's apartment building without detection.

There was no one around, but plenty of security cameras. His biometrics – the simulated biometrics created by the masking device – would be logged a dozen times before he reached the Thorn family's front door.

Whether the system would recognise the disguise was unknowable, but if Byron Sade had been interacting with a DNI agent, then everything was in jeopardy. However, he couldn't just disappear. Everything was still riding on him.

He consulted his wrist-top. The screen showed a team of people in uniform standing outside the Thorn family's apartment.

He turned on his heel and disappeared down another maintenance tunnel. This didn't mean he had been exposed, but he couldn't go through with the mission. However much it would disappoint the master, he wouldn't be of any use if he were captured.

He paced swiftly down the tunnel, glancing periodically at his wrist-top. He could see the feeds from each nearby camera, and he avoided places where he might run into people. He adjusted his masking device again just to be sure, shifting disguise as he emerged into a corridor, heading towards a public terrace.

He glanced over his shoulder and saw another team of operatives waiting at the far end of the corridor behind him. There was nobody on the camera feed and yet there they were. The DNI must be manipulating the camera feeds. That would only happen if they had discovered his backdoor into the system.

He deactivated the connection and glanced over his shoulder again. The operatives had seen him and were following him.

He pulled something out of his belt, twisted the knob until it clicked and tossed it in their direction. An explosion of light and sound hit them, knocking them off their feet as their quarry broke into a run, sprinting out onto the public terrace.

The terrace was empty and the night sky was beautiful, but there was no time to admire the view. He reach behind him and grabbed a cord, yanking it hard as he sprinted towards the edge. A set of wings extended from inside the satchel on his back and the wingtip engines fired, launching him into the sky and over the top of the safety barrier.

He felt his innards shift inside him, pulled by inertia as the sudden rush of cool air blasted against his face. The jetpack was controlled wirelessly via his wrist-top, and he used the controls to direct his path down towards the Undercity.

He never saw the stealth drone swoop down on him, but he felt the capture cord latch on and shoot a spike of electricity into his leg. His body caught fire as his nerves were paralysed and the jetpack's engines sputtered and died.

The cord began to wrap itself around his body like a coiling serpent, pulling him inside the body of the stealth drone as it soared back into the sky.

* * *

The sky was darkening. The weather instruments were warning Jezebel that a storm was closing in, so she activated the autopilot. She knew nothing about flying, and didn't want to die because of a piloting error.

The cameras were still functioning. She could see the jungle stretching out in every direction, the view punctured only by the great stone city. The landscape below was receding into the distance as the shuttle picked up speed and turned its nose skyward.

The shuttle's conventional engines weren't powerful enough to propel it into space, so the booster rockets fired. The force of their ignition forced Jezebel back into her seat and she squeezed her safety restraints.

The artificial gravity disguised the shuttle's upward pitching motion, but Jezebel still felt an uncomfortable sense of vertigo. On the video screen, the stone city shrank into an ever-expanding ocean of lush green while the clouds above dissipated into clear blue skies.

The deep blue sky darkened as the shuttle cleared the lower reaches of the atmosphere and accelerated through the stratosphere. Little pinpoints of light became visible. At one end of the display, the local star appeared as a greatly subdued orb, its blinding light tempered by the filter in the cockpit screen.

The booster rockets were still burning through their remaining fuel. It would be enough to get her into orbit towards the waiting fleet and not much more.

What if there was no fleet waiting?

That horrible afterthought struck Jezebel just as the booster rockets' fuel gauge dipped below 30%. There was no doubt that someone had sent the infiltrator to sabotage the Network's facility, but there was no reason to assume that the Navy was following close behind.

Even without booster rockets, the shuttle was still spaceworthy. She could just wait in orbit for her hoped-for saviours to turn up. If they didn't, she could turn the shuttle around and return to the facility – where the infiltrator was probably wreaking havoc.

Those were her options, and neither was very appealing. The infiltrator had spared her, but Alexander might not. At a minimum, she would have a lot of explaining to do if she returned. On the other hand, waiting around in orbit wasn't an ideal plan either.

As the shuttlecraft surged through the thermosphere, the sensors flagged another ship already waiting in orbit. It was a Q-courier, used for ultra-fast transportation of cargo between star systems. No doubt this was the ship that had brought the infiltrator here in the first place.

As the shuttle cleared the atmosphere, the comm. device squawked.

"*Transport shuttle, this is the Q-courier's pilot,*" said a man's voice from the speakers, "*we see you incoming, preparing for supply drop.*"

Jezebel froze with indecision.

"*Transport shuttle,*" the Q-courier pilot hailed again, "*are you receiving?*"

Jezebel reached for the comm. headset and put it on.

"Uh, affirmative," she replied hesitantly, "we should be making contact in two minutes."

"*Don't release the catch too soon, ok?*" the pilot said jokingly, "*otherwise our food and fuel will go floating off into orbit.*"

"Don't worry, I won't," Jezebel answered more confidently.

"*You know, you're the first girl I've spoken to who does these sorts of runs,*" the pilot added, "*are you new to this job?*"

"Is that really important right now?" Jezebel asked icily.

"*Uh, no,*" the pilot replied awkwardly, "*I was just asking.*"

Jezebel hadn't thought to make up a cover story for herself, another oversight in her hastily prepared escape plan. More importantly, it would make it difficult to convince the Q-courier crew to take her away.

The instruments squawked again, this time flashing a long-range sensor warning.

"*Transport shuttle!*" the Q-courier pilot shouted over the comm., "*There's a whole fleet bearing down on us! Get out of here!*"

"What fleet?! Where?!" Jezebel yelled back.

"*They're bearing down on us!*" the pilot shouted back, "*they must have stealth tech, we didn't seem them sneak up on us until just now! Turn around and get planet-side, now!*"

It was too late. On the display, Jezebel saw half a dozen vessels approaching. Their designs were long and winged, like finely crafted spearheads, and their hulls were as black as the void. She could only make them out because the screen highlighted their outlines.

The bulbous Q-courier was a sitting duck. It was only fast at faster-than-light speeds, ironically rendering it helpless as the flotilla manoeuvred into position.

Jezebel, meanwhile, still had a fast-moving shuttle, and could get away if she turned around in time. On the other hand, this was the rescue party she had been hoping for. Was she really going to turn tail and flee towards an uncertain fate below?

The newly arrived fleet made the decision for her. As soon as it was in range, one of the vessels locked on with a gravity well generator, and the shuttle's engines struggled and failed to resist the gravitic force.

The warship bore down like a space monster reeling in a minnow. A shuttle bay door opened on its underside and the shuttle was pulled inexorably towards it. Jezebel could do nothing but sit and await her fate.

* * *

The voice on the other end of the intercom was hushed and out of breath.

"*I think he's gone*," said a woman, unable to keep the panic out of her voice, "*but you have to let me in before he comes back.*"

The other survivors of the massacre were huddled behind the door, quietly debating whether to risk their own lives to save that of a colleague.

"As soon as we open the door the shooter could come back!" someone hissed.

"But she could be killed out there!"

"She's as good as dead, anyway! Do you want us to join her?"

"*Guys, you have to let me inside, now!*" their stranded colleague pleaded, "*He could come back at any moment!*"

They were all scared out of their wits. First the mystery explosion in the hangar, then the boss apparently disappearing, and now some commando on a murderous rampage.

"Did you see where he went?" someone asked through the intercom.

"*He looked around for a bit then went back the way he came, I think,*" the woman replied, barely more calmly than before.

"You 'think'?" someone else demanded.

"*I was hiding!*" she hissed, "*If I'd stuck my head out, he would've seen me!*"

There was silence on both ends as the survivors agonised over what to do.

"Let's vote," someone suggested, "I say we let her in."

Six other trembling hands were raised in favour of opening the door while the remaining five shook their heads in objection.

"Seven to five in favour," said the vote-taker waveringly, "the ayes have it."

With great trepidation, he entered the access code and opened the door.

A single bullet killed him as the infiltrator barged through. Screaming, scrambling, and gunshots briefly filled the corridor as he coldly executed the remaining survivors.

He left one alive. The man had been shot in the leg and he wheezed with pain as he tried to crawl to safety, leaving a trail of blood smeared on the floor. The infiltrator caught up to him and turned him over to look him in his frightened eyes.

"*Where is Alexander Thorn?*" he demanded in an electronically filtered voice.

"I don't know," the man replied, bewildered by the question.

"*Where is Mortimer Shelton?*" the infiltrator demanded.

"…Who?" the dying man asked.

The infiltrator stared at him, then fired a single round through his skull.

* * *

Oblivion. That was where he was. The darkness was so complete it was as if creation itself had been wiped out. He dimly remembered being tied down and injected with something, then the darkness had claimed him. The darkness had claimed everything. There was nothing left except the deafening echo of his own thoughts.

It was no longer dark. A tiny sliver of light was spread thin across his vision, just enough to see something of the room. There were shapes moving around him, busy with tasks he couldn't fathom, speaking to one another in voices barely above a whisper. Somehow he knew they were talking about him.

He was lying on a medical table, his wrists and ankles secured by elastic restraints. His limbs and torso were also bound to the table, holding him in place like a primeval sacrifice.

Someone up in the shadows was watching him. He could see the contours of a face, a woman's face, but all he could really make out were her eyes.

One eye, to be exact. A single crimson bionic eye regarding him without emotion. Her face was barely visible in the gloom, but the unblinking stare she was giving him was terrifying all the same. It terrified everyone – like the all-seeing eye of some omniscient deity peering into their innermost thoughts – but it terrified him most of all.

Something changed. The level of activity in the room increased as people finalised their preparations. He tried to move but couldn't, the restraints bound his body and limbs to the medical table as shadowy robotic arms descended.

Panic took over but he was powerless to move as the machines began to work on him. The stinging pain of the procedures overwhelmed his mind and what little light there was began to fade. The whispering shadows were fading away, observing in silence.

He was helpless and afraid. He had volunteered for this. He knew what the procedures were, and he had volunteered anyway just like everyone else, but he was afraid all the same. The only thing he could still see was the single red eye watching him.

* * *

Now he was having dinner. He was sitting at a table with a plate in front of him, scraped clean of food. His vision was blurred by a dream-like haze. The pain and fear of the procedures was gone, even though the memory wasn't.

He wasn't alone. Across from him were two other people, a young woman with dark hair and blond highlights. Her hair was hanging loose over her shoulders, an informal contrast to her usual cornbraid. She was doting on a toddler with jet black hair and glowing emerald eyes. He had a happy grin on his face as his mother fed him.

The little boy looked like a smaller and younger version of himself. Not only his dark hair and green eyes but the shape of his face were the mirror of his own. Hints of his mother's features were there, but it was mainly his own face that he saw, a happier and more carefree version of himself.

He wasn't involved. It was like watching an animation of a mother and son, the mother of his son, in which he was a passive observer. He knew who they were and what they meant to him, and yet somehow they seemed like strangers.

The boy knocked a cup over, spilling the contents across the table. He sat there looking mischievous as his mother scolded him and a domestic android appeared to clean up the spill.

The spilt drink caused a shift in his psyche. He felt an inexplicable fury bubble up from the depths of his mind, drowning all other thoughts. He had never felt this kind of rage before, and yet it quickly overwhelmed him.

The woman and child looked up at him and their faces changed; the mother's scolding and the boy's mischievous look melted away. They were watching him with fear.

He stood up from the table as his wife grabbed their son and fled the room. That enraged him even more and he tried to follow them. The domestic android sensed the threat and tried to block his way, but he grabbed it and snapped its cortical cord. He let the machine's limp body fall to the ground before storming out of the room.

Reality was hazy here. It had been hazy in the dining room, but it was hazier still in the hallway. The darkness was encroaching on the corners of his vision, obscuring his surroundings as if it were consciously attempting to thwart him. The door to the kitchen had vanished, and his prey was hidden from sight.

But not from hearing. His vision was fuzzy and ethereal, but he could still hear everything, including the sound of the bedroom door slamming shut.

His mind was still clouded with an overpowering urge to hunt down the source of his rage. He bared his teeth like a bloodthirsty predator and marched down the hallway, turning the corner to the master bedroom. A heavy blunt weapon appeared in his hands as he smashed the handle clean off the door and forced his way inside.

Seven flashes lit up the room and seven bangs deafened him. Seven bolts of pain struck him in the chest, stopping him in his tracks. The silhouette of a woman crouched on the floor was burned into his vision along with the sight of the boy cowering in her arms.

He couldn't move. The seven bolts of pain were still lodged in his chest and a wetness was spreading from each point. The cowering figure who had shot him slowly faded from sight as he keeled over backwards into the abyss.

* * *

Now he was trapped in a box. He couldn't see, he couldn't hear, and he couldn't breathe without the hose down his throat blasting air into his lungs.

Somewhere in the depths of his mind, a tiny voice screamed that this was nothing more than a dream. Except it wasn't a dream, it was a memory. Each time his chest moved he felt seven rivets of pain as the wounds strained against his breathing. He remembered being shot, and he remembered what he would have done if he hadn't been shot.

This was his punishment. He had died and was on his way to hell, to the place where those who murdered their own families went. This was his prison and his tomb.

The restraints tightened every time his chest moved too much, making him panic even more as he struggled to breathe. The respiration tube kept him breathing normally, but he still felt like he was choking. The panic of suffocating in a dark little box overrode the pain and he struggled against the python-like cords with all his strength.

It was no use. He couldn't break free. The cords were so strong that they dug into his flesh. His gag reflex was suppressed by the tube down his throat, and his head was becoming fuzzy as the exhaustion of fighting to be free began to take its toll.

His struggles became weaker, and the reaction of his restraints became commensurately weaker. Finally, his strength gave out, and he lay in the dark awaiting his fate. He could barely move without being punished for the slightest flinch. He was going to die in here.

The casket opened, flooding his prison with light. The silence was broken by voices shouting over his head, shouting about him. Several sets of hands reached in, scanning and prodding him. Another hand reached over and pulled a lever.

The whirling sound of mechanical strings winding back into their slots reached his ears and he felt exquisite relief as the constraining force against his body disappeared. He was free, but too weak to act on his freedom.

He couldn't see his captors' faces clearly, and as they struggled to lift him, he saw that his surroundings were fuzzy and illusory. It was enough to remind him that this wasn't real. It was a dream. A nightmare rooted in memory.

"Wake up!" someone shouted at him.

The command snapped him out of his defeatist stupor, and he obeyed by grabbing the man by the throat and squeezing.

* * *

Where was he now?

Before him was a valley of stone filled by a sea of sickly green speckled with orange. The sky was doom-laden, smothering the rays of the sun with dark clouds. The cold rain drenched the ground, pouring down in an unrelenting storm, the freezing droplets stinging his cheeks. This place certainly wasn't hell.

The view before him became clearer. The valley of stone was an immense gathering place made of walls built out of stone blocks. The sea of sickly green was an army of green-skinned amphibian aliens from the jungle world.

They had gathered in the valley of stone to see him. They were staring up at him with unblinking eyes that blazed the colour of lava. He could see that they were wearing advanced metallic armour and clutching fearsome firearms in their claws, a far cry from their usual loincloths and stone clubs.

It really was an army. His army. A million or more obedient warriors at his command. This planet was his fortress. His staging ground. A breeding ground for millions more alien warriors to replace those that were slain. They were all looking up to him as their leader. Their general. Their god. Ready to kill and die for him and him alone.

Looking up at the stormy sky, he saw a dozen dark shapes as large as the clouds. Each shape was a warship hovering low in the atmosphere, casting a great shadow over the landscape. They were ready to carry his soldiers across the galaxy, waging war across the stars and bending system after system to his will.

He wasn't the only one standing there. He was flanked by two other people watching the great army below. He recognised his wife Jezebel standing to his left, dressed in her snow-white business suit and her black and blonde cornbraid. She stood beside him like his queen, ready to reign over the space his armies would conquer.

To his right stood his mirror-image. It was his son, a younger version of himself with a well-built musculature, jet black hair, and shining green eyes. He was dressed in full-plate armour with a weapon clutched in his gauntleted hands. Gabriel looked as fearsome as the alien creatures at his command.

Flanked by his family, he turned back to the mighty army arrayed before him, standing to attention and looking up to him.

To him or at him? They were staring up in his direction, their unblinking orange eyes focused on the would-be warlord who had turned them into an army of mindless slaves. They were watching him, just standing there and watching him, backs straight and rifles poised. All of a sudden it was an eerie thing to behold.

"Congratulations, Alexander," said a woman's voice.

He froze on his pedestal. That wasn't Jezebel's voice, but he knew that voice all too well. It was a cool voice devoid of emotion and hearing it again made him tremble.

He turned to his left and saw another woman standing where Jezebel had been just a moment ago. She had jet black hair tied back in a bun and a pale face as devoid of emotion as her voice. She was watching him with a hazel-coloured left eye and a bionic right eye with a laser-red iris, her heterochromatic gaze boring unblinkingly into his soul.

"You have an army of mindless berserkers at your command," Red-eye said coldly, "just like the mindless berserker who ran away after trying to kill his own family."

Her words chilled him to the core. He turned back to the sea of alien soldiers arrayed in the valley of stone. They weren't aliens anymore, their green skin was now a light pink hue and their claws had become hands with four fingers and an opposable thumb. Their eyes were no longer blazing orange, but shimmering green.

Gabriel. In the face of every slave-soldier in the valley was the face of his own son, armed and armoured, awaiting command.

The faces all bore his likeness, but the expressions were blank and aimed squarely at him. Not one of them blinked as they looked up at their father and commander.

"I replaced you," said Gabriel's voice, still standing to his right.

A peal of thunder rumbled through the sky and the downpour redoubled in strength, creating a haze that obscured the surroundings. The rain had acquired a sticky consistency, and he held up his hand to catch some of it.

It was blood.

The blood rain poured down in a torrential flood, and soon it formed a layer deep enough to cover the slave-soldiers' feet. The valley began to fill up like a basin, the sanguinary precipitation drowning the landscape as lightning lashed through the clouds.

The army just stood there, not panicking or moving as the blood rain rose above their ankles towards their knees. They stared impassively at him, unflinching as the rain rose around them, threatening to drown them in blood.

The warships hovering just under the clouds didn't move either. They hovered in place while the blood rain continued to pour even as the lightning grew more violent, striking some of the warships. Fires broke out aboard the mighty vessels and their interiors lit up as they began to sink towards the ground.

The ground began to tremble. The whole landscape was shaking violently. Rocks came loose and tumbled down the slopes of the valley into the ranks of the statue-like army. Whole squads were knocked over or crushed, and yet still the army continued to stand to attention.

Everything was crumbling and burning around him. The storms were tearing apart the skies, the ground was in the throes of a violent earthquake, and the great warships were on fire, tumbling to their doom.

All the while, the torrential blood rain continued to pour, soaking his clothes and skin. The blood flood continued to rise past the knees of the army and up to their waists, then up to their chests. They did absolutely nothing except stand and stare, indifferent to the end of the world around them.

A violent crack tore through the air, but not from the sky. The cracking sound had come from below as an enormous fissure split the valley of stone down the middle. The bloody floodwaters poured down into the abyss and the army tumbled down with it, unmoving and unblinking to the end.

"We are building something great," said an amalgamation of Red-eye's and Gabriel's voices, "and all you want to do is destroy."

The burning warships struck the ground, shaking the earth with the force of their crash-landings and spraying fire everywhere. The whole nightmarish scene was disintegrating, torn apart by the destruction all around, and all he could do was watch.

"YOUR FURY WOULD DESTROY IT ALL!" Red-eye's voice rumbled up from the abyss and down from the clouds, "BUT MY FURY WILL DESTROY YOU FIRST!"

The stone pedestal on which he had been standing gave way and his stomach lurched as gravity disappeared. The landscape crumbled and dissolved into oblivion as the valley of stone collapsed in on itself and the skies above dissipated.

* * *

It was just him now.

The darkness enveloped him completely. He put his hands up in front of his face and saw nothing. He tried to flail about, but there was nothing to flail against, no substance to resist the swinging of his arms or the kicking of his legs. There wasn't even the feeling of gravity pulling him towards some external body.

The pure nihilism of this nightmare was maddening. There was nothing. No light or sound. No up or down. No push or pull. There was nothing but him in this endless abyss. He was the only thing that existed here.

Where was he? How had he ended up here? Why was he here? He didn't know, but he remembered everything else: the surgical procedures he had volunteered for. The family dinner and the seven gunshots. The suffocating prison and his escape. The great army he would have led and the apocalyptic ending they had met. He remembered it all.

That was all he had left; his memories and his mind. Everything else had vanished.

Not quite everything. The blackness was so total that at first he thought it was a trick of his mind; but he saw something in the dark. Far in the distance – insofar as such a concept applied – he saw a light.

Two lights. They were tiny and faint, but there were definitely two lights, looming large like the headlamps of an oncoming vessel, speeding towards him through the empty void.

He was frozen. He couldn't get out of the way. There was no way to move about in the darkness and nowhere to move to. He could do nothing as the lights suddenly arrived and loomed over him like a pair of eyes.

They *were* eyes. How had he not seen that? One eye was a shimmering organic green and the other an infernal bionic red. Only now was the colour clear, and even then he could only see the irises; the organic ridges and grooves in the one and the delicate network of circuitry in the other.

The eyes watched him without blinking, glaring down like a god regarding a bacillus, and he felt himself shrivel beneath their gaze.

Then oblivion devoured him.

THE ESCAPE

O NCE the shuttle had been pulled inside, it was held in position by docking clamps as the docking bay doors sealed up again. Then the shuttle was moved to the floor of the bay for disembarkation. Once the bay was repressurised, a squad of marines entered the bay and approached with weapons trained on the captured shuttle.

A scanner drone swept the craft from nose to engines, rendering its chassis and interior as a holographic schematic. The squad could see the contents of the supply crates attached to its underbelly as well as the outline of the pilot sitting in the cockpit.

The squad leader initiated a comm. link with the shuttle.

"Shuttle pilot," he ordered, "power down the craft."

There was no verbal reply, but the heat blooms in the schematic flickered and shifted before dying down as the shuttle's systems were deactivated.

"Exit the shuttle with your palms displayed," the squad leader ordered.

From outside, nothing seemed to happen, but on the holographic image, the thermal signature representing the pilot slowly stood up. The figure made its way from the cockpit to the hatch which unlocked and popped open with a hiss of depressurisation.

Out of the open hatch stepped a woman wearing a snow-white business suit with her black and blonde hair styled into a cornbraid. She was very well dressed for a shuttle pilot. Her palms were displayed as ordered, but she didn't look all that frightened; the look on her face was more like relief.

"Identify yourself!" the squad leader ordered.

"Uh…Jez…Jezebel," the woman said nervously, "Jezebel Thorn."

"Get on your knees with your hands on your head," the squad leader commanded.

Jezebel did as she was told while two marines moved in from either side. One marine kept his weapon trained on her as she knelt down on the floor while the other pulled out a device and flash-scanned her eyes.

Sure enough, the name and face of Jezebel Thorn appeared on the screen, adding that she was a convicted felon.

"I can explain everything," Jezebel said.

"I'm sure that'll be a fascinating story," one of the marines remarked wryly, clamping a set of restraints around her wrists and forcing her to her feet.

"He's insane," Jezebel tried to add, her voice trembling.

"Save it for questioning," another marine said sharply, "you're in the custody of the Navy now, and as far as we're concerned you're a fugitive from justice."

* * *

The marines led Jezebel through the bowels of the ship to an interrogation room; a ten-by-ten cube with a single door and a security camera in each corner of the ceiling. They sat her down and cuffed her to the table before leaving.

The last time she had been interrogated, it had been in a comparatively comfortable ACS questioning room. The setting this time was a lot more foreboding, and she couldn't count on the niceties of due process.

In fact, she couldn't really count on anything except her sob story about being a helpless prisoner in the clutches of a madman.

At best, they would send her straight back to prison. At worst, she could be sent to a DNI dungeon.

Jezebel had no idea how much time had passed when the door finally opened. A female marine entered wearing stripped-down armour and carrying a data slate. She had a military buzz-cut and a sullen, sunlight-deprived face.

"Jezebel Thorn," said the interrogator.

"That's me," Jezebel replied politely.

"You were convicted of one count of blackmail, one count of corporate espionage, and one count of murder, for which you were sentenced to a total of 30 years' incarceration at the Bentham Penitentiary Facility on Asgard," she said before looking up at Jezebel with cold grey eyes, "and yet, here you are."

The interrogator spoke with the same textbook-standard pronunciation and cadence that Gabriel and Alexander used, but her speech was still inflected with a slight accent. Humanity had settled more than a hundred worlds, so she could be from anywhere.

"I was broken out," Jezebel explained, "without my prior knowledge of the breakout, and then brought to this world."

"Who arranged your escape?" the interrogator demanded.

"I didn't escape, I was broken out," Jezebel replied, "kidnapped, effectively."

"Fine," said the interrogator, "who 'kidnapped' you from prison?"

"They call themselves the 'Network'," Jezebel answered matter-of-factly, "and their leader is a man called Alexander Thorn."

"Any relation?" the interrogator asked with a raised eyebrow.

"He's my husband," Jezebel responded, "although, he was declared legally dead after his disappearance. That was about 45 years ago."

"But he's back from the dead?" the interrogator asked with narrowed eyes, "Where was he hiding all this time and why did he reappear now?"

"I don't know," Jezebel admitted.

"Have you seen him recently?"

"Yes," said Jezebel.

"Where is he now?"

Jezebel slowed down the pace of her replies and started breathing deeply.

"If you think that withholding his location will prevent us from finding him anyway, you're deluding yourself," the interrogator informed her coldly.

"He…he'll…have me killed if…if I tell you," Jezebel said waveringly.

"What do you mean?" the interrogator demanded, unconvinced by the performance.

"The shuttle…the one I flew to get here," Jezebel answered, "I stole it so I could escape. He would never have let me go otherwise."

"So he's down on the planet?" the interrogator asked.

"Yes," Jezebel replied, "along with a private army."

"What kind of 'private army'?" the interrogator asked.

"He has a whole facility," Jezebel explained, her voice trembling, "under a mountain. There are hundreds of people down there working for him."

"What was your role in all this?" the interrogator demanded accusingly.

"I didn't have a role!" Jezebel protested.

"So he just kept you around as a pet?" the interrogator suggested with derisive sarcasm.

"…Basically…" Jezebel said, averting her gaze, "among other things…"

"So what's the nature of this private army?" the interrogator asked.

"The planet has a native population of aliens living at the foot of the mountain," Jezebel explained, "he's been experimenting on them for years."

"You say he's been engaged in xenotechnology experimentation?"

"Xenotechnology, no," Jezebel corrected, "the aliens are barely past the stone age. He's been experimenting on the aliens themselves."

The interrogator glared at Jezebel suspiciously.

"He's been brainwashing them and surgically modifying them," Jezebel elaborated, "that's how he created his army."

"Interesting," said the interrogator with more scepticism than interest.

"He's also got a network of operatives across multiple worlds," Jezebel continued, "and he's been using this network to smuggle—"

"I'm more interested in how you would know any of this," the interrogator interrupted.

Jezebel knew she would be asked that question, and she didn't have a good answer.

"Apart from the fact that I was kidnapped and held there under house arrest, I don't know how to prove that to you," she answered more-or-less honestly.

"Then how did you get away without being noticed?" the interrogator asked.

"There was an explosion in the hangar," Jezebel explained, "I snuck away during the chaos and hijacked a shuttle, the same one you caught me in."

"How did you get past the air defences?"

"I don't think the base has any air defences," Jezebel replied, "besides, the base was in chaos after the explosion. I don't think anyone realised they were under attack."

"What makes you think the base was attacked?" the interrogator asked.

"What else are you doing here in orbit?" Jezebel pointed out impatiently, her facade slipping, "There's no other reason for the DNI to be here. One of your operatives is already down in the facility, and he probably caused the explosion."

The interrogator looked at her for a moment. Then she got up and took the data slate with her as she headed for the exit.

"Is that it?" Jezebel demanded.

"For now, yes," the interrogator replied, "we'll discuss your fate later."

* * *

Alexander plunged out of the darkness and back into the waking world, gasping for air. The restraints snapped back, pinning him to the bed before he could hurt himself as Mortimer came running over. His spasmodic awakening ended as soon as it began, and he lay there in silence, catching his breath and trying not to move.

Mortimer deactivated the medical restraints.

"Try sitting up," he instructed.

Alexander sat up and found it much easier than expected. His head was completely clear and his muscles moved freely without the pain of overexertion; the exact opposite of the aftermath of a rage episode.

"How do you feel?" Mortimer asked nervously.

"Excellent," Alexander reported nonchalantly.

"Any disorientation? Memory gaps? Fuzzy vision?"

"Nothing," Alexander responded.

"Did you have any sort of dream?"

"You could say that," Alexander said wryly, "flashbacks about how I ended up here."

"Anything else?"

Alexander paused. He recalled in vivid detail the nightmare about his private alien army arrayed before him, but especially the apocalyptic ending. He wasn't so sure Mortimer should be privy to that part of his subconsciousness.

"No," Alexander replied.

"That's probably for the best," Mortimer said, "a lot happened whilst you were under."

"Like what?" Alexander demanded.

"There was some kind of explosion in the hangar–" Mortimer began to explain.

"What?! When?!" Alexander exclaimed, leaping off the medical bed.

"Shortly after you went under," Mortimer replied, "alarms went off but nobody seemed to know what to do without you around."

Alexander rushed over to the computer terminal and brought himself up to speed.

Despite the emergency and a niggling worry about whether the treatment had actually worked, Mortimer was relieved to see that his patient was still as sharp as ever.

"The explosion wiped out one of the processing chambers," Alexander said through gritted teeth, "the same one where my delivery was sent."

"What delivery?" Mortimer asked.

"Not important right now," Alexander replied, opening an internal comm. link.

"Hangar Control!" he barked, "is anyone receiving?"

There was no response.

"They must have all evacuated," Alexander hissed to himself.

The door intercom chimed, arresting the attention of both men.

"Someone came over earlier asking where you were," Mortimer remembered, "but you were still under so I refused to let him in."

Alexander approached the intercom and spoke into it.

"Identify yourself," he ordered.

"*I'm from the science labs!*" said a panicked voice, "*please let me in!*"

"I told you to identify yourself!" Alexander snapped unsympathetically.

"*I'm one of the researchers!*" the voice pleaded, "*There was a massacre! Someone entered the research labs from outside and killed everyone!*"

"Give me your name and position right now!" Alexander shouted.

Mortimer was stunned by the exchange and the claims the man was making, and he thanked his common sense for not letting the last person in.

The man still hadn't answered Alexander's question.

"Are you going to tell me who you are or not?" he demanded.

There was no reply. Instead, the interface panel began to flicker erratically. Alexander bolted for cover as the lock flashed green and the door slid open.

Mortimer's saw a tall, armoured figure wearing a combat mask with three green optical sensors. He also saw the gun and dived to one side as the barrel was raised.

The bullet missed Mortimer's head, burying itself in the opposite wall. As the infiltrator marched into the room, a metal pipe came swinging out of nowhere and knocked his gun away.

Alexander swung the pipe again, knocking the infiltrator to the ground. He swung again and again, punctuating each blow with a cry of rage. After taking enough blows, the infiltrator stopped moving and Alexander stopped swinging.

"Mortimer!" he shouted, still panting with rage.

Slowly and fearfully, Mortimer emerged from his hiding place. He kept his distance from the infiltrator and approached Alexander.

"Will getting angry hamper the effects of the treatment?" Alexander asked.

"It shouldn't do," Mortimer replied uncertainly.

"You told me the procedure needed 24 hours to work!" Alexander snapped.

"24 hours before the effects manifest fully," Mortimer clarified, "that doesn't mean that the mere act of losing your temper will undo it."

After hearing that, Alexander calmed down somewhat.

"This has come at the worst possible moment," he stated the obvious, "or the best possible moment, from the DNI's perspective."

"You think the DNI are behind this?"

"Who else could it be?" Alexander said rhetorically, crouching down and running his finger under the rim of the infiltrator's helmet, "first the hangar explosion throws everything into disarray, then this guy marches in and starts shooting people."

"We should warn the lab staff," Mortimer suggested.

"No point," said Alexander, "this guy just came from the research wing and he's clearly not one to take prisoners. Which means that everyone between here and the hangar is dead."

Mortimer was taken aback by the seeming callousness of Alexander's statement, but he couldn't argue with his logic. It wasn't callous, it was just truthful.

Alexander found the helmet's release catch and fiddled with it until it opened. Inside was a man's face with light skin and an almost square jaw. The infiltrator's eyes were closed, but his face was all too familiar.

"Sweet Terra!" Mortimer exclaimed, "That's Gabriel!"

Gabriel opened his eyes. They glowed a shimmering emerald green.

Alexander leapt back as Gabriel jumped to his feet. The metal pipe came swinging back, but this time Gabriel caught it and twisted it out of shape before yanking it out of Alexander's hands. Gabriel punched his father in the gut and sent him rolling back across the floor.

Determined to survive, Alexander hit the door's release button. As Gabriel retrieved his gun, Alexander slipped through the open door. Mortimer scrambled for the door as well, but a gunshot rang out followed by a cry of pain as the door sealed shut.

With immense agony, Mortimer rolled over to face his soon-to-be killer. He had been shot in the leg and the blood was pouring out in jets. He looked up as Gabriel towered over him and took aim at his head, staring with his father's glowing green eyes.

There was something strange about his eyes. It was hard to be certain, but the way they reflected the light wasn't quite right.

"*You should have stayed in retirement, Mortimer,*" Gabriel said in Red-eye's voice.

A chill rippled down Mortimer's spine as the infiltrator pulled the trigger.

* * *

Alexander sprinted down the corridor, locking the door behind him to slow his pursuer down. Whatever the procedure had done to him, it certainly hadn't weakened his stamina.

Mentally, he was reeling. After all this time, the DNI had finally tracked him down. The facility had been compromised, many of his followers were dead, and a naval taskforce was probably in orbit right now. Not only was the DNI trying to eliminate him, but they had dispatched his own son to do the job.

Even for Red-eye, that was a cold-blooded personal touch.

Nonetheless, he should have seen it coming. He had recruited a mole within the DNI itself, snatched one of their best ex-scientists from under their noses, and killed dozens of civilians to cover his tracks, and all within miles of the DNI's sector headquarters. Nothing in the cosmos could humiliate the DNI – let alone on its own turf – and get away with it.

And he had set himself up for it. Having broken Jezebel out of prison and deliberately implicated Gabriel, the DNI had connected the dots and used Gabriel as bait to flush him out. It was a classic wooden horse scheme, and he had fallen for it.

Mortimer was dead. That was certain. There was no way their mutual former employer would only come after him and leave a highly accomplished ex-scientist alone with a head full of secrets. No doubt Gabriel was under orders to kill anyone he found. Right now, Alexander was more concerned about not being one of them.

He reached the hangar door and squeezed through, locking it behind him to buy himself time. Then he entered the armoury, running past rows of storage cages filled with undamaged weapons, none of which he was planning to use.

At the end of the hall, he turned a corner into a staging area with a docking frame. Inside the frame was his combat platform, its optical sensor pod staring at the ground.

Alexander took a running jump and leapt onto the frame, climbing up the rungs before flipping himself over the top and into the open cockpit. When his feet hit the pedals, the safety restraints secured his legs and torso, and the hatch sealed shut. The HUD lit up and the optical display flash-scanned his eyes.

"*Identity confirmed*," the combat platform's computer announced in an electronic rendering of his own voice, "*welcome back, Seraph*."

"Likewise," Alexander replied, tapping the backs of his hands against each side.

A pair of haptic interface gloves locked around his hands, giving him full control over the combat platform's movements. The docking frame locks disengaged and the shielding was activated as the maintenance drones scattered.

A figure turned the corner and opened fire, but the bullets veered sharply out of the way as the energy shielding swiped them aside.

"You'll have to do better than that, Gabriel," Alexander sneered.

The infiltrator disappeared around the corner and Alexander stomped after him, the combat platform's footsteps echoing through the chamber. Its legs were synced to his own legs' movements, enabling him to pilot it as if it were his own body.

Alexander flipped a control on the HUD. The pulse cannon was deployed from the cradle mounted on the back, sticking up and out before orienting forwards so that the barrel was pointed over the combat platform's shoulder.

Was he seriously going to kill his own son?

That thought made him falter – briefly. Gabriel clearly had no compunctions about killing him. Furthermore, Red-eye had dispatched Gabriel specifically to kill him. If he was going to survive, he would have to kill Red-eye's assassin.

The combat platform exited the staging area just as the infiltrator reappeared. A contact warning appeared in his HUD, highlighting something attached to the combat platform's leg. He felt the explosion a split second before the display flashed red.

The combat platform barely stumbled. The limpet mine was powerful enough to damage the leg armour, but not the leg itself.

Alexander lashed out with the combat platform's arms and knocked over a pile of crates. The infiltrator was already racing across the floor, diving into cover behind some canisters as Alexander stomped after him. He primed the pulse cannon and fired.

A high powered, bright blue beam erupted from the barrel, instantly superheating the canisters to thousands of degrees and igniting their contents.

The plume of fire dissipated into a cloud of toxic smoke, but the HUD showed a figure highlighted in red running behind a line of containers. Alexander opened fire again, hitting an empty crate which suddenly glowed red hot.

The infiltrator re-emerged with a new weapon and returned fire. The projectile whizzed through the air, arcing towards the combat platform before making contact with its shielding. There was a buzz and a flash as the device reacted with the shielding, creating a feedback loop that overloaded the emitters.

Warning lights blared in the cockpit. Alexander raged at his adversary and fired another beam from the pulse cannon. The beam missed its mark again as the infiltrator dodged out of sight, leaving a superheated scorch mark on the floor where he had just been standing.

He was too fast. The pulse cannon wouldn't be of much use.

The infiltrator reappeared and prepared another shot. Before he could pull the trigger, Alexander activated the combat platform's booster engines.

The one tonne machine jetted towards the infiltrator on a pair of fiery plumes and barrelled into him. The infiltrator managed to grab a handle on the side of the combat platform, but barely held on as Alexander deliberately crashed into a storage cage.

The infiltrator lay limp and unmoving. The cage was badly dented but otherwise held up. The combat platform withstood the impact as well, and the sophisticated motion dampeners meant that Alexander was barely jolted.

Reorienting the controls, Alexander made the combat platform stand up again, using the dented storage cage to steady himself. The infiltrator slid down to the ground, still limp and motionless from the collision. The pulse cannon was primed and ready, and Alexander took aim once again, ready to finish off his assassin.

Then the sensors scanned the infiltrator's body and confusion gave him pause. If the readings were correct, Gabriel's core temperature was in excess of 50 Celsius and focused in irregular clusters throughout his torso.

Was it an android? There was no doubt that the face he had seen under the helmet was Gabriel's face, but that didn't mean it was actually Gabriel under the armour.

The infiltrator stirred as the heat sources began to shift. Alexander squeezed the trigger, hitting him square in the chest.

* * *

His ears were ringing. There was a beeping noise in the background. Several beeping noises. They were alarms, warning him of severe structural damage and critical system failures. Slowly and painfully, Alexander reached up and tapped the still-flickering HUD, coaxing it to respond, but to no avail.

The infiltrator had literally exploded, and with so much force it had destroyed much of the surrounding area. Only an android equipped with a very powerful energy source could produce an explosion that large.

He hadn't just killed his own son. What a relief.

The combat platform was damaged beyond use. That was a shame. It had served him well for many years, but its usefulness had run its course.

Alexander reached up and pulled the emergency release lever. The top of the combat platform popped open and he was ejected through the top, sending him rolling across the floor before coming to a halt staring up at the ceiling.

There was a burning sensation all across his chest and arms. The combat platform's chassis had protected him from the worst of it, but the shorting out of various systems had inflicted stinging electrical burns across his body.

Fighting against the pain, he lifted himself off the floor and looked around.

The explosion of the android had been at least as destructive as the one that had wiped out the cargo processing chamber. It had ignited volatile containers along the walls, resulting in a chain reaction that had destroyed much of the weaponry.

The DNI had exacted a devastating price. The attack had crippled the facility and left most of the staff dead, including his best scientist. Red-eye didn't do petty revenge. This was a clean-up operation, not mere retribution.

More importantly, the DNI was almost certainly about to descend to finish the job. He was the only one they might take prisoner, and that was unlikely, considering that they had just sent a robotic assassin after him. Either way, his window of opportunity for escaping was small – and closing fast.

He and the infiltrator had careened into the far end of the hangar where the entrance to the tunnel network was located. A fortunate coincidence.

Alexander's burns were still stinging and the mere act of moving about aggravated the pain, but he had to move. He navigated through the wreckage towards the door, then swiped his hand across the biometric sensor and slipped inside. From there he took a circuitous route to a separate sub-complex which only he knew about.

One more biometric lock later, and he found the place. The lights flickered on as he entered and the blast door sealed behind him with a heavy clang. The sub-complex was the size of a surface-to-orbit missile silo, which was essentially its purpose. He wiped the dust off of a long-unused console and reactivated the systems.

"*Ship diagnostics complete,*" a computerised voice announced, "*all systems green.*"

Good to know. The last thing he needed was for his getaway craft to break down. Before leaving, there was one more thing to do.

Alexander flipped the cover on a big red handle, pressing it into the slot so that it popped out again. He then turned the handle 180 degrees around.

"*Warning,*" the computer declared, "*Endgame protocol has been primed.*"

45 years. He had spent 45 years in the shadows building up this so-called Network solely to do his bidding. 45 years hiding underground pretending to be a warlord and spymaster going toe-to-toe with the very people who had made him what he was. He was about to destroy it all and start anew with the full force of Human government hunting him down.

"*Warning,*" the computer repeated, "*Endgame protocol has been primed.*"

And what about the followers he had here already? There still had to be a few hundred left inside the facility, leaderless and awaiting instructions. Their motivations for joining his not-so-merry band were many and varied, but for the most part they were loyal to him. Most of them were now dead, and the survivors would soon be joining them.

Alexander pushed the red dial back into its slot.

"*Endgame protocol initiated,*" the computer announced, "*60 seconds until launch.*"

The chamber lit up with danger red lights and a klaxon sounded as the countdown began. Completely forgetting the pain of his wounds, Alexander rushed over to the other side of the silo tube and climbed in through an open hatch, sealing it behind him. He then settled into the cockpit and strapped himself him in before checking the flight display.

"*Fifty seconds until launch,*" said the computer.

The activation of the endgame protocol triggered a facility-wide lockdown that sealed every entrance into the facility. Nothing could get in or out. Ostensibly, this was meant to keep external attackers out and dangerous specimens in – which was somewhat true.

"*Forty seconds until launch,*" said the computer.

His projected flightpath would take him up into the stratosphere before flying towards the opposite side of the planet and then finally up into space. The circuitous route would buy him time while the DNI fleet focused on his soon-to-be liquidated lair.

"*Thirty seconds until launch,*" said the computer.

Far above, a portal opened at the top of the launch silo, a perfectly vertical channel from the centre of the mountain to the peak. To the natives outside, it would resemble a volcanic eruption, a sign of impending doom – or whatever they believed about the end times.

"*Twenty seconds until launch,*" said the computer.

It did occur to him what a monumental act of cowardice he was committing leaving several hundred people to die. He wasn't sparing them a worse fate than what the DNI would have in store for them if they were captured, and he couldn't delude himself into thinking they deserved such a fate more than him.

"Ten seconds until launch...nine...eight..."

Although, both delusions had a modicum of truth. Most of the research staff had been convicted of breaking laws regulating their respective tradecrafts. Some of them were arguably dangerous criminals, and he was certainly doing the DNI a favour by getting rid of them.

"...three...two...one..."

* * *

When the countdown hit zero, a two kilometre long set of electromagnetic rails fired, propelling the craft up and out of the launch tunnel at several times the speed of sound. At the same time, the rest of the endgame protocol was activated.

Deep within the bedrock, interspersed at various depths, ten fusion bombs detonated with the force of several kilotons. The design of the bombs ensured that the explosive force was directed down and in, fracturing the roof of the long-dormant volcano's magma chamber, and creating a ready path for the magma.

The tremendous heat generated by the explosions also melted the nearby rock, instantly enlarging the magma chamber and forming a critical mass of molten rock that rose inexorably up through the base of the mountain.

The interior of the mountain was honeycombed with winding tunnels formed by similar eruptions millions of years ago. One by one, the floors of the lowermost caverns burst open as the magma bubbled up from below.

Before long, the magma flood had consumed the lower tunnels and was eating its way into the upper tunnels that led into the facility. The facility was sealed, but every door inside had been opened, allowing the magma to follow the path of least resistance and flood the entire facility within hours.

The facility and the tunnel network were large enough to contain the subterranean eruption and prevent it turning into an explosive eruption visible to the natives. The only phenomenon the natives saw was a bright star rising up from the mountain's peak, soaring into the heavens on a pillar of fiery smoke.

* * *

The force of the engines shook the cockpit, rattling Alexander in his seat. With space at a premium, motion dampeners were a luxury that he had to do without. He slowly became accustomed to the turbulence, but tightened his safety harness just in case.

His escape craft was contained inside a two-stage launch vehicle powered by a solid-propellant rocket; old-fashioned, but effective. Assisted by the magnetic rails in the launch tube, the first-stage boosters were enough to propel the craft through the lower atmosphere.

The craft was equipped with external cameras, and on the video feed he could see the vast, verdant continent below. As he gained altitude, the green on the horizon became smudged with blue as the distant sea came into view. The alien marine life was as fascinating as their terrestrial counterparts. It was a pity he wouldn't be coming back.

Alexander's mind began to wander. Mortimer's mistake had cost him plenty, but to the DNI it had cost him his usefulness to them; as a result they had disposed of him. Now, in turn, he had disposed of his surviving followers just to make a clean getaway.

Not once had he regretted leaving people to die. After each similar getaway, he had raged about the setback before accepting it and starting over. But this time, the familiar fury was gone. He couldn't feel any hint of anger at being discovered or losing his entire Network. It just wasn't in him anymore. Instead, he felt a sense of relief.

After all, once again, he had escaped.

The escape craft cleared the lower reaches of the atmosphere as the fuel gauge dipped below 50%. Now came the complicated part.

Alexander checked the flightpath on the HUD, trusting the navigation software over his own manual control, then set his destination as the other side of the planet.

The craft began to turn in an arc, its new flightpath taking it into the upper atmosphere towards low planetary orbit. He saw the movement more than he felt it, watching as the video feed tilted up towards space on one side and down to the planet on the other.

From this high up, a vast swath of the planet's surface was visible. He saw an irregular emerald landmass interwoven with a network of sapphire seas – a sprawling patchwork of green and blue broken only by strips of subtropical desert. The planet was beautiful, its beauty belying the ferocity of the life that teemed there.

Doubtless there were other planets just as beautiful or even more so. As impressive as the view was, this was no time to get sentimental.

The craft was moving fast through the upper atmosphere, its angle of attack becoming steadily shallower as it entered orbit. A warning light flashed orange, informing him that only 20% of the primary booster engine's fuel remained. He would have to switch to conventional engines soon, but for now he could coast on the momentum of the primary booster.

He couldn't prevent his thoughts from circling back around. Somewhere in the depths of his mind, below even the place where his atavistic rage used to lurk, a strange and unfamiliar feeling kept drawing his attention back.

Guilt?

Most people would agree that leaving loyal followers to die in the heart of an erupting volcano required a special degree of callous, self-serving cowardice. In the abstract, Alexander agreed, and yet it didn't make more than a ripple in his mind. If he couldn't be cold-blooded about such things, he would have met his end a long time ago.

What about Jezebel? She was the one person he might have taken with her, and yet he'd left her behind along with everyone else. It hadn't even occurred to him to go get her. It was possible she had been killed by the infiltrator or escaped in a shuttle during the chaos, neither of which could suppress the fact that he had left his own wife to die.

Then again, there was only room for one aboard the escape craft.

The warning light went from orange to red as the fuel gauge dipped below 10% and began ticking down into single digits.

Alexander kept the primary booster burning, wanting to use up every last bit of fuel. In the meantime, he prepared to jettison the first stage. When the fuel gauge hit 1%, the primary booster engine shut down, and he flipped a pair of switches.

He heard a series of metallic rattling bangs as the first stage booster was detached and blown clear of the craft, and he watched on the cameras as it floated away into the distance. It was entering an unstable orbit and before long would plummet back to the planet – a problem for the natives, not for him.

Alexander primed the escape craft's actual engines. Freed of its surface-to-orbit booster, the craft was now a conventional interplanetary shuttle. The conventional engines wouldn't get him very far, but he didn't need them to.

He activated the engines and used the planet's gravity to slingshot the craft around to the sunset side. The silhouette of the planet's moon appeared over the horizon as a diminutive body of black rock – his one and only chance to escape.

As the distance slowly closed, he began thinking of where to find refuge – certainly not beyond Human space. Preferably somewhere remote enough that direct government authority was weak but not so remote that it had no infrastructure. The former consideration ruled out all the core worlds while the latter ruled out much of the frontier.

That left a few dozen mid-tier and lower-tier planets. No matter which world he went to, the DNI would be sure to hunt him down.

Would they send Gabriel after him? That was unlikely. He may be a complete stranger to his son, but unlike his android doppelganger, Gabriel might not have the nerve to kill his own father. Even so, he couldn't quite dismiss the possibility.

Another warning light appeared, this time on the sensor array. Alexander tapped the icon and expanded it to fill the screen.

There was a ship behind him.

If the infiltrator had arrived aboard the Q-courier, of course the Navy couldn't have been far behind. More importantly, the vessel was bearing down on him. It was much larger and with more powerful engines, enabling it to close the distance at an alarming speed. The fact that it was this close already was alarming in itself.

Alexander fed maximum power to his spacecraft's engines. It was unlikely he would be able to reach the dark side of the moon before the pursuing ship caught him, but he certainly wasn't going to making it easy.

He could see the approaching warship on the camera, but the actual sensor readings were fuzzy. No doubt the vessel's hull was stealth-coated, and only its sheer size and growing proximity had given it away.

At least that meant the rest of the fleet was some distance away. All Alexander could do now was hope that he reached the moon before the ship caught up with him.

A second sensor warning appeared. Another vessel had just emerged from the far side of the moon and was also coming straight towards him.

There was no escape. If the second ship was coming from the moon, then they had already found the Q-drive frame hidden there. He was trapped between two DNI warships and was about to be captured or killed.

Alexander preferred the latter. He adjusted the spacecraft's course until it was heading straight for the second warship. He was already going at full speed, so it was just a matter of ramming into the second vessel before the first one caught up with him.

As his would-be escape craft closed the distance to the second warship, a sense of thwarted rage filled his chest.

He was so close to escaping, so damn close, and yet he'd been caught at the last moment. How had the DNI known to catch him around the moon in the first place? Had someone tipped them off? Did they have a mole inside the Network all along feeding them intelligence until the opportune moment?

The conspiracy theories bubbled up in his mind and in his angry heart he wanted to believe them. But the rational part of his mind shot each of them down.

He had screened each new joiner before allowing them into his Network, the better to weed out potential turncoats. In any case, he was the only one who knew about the Endgame Protocol, the escape craft, or the Q-drive frame concealed on the planet's moon. The simple truth was the DNI had outsmarted him.

The second ship was approaching fast, and at this speed he was going to crash straight into the hull, hopefully taking a few DNI lackeys with him. Unless its shields were sufficiently powerful to deflect the impact, in which case he would be bounced harmlessly away.

Another sensor warning began squawking at him: a gravitic disturbance warning. The spacecraft's speed dropped sharply as it was caught in a gravity well.

He should have known better. If the DNI was going to take him alive, of course they weren't going to let him crash into one of their own ships. Now there really was nothing he could do – except, of course, resign himself to his fate.

Before the procedure, this situation would have plunged Alexander into another one of his rage episodes. This time, however, he felt nothing…just the bitter taste of defeat.

THE AMBUSH

IT was pitch black. He could hear his own breathing and nothing else. He could also feel bindings holding his body down. They were reactive restraints, judging by the way they tightened every time he tried to move. He had no idea how long he had been awake, let alone how long he had been trapped in here.

Without warning, a series of mechanical latches unlocked and a hatch opened in front of him like the lid of a sarcophagus. On the other side was a face he recognised instantly.

"Did you enjoy your nap?" Red-eye asked.

The quip was very uncharacteristic, and Gabriel glared at her in response.

"You are still on Asgard, by the way," Red-eye informed him.

"You set me up to be captured by Byron Sade," Gabriel said accusingly.

"You were never captured by Byron Sade," Red-eye corrected him, "You were captured by Colonel Starborn who was posing as an agent of the Network."

"And what was the point of that?" Gabriel demanded.

"The Network has shown an inordinate interest in you from the beginning," Red-eye explained, "the original mole who facilitated Mortimer Shelton's escape named *you* as the orchestrator. Clearly, that was a lie, but one intended to cast aspersions on your loyalty, just like the message at the prison system sending you your father's regards."

Gabriel knew much of this already but kept listening.

"Combined with the fact that your mother was broken out of the same prison on the same day as the attacks," Red-eye concluded, "he was going to come after you eventually."

Having been presented with the dots, Gabriel connected them.

"So it's true, then?" he asked in disbelief, "my father is alive?"

"Yes," Red-eye replied, "and I used you as bait to flush him out."

"So what did you actually do with me instead of handing me over?" Gabriel asked.

"Colonel Starborn switched your container with another container prepared by the Rand Block," Red-eye answered, "that second container was taken away by the Network smuggling team with a naval taskforce in covert pursuit."

"I see…" said Gabriel.

"Did you really think I would hand over one of the Directorate's best operatives to one of its worst enemies?" Red-eye asked rhetorically, "Aster would be furious."

Gabriel bristled at the mention of Aster's name, but held his anger in check.

"As grateful as I am for you not handing me over to the enemy," he said sarcastically, "why didn't you just brief me about the plan to begin with?"

"The fact that the Network's leader is your own father would have made that awkward," Red-eye explained, "for you, at least."

"That doesn't mean you had to keep me locked up in here!" Gabriel pointed out angrily.

"Of course not," Red-eye replied, "consider that your punishment for interfering in this investigation despite my explicit orders not to."

Her reply left Gabriel fuming.

"I'm letting you out in time for the final stage of mopping up the Network," Red-eye said, "namely: storming Sheraton Biopharma and eliminating Byron Sade."

"Why can't Colonel Starborn handle that?" Gabriel asked.

"Because she's been captured," Red-eye replied, "we captured the influencer, but it seems he informed Byron Sade that Colonel Starborn was impersonating him."

"So the influencer blew her cover…" Gabriel said.

"Yes, albeit by chance," Red-eye replied, "so now, you and a team from the Special Operations Division will be sent in to rescue her and capture Byron Sade."

"I'm sure that the SOD operators can handle it without me," Gabriel said.

"They can," agreed Red-eye, "but since this whole affair in many ways started with you, it may as well be ended by you. Besides, Aetherea is a fellow voidstalker."

"I'm surprised you ordered a second generation to replace us," Gabriel remarked.

"Of course I did and don't be ridiculous, respectively," Red-eye responded, "the Rand Block is constantly making advancements, and I would be a fool not to take advantage of them. As to being replaced, if the voidstalkers were disposable they would be an army of robots. The second generation are an improvement on the first, not your replacements."

Red-eye had been standing only a few steps away from Gabriel the whole time, but she took another step closer, fixing her eyes on Gabriel's own.

"Do you trust me?"

"What do you mean?" Gabriel asked, flinching at the question.

"You've been quite the maverick ever since the Loki mission," Red-eye told him, "and it seems that your yearlong cooling off period soured you instead."

"Don't forget kidnapping and interrogating me as a possible traitor," Gabriel added.

"A regrettable but unavoidable precaution," Red-eye conceded, "one which your father hoped would undermine your trust, not just in me, but in the Directorate."

Gabriel had no polite answer to that.

"It would be extremely problematic if one of my best operatives did not believe that his superior's decisions could be fully trusted," Red-eye continued, "especially when his vocation requires him to risk his life in the depths of space."

She took another step towards him until she was only inches away. The closeness was unnerving, even for Gabriel. Her heterochromatic stare held him transfixed, and he could even see the delicate circuitry in her bionic eye as it blazed an infernal red. His heart began to race as she strained his ability to stay composed.

"Everything I have ever done or ever will do," she said with stone-cold conviction, "has been to ensure the continued existence of the Human species. Believe me."

Red-eye's mere proximity robbed people of their presence of mind. Gabriel certainly felt it, wanting to demand answers to questions he couldn't bring himself to ask. She was still staring at him, and so he finally managed to muster the words.

"What do you have planned for my children?" he asked.

"The same thing I have planned for all of Humanity's children," Red-eye replied, "a happy and fulfilling life within the safety of a strong and thriving Human civilisation, a goal to which you have made invaluable contributions."

Gabriel was mystified by that vague answer, but felt that he shouldn't be.

"I have no plans to kidnap them or conscript them into the Directorate," Red-eye added coolly, "but my plans are not for your children, they merely involve your children. Just as they involve you and all the other voidstalkers as well as their respective families."

"With an answer like that," Gabriel remarked, "of course I don't trust you."

"You have no choice but to trust me, Gabriel," Red-eye replied, "but I hope that you will of your own accord. Our future depends on it."

* * *

The building was in lockdown with minimal power except to operate the doors. Byron Sade could see where he was going, and presumably the androids had night vision, but there was little or no light. The only sounds to be heard were the androids' footsteps and the capture net scraping against the floor.

The androids were dragging Aetherea down the corridor as Byron Sade led the way, swiping through biometrically-locked doors as they moved deeper into the facility. She didn't bother to struggle; the slightest movement caused the capture net to tighten in response, so she bided her time.

After a while, she was brought to a detention block and dragged into an interrogation room. Something pricked her skin and a wave of weakness swept through her muscles. She could barely move a finger as the androids disentangled the netting and strapped her to an X-shaped restraint board.

Her strength returned rapidly and she lashed out, but most of the restraints were already in place, enough for the androids to pin her down and finish securing her.

Byron Sade stepped forward, glaring at Aetherea with burning suspicion.

"What the fleek are you?" he demanded in angry disbelief.

"Could you elaborate?" Aetherea requested smugly.

"That was one of the most powerful muscle relaxants in my company's inventory," he said, "and you shrugged off the effects after less than a minute."

"Is it legal to use?" Aetherea asked, knowing that it probably wasn't.

"*I* will be asking the questions," Byron Sade countered, "and if you fail to answer them, I will do truly horrible things to you."

"Like you do to your drugged sex slaves?" Aetherea asked.

"You sound awfully calm for someone who's going to be dead in the next few hours," Byron Sade said as he activated a control panel.

"In which case, I don't have much incentive to tell you the truth," she pointed out.

"You don't have to," Byron Sade answered, tapping a set of keys on the panel, "I'll ask questions and the machine will decide whether you're telling the truth."

"Then why bother torturing me?" Aetherea asked him.

"Because I can," he replied with sadistic menace, "although I might spare you that part if you tell me your real name."

"How do you know it isn't really 'A'?" she suggested with a grin.

Byron Sade glowered at her before continuing.

A set of folding panels descended from the ceiling and closed around Aetherea's head. Once in position, they began to glow softly as they scanned her brainwaves in real-time.

"Are you female?" Byron Sade asked.

"Yes," Aetherea replied.

"Are you Human?"

"More than you," she responded.

Byron Sade took a fine cutting device and sliced open the front of Aetherea's suit. The superheated blade cut through the fabric with ease, leaving her chest exposed.

"So we're playing the strip version, are we?" Aetherea smirked.

"Next time, it'll be your flesh," Byron Sade snarled through gritted teeth, "do you work with the Directorate of Naval Intelligence?"

"No," Aetherea replied.

Byron Sade scowled at the control panel, perplexed and frustrated by the inconclusive reading he was getting. Aetherea, meanwhile, simply smirked at him.

"Are you an operative of the Directorate of Naval Intelligence?" he demanded.

"Asking the same question twice usually doesn't–"

Byron Sade lunged at Aetherea and grabbed her by the throat.

"Answer the fleeking question, you little bitch!" he snarled dangerously.

"Why so angry?" Aetherea asked mockingly, without a hint of terror, "I'm just trying to give you some tips on how to do it properly."

Byron Sade's thwarted rage was steadily giving way to incredulity. He simply couldn't believe this woman's shameless bravado and intentional goading. Slowly, the taut expression of anger on his face loosened.

"Fine," he hissed threateningly, preparing the cutting tool again, "we can go straight to the fun part if that's what you really want."

An alarm sounded.

* * *

Given what had happened last time, Gabriel wasn't keen on being accompanied by a team. For this mission, however, he was the one accompanying them, and that sat even less well with him. He also had mixed feelings about seeing Aetherea again. He didn't exactly want to leave her to die, but their past interactions would make a reunion awkward.

"*ETA 60 seconds!*" shouted the pilot over the intercom.

There was a rush of activity as everyone checked their equipment one last time, putting their helmets on and priming their weapons.

Gabriel was already ready, but he checked his equipment again just to make sure.

In the middle of the crew compartment, a display showed the team a rendering of Sheraton Biopharma. The headquarters themselves occupied a dozen of the uppermost levels of the building, along with Byron Sade's fortified penthouse.

"*One of our agents was captured infiltrating this place in preparation for the raid,*" Gabriel reminded everyone over the comm., "*Byron Sade knows we're coming and he's not going to surrender meekly, so expect an ambush and a vicious fight.*"

Everyone nodded.

The first team, accompanied by Gabriel, would infiltrate through the cargo elevator on the roof and storm the labs. The second team would secure the front entrance and a third team would enter via the cargo delivery hatch to secure the penthouse.

"*ETA 30 seconds!*" the pilot announced.

The squad members glanced at their weapons one last time as the ETA counter ticked down towards zero. They showed no sign of what they were thinking or feeling. Gabriel had few real feelings to express, and what little emotional capacity he had was slowly suppressed until he felt pure focus.

"*ETA ten seconds!*" the pilot declared, "*coming in for the drop!*"

Gravity and inertia shifted as the transport craft decelerated, coming to a hovering halt just above the roof. The rear door unlocked and folded down into a ramp, releasing a rush of howling wind into the compartment. The squad unlocked their restraints and stormed out with their weapons raised.

The sun had long since set and yielded to the gloaming. The transport craft had no lights except for a thin ring of fire crowning the exhaust port of each engine. The only other light came from the city centre in the distance.

The gale force winds howled like a chorus of demons, battering the squad's armour as they gathered around the cargo elevator pad. Someone overrode the controls and the squad stepped onto the pad as the transport soared up into the night sky.

"*We'll be a short distance away,*" the pilot informed the squad, "*but we won't be of much help whilst you're inside the building.*"

"*Acknowledged,*" said the squad leader.

* * *

The facility was completely dark, requiring night vision to see anything. As the cargo elevator descended, the squad saw a deserted staging area with robotic cranes lining the walls. The cargo had been cleared away, leaving no cover if they were ambushed.

As the elevator descended, the safety lights were flashing, creating dull flashes in their false-colour visual enhancement filters. The squad scanned around for movement or signs of anything suspicious, but they saw nothing.

When the elevator reached the bottom, the heavily armed operators spread out across the floor. Someone pulled a support drone from his backpack, laid it out on the floor, and hit the activation switch. The drone launched itself off the ground and flew away, scanning the area for threats.

"*Libra team has arrived,*" the squad leader announced over the comm., "*we've secured the cargo entrance and are advancing through the cargo facility.*"

"*Acknowledged,*" the second squad leader answered, "*Puma team is in the service corridor heading to the penthouse now.*"

"*Echo team is at the front entrance,*" the third squad leader reported, "*it's heavily reinforced, it'll take us a while to get through the door.*"

Libra for laboratory. Puma for penthouse. Echo for entrance. Easy enough to remember.

"*The facility looks powered down,*" Libra leader informed the other squad leaders, "*this definitely feels more like a trap than anything else.*"

The support drone finished scanning the cargo processing area. Having found nothing amiss, it moved on down the service hall. The squad went after it, following the transport tracks leading to the far end. Gabriel took point with two other operators flanking him and the rest of the squad following close behind.

"*Puma team has entered the penthouse,*" Puma leader informed everyone, "*we're in the living room. Moving to secure the other rooms.*"

"*Is there a strange, animated tapestry on the walls?*" Gabriel asked.

"*No,*" was the bemused reply, "*Why?*"

"*You're in a side room,*" Gabriel explained, "*the living room is much bigger.*"

"*Acknowledged,*" Puma leader answered.

"*This is Echo team,*" said Echo leader, "*the front door is built like a vault. Even with plasma-torching, it'll take us an hour or more to cut through it.*"

"*Our operative was supposed to disable the security systems,*" Libra leader fumed.

"*Her cover was blown and she was caught,*" Gabriel reminded him.

The squad emerged into another multi-storey staging area. The support drone had already arrived and was sweeping the chamber.

"*We've made it to the actual living room,*" Puma leader reported, "*I see what you mean about the weird tapestry.*"

The sound of metal grinding against metal arrested Libra team's attention. They turned around just in time to see the blast door slam shut behind them.

"*We've just been locked inside the processing area!*" Libra leader warned.

"*The living room just sealed up,*" Puma leader reported, "*We're trapped in here.*"

A set of stasis pods descended from the ceiling on magnetic rails, and the support drone whizzed through the air to scan them.

"*Alien DNA!*" someone shouted, "*There are alien lifeforms in there!*"

The squad closed ranks until they were concentrated in the centre, forming an outward-facing ring of guns as the pods were lowered into place around them.

They could see the aliens through the observation windows. Each one was wearing a full-body suit and their eyes were closed in placid dormancy. They watched as the creatures slowly awoke, their eyelids flickering open to reveal blazing orange eyes that quickly narrowed and focused on the interlopers in the centre.

The stasis pods opened one by one and the creatures burst out, shrieking like animals. The squad opened fire but their bullets were deflected by shield emitters embedded in the aliens' protective suits. The rattle of gunfire clashed with the crackle of emitters, and the aliens raged and thrashed about as if they could swat the bullets aside.

The support drone buzzed into action, swooping down on the aliens. Its outer edge contained two contra-rotating circular blades sharpened to a nanomolecular finish, and they achieved what the bullets couldn't.

The drone took down one of the aliens, slicing through its neck before taking flight again. The creature's severed head fell to the ground followed by its body as the drone swooped down again and cut through the abdomen of another alien.

The squad couldn't keep up a continuous barrage, however, and the aliens ultimately closed the distance. Gabriel was ready and he swung his fist as a screeching alien lunged at him, the clenching action activating a set of nodes along the knuckles.

The nodes transmitted a spike of electricity and antigravity as they connected with the alien's head, shattering its jaw and killing it instantly. There was a crackle and boom followed by a reactive flash as the alien was sent flying towards the far wall.

Other members of the squad were too slow to react, and the alien berserkers barrelled into them, knocking them to the floor and slashing viciously at their armour.

The support drone swooped down and cut through one alien's spine, paralysing it from the shoulders down, but its secondary nervous system continued animating its limbs. The one-sided gunfight quickly became a one-sided brawl with the aliens mindlessly trying to tear their targets to pieces.

Gabriel swung his weapon like a club, hitting one creature in the side of the skull with the butt and knocking it off one of the operators. As soon as he had helped the operator off the floor, he was attacked by another creature. He lost his gun in the fray but managed to swing his fist at his assailant.

There was a flash as the shock-fist connected with the alien's eye socket, shattering the front of its skull and propelling its corpse off of him.

The brawl was still going on and Gabriel retrieved his gun before re-joining the fight. Eventually, the squad managed to neutralise all of the alien berserkers, but despite their heavy armour, many of the squad were badly injured and needed medivac.

"*Libra! Echo! This is Puma team!*" the Puma leader shouted over the comm., "*we're under attack in the penthouse!*"

Libra team had been so pre-occupied with their own ambush they hadn't heard their comrades calling for help.

"*Puma team! This is Libra leader! We've been attacked as well! Hang in there!*"

"*We still need to clear out the labs,*" Gabriel reminded Libra leader.

"*What about Puma team?*" Libra leader objected, "*They're under attack by the same things as us, we can't leave them!*"

"*We don't have to,*" Gabriel said, "*Once you've evacuated the wounded, go and help Puma team. I'll head down to the labs and clear them out alone.*"

Gabriel couldn't see Libra leader's face, but he seemed conflicted. Gabriel outranked him, but it was a suggestion not an order.

"*If you think you can do better alone, I won't contradict you,*" Libra leader said less-than-enthusiastically, "*but I don't like the idea of splitting up.*"

"*Neither do I,*" Gabriel lied, "*but we can't let Byron Sade stall us. Get the wounded out of here for medivac, then go and help Puma team, then search for and rescue our captured operative. Once you're done with that, feel free to come join me down in the labs.*"

"*Yes sir,*" Libra leader replied reluctantly.

* * *

The elevator doors opened onto a disaster zone. The labs had been torn apart. Gaping holes had been ripped out of the walls, valuable equipment had been destroyed, and power conduits had been gutted by electrical overloads.

This seemed like more damage than the green-skinned aliens were capable of.

Gabriel stepped out of the elevator and into a puddle of clear fluid. It was leaking out of the smashed chemical tanks at the far end. It also looked electrically active, judging by the sparks dancing intermittently across its surface.

He moved deeper into the labs, sweeping his weapon from side to side and ignoring the unpleasant squelching sound his boots made in the fluid. There weren't any other signs of life as far as he could tell, but the atmosphere was eerie nonetheless.

A shadow whooshed across the far wall, catching Gabriel's eye. His HUD was faster than he was and flagged up a briefly captured image, highlighted by its thermal signature. The digitally reconstructed shape was too distorted to get an idea of what it looked like. It was roughly Human-shaped, but that was all his HUD could tell him.

He continued forward, the electrically active fluid sucking at his boots with each step. Some of the equipment was still intact and looked mostly functional. At least one console was still working, but it was displaying a set of readings on a loop.

The temperature was warm, almost tropically warm; close enough to Human body temperature to make regular thermal vision useless. His HUD's thermal vision was more sophisticated, but it was still hard to make out distinct shapes.

Gabriel continued through the chamber, passing a row of glass tanks on the left. Each tank was fitted with elaborate supporting machinery which reached up to the ceiling, and each one had been smashed open from the outside.

Presumably the containment tanks had been used to hold more of the green-skinned berserkers. Someone or something had broken the tanks in order to free them. Why not simply disable the safety protocols and open the tanks? And what could be strong enough to shatter reinforced safety glass?

The shadow zipped back along the opposite wall, disappearing through an open door on the far side of the chamber. It moved too fast for Gabriel to get a shot at it, but his HUD caught a clear image of it this time. The creature in the image had a more-or-less Human shape, but with distended limbs and dark, glossy skin.

It was definitely not one of the alien berserkers.

Gabriel was tempted to just seal the creature inside, but he wasn't sure if that would actually contain the monster – whatever it was. He advanced towards the far end of the labs, keeping his gun aimed squarely at the open door.

He could hardly see anything on the other side, even with the visual enhancement filters. The thermal readings were distorted as well, this time by a mass of cold air. It wasn't quite refrigerated, but it was still cold enough to give the room a cool blue colour in his HUD.

Gabriel reached the far end of the chamber and paused outside the open door. To his left was a long corridor that split off into a T-junction down which the shadow had dashed earlier. To his right was another bank of still-functioning computers.

The door itself was a heavy containment door, about an inch thick with biohazard seals around the edges. Gabriel gripped the door handle and pulled on it experimentally. It swung open easily enough and he stepped over the threshold.

On the other side, his thermal vision readjusted, giving him a clear image of the room. It was a smaller chamber with a circular shape, a low ceiling, and a metal rim ringing the edge. In the middle of the floor was a single pane of glass below which was a mass of water.

The water looked cool blue in his HUD, but not uniformly so. Below the glass, he saw a pair of long slithering shapes swimming around in the tank, exhibiting graceful undulating movements. Their bodies were tinged orange in his HUD, making them stand out in the mass of cold water in which they swam.

At the opposite end of the chamber, he saw something else.

It was the shadow monster, standing there and watching him. It was so tall the top of its head almost touched the roof. Despite its fuzzy thermal profile, there was no mistaking the swollen limbs or the abnormal distribution of body heat. Gabriel didn't wait for the creature to make the first move. He took aim and squeezed the trigger.

The monster's chest lit up with blue flashes of energy as the hail of hypersonic bullets made contact with its shielding. Some rounds hit home, grazing the target's flesh, but most were sent swerving off to the side.

The shadow monster was unharmed.

Then it moved. It moved so fast that Gabriel barely had time to react. He managed to fire another burst of rounds into the creature's chest, but it closed the distance in a heartbeat and slammed into him.

Gabriel was struck so hard he was pushed out of the doorway, but even before he had hit the ground again, the monster caught him by his ankles in mid-air. He found himself pulled back inside and thrown across the chamber like a discarded toy, but managed to kick back off the wall and roll back to his feet.

The monster was already coming back. It raised a bloated fist in the air and slammed it into the floor. The glass floor separating the chamber from the water tank was smashed, causing the floor to disintegrate beneath Gabriel's feet.

* * *

He was drowning. No, he wasn't drowning. There was no feeling of liquid suffocation. No water pouring in as the air bubbled out. But he was definitely underwater. He could feel his body moving at half normal speed. His suit was still secure and had its own independent supply of oxygen, but he was sinking towards the bottom.

Something else was in the water. It attacked as soon as he fell in. He was thrashing and struggling against its coils. It was trying to wrap itself around him and crush him to death, all the while dragging him down to the bottom.

It was so dark he couldn't see without his HUD, but his HUD was having difficulty locking onto the wriggling monster. Its body was as thick as a utility pipe and he could almost feel its slimy skin slipping against his armour as it struggled to get a purchase.

Orange pressure warnings appeared in his HUD. The creature was squeezing his armour so hard it was actually damaging his suit. His gun was gone, leaving only his own strength and the shock-fist. Still struggling not to be crushed, Gabriel pressed the back of his hand against the creature's body and clenched his fist.

The nodes along his knuckles activated, delivering a lethal pulse to the monster's flesh. The creature relaxed its crushing grip and swam away, disappearing into the surrounding water, and leaving Gabriel to flail on his own.

His armour made it difficult to swim, but now that the sea serpent was gone, he could see the tank clearly. Above him, he saw the broken observation glass where he had fallen in. Below him, he saw his gun lying on the bottom of the tank amongst hundreds of glass shards.

He also saw the sea serpent on the far side of the tank. Both of them. Their outlines and movements were highlighted clearly by the HUD, but their bodies were a riot of thermal shades. One of them had a swollen blotch of red in its mid-section and was twitching awkwardly. The other one was coming straight at him.

He saw its spear-like snout first, flanked by a pair of side-facing eyes that glowed in the dark. Then he saw its mouthful of dagger-like teeth as it opened its jaws and tried to close them around his head, and he raised his hands just in time to grab them.

The sea monster struggled and failed to close its jaws around Gabriel's head, but it did manage to wrap its coiling body around him, and he found himself smothered once again. He kept a grip on its jaws but could scarcely move the rest of his body.

"*Shield! Over-pulse!*" Gabriel shouted into his suit comm., "*Now!*"

The shield emitters in his armour were instantly and simultaneously overloaded, forcing a wave of artificial gravity outwards from Gabriel's body. The sea serpent bore the brunt of the over-pulse as its internal organs were pulped, but the over-pulse also violently repelled all nearby matter, including the surrounding water.

The explosive change in pressure forced a column of water outwards in all directions, smashing a second observation window near the bottom of the tank.

For the briefest moment, Gabriel was in freefall, dropping through the vacuum created by the over-pulse. The same vacuum sucked all of the water back down and out through the path of least resistance. He found himself carried along by an indoor tidal wave and spat out through the shattered observation window at the bottom.

He ended up sprawled on the damp floor of a new room which resembled the viewing room of an aquarium. An emergency drainage system was activated, sucking the water out through the floor. Within seconds, the water was gone, leaving only Gabriel and the twitching corpses of the two sea serpents.

His shielding was gone. Most of the emitters were fried by the over-pulse, leaving them too damaged to use. His armour was still intact, but it wouldn't afford as much protection, especially against the shadow monster. His gun was lying around in the hall somewhere, but it hadn't proven very effective either.

He heard a thump as something landed on the bottom of the tank. Gabriel saw the shadow monster and he scrambled to his feet as it bolted towards him. It moved so fast that he barely had time to swing his fist. The electrical nodes of his shock-fist activated just as his knuckles connected with the shadow monster's chest.

There was a liquid squelching and hissing sound like the instant boiling of fluid, and the reverberation from the impact caused Gabriel to lose his balance and fall backwards.

The shadow monster was rendered insensate by the blow. It didn't move or topple over. It simply stood there, paralysed by the impact. It was frozen in mid-lunge, balanced awkwardly on two swollen legs with its bulging arms outstretched in a body-tackling motion.

Gabriel found his gun lying on the floor. He picked it up again as he climbed back to his feet before confronting the shadow monster.

It looked almost like a living creature, albeit a grotesquely deformed one, but not quite. There were wisps of smoke coming from the point of impact, and a scan by Gabriel's HUD detected circuitry just below the slimy skin.

An organic machine?

It wasn't that farfetched. The Hive-dwellers used organic technology for certain critical parts of their spaceships, and it was certainly within Humanity's technological capacity. Even so, this was the first time he had ever seen organic technology used in this way.

How was it controlled? Was it being operated remotely? Was there a combat AI inside? All fun questions for the scientists down in the Rand Block to investigate. Either way, it was no longer a threat, and in the meantime he still had to locate Byron Sade and find out where Aetherea was being held captive.

A cracking and squelching noise arrested his attention. Slowly and disgustingly, the back of the shadow monster's carapace burst open as something inside struggled to emerge. Colourless fluid leaked out of the back, forming a sticky puddle on the floor, and Gabriel circled around the back, keeping his weapon trained on the shadow monster.

Like an insect growing out of its old skin, the pilot's torso emerged from inside the carapace. He had an unmistakeably Human head, and after freeing his two humanoid arms he tried to extricate the rest of his body from the shadow monster carapace.

Gabriel made no effort to assist the pilot who had tried to kill him just a moment ago, but kept his gun trained on the pilot's head, preparing to execute him on the spot. He watched in disgust as the pilot leaned backwards and tipped out of the carapace, landing on the floor in a mess of organic fluid.

Was that really Byron Sade sprawled on the floor? It was hard to imagine the cultured and snobbish pharmaceutical industry titan personally climbing into a grotesque suit of organic armour to fight the DNI. Most corporate sybarites would rather force their lackeys to fight to the end while they fled to safety.

With much effort, the pilot rolled onto his back. He was wearing an organic respirator which resembled a living creature hugging his face, smothering his nose and mouth, and leaving only his eyes visible through a translucent glaze.

The pilot reached a web-gloved hand up to his mouth and gripped the respirator. His fingers struggled to find purchase on the slime-covered device, but he eventually managed to squeeze a pair of release triggers.

There was a grotesque sucking noise as the respirator relinquished its fleshy grip on the pilot's face, and he plucked it away. He heaved and gasped for air as he let the device roll out of his hand before peeling back the translucent glaze covering his eyes.

Gabriel could now see the man's face: a gaunt face with a pallid complexion, a pair of jet black eyes, and surgically refined features.

"…You…got me…" Byron Sade wheezed, trying to sit up on his elbows.

"Where is the prisoner?" Gabriel demanded through his helmet speakers.

"…and…the bio-suit…it works…"

Gabriel fired a single round into his kneecap. The bang of the gunshot combined with the sound of the bullet passing through bone and flesh.

Byron Sade gasped in shock, his eyes and mouth fixed wide like a fish, then he reclined back onto the floor with a bizarre look of contentment on his face.

"That felt...stimulating..." he wheezed.

Gabriel guessed that a self-made bioengineering magnate would have the resources to tinker with his own biology. Having connected the dots, he immediately wished he hadn't.

"The neurochemistry behind...pleasure and pain...is remarkably...similar," Byron Sade purred, basking in the 'pain', "my researchers...created a drug...which temporarily crosses...the two wires..."

"I asked you where you're keeping the prisoner," Gabriel repeated.

"So she really was a DNI spy," Byron Sade chuckled, starting to catch his breath, "such a devious little snake, posing as a representative of my business partners."

"You mean the Network?" Gabriel asked.

"Correct," Byron Sade confirmed, "they've been a remarkably useful source of research material, although they're not the most forthcoming people. They're also not terribly competent if someone can pose as one of their own."

"Did they supply you with the alien creatures that attacked us?" Gabriel demanded.

"Yes," Byron Sade replied, "they even came pre-modified with cybernetics. Although, I have no idea why they sent them to me."

"So where is the prisoner?" Gabriel repeated.

"She's in the detention block at the far end of the building..." Byron Sade wheezed in grotesque satisfaction, "...I suggest you run."

* * *

Gabriel ran from the room as fast as he could, following the map of the building in his HUD towards the detention block. If Byron Sade really was that injured, he wouldn't be going anywhere, but in the meantime Aetherea was in danger.

"*Libra leader! This is Thorn!*" Gabriel barked into his comm., "*Byron Sade has been located and subdued, I'm going after the captured agent!*"

"*Acknowledged, Colonel,*" Libra leader replied, "*we're in the penthouse now, I'm afraid we can't reach you any time soon.*"

"*Why? What happened?*" Gabriel asked, arriving at a sealed door.

"*Puma team is in very bad shape,*" Libra leader explained, "*they'll need medivac as well, those that are still alive, anyway.*"

"*Acknowledged,*" Gabriel answered grimly, "*I'm at the entrance to the detention block now. Byron Sade is in the observation chamber nearby, one level below the labs. Thorn out.*"

Gabriel came to a locked door and planted his palm on the sensor pad. It flickered as his suit computer worked to bypass the encryption before flashing green and opening the door. He stormed in with his gun drawn as the door sealed shut behind him.

Unlike the rest of the building, the detention block was fully lit, with a small processing area and several hallways leading off to various holding cells.

A signal appeared in Gabriel's HUD as soon as he entered. It was a DNI tracking beacon, and he followed it down one of the corridors to the end of the block. At the entrance to the holding cell, he found another scanner and a viewing screen.

Inside the cell, he saw a woman strapped to an X-shaped frame secured to the wall and surrounded by probing equipment. She didn't look conscious, but he recognised her blonde hair and the tracking beacon was inside the room. It was definitely Aetherea.

"*Colonel Thorn,*" said a voice crackling over the comm., "*this is mother-bird. We've located the captured agent and are standing by near your location.*"

"*Acknowledged mother-bird*," Gabriel replied, "*I can bypass the lock but there might be any number of booby-traps in the holding cell.*"

"*Affirmative, Colonel*," the mother-bird pilot confirmed, "*We're detecting chemical canisters inside the cell. As soon as you try to open the door, they'll be triggered.*"

Gabriel gritted his teeth. That was an insidious setup, and of course Byron Sade hadn't intended to make it easy. With the holding cell booby-trapped, the challenge was how to get Aetherea out without triggering it.

"*We have equipment to breach the wall of the building*," the mother-bird pilot suggested.

"*I want to call that insane*," Gabriel responded, "*but I can't think of a better plan.*"

"*It's even more complicated*," the mother-bird pilot warned, "*we can't breach the wall and then enter the holding cell without triggering the canisters.*"

"*So what are you suggesting?*" Gabriel asked.

"*Breaching the wall around the frame she's shackled to and then taking the whole thing away in one go*," the mother-bird pilot explained.

"*That's even more insane*," Gabriel remarked.

"*By the way*," the mother-bird pilot added, "*as soon as we breach the cell, she'll need to be physically pushed out of the building.*"

"*What do you mean 'pushed out'?*" Gabriel asked.

"*The transport craft has grappling equipment for physically carrying the piece of the wall away*," the mother-bird pilot explained, "*but it will need an extra shove.*"

"*I don't have a jetpack for when I fall*," Gabriel pointed out.

"*We have a capture drone on standby*," the mother-bird pilot assured him.

Gabriel thought it over for a moment.

"*Fine*," he agreed, "*let's do it.*"

"*Preparing breaching tool*," said the mother-bird pilot.

Watching through the display, Gabriel saw a dark spot appear at the top of the far wall, just above the X-frame. The spot began to glow red and then bright orange before moving in a slow circle around the frame, cutting swiftly and precisely through the wall.

Gabriel stowed his weapon away, securing it to his back before preparing to open the door. His own armour was atmospherically sealed, so it would protect him from whatever toxins were released into the room. He couldn't be so sure that Aetherea wouldn't be affected. The faster he charged in and pushed her out through the breach, the better.

The glowing orange dot completed its circular path around the X-frame.

"*Breach complete,*" the mother-bird pilot announced, "*deploying spikes.*"

A pair of hooked spike were fired at high speed into the wall, punching straight through and lodging inside the metal.

"*Spikes deployed,*" said the mother-bird pilot, "*ready when you are, Colonel.*"

Gabriel planted his hand on the biometric scanner. It flickered and flashed awkwardly as the bypass program wormed its way into the system. After a minute of waiting, the scanner flashed green and the door slid open.

"*Go!*" Gabriel shouted, charging into the room.

As the door opened, the breached wall was pulled out by several inches, but not enough to yank it completely out of the superstructure. Gabriel charged into the room at full speed, slamming both palms into the wall with superhuman strength augmented by the exoskeletal motors in his armour.

He heard the hiss of escaping gas and the screech of metal on metal. The transport's engines were firing at maximum power, and with Gabriel's shove, the slab of metal gave way, falling and swinging down underneath the craft like a pendulum.

Gabriel plummeted.

The pull of gravity on his body was pitted against the disorienting sensation of spinning in awkward circles as he fell. He could see the city spinning all around him, the lights flashing past his vision as he fell like a rock towards the ground not far below.

A dark shape swooped down and fired a capture cord at him. Gabriel felt himself being yanked out of the air as he was pulled into the drone's capture bay. Before he knew it, the bay doors had sealed him inside and the drone was flying him home.

Gabriel found himself wrapped up in a constrictor-like embrace, but at least he was no longer falling to his death.

That and Aetherea was alive.

THE ANALYSIS

DEBRIEFING sessions at the Spire were usually quick and to-the-point – unless something went wrong, in which case a detailed account was required. Gabriel recounted exactly what had happened from start to finish while his words were noted down for the record. Once he was done, he was sent on his way.

Byron Sade, he had been told, had been working on a biome-chanical suit and had used the opportunity of the Directorate raid to take it out for a test run. It was probably the first example of a living machine ever created by Human science, requiring partial symbiosis with its pilot in order to function.

The inventor himself – so the debriefing team claimed – had survived the injuries he had sustained from the shock-fist. The wealthy hedonist was probably sitting in a maximum security cell in a DNI detention facility awaiting his own 'debriefing'.

Libra team had taken six casualties in total, but with no fatal-ities. Puma team, on the other hand, had found itself trapped in the penthouse with a dozen of the green-skinned berserkers with little room and no exits. Three of the squad had been killed and most of the rest were badly wounded.

Gabriel was leaving with so many questions, and Red-eye wasn't likely to answer any of them. She hadn't even shown up to the debriefing. Why should she? She was the most powerful woman in the sector, and Gabriel was just one of a few hun-dred voidstalkers. She couldn't spend all her time and energy attending to one discontented operative.

Although he wasn't looking forward to explaining his absence to Aster, all he wanted to do was go home. The Directorate had arranged for a sky-car to take him home; it was the least they could do after locking him in a box for several days.

When he arrived at the landing pad, sure enough, there was an armoured sky-car waiting for him. Gabriel opened the door and climbed inside, strapping himself in as the door shut and locked automatically.

"If we crash, a safety belt probably won't save you," said a female voice.

Gabriel span around.

"Sorry to disappoint you," said Aetherea, "but we'll be carpooling tonight."

"What are you doing in here?" Gabriel demanded.

"Are you hard of hearing?" Aetherea replied as the sky-car took off, "we're sharing a ride home. So sit back, relax, and deal with it."

She didn't seem all that happy with the arrangement either.

"How was the box?" she asked.

"How about I lock *you* in one?" Gabriel suggested, "Then you'll find out for yourself."

"Careful," Aetherea smirked, "remember the last time you put your hands on me?"

Gabriel scowled at her.

"Of course you remember," Aetherea continued, "You can't get it out of your head."

Gabriel opted not to reply, watching the buildings zip by on the display.

"The silent treatment again?" Aetherea remarked.

Gabriel said nothing.

"You never actually thanked me for coming to get you when the hive-ship was about to blow up," Aetherea reminded him.

"I saved you from being raped and murdered by Byron Sade," Gabriel reminded her in turn, "consider that my thanks."

"You got me there," Aetherea conceded.

"Why do you keep baiting me over a one-time mistake?" Gabriel demanded.

"A mistake for you, maybe," Aetherea replied.

"I'm not leaving Aster for you, ever," Gabriel told her, "the only reason it happened was because you reminded me of her."

"Yes," Aetherea grimaced, "it's painfully obvious that you have a type."

Gabriel didn't answer. She was right, but he would rather not give her anything.

"Were you thinking of her when you and I were together?" Aetherea asked.

Gabriel kept his mouth shut.

"Or do you think of me when you're with her?"

"You poisonous little bitch," Gabriel muttered.

He hardly saw her move, but he found himself pulled off the seat until she was on top of him and holding him in a headlock.

"Don't you dare call me a bitch," she hissed angrily.

"Why not? It suits you so well," Gabriel snarled in defiance.

"Why do you have to be so fucking rude?" Aetherea hissed into his ear, keeping his body pinned to the floor of the sky-car.

"What the fleek do you want from me?" Gabriel demanded, struggling against the arm around his throat, "an acknowledgement of the fact that we had sex?"

His question made Aetherea pause.

"Or is this your way of begging for attention?" Gabriel taunted her, sensing weakness, "Is that why you came onto me in the first place?"

Aetherea didn't answer immediately. She didn't loosen her grip on his neck, but she pulled his head close before answering.

"Seven months," she said softly, "that's how long I was in deep space with no one to back me up. I was completely alone. Finally being reunited with members of my own species, especially someone who's like me, meant a lot."

"So all of that was out of sheer loneliness?" Gabriel asked.

"Maybe you first generation voidstalkers would be happy all alone," Aetherea replied, "But the second generation didn't have our emotions dulled for the sake of 'combat efficiency', so it's nice to have another Human to interact with."

"So you tried to steal someone else's husband for the sake of fun?" Gabriel demanded.

"I have no intention of stealing you and never did," Aetherea responded, "All I did was borrow you. Besides, it wouldn't work out between us. I drive you up the wall."

"Deliberately," Gabriel pointed out.

Aetherea laughed.

"Of course, I do," she answered, turning her stranglehold into an embrace, "and your reactions are as predictable as the colour green when you open your eyes."

"How poetic," Gabriel said, "now let me off the floor."

"Only if you ask me nicely," she answered, tightening her grip.

"Let me go," he growled dangerously.

"Ask nicely…and use my name," she instructed.

Gabriel huffed.

"Please let me go…Aetherea," he said finally.

Aetherea purred with satisfaction and relaxed her grip on Gabriel's neck, standing up and getting off him. Gabriel picked himself off the floor and sat back down on the seat.

"I'm not a bitch, by the way," Aetherea added with an edge of bitterness.

* * *

The front door opened and Gabriel stepped into Aster's waiting arms.

"The Directorate phoned to tell me you were coming back," Aster said, resisting tears of relief as she embraced him.

Gabriel pushed the door shut behind him, locking it for good measure.

"Did they also tell you they locked me in a box for days on end?" he asked bluntly.

"No…" Aster replied, her jaw tightening, "They didn't."

"It was partly to punish me for nosing around an ongoing investigation," Gabriel added, "or so they claimed after the fact."

"Well, you're back now," Aster directed him to the bright side, "and you look fine."

"How is everyone?" Gabriel asked.

"They panicked when you vanished," Aster admitted, "but everyone's asleep now. You can reassure them you're not gone in the morning."

Aster led Gabriel back to the master bedroom and pushed him down onto the bed, climbing on top of him and entangling herself in his arms. Gabriel embraced her and pulled her close, running his fingers through her hair.

"I'm getting really fucking sick of the Directorate taking you away from me without notice like this," Aster murmured bitterly.

"You're not alone in that," Gabriel agreed.

There was silence as they lay together in the dark.

"Do you remember when the Directorate called to place you on leave?" Aster asked.

"Yes," Gabriel responded.

"Do you remember that security incident at Bentham Prison?" she asked.

"Yes," he replied.

"Were you there?"

Gabriel didn't answer, and Aster slid her hand down between his thighs.

"So you weren't actually at an all-day debriefing," said Aster, keeping her grip gentle but firm, "which makes me wonder what else you've lied about."

An image of Aetherea's smirking face flashed through Gabriel's mind and he shifted uncomfortably in his wife's grip.

"So what were you really doing that day?" Aster asked.

"I posed as a member of an off-world delegation so I could question my mother about the conversation you had with her," Gabriel admitted.

"About who your father was?" she asked.

"Yes," Gabriel confirmed, "but someone had already broken her out and replaced her information with mine, making the system think that I was an escaping convict."

"Leading to a security incident which caused the prison to shut down," Aster concluded, "and probably a lot of trouble for your bosses."

"Are you saying I got what I deserved?" Gabriel asked.

"I did not say that," Aster replied emphatically, "I'm just saying that I'm not surprised the Directorate wanted to teach you a lesson."

"So you *do* think I got what I deserved," Gabriel said.

"Don't twist my words, sweetheart," Aster replied, giving him a gentle squeeze, "it's even worse than a straightforward lie."

"I know it wasn't the best plan," Gabriel said defensively, "but I had to investigate."

"No, you didn't," Aster said tensely, "you could have just done as you were ordered and stayed at home to take care of your wife and children."

Gabriel was in no mood for a fight and cradled Aster's head close to his shoulder.

"That's the right response," Aster purred, kissing him on the cheek.

She began stroking him until she got a physical response. Gabriel couldn't help the response, but that didn't mean he was in the mood for it.

"Five is a good number," he said.

"Sweet fucking Terra," Aster said in half-joking exasperation, "I'm not trying to trick you into expanding the family again."

"You keep saying that," Gabriel replied, rolling her over until he was on top of her, "and yet the number keeps creeping up."

"We've had this conversation before," Aster told him, locking her legs behind his hips, "If you don't want a bigger family, get snipped."

* * *

A team of androids moved a biohazard container into an observation module on the other side of the room. Once the container was inside, a containment shield was activated. Then a pair of robotic manipulator arms opened the container, allowing the contents to fall out.

The glossy black, slimy thing inside was a suit made of organic material and stood taller than a Human. Its face was a formless lump and the back was split open.

The biohazard container was moved out of the way and extracted through a quarantine gate to be sterilised. Meanwhile, the organic suit was suspended in the air by an antigravity projector in the floor, enabling the scanners to sweep it up and down.

The doors opened and a visitor arrived, approaching the central display and regarding the readings with a cold and calculating, heterochromatic gaze.

"It really does seem to be a functioning example of organic technology," explained the chief researcher, bringing up a 3D schematic of the suit.

"Has the Rand Block ever studied organic technology of this sort?" Red-eye asked.

"Only on a theoretical level," the chief researcher explained, "we've always maintained the separation between life sciences and physical sciences. While the engineering teams take plenty of inspiration from nature, they've never actually crossed that line."

"That's probably for the best," Red-eye remarked.

The sensors completed the first round of scans and commenced the second round, bathing the organic suit in a kaleidoscope of artificial light. The specimen itself hung limply in the air, like a damp set of clothes fresh from a washing cycle.

"We'll have to examine the pilot if we want to understand how the suit was operated," the chief researcher said, "but the preliminary data we have is a good start."

"Another research team has the pilot in their care," Red-eye informed him.

"To have created something like this," the chief researcher remarked, "the designer was either a genius or dabbling in xenotechnology or both."

"Dismantle it completely," Red-eye ordered, "right down to its most basic components. Scrutinise every piece of it for xenotech, then pass on your findings to the relevant departments. Once you've done that, start working on reverse engineering it."

"Understood, director-general," the chief researcher acknowledged.

Red-eye departed the laboratory without another word. She took the elevator down a dozen floors and stalked down the corridor, barely acknowledging the frightened staff who caught sight of her. Seeing the director-general was like seeing the queen of the underworld, and they hurried about their duties.

Red-eye arrived at the entrance to another laboratory, officially designated as a medical examination suite – which, technically, it was.

She appeared on a balcony-like viewing platform that formed a ring around the upper level. The lower level was an operating theatre sealed off by a thick layer of glass, keeping it under environmentally secure quarantine. A set of robotic surgical arms formed a circle around the operating table in the centre.

No one saw her enter. The research team was too busy watching the dissection as Red-eye stood next to the research leader.

"We've only just started the actual dissection," the chief medical researcher informed her, "it took us a while to determine the right cocktail to keep him alive and pacified, but his condition is stable enough to proceed."

"Is he conscious?" Red-eye asked.

"Yes," was the matter-of-fact reply, "and he has to be for us to examine the neural interface mechanism he used to control the suit."

Having been found barely alive by one of the backup teams, Byron Sade had been given enough medical treatment to keep him alive until he was transferred to a specialist trauma unit. Once the trauma unit had stabilised him, he had been transferred to the 'care' of the Rand Block's scientists — a fate worse than death.

Live video footage of the dissection filmed from various angles was being displayed on the screen. Everyone except for the chief medical researcher preferred to watch the sterile digital simulation, even though the subject's vital signs displayed on the screen reminded them that he was still alive.

The medical team barely noticed when their immediate superior pulled out a data slate and walked away to a secluded corner. He was joined shortly by Red-eye who watched him expectantly. His mask of professional calm had slipped and he looked nervously at the data slate before speaking.

"We conducted the new test on Byron Sade," he began in a quiet voice, "he's clean."

"That's reassuring news," Red-eye replied without emotion, "which makes me wonder why you don't share the sentiment."

The man hesitated for a moment before continuing.

"The evidence is crystal clear," he acknowledged, not wishing to second-guess his own results, "but given Byron Sade's behaviour and...creations...the similarities with what Colonel Thorn reported about the Swarm are disturbing. Not remotely conclusive, but disturbing."

"You are right to fear he might have been enthralled," Red-eye answered coolly, "but your own results should assuage your concerns. They've certainly assuaged mine."

"It's certainly a vital precaution to take," he agreed, "although ...I'm still disturbed that it was necessary to use it on Colonel Thorn himself."

"The theory that he might have been corrupted by the Swarm was never a credible one," Red-eye remarked, "however, as the old saying goes, 'better safe than sorry.'"

"Indeed," the chief medical researcher responded.

"Keep me appraised of your progress on the dissection," Red-eye ordered.

"I daresay," the chief medical researcher remarked, "I don't feel all that sorry for Mr Sade in light of the horrific things he did in his personal life."

"If he had been a saint of probity and charity I would still require the dissection," Red-eye said with sociopathic coolness, "as well as regular appraisals of your progress."

"Y...yes...of course," was the halting reply, "we shall, director-general."

* * *

A patch of starlit space blackened into a Q-rift as a vessel emerged back into real space. It was a warship, but without the markings associated with the Navy. Its jet black hull matched the void in which it travelled, marking it as a DNI warship.

Deep within the vessel was a secure block with a dozen holding cells and a super-max cell at its centre with a lone prisoner inside. Each of his limbs was being stretched taut by his restraints, keeping him suspended in an X-shaped stance.

The door to the super-max cell opened and a group of DNI operatives entered. One of them was carrying a helmet of some kind, but with a tangle of wires protruding from the scalp and back. He hooked it up to a robotic arm that descended from the ceiling, checked that all the wires were in place, then let the robotic arm re-ascend.

They had flash-scanned his eyes and tested his DNA every hour throughout the voyage just to be sure that the man they had expended so much effort to capture hadn't broken loose. But this device wasn't a DNA sensor, it looked more like a neural scanner of some kind.

The robotic arm did an arcing motion before lowering the helmet down over his head. Then a set of straps tightened themselves around his chin to keep it in place. Once everything was ready, the operatives pulled up a screen and activated a pre-programmed routine before stepping back and watching.

The whole process lasted about ten minutes, but once it was done, the operatives looked at the results and nodded in satisfaction before leaving. One member of the group stayed behind and approached the prisoner.

"Colonel Alexander Thorn," said the interrogator, "I have a few questions."

"I have plenty of my own," Alexander muttered.

"I'll ask the questions and you'll answer them," the interrogator made clear.

He returned to the screen and reactivated the helmet scanner.

"Why did you scan my brain *before* questioning me?" Alexander asked suspiciously.

"As I said," the interrogator replied, rebuffing his question, "*I* will be the one asking the questions and *you* will answer them."

The helmet scanner reactivated and Alexander stared at the opposite wall.

"Is your name Alexander Thorn?" the interrogator asked.

"No," Alexander answered, causing a spike of red on the screen.

"Were you ever inducted into the Voidstalker Programme?" the interrogator asked.

"No," Alexander responded, creating another red spike as his lie was flagged up.

"Are you going to take this seriously or do I have to bring out the shock-stick?" the interrogator demanded threateningly.

"No and feel free, respectively" Alexander replied defiantly, "I can endure a lot more pain than you, and since you're probably planning to lock me away forever or dispose of me altogether, I don't really see why I should cooperate."

The interrogator paused, keeping his composure but clearly stumped.

"Shame you can't just torture me," Alexander said sardonically.

"How about the chance to speak to your family?" the interrogator suggested.

"I don't have any family," Alexander retorted, "my wife died when the volcano erupted, and you tried to use an android facsimile of my son to assassinate me."

"We captured Jezebel a few hours before we captured you," said the interrogator, "like you, she fled the planet in a shuttlecraft. Unlike you, she didn't try to take a circuitous route around the planet, so we managed to scoop her up as soon as she entered orbit."

"Sorry for the inconvenience," Alexander replied sarcastically.

"More importantly," the interrogator added, "your son is on Asgard. We can arrange a video-call, or even a face-to-face meeting, depending on how much you cooperate."

"And I'm supposed to believe a word of that?"

"You can do," the interrogator replied, "or we can move you to the interrogation room and test your claims about pain endurance."

* * *

It was early in the morning when the doorbell rang. The household android moved to answer the door, first activating the intercom and security screen.

"*This is the Thorn residence,*" the android announced in a digitised voice, "*please state your name and the reason for your visit.*"

Instead of answering, the visitor allowed the security panel to flash-scan her eyes. The android stood still for a moment before opening the door just as Aster was turning the corner. She froze, fearfully wondering why the android had opened the door to a stranger.

"Is Gabriel home?" asked a woman's voice.

"What do you want?" Aster demanded.

"I'm a work colleague," the woman replied.

Against her better judgement, Aster approached the front door to confront the stranger. She saw the woman's eyes and furrowed her brow.

"Wow, blue instead of green," she remarked.

"The sensor flash-scanned my eyes," the blonde visitor added, smilingly pleasantly, "so you can check my identity if you want to."

Aster looked at the security screen and saw the name '*Aetherea Starborn*' displayed above the words '*Access Denied: Tier 2 Classification.*'

"So what can I do for you?" Aster asked.

"I just wanted to return this," Aetherea replied, pulling something out of a bag and offering it to Aster, "he forgot to take it with him after his most recent mission."

Aster accepted the package.

"And you couldn't just mail it to our home?" Aster asked suspiciously.

"I wanted to give it to him in person," Aetherea admitted, "given what happened."

"And what exactly happened?" Aster asked, keeping her voice from wavering.

"He can tell you himself," Aetherea answered, "although, I suspect he won't."

Aster looked at the package.

"Thanks for stopping by," she said, flashing a polite smile.

"You're welcome," Aetherea replied, smiling back, "give Gabriel my regards."

Aetherea departed and the android shut the door.

"Who was that?" Gabriel asked as he turned the corner.

"A fellow voidstalker of yours," Aster replied, "although her eyes were blue."

Gabriel flinched at that detail.

"What did she want?" he asked apprehensively.

"Why so paranoid?" Aster said, punching him in the ribs, "she came by to return this."

Aster showed him the package and Gabriel took it, opening up the box and removing the contents. The tension in his face softened.

It was the family photo he had taken almost a month ago. He and Aster were seated in the centre of the couch with Leo sitting next to Aster, Orion sitting next to Gabriel, Violet sitting on Gabriel's lap, and Rose perched on top of his shoulders. Aster was holding baby Emerald in her arms as the family huddled together.

"I can't believe you forgot to bring that back home with you," Aster admonished him as she smiled at the photograph, "still, it was nice of her to return it."

"Yes," he murmured, "it was."

* * *

Alexander lay in darkness. The DNI liked to play disorienting games with its prisoners: turn out the lights and confuse their sense of direction and time. He could still feel the restraints clamped over each of his limbs. The DNI would sooner kill him than let him move a muscle without permission.

Understandable. He was the biggest threat they had faced in decades. They weren't going to risk him escaping from another prison ship like he had the last time.

Being held captive brought with it a strange kind of relief. With the disintegration of his Network, he was absolved of any responsibilities. No more hiding in the shadows and no more tugging on the threads of a poorly constructed web of influence and subterfuge.

Best of all, Mortimer's cure had worked. The dormant volcanic rage that had lurked for so long in the back of his mind was finally extinct. For the first time in nearly half a century, his head was truly calm and clear.

A screen flickered on in front of him, temporarily blinding him until his eyes adjusted. He could hardly believe the face he saw on the other end.

"*Hello, Alexander,*" said Red-eye.

A tsunami of conflicting emotions welled up inside him, all of them negative.

"*You should have stayed in hiding,*" she said coolly.

"Don't you have better things to do than gloat?" Alexander demanded.

"*I have no need to gloat,*" Red-eye replied, "*I just wanted to speak with you.*"

"So the DNI's legions of interrogators gave up and now they're sending in their ultimate last resort," Alexander sneered.

"*I will tell you my theories and all you have to do is tell me if they are accurate,*" Red-eye answered, ignoring the taunt.

"I take it you're scanning my neural patterns now?" Alexander asked.

"*Contrary to what you may suspect, I have no reason to lie to you,*" Red-eye responded, "*so the answer to your question is your neural patterns are under constant surveillance.*"

"Alright then," Alexander said, "fire away."

"*First, I believe that you orchestrated the gas attacks in Asgard City as cover to smuggle Dr Mortimer Shelton off the planet,*" Red-eye began, "*and that you had him concoct the toxin in order to implicate him should he have second thoughts about joining you.*"

Alexander didn't answer. This was different from the standard yes-no interrogation method, but if she really was watching his neural patterns, she could tell whether her theories were true or not. It was unnerving just how accurate Red-eye was.

"*Second, I believe that you recruited Dr Shelton in order to correct the chemical imbalance that caused periodic episodes of rage,*" Red-eye continued, "*having searched in vain for a cure, you concluded that only the man who caused it in the first place could fix it, and it would appear he succeeded.*"

Still, Alexander said nothing.

"*Third,*" Red-eye continued after a brief pause, "*I believe that you broke your soon-to-be ex-wife out of prison and arranged for one of your agents to monitor your daughter-in-law and your grandchildren because you hoped to be reunited with your family.*"

Alexander raised an eyebrow.

"What do you mean by 'soon-to-be ex-wife'?" he asked.

"*Jezebel Thorn filed for divorce from you as soon as she was back in the custody of the civil authorities,*" Red-eye explained, "*of course, it will be difficult to divorce a man who is still officially dead, but after all this time, I see no reason why it shouldn't go ahead.*"

Alexander wanted to be angry that Jezebel would leave him, but after being presumed dead for decades, he had kidnapped her from prison just to have her around. Then, after all that, he had left her to die in the mountain facility.

Of course, if she was alive, that meant she had fled the facility long before the endgame protocol's activation, which meant that technically *she* had left *him* to die. However, the details did nothing to alter the bigger picture.

"*Your desire for family reunification, in turn, explains part of your working relationship with Byron Sade,*" Red-eye continued, "*we now know from a separate investigation that Byron Sade was deeply involved in the smuggling of xenobiological samples, and that some of those samples came via your Network.*"

"And so I roped him into a scheme to kidnap my own son and have him brought to me," Alexander finished, getting bored of the explanation, "which you already knew because you swapped Gabriel out for an android duplicate programmed to assassinate me."

"*Correct,*" Red-eye confirmed.

"Your android assassin also gunned down a hundred others," Alexander added.

"*As it was programmed to do,*" Red-eye replied without even the pretence of remorse, "*all of them were criminals of one kind or another before you recruited them, and even if they hadn't been, they became threats to be neutralised as soon as they joined your Network, Mortimer Shelton included.*"

"Any other theories you want to run by me?"

"*Fourth,*" Red-eye continued, "*you were experimenting on the native population of the planet where you were hiding, and a number of them were smuggled to Asgard as corporate industrial shipments intended for Sheraton Biopharma.*"

"All dead on the money so far," Alexander admitted, trying not to sound impressed, "how many more theories are there?"

"*Fifth,*" Red-eye concluded, "*I believe that you intended those modified aliens to be used as shock troops in some kind of follow-up attack on Asgard City.*"

That would have been one use for them, although she was assuming a bit too much.

"*What I didn't understand,*" Red-eye continued, "*was your endgame.*"

The admission caught Alexander by surprise.

"*You spent so long in hiding and amassed a vast arsenal and an intelligence network loyal to you,*" Red-eye summarised, "*you were even building a private army of alien slave-soldiers right under the noses of the Directorate, and yet you put it all at risk for this gambit to be reunited with your family. What was your plan?*"

Alexander looked at Red-eye in bemusement. Then he burst out laughing.

For the briefest moment, a look of confusion crossed Red-eye's face. Alexander was too busy laughing to notice it, and it was gone as soon as it appeared.

Alexander's fit of laughter subsided and dissolved into a look of hatred.

"I never once had a grand plan in mind," he seethed, "only goals; to quell the unbearable fury you planted in my head. To be reunited with the family you almost caused me to murder. To get revenge against you."

"*All of which sound like compatible elements of a single overarching design,*" Red-eye replied, "*a design which you're claiming never existed.*"

"Not everyone in the galaxy is a calculating bitch like you," Alexander spat, "I always had those goals in mind, but for the most part, I just made it up as I went along."

Red-eye paused in thought.

"*That would explain a lot,*" she said thoughtfully.

"Any other questions about my 'grand designs'?" Alexander asked.

"*No,*" she replied, "*You've given me everything I need, for which you get a reward.*"

"Like what? A cookie?" Alexander asked sarcastically.

Red-eye terminated the link and the video-screen was replaced by an image that made Alexander's breath catch in his throat.

He recognised Gabriel's face instantly, the spitting image of his own, but he wasn't alone. He was sitting on a couch next to a woman cradling a baby in her arms. Around them were seated four other children, one of whom was perched on Gabriel's shoulders.

All of the children had their father's patrilineal green eyes.

* * *

Red-eye reclined in her seat. The results of the earlier neural scan had confirmed that his condition had been cured – Dr Shelton's final achievement before his death. Alexander really was free of the rage condition accidentally inflicted on him.

The results of her own questioning were even more intriguing. Alexander Thorn had always been something of a maverick; it was one of the things that got him inducted into the original

Voidstalker Programme. It also limited his aptitude for strategic planning, a fact which explained the ease with which his Network had been dismantled.

That he had built up such a formidable network of agents was impressive – doubly so given that he had been struggling with mental illness throughout.

Someone else was present in the room. One of the more senior intelligence directors. His skin looked pale and waxy, and his bald head reflected the light. His eyes resembled black coals, intimidating people almost as much as Red-eye's gaze.

He wasn't her second-in-command – no such position existed – but they called him Cypher. 'They' being the small number of high ranking Directorate operatives who knew about him. Few people were privy to the details of deep space operations. Cypher oversaw all of them, reporting directly to Red-eye.

"His erratic behaviour may have aided us in neutralising him," he said in a deceptively soft voice, "but it also makes him too dangerous to keep alive indefinitely."

"His erratic behaviour and loathing for the Directorate are harmless as long as he remains a prisoner," Red-eye responded.

"Were it not for the earlier neural scan," Cypher said, shifting the topic, "I wouldn't have believed that he hadn't been enthralled by the Swarm, given his behaviour and the nature of the experiments he was performing."

"That's similar to the assessment of Byron Sade," Red-eye answered, "but it seems that both men are merely sick – albeit in very different ways. We can rest assured that this incident had nothing to do with the Swarm."

"Speaking of which," Cypher said, producing a flexi-tablet, "we have new intelligence regarding the hive-ship."

"The one that Colonel Thorn destroyed?"

"Yes," Cypher confirmed, "it seems that at least a thousand escape pods made it to safety before the hive-ship met its end."

He handed the flexi-tablet to Red-eye who took it and began to read.

"The antimatter explosion destroyed most of the pods," Cypher explained, "which means that there were no more than a few thousand adult Hive-dweller survivors and perhaps ten times that number of Hive-dweller larvae."

"How many pods contained Swarm fragments?" Red-eye asked, continuing to read.

"None," Cypher responded, "the Krakenscourge was able to track the Swarm's unique signature throughout Colonel Thorn's infiltration. It remained within the hive-ship until it was snuffed out by the explosion."

"It's possible that the surviving Hive-dwellers smuggled some portion of it away and managed to conceal the signature, is it not?" Red-eye suggested.

"Possible," Cypher admitted, "but unlikely as well as unprovable for the time being."

"This comes from third party sightings picked up by SIGINT," Red-eye noted.

"By tabulating reported encounters and eliminating duplicates," Cypher answered, "we can be 99% certain that no more than a thousand pods survived the hive-ship's destruction."

"Out of all the reports you recorded," Red-eye inquired, "how many of them suggest to you that the Hive-dwellers somehow smuggled a piece of the Swarm away with them?"

"None," Cypher replied, "although, the Hive-dwellers would certainly keep something like that concealed from anyone they encountered."

"Then we can be 99% certain that the Swarm fragment the Hive-dwellers discovered did not survive the destruction of their vessel," Red-eye concluded.

"That leaves the Water-skins and their trading barge," Cypher continued, "specifically where they discovered the Swarm fragment in the first place."

Red-eye scrolled through the rest of the report.

"It also leaves open the question of what attacked them in deep space before they made it to the Nexus," Cypher added, "not to mention how the Hive-dwellers knew they were in possession of a fragment of the Swarm."

"So what is your theory?" Red-eye asked, still reading.

"Colonel Thorn was convinced that the Hive-dwellers were behind the attack on the trading barge," Cypher answered.

"You think he was wrong?"

"He *was* wrong," Cypher replied, "Not only the trading barge's vital systems, but also every single one of its exits was targeted. Not the sort thing one would do if the intention was to board the ship and steal a piece of cargo."

Red-eye finished reading the report and waited for the rest of the explanation.

"It is highly improbable that the Hive-dwellers would first try to seal the Water-skins inside their own ship and kill them all," Cypher continued, "only to board the Nexus station and attempt to capture the survivors alive."

"So if the Hive-dwellers weren't behind the trading barge attack, who was?"

"A fourth party attacked the trading barge in deep space to contain the threat of the Swarm," Cypher surmised, "and transmitted the word 'voidstalker' – in our language, no less – in order to warn us specifically."

Red-eye waited for Cypher to connect the dots.

"Furthermore," Cypher finished, "this fourth party used the backchannel to assist the Krakenscourge in locating and destroying the hive-ship."

Red-eye returned the flexi-tablet to him.

"You are correct," she confirmed, "Although, this is the first time it has ever been used."

"And this fourth party," Cypher inquired, "I presume it was a voidstalker who set up the backchannel at some point in the past?"

"Yes," Red-eye replied, "Unfortunately, not all threats can be avoided by simply hiding ourselves away. Hence, some contact must be authorised from time to time. I'll be giving you clearance to view the relevant files shortly."

"I presume Colonel Thorn already knows?" Cypher asked.

"He doesn't have access to those files," Red-eye replied, "but he was onboard when the Krakenscourge was contacted by the 'fourth party', and he confronted me about the incident a few days ago, so he definitely knows."

"Very bold," Cypher remarked distastefully.

"He believes that I, and by extension the Directorate, are keeping him in the dark in order to retain his loyalty and services," Red-eye explained.

"Thorn is the ideal operative for this," said Cypher, "but his loyalties—"

"Are not in question," Red-eye cut him off smoothly, "Thorn's case is a delicate one to be handled with care. It is also beyond the scope of your responsibilities."

"Understood," Cypher acknowledged before departing.

Red-eye sat back in her seat. She always had many plans progressing simultaneously, some over the very long term. Gabriel's suspicions were misplaced, but she had done little to assuage them. Having just neutralised one threat, the Directorate could ill afford to lose one of its best operatives to disillusionment.

Humanity's enemies were always circling.

THE END

About the Author

I'm not a full-time author, few of us are that lucky. I have a five-day-a-week job which pays the bills, including the book-related bills. I enjoy writing and science fiction as a hobby and an escape, and the result of unwinding at the end of every day, and over every weekend, are the stories I write.

CPSIA information can be obtained
at www.ICGtesting.com
Printed in the USA
LVHW021305111119
636960LV00002B/530/P